PENGUIN BOOKS

Then. Now. Always.

Isabelle Broom was born in Cambridge nine days before the 1980s began and studied Media Arts at the University of West London before starting a career first in local newspapers and then as a junior sub-editor at *heat* magazine. She travelled through Europe during her gap year and went to live on the Greek island of Zakynthos for an unforgettable and life-shaping six months after completing her degree. Since then, she has travelled to Canada, Sri Lanka, Sicily, New York, LA, the Canary Islands, Spain and lots more of Greece, but her wanderlust was reined in when she met Max, a fluffy little Bolognese puppy desperate for a home. When she's not writing novels set in far-flung locations, Isabelle spends her time being the Book Reviews Editor at *heat* magazine and walking her beloved dog round the parks of north London.

You can follow her on Twitter@Isabelle_Broom or find her on Facebook under Isabelle Broom Author.

Then. Now. Always.

ISABELLE BROOM

PENGUIN BOOKS

For my sisters, Coralie, Heloise, Felicity and Bryony

PENGUIN BOOKS

UK | USA | Canada | Ireland | Australia
India | New Zealand | South Africa

Penguin Books is part of the Penguin Random House group of companies
whose addresses can be found at global.penguinrandomhouse.com.

First published 2017

001

Copyright © Isabelle Broom, 2017

The moral right of the author has been asserted

Set in 12.5/14.75 pt Garamond MT Std
Typeset by Jouve (UK), Milton Keynes
Printed and bound in Great Britain by Clays Ltd, Elcograf S.p.A.

A CIP catalogue record for this book is available from the British Library

ISBN: 978–1–405–94151–8

www.greenpenguin.co.uk

Penguin Random House is committed to a sustainable future for our business, our readers and our planet. This book is made from Forest Stewardship Council® certified paper.

Then...

The wind is the first thing.

It greets her like a warm breath as she steps tentatively out from the foggy interior of the bus, and she pauses for a moment to savour the sensation. It has taken her so long to reach this place, and she feels dusty, sticky and worn down. The bus doors close behind her, the hinges squeaking weakly in protest as metal brushes against rust.

It is safe here, a voice from inside her soothes. He cannot find you here, and neither can she.

She turns her head and sees the dark ribbon of the sea far below, its rich blue canvas punctuated by the pale tops of broken waves. If she strains her ears, she imagines that she can hear the sound they make as they buffet against the shore — a gentle swoosh, a soft crackle.

The sun is almost in bed now, it's lounging sleepily in the sky, and she squints as she gazes at it, a single hand raised to shield her eyes. The tears have dried across her cheeks, the skin beneath them tight and sore. She wonders if they will ever cease. Will she ever be able to forget?

The bus has moved away from her now, a cacophony of rumbling engine, crunching gears and then a lingering swarm of dust. In its wake looms a vast hill. When she sees it for the first time, the scatter of white dwellings turned a soft lilac colour in the fading light, she feels a twinge deep inside her chest. Plenty of places to hide up there. A labyrinth in which to lose her former self.

As she stares upwards from her place on the stony path, a scent assails her — an aroma of pine, lemon and salt. A rustling sound rises from the undergrowth by the road, the murmur of insects, tiny and busy. Life goes on, the earth turns over. Birds fly and waves crash, the sun sets and the wind blows. And she is here. She is alive.

She has yet to set eyes on another soul, but the fear is dripping away. The darkness that had enveloped her is pierced now with brightness: the future contains hope. There will be a way to continue. She does not need to be afraid.

The hillside beckons her with invisible fingers, the distant lights twinkle like stars.

'Goodbye,' she whispers, and begins to walk.

I

Now . . .

I know it's a total cliché to fancy your boss, but I can't help it. I've fancied Theo since the first moment I set my young, eager-to-please eyes on him during my internship five years ago, and my devotion hasn't wavered since. I would argue that it's his own fault, though, for being so utterly delicious, awe-inspiringly brilliant and, well, just perfect in every way.

'Are you feeling all right?' Tom asks, peering at my flushed face in concern as the object of my unbridled desire strides past us into the meeting room. He's wearing a pale blue shirt today, and he looks sexy as hell.

'I'm fine,' I assure him, fanning my face with my hand for effect. 'It's just really hot in here. There are too many computers on at the same time.'

'If you say so.' Tom shrugs and turns back to his screen.

'I don't look that bad, do I?' I mutter, and he swivels around to face me.

'A bit like a radish,' he informs me. 'Only hairier.'

Tom does this occasionally, winds me up with his silly banter just to pass the time between our three p.m. cuppa and our six p.m. after-work pint. I shouldn't really be surprised, because when it comes to Tom, I give just as good as I get, but I dread to think how much he'd rib me if he knew about my pathetic crush on Theo. And it really is a bit pathetic, not that I'd ever admit that to anyone other than my own self in the mirror. Yes, I talk to myself in the mirror, too. Hannah Hodges: walking, talking tragedy.

'Did we get any bite-backs on Twitter about Mojácar?' I ask him now, firmly changing the subject back to work.

Tom clicks his mouse and sniffs with disgust. 'Only from people who think I've spelt "Majorca" wrong.'

'Those people are philistines,' I grumble, rolling my eyes as I take in the snarky tweets on his screen. Secretly, however, I'm quite thrilled. I'd pitched my documentary idea to Theo partly on the basis that little is really known about the small Spanish town of Mojácar, and these tweets are proving my point.

Theo had lit up like a department store Christmas tree when I talked about the time I spent there as a teenager, his beautiful brown eyes widening as I turned my laptop around to face him and flashed up images of little white buildings cut out of the hillside, trailing bougainvillea, and the wide, sandy beach. When I explained why it fitted so well with the brief we'd been working on, he'd actually clapped his hands with pleasure. It was definitely one of the best days of my professional (okay, and personal) life so far, and I've been happily reliving the moment over in my head at least twelve times a day ever since. Turns out I'm not that bad at presentations after all, even if I was so nervous in the run-up that I almost swallowed myself whole.

'Do you really think we're going to get everything ready in time for the shoot?' Tom asks me now. He's a worrier, my best friend, but sometimes I wish he'd be more of a warrior – fierce and fearless rather than fretting about things all the time.

I turn to him, an expression of mock outrage on my face. 'Of course we will. Theo has put me in charge of researching everything about the location and Mojácar's history. Trust me, I'm not going to let hi— I mean, the company down. This film will have everything: beauty, an exotic location, magic.'

'Magic?' Tom frowns. 'That cave painting again?'

'Oh, it's a lot more than that,' I reply, looking down instinctively at the little symbol tattooed on the inside of my left wrist. The ink has faded over the years; more a muddy blue now than black, but it still makes me smile with nostalgia. My Indalo Man, with his simply drawn, stick-man body and outstretched arms. As soon as Theo had gathered us into the meeting room and explained that a series of documentaries had been commissioned on the subject of modern folklore and myths, I knew exactly which place would work – and it had, too. We had been awarded funding not long afterwards, and were now on a seriously tight race to meet our deadline.

I run a protective thumb over my Indalo Man. 'I believe in him,' I admit.

Tom looks down at the tattoo and back up at me. For a brief second, I see something in his eyes that looks like affection, but he blinks it quickly away.

'You're mad.' He smiles.

'But you love me all the same, right?'

Tom rolls his eyes, and turns back to his screen.

I've lost count of the number of times over the years that people have assumed the two of us are a couple, though I suppose it's an understandable assumption to make. Ever since Tom and I met at the Student Union bar during our university's Freshers' week, we've been pretty much attached at the hip. I know all his faults and he knows all mine, but we still love each other like family. In fact, I often like to think of Tom as a brother, probably because I like him a hell of a lot more than my actual sibling. Well, half-sibling.

He looks more like me than my actual relative does, too. While my beloved Theo is olive-skinned, broad-shouldered and dark-haired, Tom is lanky like me with long, pale limbs and a messy, straw-like thatch on the top of his head. We'd look at home in the middle of a field, scaring crows away from the crops – a fact that I remind him of on the rare occasion that he does something to annoy me.

'Hannah – can I have a word?'

Oh God, Theo is calling me. I get hastily to my feet, feeling my heart leap up into my throat.

'Of course – coming!'

I squeaked out that sentence like some sort of mouse-human, which I know Tom will definitely have noticed. Great.

Theo is sitting on one of the six leather chairs in the glass-walled meeting room, one casual foot resting on the opposite knee. There's an iPad propped up against his thigh. Lucky iPad.

I take a deep breath and exhale my ridiculous anxiety. 'What can I help you with?'

Theo smiles at me, pointing to the chair next to him. 'Come and sit down, Hannah.'

I sit down, trying my best not to blush as my bare knee brushes against his trouser leg.

'How's the research coming along?' he asks.

'Good,' I chirp, filling him in on the sarcastic Twitter replies. 'I think we can safely assume that Mojácar is an area of Spain that not many people know much about.'

'Music to my ears.' Theo grins. His Greek upbringing has left him with a slight accent, and I can't help it – every time I hear it my insides turn into something resembling mushy peas.

'I think you'll love it over there,' I tell him, crossing and uncrossing my ankles. 'When are you planning to go?'

'Well, that's just it.' Theo smiles at me again and I instinctively grip the arms of the chair. 'That's why I called you in here. I wondered if you'd like to come along, too?'

'Me?' The mouse-human has taken over my body again.

'Yes. You and me, and Claudette and Tom, of course.'

'All of us?' I'm beginning to sound like an imbecile.

Theo is bemused now, but he laughs good-naturedly. 'You are the one who pitched the idea, and you are the one who has spent time in Mojácar before, so you must come,' he explains, clapping his hands together as if to prove the point.

Meanwhile, I'm trying to reassure myself I'm not dreaming. In all my five-and-a-bit years as a researcher here at Vivid Productions of London, England, I have never once been invited along on a shoot abroad. I'm not a fancy cameraman like Tom or a hot, French-accented presenter like Claudette; I'm a mostly office-based researcher, good for chasing leads, organising interviews and dredging up forgotten footage from the deepest, darkest TV archives of the world – but this? This is new territory for me, but it's something I've been hoping will happen for as long as I can remember.

'We'll be leaving in two weeks,' Theo continues, swiping the screen of his iPad with a long, tanned finger. 'Is that okay with you?'

'Yes, of course.' It takes all my effort not to hug him.

'You'll be my right-hand woman out there, so there won't be much time to sunbathe or drink sangria,' he warns. 'We've got a very tight deadline for the project, so I'll be editing the footage myself as we go along. I'll need you to help with continuity and any interviews we may line up.'

I bob my head up and down in the manner of a nodding dog that's been stuck to the top of a washing machine during its spin cycle.

'What we really need to do in the meantime is track down some people who were part of that artists' colony you mentioned,' he continues. 'Have you had any luck so far?'

I shake my head, devastated to be sharing bad news.

'I read that the colony broke up in 2013,' I remind him. 'So unfortunately there's a chance that they've all left the area, but I'll keep trying.'

Theo nods. 'Good stuff, Hannah. I knew I could count on you.'

He did? I turn beetroot with pride.

When I float back to my desk a few minutes later, Tom has abandoned Twitter and is checking Facebook while he has a tea break.

'Sissy Martin got married,' he announces.

'What? Again?'

Sissy was a girl we'd both known at university who, putting it as delicately as possible, was the human equivalent of the slide in the local park. Everyone and their uncle had a go on her.

'To an army officer this time, by the looks of things,' Tom adds, pointing a huge hand at his screen. 'And they're honeymooning in Sri Lanka, of all places. That's at the top of my list.'

Tom has been talking about travelling around the world since I met him, but aside from a few trips overseas to film with Vivid, he hasn't ventured very far. Selfishly I'm happy about that fact, because I'd miss him horribly if he went away for any extended periods of time. But then again, I want him to follow his heart.

I peer over his head to look at the photos and snort. 'How can it be that Sissy bloody Martin has been married twice since we left uni, and I haven't even had a sniff?'

'You're too fussy,' Tom says, which is only partly true. It's not my high standards that are keeping me cold and lonely at night; it's my inability to see past my delectable boss.

'Well, maybe I'll meet the love of my life in Mojácar,' I tell him, throwing a cartoon wink in for good measure. 'Yours truly has just been invited along on the shoot.'

'No way?' Tom's whole face has lit up and he's flapping his pipe-cleaner arms around now like a tree on a windy day.

'Way. Apparently, I'm to be Theo's *right-hand woman*.' Unfortunately, I say the last part in a very obviously dreamy voice, and Tom scrunches up his face in suspicion.

'He obviously needs someone there aside from you,' I add quickly. 'You know, someone with incredible talent and amazing people skills and . . . Ow!'

Tom has retaliated with a playful but actually quite hard punch on my thigh.

'Don't make me take you down, Robertson,' I warn. 'I've done it before and I'll do it again.'

It was true. I had.

'I surrender!' He laughs, holding his hands up. There's blue ink all over one of them where his pen has leaked.

'You can bring me a tea to make up for it,' I reply, turning to my own screen and opening Facebook, even though I know it will annoy me in a matter of minutes.

'Oh my God – vomit!' I snarl at the computer a few moments later.

'What?' Tom has used his beanpole legs to propel his chair over at an alarming speed.

'That.' I point. 'My half-sister looking annoyingly smug as always.'

Tom examines the photo and shrugs. 'She looks happy.'

If I wasn't so consumed by irritation towards my younger, prettier, darker-haired and far-more-confident-than-me sibling, then I might agree with him, but as it is, I find the picture of Nancy with her blond-haired, blue-eyed boyfriend, both of them smiling like a pair of deluded in-love idiots, utterly revolting.

'Remind me again why you hate her so much?' Tom asks, wheeling backwards, a certain amount of bemusement in his expression.

'She's spoilt, boring, self-involved, dull.' I count the insults off on my fingers.

'Pretty sure boring and dull mean the same thing,' Tom informs me.

I glare at him.

'In all seriousness,' he says, giving me a half-smile. 'She's actually very sweet, your sister. I had a really nice chat with her when I met her at our graduation ceremony. And, you have to remember, it's not actually her fault that she was born.'

I open my mouth to retort, but at that moment Theo emerges from the meeting room, wafting his lime-scented aftershave all over the place and reducing my loins to molten lava.

'Everything okay?' he asks as he passes.

'Yes, boss,' Tom and I chorus, immediately closing down our respective Facebook pages with a swift click.

I watch as he heads across the office, turning every female and male head of our fifteen-strong team as he goes, and let out a contented sigh. I'm going to go to Spain with him and he is going to fall in love with me. It is finally going to happen. It must happen.

And in that moment, as the May sunshine shrugs off its robe of clouds and beams in through the window, I actually believe that my wish might just come true.

2

The next fortnight passes by in a blur of late nights at work and even later nights at various waxing appointments. There is no way I can risk Theo seeing any stray hairs escaping from any part of the new bikini I've just bought myself. Even though he's warned us that the trip will be all work, work, work, I've been indulging myself in a little fantasy involving the two of us, a hot tub and some champagne on ice. Where we'll even find a hot tub is beside the point – it's a really good fantasy and I refuse to believe that it's not at least sixty-two per cent attainable.

It's the night before we depart for Mojácar, and to celebrate, Tom and I are meeting our friends Rachel and Paul in our favourite pub in Islington. Well, I say 'friends' plural, but really we just love Rachel. As far as I'm concerned, Paul is only permitted to socialise with us because he is her boyfriend. That is literally the sole reason.

They're already waiting for us at the pub when we arrive, typically late, and Rachel stands up to give us both a hug of greeting, going into loyal ecstasies over my new haircut (I was worried it made me look like a *Blue Peter*-era Anthea Turner; she assures me it does not) and telling Tom he looks handsome with a beard (he does not).

'You're just in time to get a round in,' grins Paul from his seat, earning himself a giggle from his girlfriend and a tut from me.

'Shut up and go to the bar, Pauly,' she tells him sweetly, winking at me as we all shuffle our bottoms along the bench seats they've chosen.

'So,' she begins, lacing her slim fingers around her half-empty wine glass. 'Are you all set for your trip?'

'Hannah is completely hair-free, if that's what you mean?' Tom tells her, moving his foot to one side just in time to stop it being crushed under my boot.

'I'm never telling you anything ever again,' I mutter, and they both laugh at me. Paul is back with three pints of what looks distinctly like ale. I asked for lager.

'And this is?' asks Tom, raising his own glass to his nose and taking a tentative sniff.

'On special offer,' replies Paul, grinning at us as he sits back down. I resist the urge to pour the contents of my own pint over his head, although it would be very amusing to see that perfectly coiffed hair of his collapse across his face. Paul is a very good-looking man and he knows it. Presumably he has used this fact to avoid having to develop a personality beyond telling often-sexist and always very bad jokes. Rachel is far too besotted with him to notice any of this, apparently, and the fact that neither Tom nor I have pointed it out in the year since they've been an item is a real testament to how much we care about her as a friend. She's even more beautiful than Paul, of course, with a tumble of red curls, pale green eyes and flawless skin, but for some inexplicable reason she feels inferior to him – another fact that I've become convinced he does his best not to discourage.

'So, will you two be bunking up over there?' Paul asks now, throwing Tom and me a look as if to say, 'I know you two are at it, hammer and tongs.'

I don't bother to reply and bring the disgusting ale up to hide my sneer. Tom, on the other hand, mumbles something unintelligible about not wanting to cramp my style. I wish he wouldn't be like this around Paul, so nervous and eager to impress. He's worth about seventeen billion of that self-satisfied dingbat.

'How did your housemates take the news?' Rachel asks me now. I live in an enormous run-down Victorian pile in Acton with about nine other people, most of whom I never see and a few of whom I'm pretty sure I didn't even meet before they moved in.

I shrug. 'I left a note pinned to the kitchen cork board and bought a lock for my bedroom door. I doubt any of them will even notice I'm away, to be honest.'

'I don't understand why you stay there,' Tom says, as he always does when the subject of my chosen place of dwelling comes up in conversation. 'You're still living like a student.'

'Oh, I'm sorry, Mister "my stinking rich parents gave me a deposit",' I say lightly, pulling a face at him so he knows I'm not being serious. 'We can't all afford to live in luxury.'

Rachel laughs at this, because she knows as well as I do that Tom's grotty studio flat above a Chicken Stop takeaway in South Ealing is very far from anything resembling luxury. It still irks me that he's a homeowner, though. I don't know anyone who's managed to buy their own place without help from a generous relative. My Acton abode might be overcrowded and ramshackle, but I only pay £450 a month — and that includes all my bills. When I accidentally (on purpose) sneaked a look at Tom's bank statement once when he left it on the desk at work, I almost choked on my ham and tomato baguette. No wonder he's so skinny, what with having no money left after the mortgage to afford food.

'On the subject of living arrangements,' Rachel puts in before Tom has a chance to reply, 'we have a bit of news, don't we, Pauly?'

I wish she wouldn't call him that.

For the first time since I've met him, Paul looks a little bit uncomfortable. It's only a passing sense of awkwardness, but I spot it. And he sees me spot it, too.

'I'm moving in with Rach,' he declares, coughing slightly as she reaches across to take his hand.

Rachel is another one with a generous relative. Well, a granny who was generous enough to save every penny she ever had and hand it over to her own daughter's children after she died. Rachel lives in a two-bedroom actual house in Willesden, which is about five thousand miles away from anywhere, so we hardly ever visit. Now that Paul and his amazing hair are moving in, I doubt I will ever go there again.

'That's great news,' I manage to say through gritted teeth. 'How lovely for you both.'

Is it lovely, though? I can't imagine living that closely with any man, let alone an oaf like Paul. Rachel is a lot braver than I am. And what's the big rush, anyway? She's only just turned twenty-eight, like Tom and me. It all feels a bit overly serious and grown-up.

True to generous form, Tom is now shaking Paul's hand across the table. I don't think he should be congratulated. Rachel is a goddess; too good to shine his boots, which I'm sure she'll actually start doing now, along with ironing creases into his underpants and leaving chocolate hearts on his pillow. I'm not sure if it's the cheap ale or the sense of impending doom for one of my best friends brewing in the depths of my gut, but I suddenly feel very sick indeed.

Rachel, as if sensing this, swiftly changes the subject. 'I can't believe you're going back to Mojácar!' She beams at me. 'I wish I could come with you. I'd love to see the place again.'

As she says it, she looks down at her own tiny tattoo on the inside of her left wrist. We had them done at the same time, each paying for the other one to ensure the symbol was given as a gift. The legend goes that if the Indalo Man is bestowed by its recipient then it will not act as a talisman. Back when we were teenagers, Rachel and I believed this wholeheartedly, hence the complicated payment method. It worked out well for me, though, because mine is about four times the size of hers, and so cost about four times as much. Poor Rachel.

I trace my own tattoo now with my little finger, going over the clean lines of my inky friend's body and around the crest of the semi-circle joining one arm to the other over his head. According to the history books, this half-hoop represents a rainbow, but I chose to have mine done in plain black. I've read so much about this symbol and done so much research into the legend surrounding him over the past month, that at the moment this tattoo feels more important and significant than it ever has before. I just hope all the things I've read about him are true – even those that sound suspiciously like a load of old gobbledygook.

I visited Mojácar for the first time when I was fifteen, and I can still remember how excited I was. It was the first time I'd ever been away from my mum for more than a few days, and there were lots of tears when she waved me off in Rachel's dad's car. It was very generous of her parents to let me tag along on their family holiday – especially because at the time Rachel and I used to enjoy communicating with each other in a weird language that we'd made up ourselves, which consisted of grunting noises and exaggerated hand movements. We thought we were so clever; in reality, we must have looked like a pair of deranged gibbons.

That first year, we weren't allowed out in the evenings alone, but by the second summer, when we had both turned sixteen, Rachel and I were permitted to have dinner out on our own and to head down to the beach bars unsupervised during the daytime. Rachel's parents were fond of excursions and her mum loved to set up her foldable easel in remote locations so she could paint. The two of us, on the other hand, were only interested in giggling at the Spanish waiters, reading copies of *Just Seventeen* while we sunbathed and talking about all the boys we fancied from school.

The third year was when we began sneaking into the bars and kissing some of the local lads. It was all very innocent, but at the time it felt like we were so grown-up. Everyone in Mojácar was so laid-back, and the way of life so relaxed compared to how it was back in dreary old England. I came out of my shell in Mojácar, worried less about things, and relished the distance it provided from the stuff I was struggling with back at home. I loved having a place that was mine, somewhere that my mum and dad had never been to, and what I loved even more was having a version of myself that they never saw, either. Only Rachel really got to see both sides of me, but it had been a very long time since even she had been in the company of Mojácar Hannah. We had been planning to go back the year we turned eighteen – in fact, for months it was all we talked about – but then they found Rachel's dad's tumour and my poor friend's world fell apart overnight. I guess, ever since then, life has just got in the way of us ever making a return trip, but now that I'm sitting here talking to her about it, I can't believe we've never done it.

'I wish you could come too,' I tell her honestly. 'It's going to be strange being there without you.'

'Oh no, it won't,' she assures me, meeting my eye. 'I'm sure you'll find ways to pass the time.'

Rachel is the only person who knows about my crush on Theo, so I know what she's getting at even if the two boys have no idea.

'Maybe I will,' I agree, giving her a loaded look.

'If I was single, I'd definitely be up for a holiday fling,' says Paul, rather too wistfully. There's an awkward silence while we all wait for Rachel's displeasure to waft down the bench and into her boyfriend's subconscious. It takes longer than it should.

'Not that I miss being single,' he adds at last, smiling at her furious expression. 'You know I only have eyes for you, Rachy.'

The ale is definitely in danger of making a projectile reappearance.

'From what I remember,' Rachel says now, looking at me with amusement, 'you never had any trouble attracting the men over in Mojácar.'

Tom rudely guffaws into his pint.

'I don't see why it will be any different this time around,' Rachel continues, ignoring his interruption. 'Just channel that sexy, confident seventeen-year-old version of yourself and you'll be golden.'

'I definitely wasn't sexy,' I reply, picturing my flat-chested and spotty teenage self and grimacing. 'And if I was confident, it was only because we were stealing from your mum and dad's vodka stash every night before we went out.'

'You can buy your own vodka this time – even better!'

At the mention of alcohol, I notice everyone's glasses are running low and head to the bar to get another round in.

As I stand up to leave the table, Paul gives my hand a quick squeeze. 'Get me a Peroni, will you, Han?'

A bloody Peroni? He's getting the cheap, nasty ale and liking it.

Despite good intentions, it's past eleven by the time we all stumble out on to the pavement and give each other clumsy hugs goodbye. Rachel draws Tom to one side and whispers something into his ear, but before I can barge over and find out what, Paul has blocked my path and pulled me into a rather stiff embrace.

'Have a good time in Majorca, yeah,' he slurs into my ear.

'It's Mojácar,' I reply through gritted teeth, patting him lightly on the shoulder.

What. A. Wally.

Thankfully, I'm saved by the bell. Well, the ringing of my phone, which is a bit bell-like. Who the hell would be calling me at this time? For a brief, fleeting, ecstatic second, I allow myself to believe it might be Theo, ringing to tell me he can take it no longer, that he must give in to the feelings of love and abundant lust that have been coursing through his veins for months.

It's my mum.

'Hi, Mum,' I say, slightly cautiously, as I disentangle myself from Paul's drunken spaghetti arms. 'Why are you calling me so late?'

'Is it late?' comes the reply. I sense I may not be the only one who's indulged in a few cheeky bevvies this evening.

'It is for someone your age,' I joke, smiling at the shriek I get in response.

'Well, I know you're flying out tomorrow, and I've got that zoga class down at the leisure centre first thing.'

'Zoga?' I ask, waving and blowing a kiss at Rachel as she and Paul head off hand in hand towards the tube station. Tom stands by the kerb waiting for me, staring at his shoes and pretending not to eavesdrop on my conversation.

'It's a new thing,' she informs me cheerfully. 'Like a mixture of yoga and zumba.'

'Right,' I manage, wondering how the hell such a thing could ever remotely work. Do you dance first, then yoga after? Or are you meditating to hard house? Nope, total nonsense.

'Have you spoken to your dad?' she asks now, her voice

getting that slight edge that it always does when my other parent comes up in conversation.

'No.'

'Oh. But he does know about this trip, doesn't he?'

'Not unless you've told him,' I sigh, kicking a stone along the street so hard that it causes Tom to look up at me in alarm.

'Of course I haven't,' my mum says. 'I haven't spoken to him in months.'

'I'll send him a text,' I lie, feeling irritated. I'm twenty-eight, for God's sake. I don't have to tell my dad everything I'm doing. It's not like he'd care anyway, even if I did.

'I'm very proud of you,' Mum says then, swiftly bursting my bubble of anger. 'I just wanted you to know that. I know how long you've been waiting for this, so make sure you enjoy every single second of it.'

I picture Mojácar, its narrow cobbled streets, the sunlight sneaking through gaps in the trailing flowers, the wide expanse of beach, the fresh and frisky Mediterranean, and I feel a grin start to lift the edges of my mouth.

'I promise I will,' I tell her. 'I'm going to make sure I do.'

We continue chatting as Tom and I make our way to the bus stop, and he waits for my number sixty-four to turn up even though his bus arrives first. He can be very sweet sometimes. It's easy to forget when we seem to spend a large percentage of the time winding each other up.

'Your mum okay?' he asks, when I finally hang up.

'She's taken up zoga,' I tell him, my eyebrows raised,

and he laughs with affection as I explain what it is. Sometimes I think Tom loves my mum even more than I do.

'What do you think about Paul moving in with Rachel?' he says then, even though he knows full well what I think.

'I think she's crazy,' I say simply. 'And I think she can do better.'

'But she does seem happy . . .' Tom begins, stopping mid-sentence when he sees the look on my face.

'He's just such a typical boorish lad, though,' I argue. 'He's so self-involved and he has no social skills and he doesn't appreciate her and I bet he's cheating on her.'

'Whoa, whoa, whoa!' Tom holds up a dinner-plate-sized hand. 'That's not fair, Hannah.'

I hate it when Tom tells me off – especially when I know that I'm right and he's wrong.

'Okay,' I allow. 'He might not be cheating yet, but I bet he will soon.'

Tom just shakes his head at me. 'You shouldn't think like that,' he says quietly. 'He's not all bad. What about the time he got those free passes to go up the Shard and took us with him? Or when he whisked Rachel off to Rome for the weekend when they'd only been dating for a few weeks? You might not like him much, and I agree he can put his foot in it sometimes, but Rachel is your oldest friend and she loves him. That has to count for something.'

I hate it even more when Tom tells me off and I know that he's right and I'm wrong.

'Sorry, Dad,' I retort childishly, hurling my arm out to one side just in time to get the attention of the bus driver. Tom still looks a bit sad when I wave goodbye to him through the window of the bus, and as we move off around the corner and he disappears from view, I'm hit with a small but very sharp pebble of guilt.

I am so over London. The sooner we get to sunny Spain and away from all this dreary, day-to-day real-life stuff, the better.

3

'Why do all airlines think that only midgets travel in their planes?'

Tom is unusually grumpy. Like me, he feels a huge injustice at having been born slightly taller than the average human, and moans about it at every possible opportunity.

'Seriously, though,' he mutters, trying for the forty-eighth or so time since we took off from Gatwick airport to rearrange his ridiculously long legs into a comfortable position. It doesn't work.

'Just suck it up, boy,' I tell him, wondering if I'll ever get the feeling back in my own feet. 'I think the man in front of you will actually kill you if you bang your knees against his seat one more time.'

There's a grunt from the bald chap in question confirming this, and Tom goes bright red.

Claudette nabbed the aisle seat, despite being only five foot one in heels, and promptly fell asleep just after take-off. For someone so petite, French and beautiful, she can't half snore. As we were crossing the Channel, she even snorted herself momentarily back awake. Tom and I were still laughing about it when we'd cleared France.

Theo isn't with us; he flew out a few days ago to make sure all our equipment arrived safely, and it's completely pathetic, but I miss him. I'm almost as excited about seeing him as I am about setting foot in Mojácar again after all these years. I really need to get a grip.

'Look.' Tom nudges me out of my drooling delusion and points out of the window. We're nearing Almería now, and he's spotted the corrugated roofs of all the farm buildings next to the airport. From road level, they're nothing special at all, but from up here they look like scattered pieces of a broken mosaic. It's actually quite beautiful.

'I remember these,' I tell him. 'We're almost there.'

I feel the fingers of nervous excitement start to tickle my insides. My very first location shoot, in a place that means so much to me – and Theo is going to be waiting for us at the airport. As the plane starts to slip through the thin clouds towards the Spanish runway, I feel as if my smile alone could keep it up in the air.

'Did I sleep the whole way?' asks Claudette as the wheels hit the tarmac, yawning and stretching out her tiny limbs in all directions.

'Yes,' Tom informs her. 'And you snored the whole way, too.'

Claudette merely smiles sleepily at him, and then turns to me. 'He is so funny, that boy, always making such silly jokes.'

'Hmmm,' I reply, doing my best not to laugh as she runs her minuscule hands through her neat, dark bob. It seems cruel to tell her the truth, which is that she snores like a warthog with severe asthma, so I keep my lips sealed as we get ready to disembark. Tom is making a big show of rubbing the circulation back into his legs, grumbling all the while, and Claudette is tapping her foot impatiently behind our friend the bald man, who is in turn wrestling with his case, which has become stuck in the overhead locker.

'This man is an imbecile,' she remarks, not bothering to lower her voice.

'What?' asks Tom, shooting up from one of his extravagant bend-and-stretches and promptly cracking his head on one of the airflow nozzles above the seats.

'You are an imbecile, too,' she adds with disdain, as Tom rubs the back of his messy blond head and recites every swear word known to man – plus a few inventive extras of his own. How the hell these two manage to go on foreign shoots together all the time, I'll never know. In the past year alone, they've been to Canada, Australia and France – and every time I've had to pretend I'm not gut-squirmingly jealous.

By the time we've queued to get our passports checked, waited half an hour for Claudette's three suitcases and then waited another fifteen minutes for her to redo her make-up in the bathroom mirror, my frustration and excitement has reached such an intense level that I'm about ready to climb up the wall of the arrivals lounge, scramble across the ceiling and come back down the other side.

'What's up with you?' enquires Tom, frowning at me as I hop from one foot to the other. 'You look like you're about to wet yourself.'

'I am!' I practically yell at him, glancing towards the doors leading out to the exit. Mojácar is waiting for us on the other side of that frosted glass, and so is Theo.

'Just go to the toilet then,' he says, confusion evident in his voice. Men don't understand anything.

Of course, when the moment arrives and we finally make it through to where Theo is indeed waiting, a newspaper open across his lap and a pair of sunglasses keeping his dark curls off his face, the only thing that happens is a series of polite hellos. I'd hoped for a kiss on each cheek at the very least – we are in bloody Spain after all – but no. He just smiles at me and beckons us outside to where the car is waiting.

My senses are reeling as I look around and take it all in. I'm actually here, back in Almería, less than an hour away from the beautiful and magical Mojácar that I've never been able to forget. It all feels so strange yet familiar at the same time.

'Bit hot, isn't it?' remarks Tom, taking off his hoodie and squinting up at the cloudless azure sky. Theo, who is wearing an immaculately pressed white shirt and smart black trousers, and who doesn't have a single bead of sweat on him, shrugs.

'It is summer,' he says, by way of an explanation. I decide not to say anything about the fact that my cropped jeans and vest top seem to have morphed into an eighteen-tog duvet in the hour since we landed, and instead sneak a tissue out of my bag to wipe the sweat off my face. It's just past four in the afternoon, and I know the sun will soon start to lose its intensity, but at the moment it's almost stifling. It's a huge relief to clamber into the air-conditioned haven of Theo's hire car, even if Tom – traitor – does bagsy the front seat.

The overwhelming sense of déjà vu intensifies as Theo puts the car in gear and heads out of the parking lot on to the motorway, and I feel my eyes widen as they take in the surrounding mountains. We're on the south-east coast of the country, and the landscape is arid and roasted brown by the year-round sunshine. Below me to the right the Mediterranean is spread out like a navy blanket, its canvas interrupted by only a very occasional flash of white-topped wave. There is almost no wind, and clumps of cactuses sit fat and unmoving by the side of the road. It's no wonder that this area of Spain is often used as the setting for Westerns, another fact that I've discovered since I began my research.

Tom has fallen silent in the passenger seat, as mesmerised as I am by the alien landscape. Claudette, meanwhile, is nattering away to Theo about the filming schedule and doing her best to persuade him that a few days off to work on her tan would be beneficial to the documentary.

'I just think people like to see me looking healthy,' she tells him. 'They don't want a ghost telling them about this beautiful place – my skin is so pale it will scare the audience.'

Theo, who has clearly spent the last few days in the sun himself, chuckles along, humouring her, but I know he won't budge when it comes to the schedule. His serious-boss side is one of the things I love most about him. When he puts on that stern face of his and gets those angry wrinkles across his forehead . . . Sigh.

'Hannah, did you hear me?'

Oh hell, he's actually talking to me.

'Yes! No. Erm, sorry. What was that?'

Moron.

Theo smiles at me in the rear-view mirror. 'I said that Mojácar is absolutely perfect. I looked at so many photos before we came here, but nothing could have prepared me for how beautiful it is. You have found us an amazing place.'

Is it possible to actually combust with pride? If it is, then the interior of this hire car is about to get very messy.

'Thanks.' I grin back at his reflection. 'I can't wait to see it again myself – I imagine it's changed loads over the years.'

'I thought we could all have dinner in the Old Town this evening,' Theo continues. 'Then afterwards you can show us where you used to party when you were a teenager.'

He's definitely poking fun at me now, but I love it.

'Do you think any of the Spanish barmen will recognise you?' asks Claudette, making me instantly regret telling her tales a few nights ago about some of my teenage antics. I knew that second bottle of wine was a bad idea, but I was so thrilled to be invited out for a drink with her. She's done a few projects with Vivid now, but because she's a freelance presenter and sometime actress, she isn't based in the office with the rest of us, and so I haven't spent much one-on-one time with her. Claudette is effortlessly cool and radiates the sort of self-assured charm that I have never managed to convey. She's thirty-seven, but her skin is flawless and her make-up always immaculate so she looks about ten years younger. She's the kind of woman that doesn't even own a pair of ratty old tracksuit bottoms, let alone wear them to the pub on a Sunday afternoon like I often do.

'Why would they?' I reply, through gritted teeth. I don't want to discuss Spanish barmen in front of Theo. He must see me as professional and sophisticated at all times.

'True,' she says, her tone making it clear that she's enjoying toying with me. 'They must get off with so many English girls that they all blend into one.'

'I did *not* get off with any Spanish barmen,' I squeal. It's a total lie, of course, and I know Claudette's only teasing me, but I wish she'd rein it in around our boss.

'Greek barmen are the same,' Theo agrees, overtaking a lorry with just a single hand on the wheel. 'I can't remember many English girls from the summer I spent working in my uncle's bar.'

Oh my God – Theo was a teenage tramp, too. Now all I must do is invent a time machine, then go on holiday to the Greek island that he was working on about twenty years ago and make him fall in love with me. Simple.

'Men are disgusting,' Claudette announces in response, causing Tom to boo loudly at her from the front of the car. Theo is laughing now, and he catches my eye in the rear-view mirror again. Is it my imagination, or does he linger a little longer this time? I dare myself to look again, but the moment has passed. Either that or I simply imagined it.

'We're coming up to the turning,' Theo says. 'The first time I drove around this corner and saw Mojácar, it took my breath away, I'm telling you.'

He's right. Even though I've been here before and seen the honeycomb-shaped village appear in the distance, its white stone buildings shining like an enormous toothy grin against the tanned backdrop of the mountain, I still get major butterflies when it eventually comes into sight.

The car falls into a reverent silence, with even Claudette lost for words as she gazes up at the magical village nestled snugly in the distance. As we speed up and veer towards our exit, she mutters something romantic-sounding in French, putting her slender hand on my arm and giving it a squeeze. This is exactly what I'd hoped for. I knew that Mojácar would get them all under its spell, just as it had done to me all those years ago. There's just something about this place, something that makes it special, unique and different to anywhere else I've ever been in the world.

'I've got the goosey bumps,' Claudette admits, saying what we're all thinking. Assuming she's cold rather than moved, Theo stretches over and switches off the air conditioning, and for a few minutes we continue to drive in silence. The spell is only broken when we turn again and the view of Mojácar is momentarily lost, obscured by the bulk of one of the many surrounding hills.

'Where are we staying again, Han?' asks Tom, turning in his seat. I open my mouth to reply, but Theo beats me to it.

'In the Old Town,' he says, coughing slightly. 'Hannah and Claudette are in one apartment, and you are in a studio flat.'

'I'm not sharing with you this time, boss?' Tom fails to keep the joy out of his voice.

'Unfortunately for you, no.' Theo grins. 'I am staying down at the beach. I prefer to be next to the sea and I need space for the editing equipment, but it is better for you to be up in the town, I think. Close to the bars and shops.'

Because I made all the bookings, I know just how small Tom's place is compared to the entire villa that Theo has secured, but I know he won't care. The laid-back way of life here is going to fit my best friend like a well-tailored suit, and I'm gripped by a new elation as I envisage showing him around. I'm looking forward to sharing an apartment with Claudette, too. I'm hoping that some of her French magnetism will rub off on me.

It makes a change from sharing with Tom, anyway, which I've done at a fair few festivals over the years. His feet smell like centuries-old Brie after a day spent in wellies and he talks in his sleep when he's drunk – and I mean really chatters away. I had an entire conversation with him in complete gibberish at Glastonbury one year and he didn't remember anything about it.

I hear Claudette gasp next to me and look up to see that the village of Mojácar – or Mojácar Pueblo, as the locals call it – is now right above us. Incredibly, it's exactly how I remember, with narrow cobbled roads snaking up and around the hill, white stone houses sitting at jaunty angles and, as Theo edges the car higher, magnificent sweeping views of the mountains and beach below. Something stirs deep inside my belly, and I'm unable to keep the smile from forming on my lips. The fatigue I felt after the three-hour flight vanishes as I wind down the window and inhale the warm air. I can smell lemons and there's an earthy scent, too – even the dust here smells deliciously fragrant to me. Poking my head out through the gap, I suck more of the air into my lungs like a greedy child.

'You look like my parents' old Labrador,' Tom quips, laughing at me in the wing mirror. I slyly give him the finger.

'Parking around here is a nightmare,' Theo complains.

We've arrived at the rather unimaginatively named Vista Apartments, where Claudette and I will be living for the next four weeks, but all the parking spaces, plus a lot of the road alongside them, are full.

'Just drop us here,' I say sweetly, ignoring the look of total disgust on Claudette's face. 'We'll meet you up in the square at, say, half seven?'

Theo nods and flicks on the hazard lights long enough for me to heave Claudette's entire collection of luggage – plus my own, single case – out from the boot, before giving us both a quick wave and driving off up the hill towards Tom's place.

'I am all sweaty,' grumbles Claudette, sniffing at the bougainvillea that's trailing down from the top of our apartment block. Like so many of the buildings cut into the side of the vast hills here, its roof is level with the road, and each apartment is reached by climbing down a scarily narrow and steep set of stone steps. Luckily, given Claudette's increasingly fractious mood and the multiple number of suitcases she's brought with her, we only have to go down to the second level of five. The key is, as promised by the owners, hidden under the doormat, and there's a large Indalo Man symbol painted on the wall next to the door.

I didn't tell any of the others this, but I stayed in this very same block of apartments with Rachel and her folks. We're higher up this time, but the layout is exactly as I remember it, with a hallway, large living area and kitchen, plus a separate bathroom and two good-sized bedrooms.

While Claudette crashes around in her chosen bedroom and mutters French obscenities at the lack of wardrobe space, I head straight out through the glass doors and on to the wide, tiled balcony. There's a beautiful wrought-iron table and two chairs out here, and someone has strung a makeshift washing line from the back corner to a pipe that's running down the length of the whole block. A large clay figurine has been fixed to the sloping stone wall on my left, and I smile as I sneak a look down at my matching tattoo.

If I peer over the side of the far wall, I can see the very edge of the balcony belonging to the apartment below our own, each one in the block stacked against the hillside like seats in a stadium.

I'm still standing there, enjoying the citrusy air and the feel of the warm tiles beneath my bare feet, when Claudette bustles out. I think she's saying something about forgetting her travel iron, but as soon as she looks up and sees the view spread out in front of us, she shuts up.

'Mon dieu,' she whispers, and I see the hairs rise up on her arms.

We stand there for a time, side by side, drinking it all in. I realise I can feel a strange something stirring inside me, the same something that's been bubbling away since I began reading up on this place again. There really is magic in Mojácar, I decide. And I intend to find out where it comes from.

4

The first thing that strikes me as Claudette and I make our leisurely way up the steep hill and into the Old Town later that evening is that Mojácar has barely changed at all. It's over ten years since I was last here, but it feels like it could have been last week. Everything is so comfortingly familiar, from the immaculate whitewashed buildings to the decorative pots of flowers fixed to walls and lined up along window sills. The little gift shops selling postcards, maps and hundreds of Indalo Man souvenirs look utterly unaltered, as if time has ceased to pass up here. With every step, my enchantment swells, and I have to quell a ridiculous urge to skip along the path like a playful goat.

It isn't long before Claudette gets fed up of stopping every few yards to wait for me while I take photos to send back to Rachel. I can't help it, though, despite her unsubtle tutting — everything is just so beautiful.

'My legs are hurting,' she grumbles now, reaching down to massage her non-existent calves. It's not surprising, really. The winding road that leads up from the beachfront, right up the side of the hill, past our apartment block and into the Old Town, is very steep — especially on this last section just below Plaza Nueva, the main square.

Often when people think of Spain, they picture the fiery golds and reds of a matador's costume and the rich orange of the setting sun over one of the country's many beaches, but the dominant colours here in Mojácar are white, blue and pink. The buildings in the town are almost all painted a bright, unapologetic white, a shade that is made all the more vibrant by the contrasting deep blue of the sky above and the many cerulean-blue shutters and doors. The pink comes from the clusters of bougainvillea that are spilling out over the balconies of every house we pass, their scent clashing deliciously with the strange fragrant dust in the air. I could quite happily sit down on the wall by the road and let my senses devour the lot, but Claudette has other ideas. She is hungry, she is thirsty, she is worn out and she needs to empty her bladder – all things she's told me at least ten times in the last three minutes. I had no idea she was this high-maintenance.

We pass the tiny post office just below the Plaza Nueva and Claudette, spotting several open bars, dashes off across the cobbles in search of a bathroom. There's no sign of Theo or Tom yet, so I decide to take the steps to my right and head up to admire the view from the Mirador de la Plaza Nueva, a wide, tiled platform set along one side of the square.

I have to navigate a few tables and chairs outside the platform's one neighbouring restaurant to reach the stretch of black railings along the far edge, but it's worth it – the view below is nothing short of spectacular. The brown, desert-like earth seems to stretch on into the distance as far as my eyes can see, and the road we drove in on earlier snakes its way between white buildings that are scattered like discarded Scrabble pieces against the dusty horizon. To the far right is the shimmering blue line of the sea, and immediately in front of me is a very distinctive flat-topped hill, which I know from my research to be Mojácar la Vieja, or Old Mojácar. It was here that the ruling Moors of the Bronze Age built a garrison to watch over their land, and what a view they must have had.

There is such a sense of history here – not only in the surrounding buildings and landscape, but also in the air, particles of distant memories swept up by the persistent wind and chased around this beautiful old town in a never-ending dance of then and now. Perhaps it is this element that makes Mojácar such an unmistakably magical place.

There is all of a sudden a delicious scent of limes, and I turn to find Theo approaching. He's looking at the view instead of me, thank God, because I'm pretty sure my jaw just dropped low enough to leave a clear mark in the dusty blue and white tiles beneath my feet.

It's a warm evening, but there's a pleasant breeze easing its fingers across the bare skin of my arms and legs and through my still-damp hair. Theo must have showered, too, because his dark locks are free from the earlier gel and he's swapped his white shirt for a plain grey T-shirt. Like me, he seems to have instantly relaxed into the sleepy atmosphere of the place, and looking at his contented expression as he gazes out towards the flat top of the Old Mojácar hill fills me with pleasure.

'Is it just as you remember it?' he asks, turning to meet my eyes for the first time since he walked over.

'Exactly.' I smile at him. 'I was worried that I'd get here and find a Pizza Hut in the middle of the square, but thankfully that wasn't the case.'

'I have been exploring the village up here,' he tells me, that gorgeous half-smile still playing around his mouth. I make a concerted effort not to stare at his lips, but it's not easy. I have never wanted to kiss anything more in my entire life.

'You were right, Hannah – it is a very special place.'

He looks almost thoughtful as he says this last part, and I wonder what he's thinking. There is so much depth and wisdom in those dark brown eyes of his. They more than rival the view spread out below us.

Just as I open my mouth to offer a penny for his thoughts, Tom bounds towards us, a still-irritable Claudette scuttling along behind him like a grumpy Chihuahua.

'I had no idea where you'd gone,' she admonishes, wagging her finger in my direction.

'You've found me now,' I shrug, keeping my eyes firmly on the floor rather than Theo. Tom is wearing the same hilariously bad shorts that he rolls out every time there's a bit of sunshine, which are black with big orange flowers on them. I make a mental note to show him the shopping centre down by the beach. Still, at least he's shaved off that grotty beard.

Theo tells us he's booked a table at a pizza place about ten minutes' walk away, so we head off through the labyrinthine cobbled streets, Tom and I falling into step beside each other as the other two stride ahead. I notice with a certain amount of disgruntlement that Claudette seems to have recovered from her earlier leg pains and is now skipping along next to Theo, chatting shop with him. The sun is very slowly starting its descent, and as we make our way through the heart of the town, golden ribbons of light appear around corners and across the curved roof tiles of the buildings. Shop owners smile a greeting from their doorways as we pass, and I notice that Tom has again been uncharacteristically wowed into silence by the surroundings.

'I feel like a marble in a marble run,' he whispers, as we turn a sharp corner to find yet another steep cobbled path ahead.

'There's nothing remotely marble-like about you,' I whisper back.

'But if I was a marble, I'd have a lot of fun rolling around these streets,' he hisses.

I shake my head at him, the loon. If anyone ever overheard some of the bizarre conversations Tom and I have, they'd be calling the men in white coats to come and cart us off. Thank God we're both as odd as each other, though. It would be very boring if I couldn't be myself around him.

Theo leads us round three more corners and finally, at the top of a set of steps steep enough to render even him slightly out of breath, we reach our destination.

'I know this place!' I blurt in surprise, my mouth reaching the finish line before my brain.

It may be a pizza restaurant now, but these decorative metal gates in front of us used to lead into a bar. And not just any bar, *the* bar where Rachel and I spent almost every night of our last holiday, lusting over the Spanish owner and drinking endless glasses of Coke topped up with our stolen vodka. It would be fair to say that I may have embarrassed myself in here a few times.

Perhaps more than a few.

'Was this one of your hangouts?' guesses Claudette in delight.

'No. I mean, I thought it was, but I must be mistaken.' I give her a look that I hope is suitably convincing, but she's not falling for it.

'Whatever you say,' she replies, stepping over the threshold. Theo has gone on ahead and is now beckoning to us from across the open courtyard. There are several wooden tables and chairs arranged out here, each one adorned with a red umbrella, and as I pass the open doorway of what used to be the bar, I sneak a quick glance inside. In contrast to everywhere else in this town, this place actually has changed, but only from a bar into a restaurant – the layout is the same as I remember, and a rush of lovely nostalgia flows through me.

God only knows what that poor barman thought of us back then. He was far older than Rachel and me and barely spoke any English, but that didn't deter either of us in our pursuit. We'd spend literally hours getting ready down in the apartment, dismissing every single item of clothing we'd packed in our suitcases until teetering piles of dresses, miniskirts and boob tubes covered the floor. What little horrors we were. I like to think I'm much more sophisticated these days.

'Hannah, are you going to sit down?'

Theo is standing up at the table, his hand on the back of my vacant chair and an expectant look on his face. Rushing forwards from my spot by the gate, I promptly trip over my own feet and stagger into him sideways. Like I said, sophisticated.

'Shit! I mean, sorry.'

'Have you two been drinking?' Tom asks Claudette, as Theo steers me carefully into my seat.

Claudette is peering at me and totally ignoring Tom, while Theo is oblivious to all of us, consulting the wine list. We all nod along with his suggestion of a fruity red.

The courtyard of the restaurant looks out over yet another stunning view, and I watch as a pair of birds wind their way gracefully through the treetops. I had forgotten just how deafening the crickets and cicadas can be here – especially at this time of day. The chirping coming from the prickly undergrowth is constant, shrill and insistent, but it's also a comforting reminder that we're a very long way from boring old England. I still can't quite believe that I'm here, back in Mojácar. And it still feels as special as it always did. I'm so glad that I'm getting to share it with Theo. And Tom, too, of course.

We all order pizza except for Claudette, who asks the waiter to list all the salad ingredients they have on offer before designing her very own creation, much to his gratification, I'm sure. Anyone else would be embarrassed, but Claudette gets away with it. She should bottle that confidence of hers and sell it – she'd make an absolute killing, and I'd be her best customer.

I'm not sure whether we're all simply tired from the travelling we've done today or if it's more to do with the strange ambience of this place, but there isn't much chatter going on at our table. It occurs to me then that this is the first time the four of us have ever had dinner together. Obviously there's the work Christmas lunch and the odd leaving party down at the local pub, but those involve everyone. I'm not used to spending so much time with Theo, and my nervous jitters are increasing every time I look up and find him staring at me. I'm fine when we're at work, because I'm confident that I can do my job, but it's very different being in a social setting with him. It's as if I'm getting to know a whole new version of him that I never knew existed.

By the time the food arrives, I've wound myself up about it all so much that I can barely chew my cheesy topping. Of course, I want Theo to notice me, but not when there's a serious chance that I'll either choke to death on a strand of melted mozzarella or dribble tomato sauce down my chin. I want him to think of me as demure, not demented.

'They have forgotten my avocado,' grumbles Claudette, pushing her collection of leaves around with her fork.

I look up just in time to catch Theo rolling his eyes at her, and then he sees me, and smiles.

'Hola, amigos.'

A man has joined us at the table and is standing right behind me, his hands on the back of my chair in the typically over-familiar manner that I learned to associate with the Spanish a long time ago. Before I crane my head around to look at him, I notice a flush of colour wash across Claudette's cheeks and feel a tiptoe of foreboding creep through me.

'Hola!' Tom replies cheerily, reaching over to shake the man's hand. Typically, he's not remotely fussed about the fact that he's a complete stranger.

The man's hairy arm is right by my face now, but I'm still too scared to turn around. If this is who I think it is, then someone had better have a bulldozer handy, because I'm going to require the ground to swallow me whole.

Theo is chatting away to the man now in fluent Spanish, which, despite my feeling of sudden dread, is pretty damn sexy to behold – is there nothing that man can't do?

'Ah, you are making a film.'

The newcomer has reverted into broken English, presumably in an attempt to include the rest of us in the conversation, and again I feel his knuckles against the bare skin of my back.

Oh hell, now Theo is introducing each of us in turn.

'This is Hannah,' he says, coming to me last, and finally I take a deep breath and force my eyes upwards.

'Diego.' The man smiles at me.

Of course it's Diego. The very same Diego that I used to daydream about on a daily basis, possibly with added drool; the man that Rachel and I were both convinced we would one day marry and have babies with; the man who turned a blind eye to our illicit vodka consumption and pretended not to notice when we took photos of him on our disposable cameras. *That* Diego.

'Hola,' I manage, inwardly cursing my Anthea Turner crop yet again. I should have kept my overgrown fringe – it would have been perfect to hide behind.

Diego is now looking at me with a mixture of mild bemusement and recognition. He can't remember me, can he? It's been over ten years since I last saw the guy – a whole solid decade that I've been tossing shovelfuls of dirt into the very deep hole where I buried my pride after that fateful night.

'You have been here before, I think,' Diego says now.

'Yes, she has!' Tom exclaims happily, just as I shake my head to disagree.

Please don't let him remember what I did. Please, please, please.

'It was a very long time ago,' I mumble, wondering seriously if there's enough topping on my pizza to drown me if I shove my face into it.

Diego has crouched down on his haunches now and is

staring right at me. Back when I was seventeen, I would have happily swapped my signed Take That poster for the chance to get this close to him. Now, however, I wish I had the poster just so I could tear it into tiny pieces and build a fire as a distraction.

Just as I think Diego is going to admit defeat, he leans back on his heels and starts laughing.

'Hannah!' he says, slapping his meaty Spanish thigh in delight.

'Have you two met before?' Theo asks, putting down his fork.

Oh no. Oh shit. Oh help.

I turn to look at Diego now properly for the first time. He's still got the same almond-shaped eyes, dark and brooding and sparkling with mischief. His black hair is peppered with grey now, but the exquisite bone structure of his face and that generous mouth are still just as heavenly a combination as they ever were. My only option is to stare back at him so beseechingly that my yearning to keep the past a secret transcends the language barrier and somehow penetrates his brain. It's a long shot, but it's all I've got.

There's a small beat of silence interrupted only by the sound of Claudette's cutlery scraping against her plate, and then Diego stands up.

'It is nice to see you again,' he says, patting me on the back.

Oh my God – my mind trick actually worked. I must be a Jedi.

'You too,' I mutter, downing about half a glass of wine in a single gulp.

'Good luck with the film.' He addresses this to the whole table, and then tells us that we must come back and eat here at his restaurant again.

You can dream on, I think, but smile at him politely.

'He is gorgeous,' Claudette says loudly when Diego is less than a metre away. 'So many Spanish men are small, but that one is like a delicious man mountain.'

Theo, who is a very delectable – in my mind – five foot nine or so, shifts in his seat.

'How do you know him?' Claudette demands, craning her head around so she can watch Diego saunter back inside.

'He used to work here when it was a bar,' I inform them. 'I don't know him that well at all.'

'Yeah, yeah,' says Claudette, and I feel rather than see Tom look at me.

'He is gorgeous,' she repeats, her salad long ago abandoned. Without waiting for the rest of us to finish eating, she has extracted a thin cigarette from a silver packet and is now fishing in her bag for a lighter.

For a second, I picture my seventeen-year-old self, stumbling across this very courtyard in the high-heeled sandals that Rachel's dad used to compare to a North Sea oil rig, patches of sunburn decorating my legs and a complicated sculpture made from twisted plastic straws stuck in my hair. Diego is in the memory, too, leaning against the outer wall smoking and regarding me with amusement. What happened next is too humiliating to relive, and I smother the image with a fistful of pizza.

'You've gone a very strange colour,' Tom tells me.

'We must all leave the poor girl alone,' says Theo,

smiling at me as I chew on my dinner forlornly. 'If a lady has secrets that she does not want to share, then who are we to question her?'

Claudette has the grace to look mildly sheepish at Theo's words, but they almost cause me to splutter in surprise. I don't even care that Theo now assumes I have embarrassing secrets – all I can think is that he stuck up for me. He defended my honour, and he wouldn't do that unless he cared about me, would he?

I brave a look at the man in question to find that disappointingly he's looking not at me, but at the stunning view that fills one side of the open courtyard. The earlier chorus of cicadas has been replaced by the distant ringing of church bells, and the persistent breeze of the day has eased, its gentle fingers lifting only the very tips of my hair. In this moment, everything suddenly feels peaceful and calm again, as if the drama of bumping into Diego has been wiped away like chalk off a board.

Claudette blows a smoke ring up and the four of us watch transfixed as it breaks slowly into pieces before vanishing into the dusty air. I feel my eyelids sag under the weight of the day, and stifle a yawn at the exact same moment as Tom.

Theo must have noticed it, too, because after a beat he stands up and drops a heap of euro notes on to the table.

'Come on, team,' he says, meeting my eyes for less than a split second before glancing away. 'I think we must all call it a night.'

5

I've always been an early riser. Back when I was a child, our family dog used to wake me up by licking first my feet and then, if I didn't stir at that, my face. He was a Border collie called Chewy – named not after the *Star Wars* character as most people assumed, but solely because of his love of chewing up anything and everything he could get his grubby little muzzle around – and I loved him with every fibre of my innocent soul. I say innocent, but in actual fact, Chewy and I used to get up to all sorts of mischief during those early morning jaunts we'd go on together. There was the time I tried to teach Chewy to climb a tree, only to fall over Mr Harding's garden fence and destroy his prize-winning patch of strawberries. Then there was the time Chewy decided that an old lady's bag of knitting was a toilet. That one was definitely worse.

When Chewy died very suddenly from prostate cancer when he was only eight, I roared my miserable head off for days on end. I still miss that dog.

I grew up eventually, of course, and moved to London, where the mighty volume of the capital city's traffic replaced my licking-dog alarm clock. Everything is louder in London, and as much as I love living there, I also hate being shaken awake by a vibrating bedframe – not least because it's a passing lorry causing it to quiver, as opposed to the naked and randy Theo from my dreams.

Here in Mojácar, however, I am pleasantly surprised to be woken by the sound of birdsong. I closed the wooden shutters across the window just before crashing out last night, but there's still a trickle of sunlight seeping into the room around its edges. Feeling not unlike Snow White when she conjures up an entire woodland population just by whistling a mediocre song, I kick off my tangled sheet and skip happily through into the kitchen, where I decant water from the bottle in the fridge into the kettle and ready a mug for tea.

Being careful to stir in my sugar quietly so as not to disturb Claudette, I pad silently across to the balcony doors and slide them open, immediately smiling a greeting to the sun which has started to warm the terracotta tiles beneath my feet. This time of day feels so bewitching, when possibilities seem endless and my enthusiasm has been recharged, ready to fire out at full throttle. This is the best time, before anyone else has had a chance to puncture my serenity with their worries or complaints. It's taken me twenty-eight years to know for certain, but I can say with full confidence now that I'm definitely a morning person.

Lifting up one of the beautiful wrought-iron chairs, I carry it carefully to the edge of the balcony before retrieving my tea from where I left it on the table. I put my feet up on the low painted wall and wiggle my toes, enjoying the feeling of the clean morning air tickling between them. I painted my toenails seashell pink to match one of the three new bikinis I bought specially for the trip, and the iridescent top coat I added keeps catching the light.

Closing my eyes, I take a deep breath in, detecting the

scent of pine and a hint of last night's perfume. The tea is sweet and has reached that perfect temperature just below scorching, where you can sip it without feeling the need to gulp. The sound of more birdsong draws my attention away from the view and up into the pure blue sky above the mountains. Two birds are taking it in turns to dive down to the swimming pool right down at the base of the apartment block, presumably picking off insects that have become marooned on the surface, and each time one soars back up, the other squawks its applause. I only realise how much I'm smiling when I crash my mug against my teeth.

Last night Theo gave Tom, Claudette and me strict instructions to meet him at La Fuente, Mojácar's public water fountain, at nine a.m. sharp this morning, but a glance at my watch tells me that it's only just gone seven. If I get a wriggle on, I could pop down there first to check the place out, maybe pick up some breakfast bits on the way back. After her pathetic salad last night, Claudette is bound to wake up ravenous, and a hangry – a combination of hungry and angry – French presenter is not what we need on the first day of the shoot. Mind made up, I leave my empty mug in the sink, throw on a red sundress that I found languishing in the back of my wardrobe with the tags still attached, and stick my sunglasses into my nest of hair, opting for plimsolls over flip-flops at the last minute. Hazardous shoes and steep hills do not mix.

Outside, the mounting heat of the day has already strung a shimmering line across the horizon, and I have to squint when my eyes find the tinsel-like strip of the distant sea. As I walk downhill, my flat shoes making a pleasing slapping sound against the smooth pavement tiles, I promise myself that tomorrow I'll get up even earlier and go for a swim. Hopefully this won't be the one and only location shoot I ever get to go on, but I intend to make the most of it just in case.

I imagine that I can feel my eyeballs expanding to take in the higgledy-piggledy clutter of whitewashed buildings, the uneven landscape unfolding in front of me so unlike the comparative flatness of London. Again I experience that sensation of contentment, acute yet comforting at the same time. It makes me even happier to know that Theo feels it, too. We have so much in common, the two of us, I think, turning another corner and encountering a steep downward slope. It hadn't even occurred to me that I already know the way to La Fuente, but clearly my body remembers exactly where to go, because I can see it now coming into view below me.

Arguably one of the most important landmarks of Mojácar and certainly the most famous, the fountain is as vital now as it was back in the fifteenth century, when the folk in this area were living solely off the land. In those days, women from the village would journey down the hillside with their large clay pots on a daily basis, making a pilgrimage to collect water for themselves and their livestock. There's even a statue of a Mojácar water woman up in the village by the church, which I must make sure I remember to show the others.

What a life it must have been for those women, I think, smiling at a small old man who's pulling up the shutters of his tobacco store as I pass. It seems bizarre to think of the lifestyle they must have led, living hand to mouth and balancing these vast urns of water on their heads as they trudged back up the side of the hill. I feel as if I'm hard done by when I have to struggle back from the supermarket with washing powder and orange squash, but I bet the ladies living here never complained. We really do have it so easy these days.

I can hear the sound of running water now, and as I round the last corner and finally reach La Fuente, the air around me takes on a new clarity, as if the hovering particles of liquid have washed away that ever-present dust. The fountain itself is large, rectangular, and paved in white and brown stone, each edge bordered by low stone basins. The walls are painted white and decorated intermittently by terracotta pots full of flowers, each one a vibrant splash of colour against the plain backdrop. I take the steps down into the centre, counting the spouts as I go. There are thirteen in total – unlucky for some – and clean spring water tumbles merrily out of them, filtered not by chemicals but by the insides of the very mountain that stretches up above me now. It's pretty bloody amazing, if you think about it.

I decide to stay here for a while and drink in the atmosphere, smiling at the aptness of that description as it passes through my mind. There's a plaque at the far end of the fountain, below which the word 'Mojácar' has been sculpted and fixed into the stone, and I step across the marble trough to run my finger across each of the letters in turn. The whole place is so clean and well maintained, and I feel a surge of affection for the people living here. There is clearly much pride associated with this fountain, saturated as it is by history and importance, and I love that it's remained such a focal point of the village. It won't be long now until Claudette is standing right where I am, talking about this legendary place, her pretty head tipped slightly to one side as she flirts effortlessly with the lens of Tom's camera, expertly enticing the audience which I know she must always imagine are watching. Theo will be here, too, his own even prettier head also on one side as he concentrates not just on what Claudette is saying, but also how the light is falling across her face, whether the pots of flowers look right in the background and how best to frame the shot. I won't be doing any of that; I'll be watching him, just like I always am whenever I can get away with it.

I sit down on the low wall and take a deep breath, enjoying the sensation of the cool, moist air as it rushes into my nose and down into my lungs. I feel so awake and alive, but not agitated like I usually would – more in a measured and focused way. It's probably this strange sense of alertness that prompts me to say good morning to the woman who has just wandered over to fill up her empty bottles. I say it in Spanish – *buenos días* – but when she turns and sees me, she immediately replies in English.

'Good morning to you, too.'

'You're English?' I ask needlessly, as it's very plain from her accent that she is.

The woman nods. 'I am. Although I've been here so long now, I like to think I've become at least a bit Spanish.'

'Well, you look the part,' I tell her, taking in her messy upward swirl of dark hair and bohemian-style orange kaftan. Her feet, which are encased in cracked, gold sandals, are tanned a rich dark brown.

She must have noticed me looking, because after a pause she glances down at herself and grimaces.

'I look a right state, I know,' she says, running a hand into her untidy stack of curls. 'There's never usually anyone here this early on a Sunday, so I didn't bother getting properly dressed.'

'I think you look great,' I say, meaning it. I've always admired people who have their own style, and I suppose I must have one, too, although the majority of my outfit choices are based more on comfort than trend. Give me jeans and a checked shirt and I'm happy. Hand me anything tight-fitting that finishes above the knee and I'm instantly uncomfortable.

'I like your dress,' the woman says kindly. 'Red is definitely your colour, which is actually quite a rare thing. Most people look awkward in red, but on you it looks right.'

'Really?' I say, automatically self-conscious. I'd never given much thought to a particular colour suiting me better than another one. I just picked up this dress on a whim because it was in the sale.

The woman nods at me, certain enough for the both of us, and in that moment, I decide that I like her very much. She's one of those people who could be any age from around thirty-five to fifty, her clothes and hair hinting at youth but the lines around her eyes suggesting the opposite. Luckily my politeness mutes the question before I blurt it out. Instead, I comment on the weather like some sort of society bore from a Jane Austen novel, and we chat for a while like true British people about how nice it is to be somewhere with real sunshine.

'You've been to Mojácar before,' she states, setting down her now-full bottles and taking a seat beside me on the wall.

'Yes,' I reply, surprised. 'How did you know?'

'You seem at home here,' she tells me, with a genuine smile. 'Most tourists that come to the fountain stand around making oohing and ahhing noises for a while, pose for a few photos and then bugger off, but you seem content just to sit here.'

'I am!' I say, delighted with my new status as a Mojácar local.

'I like to sit here, too,' she says, a wistful edge entering her voice. 'If you pick just the right spot, you can watch all the rainbows dancing in mid-air.'

I must have looked intrigued by her words, because the next thing I know she's leapt up and is reaching for my hand.

'Come on, I'll show you.'

I let myself be towed across the courtyard to the far corner, where the sunlight has sneaked through the trailing ivy and is bouncing buoyantly off the surface of the water. Sure enough, after a few seconds I can see what she was talking about – there are rainbows in the air, loads of them. So many that I feel like I've stumbled into a fairy grotto, and I beam across at the woman.

'Beautiful, aren't they?' she says, her eyes lighting up as she looks at me.

'Magical,' I confirm, wondering to myself if there's a way we can capture this spectacle on camera. Tom will know how.

'I come here every morning to watch the rainbows,'

she tells me. 'I've been here for more than forty-two years now and I've never known a day pass without some sunshine. Even the rainy days are sunny in Mojácar.'

'Forty-two years?' I exclaim, my tact groaning with exasperation as my disbelief stomps all over it.

'Oh yes.' The woman is clearly more amused than offended. 'I was sixty on my last birthday, although don't go spreading that around, will you?'

'You look amazing for sixty,' I can't help but blurt. This woman is ten years older than my mum, but she looks much younger.

'You flatter me.' She flushes slightly and glances down at her feet. There's a heap of cheap-looking metal bangles on one of her slim wrists, and they clatter together as she brings up a hand to rub her eyes. More people have begun filtering into the fountain courtyard, empty water bottles of all shapes and sizes bashing against their bare legs. A rather harassed-looking man with curly grey hair smiles a greeting at my new female companion, and the two of them begin to natter away to one another in rapid Spanish. Feeling rather like I'm eavesdropping, even though I can't understand a word of what they're saying, I inch away towards the steps.

There's a bakery on the opposite side of the road, and the smell drifting out is reeling me in like a fish caught on a line. Just as I'm about to push open the door, I feel a hand on my arm.

'Sorry.' It's the woman again, grinning apologetically. 'I didn't mean to ignore you back there. Josef, that's the old man you saw, he loves a good moan of a morning.'

'I should introduce him to my friend Claudette,' I say,

thinking as I do that it's high time I trudged back up the hill and woke up the angry little French maniac.

The woman gestures through the window of the bakery.

'I know it's a bit early in the day, but the miniature doughnuts are delicious,' she tells me. 'If you've got a sweet tooth, there's honestly nothing better.'

'Thanks,' I say, for some bizarre reason giving her a thumbs up.

'Is that an Indalo Man?' The woman has spotted the tattoo on my wrist.

'Yes,' I admit sheepishly. I always feel absurdly embarrassed about my little inking whenever anyone of my parents' generation notices it, almost as if I'm bracing myself for the same telling-off that my dad gave me when he found out about it. But this woman appears to be enchanted by it.

'So, you *really* know Mojácar, then?' she exclaims, her pleasure evident.

'I used to come here when I was a teenager,' I explain.

'I was barely an adult myself when I moved here,' the woman replies, and again I detect that brush of wistfulness.

'Hang on, you've lived here all that time?' I ask, goosebumps of excited possibility popping up on my arms, despite the rising temperature.

She nods slowly, less sure of herself than she was just a few seconds ago.

'This is going to sound mad,' I babble, 'but please hear me out – I've got a proposition for you.'

And so I tell the woman why I'm here in Mojácar, about

the documentary we're making and – most importantly – how keen we are to interview someone who remembers what the place was like during the seventies, when artists travelled from all over the world to join the colony here.

'It would be beyond amazing if we could interview you,' I continue, not even bothering to keep the pleading tone out of my voice. I can see that she's not thrilled by the idea, but at least she hasn't said no yet.

'I've been trying for weeks to track down someone who would be willing to do it, and now meeting you suddenly feels like fate. You'd be perfect! And you'd look great on camera, too,' I add. Flattery gets you everywhere, right?

'I'm not sure,' she mumbles, looking anywhere but at me. 'I don't know if I'd even have anything that interesting to say.'

'Let me be the judge of that,' I urge, with perhaps a smidgen more confidence than I actually feel.

There's a pause as she deliberates, and I rub my thumb against my Indalo Man tattoo out of habit, wishing silently in my head.

'Okay,' she finally agrees. 'But I'd prefer it if it's just you and me. And can you do that thing, you know, where you disguise someone's face?'

This surprises me. She doesn't come across as a particularly shy person, and it's not as if she's going to be telling me anything that scandalous, surely? However, at this stage she's the closest I have to the vital Mojácar insider that Theo is insisting on for the documentary. Perhaps I can talk her into revealing her face later down the line, when there's a bit of footage to show her.

'That can be arranged,' I say vaguely, smiling to reassure her. 'We'd do it all officially and you'd never have to do anything that you weren't comfortable with.'

'And it's okay that it's just me and you?' she asks again.

'Of course,' I say, wondering how long it will take Tom to teach me how to use his bizarre collection of equipment.

After I've answered a few more questions, we arrange to meet here at the same time in a few days, after which she'll take me to her house or to a café to do the chat. I have no idea if this new plan will work with Theo's rigid filming schedule, but I have to believe that he'll be so thrilled I've found this woman that he won't mind moving the odd thing around.

'You have no idea how grateful I am to have met you,' I gush, deciding to lay it on as thick as tarmac. I don't want her going away and having second thoughts. Mojácar isn't a big place, but she could easily hide from me for the next month if she so chose.

'I don't even know your name!' I practically shout, delight at having good news to tell Theo making me shrill and giddy.

The woman laughs good-naturedly at this and offers me a tanned hand.

'I'm Elaine,' she says.

'Hannah. Hannah Hodges at your service!'

At her service? I'm such an idiot.

After hugging Elaine far too enthusiastically and returning her kiss on each cheek with a gusto that would make even Russell Brand blush, I wave goodbye and bounce happily back up the hill to the apartment, shoving miniature doughnuts in my mouth as I go, which is a good thing, because it stops me actually singing out loud with joy.

I have found the perfect person to take this documentary to the next level, and Theo is going to love me for it. In fact, it's such insanely great news that he might immediately insist on whisking me straight back to his villa down by the beach so he can make wild, passionate love to me.

I'm so buoyed up by the events of the morning and the seventeen or so sugar-coated nuggets of heaven that I've shoved in my gob between La Fuente and the apartment, that it doesn't even faze me when I get back to find that Claudette's hairdryer has blown a fuse, taking all the power in the block with it.

According to Tom, who was passing by at road level when the incident happened, the resulting torrent of French obscenities was loud enough to shatter all the windows in a six-mile radius.

6

Despite Claudette's hairdryer drama, the morning's filming at La Fuente is a huge success, and Theo is so thrilled with the first chunks of footage that he offers to treat us all to lunch at the beach.

'I might walk down,' Tom says, looking up to where the sun has settled itself proudly high above us, a white-hot hole in the immaculate blue canvas of the sky. 'Will you come with me, Han? Make sure I don't get lost?'

Normally I would roll my eyes at such a suggestion, given that it will mean a thirty-minute separation from the object of my unbridled desire, but I need to pick Tom's brains about how best to do the interviews with Elaine. Theo was, as predicted, very impressed that I had managed to find her. I'll be dining off the look of pride he gave me for at least the next month. Being assured that I'm good at my job means just as much to me as Theo's attention, so to receive both at the same time feels like winning the life lottery.

Theo gives us the name of the beach restaurant next door to his villa, then Tom and I stand watching as he and Claudette drive off down the hill.

'Sorry.' Tom turns to me once they're out of sight. 'I know you would probably rather have gone in the car. I just needed a break from Claudette.'

I nod, sympathetic. Our French friend is such an

angelic presence on screen that you'd never guess at her behaviour once the camera is switched off. Tom has been barked at and needled all morning, and by the look of resigned dismay on his face, this is something that happens to him on every shoot.

'She doesn't mean to be so stroppy,' I tell him, as we nip into a local shop to buy a bottle of water each for the walk. 'She's just a perfectionist. And my mum always tells me that overly confident people are usually just hiding the fact they're insecure.'

'Claudette, insecure?' Tom almost coughs his sip of water all over me. 'Fat chance!'

We've made our way up from La Fuente to the main road, and Tom points as a small black and white cat picks its way daintily across the roasting hot tarmac in front of us. The wide pavement leading down the hill is paved in caramel-coloured stone, and metal railings separate the path from a mess of tangled undergrowth. Every few metres, there's a large Indalo Man symbol set into the fence, each one casting a warped shadow against the ground.

'You weren't wrong about the Indalo,' Tom says, gesturing downwards. 'It's everywhere around here.'

Like me, he's wearing red today, but unlike my dress, his T-shirt has been washed about ten times too often, and it's clashing with his bright pink neck.

'Have you put any sun cream on?' I ask him, tutting affectionately when he shakes his head. 'Here, squat.'

Tom does as he's told and hunkers down in front of me. Rooting through my bag, I find a tube of factor thirty and squeeze a dollop on to his exposed skin. I notice that the tops of his sticking-out ears are starting to turn red, too, so I smear a bit on them as well.

'Thanks, Mum,' he quips, standing back up.

I ask him about Elaine as we walk, and Tom assures me that his small camera will be the perfect thing to use. It's portable and has a good battery life, so I shouldn't have to worry about plugs and wires and all that nonsense. He even has a foldaway tripod that he can give me.

'If you go bowling in there with bags of equipment, you'll only scare her off,' he tells me. 'Trust me, when it's a one-on-one situation, it's better to keep things intimate.'

I can't hear the word 'intimate' without my mind conjuring up images of Theo, but I keep my mouth tightly shut.

It takes us about twenty minutes to make our leisurely way down the hill, both of us enjoying the feel of the sun against our London-weary joints and the incessant cacophony of cicadas, grasshoppers and crickets coming from the surrounding trees and scrub. Someone has gone to the trouble of planting roses in the flower beds next to the road, and every so often a gust of particularly determined breeze will shower little heaps of petals on to the soil. Everywhere I look there is vibrant colour, from the impenetrable cobalt sky to the pale gold stone of the distant buildings and the pinks, reds, yellows and peaches of the flowers. There are no shades of grey here, nothing that looks tired or washed out, and again I feel a rush of energy, as if my senses are on a dial that has been switched around as far as it can go.

Tom is nattering away about his plans to record a montage of shots up in the Old Town at sunset, when he's interrupted by the sound of my phone ringing. Pulling it out and glancing at the screen, I pull a face.

'Who is it?' Tom leans across to get a look.

'My horrible half-sister,' I grunt, switching off the ringer and putting the phone resolutely back in my bag.

'It might be important,' Tom protests.

'It won't be,' I reply, immediately irritated as I always am whenever I'm forced to talk about Nancy. 'It will just be her calling to boast about something. That's all she knows how to do.'

'That's a bit harsh,' Tom argues, but I notice that he's careful to keep any judgement he might feel out of his voice. He's only met Nancy twice before – once at our graduation ceremony and again at my dad's fiftieth birthday party – and he may have fancied her on sight, but he clearly doesn't know her well enough to see through her act yet. The reverse is true in my case.

'You're one of the kindest people I know, Han. I guess it just jars to hear you talk about your own sister like she's an enemy.'

'Half-sister,' I parrot automatically.

He frowns, coming to a halt on the warm pavement.

'You know she never says anything bad about you.'

'You've spoken to her all of twice,' I point out, and Tom looks down, avoiding my eyes.

'Well, she's always liking your Facebook photos – and those ridiculous videos of dogs on trampolines that you post all the time,' he mutters into the collar of his T-shirt.

It's true, and it irks me that he's noticed. The fact is, I actually spend a lot of time online looking at Nancy's profile and photos, too – but only late at night when nobody can see me. And I've certainly never liked anything that she's posted. I don't even know why I do it – call it a morbid fascination.

'We may share genes,' I inform Tom grumpily, 'but that's where the similarities end. We're never going to be friends, so there's no point in making the effort.'

Tom looks as if he's going to open his mouth and disagree again, but then he just sighs instead, which is only marginally less annoying. To him it might seem as if I'm being unreasonable, but he doesn't know what it feels like to look at a person and be reminded so acutely of so much misery. Nancy represents the final nail in the coffin of my parents' marriage, and for that I'm unable to forgive her. And anyway, she *is* all the things I'm always telling Tom that she is: selfish, spoilt and self-involved. Everything has always been about her, for as far back as I can remember, and I don't want to be around someone like that, even if they do happen to be family.

We carry on walking, and when my phone starts ringing again a few minutes later, silently this time but with just enough vibration for me to feel it through the canvas shell of my bag, I resolutely decline to mention it.

Mojácar Playa consists of seventeen kilometres of wide, clean, sandy beach, an array of bars, restaurants, shops and tavernas, and an eclectic variety of plant-life. Majestic palm trees peer down at us, their sun-shrivelled leaves cracking noisily as they are buffeted by the wind, while down at ground level, cactus sit heavily in their beds, their bulbous, elongated bodies so distinctive yet alien in appearance.

Theo's villa is a short walk from the roundabout where the main road down from the Old Town comes to an end, and I point out its bright blue door to Tom as we hurry towards the restaurant. If only I was staying in there, too, I can't help but think. Being the one that booked it for him, I know just how beautiful it is inside, with its wooden decking complete with plunge pool and a bedroom window looking out over the water. A girl can dream, right?

We spot Theo sitting alone at an outdoor table and he stands up to greet us. After more than half an hour of walking in this heat, both Tom and I collapse gratefully into the two chairs that are in the shade, while Theo sits down comfortably in direct sunlight, his heavenly Greek complexion turning darker by the minute.

'Claudette is over there,' he informs us, pointing down at the beach to where our French friend has indeed stretched herself out on a sun lounger, her eyes closed and her bikini top tossed aside like a discarded sweet wrapper.

'Ooh la la,' Tom can't help but joke, and I quickly avert my gaze and study the menu.

'I would recommend the grilled sardines,' Theo says. He's leaning back in his seat now, the sleeves of his pale blue shirt rolled up and his fingers laced behind his head. He looks so gorgeous that I almost sob tears of lust into the pint of lemonade that's just arrived.

'Okay!' I trill, chuffed to have the decision taken out of my hands while also making him happy at the same time.

Tom is still studying the menu, and I take advantage of his attention being elsewhere by sneaking a more lingering look at Theo, who is busy reading something in a tatty old book that had been face down on the table. The spine is faded yellow and the Sellotape holding the pages together has turned amber with age. There's no cover, but I can see the word 'Mojácar' on the first page. Theo's brow is knotted in concentration as his eyes skim from side to side, and I watch as his fingers caress the fragile paper.

'Should we order for Claudette?' Tom asks as a waitress approaches.

Theo puts the book down. 'She'll come and join us if she's hungry.'

The sardines, as it turns out, are grilled outside on a barbecue that has been built inside the shell of an old fishing boat. You're even invited to go over and choose which ones you'd like for your lunch, and I'm thrilled when Theo puts me in charge of the selection. When I return, the bread has arrived, along with what looks suspiciously like a ramekin full of mayonnaise. Suddenly ravenous, I break open a roll and stick my knife straight into the sauce.

'Bloody hell!'

It's garlic mayonnaise. Of course it is.

'Fragrant, isn't it?' Tom announces, amused by my mortification. It's not that I dislike garlic mayonnaise. I mean, who does? But Theo is sitting right here. He's close enough to smell my breath. Close enough to recoil and die if I breathe on him. To make matters worse, he isn't even eating any of it himself.

A short while later, the fish arrives, along with a tomato and onion salad thoughtfully ordered by Tom. So, to recap, that's garlic, fish and onion breath. The only thing I'll be snogging tonight is my toothbrush.

'What are you reading, boss?' asks Tom between

mouthfuls. He opted for lasagne, and has already managed to drop stringy cheese into his lap.

'A history of Mojácar,' Theo says, holding up the book to show us. 'I found it on the shelf in my villa, and it's very interesting.'

I know from my own research that there aren't many books in existence about Mojácar, and I feel a rush of irrational jealousy towards the villa bookcase for providing something for Theo that I couldn't.

'I had no idea how many legends are associated with the place,' he adds, frowning slightly as he flicks through to find the right page. 'The Indalo is just one of many.'

I use the time while he's searching to subtly remove a sardine bone from between my teeth.

'Ah, here we are,' Theo says, shifting to get comfortable in his plastic chair and clearing his throat. 'Just before you reach the Plaza Nueva in the Old Town, you will see the cave of Mariquita the Betrothed.'

'I don't remember any caves,' says Tom, but I shush him.

'The legend says that the fairy godmother of Mojácar lives in this cave,' Theo continues, his rich, self-assured voice running over me like warm honey. 'Once upon a time, many years ago, there was a plague in the village that had killed hundreds of local people. One day, an old wizard declared that he had found a cure for this disease, but that he would only share it on the condition that he was permitted to marry one of the beautiful young virgins in the village.'

'Brilliant,' says Tom, just as I mutter the word 'pervert'.

Theo raises an eyebrow and continues reading.

'Mariquita offered her hand to the wizard, but once he had her up in his cave, he refused to relinquish the cure, thinking that if he did, she would leave him. In order to save everyone from certain death, Mariquita waited until the wizard was asleep, then stole the jar containing the cure and healed the sick.'

'Bravo!' Tom cheers, tomato sauce on his chin.

'Alas.' Theo looks at us solemnly. 'Mariquita was desperate to leave the wizard after what he had done, so she opened another jar of his spells and tried to kill him by pouring them into his open mouth. In her haste, she spilled some on her own hand, burning a hole right through the flesh and unleashing magic which meant she was cursed to stay up in that cave for eternity. According to this book, she's still up there with her wizard even today.'

I put my knife and fork together and toss down my napkin.

'That's a creepy story,' says Tom. 'Do you reckon the wizard had experience of dating in London, so knew he had to take desperate measures?'

Theo chuckles at this, then turns to me.

'How about you, Hannah?' he asks.

I smile nervously. 'How about me what?'

'How do you find dating in London?'

'Oh, you know, it's a bit hit-and-miss,' I tell him nonchalantly, but I can feel myself turning redder than the bowl of tomato and onion salad. Tom isn't saying anything, perhaps because he knows full well that dating is something I haven't done for a long time.

'I think finding someone to date is the easy bit,' Theo admits. 'But finding someone who has the same mindset as you, that is far more difficult.'

I think about that shared moment between the two of

us up in the square yesterday evening, and how for the first time since I met Theo, I felt like we were thinking and feeling the same thing. Do I have the right mindset for Theo? If not, I must find a way to get it.

'I'm just very fussy,' I say slowly, watching his eyes skate over me. If I was more like Claudette, I'd say something suggestive now and flick my hair, something to leave Theo in no doubt of how I feel about him. But I'm not, so instead I look away towards the sea.

Theo is silent until the plates have been cleared away and Tom has gone down to the beach to rouse Claudette. She's fallen asleep and has been snoring like an idle bus for the past ten minutes.

'I think it is good to be fussy,' Theo says, casually picking the conversation back up.

'You do?' I ask.

He regards me through his sunglasses.

'I think too often women settle for something comfortable – and men do, too. It is better to be happy alone than with the wrong person, no?'

He's never once asked me about my love life. Not once. What the hell should I say? I don't want him to think that I'm a prude, but then I'm not sure I agree with what he's saying. My dad left my mum because he didn't think she was the right person, and that decision has caused so much unhappiness.

'Um . . .' I begin, attempting to speak but only managing to gargle like a patient in a dentist's chair.

'The first English woman I dated was older than me,' Theo goes on, smiling as he dredges up a no doubt pleasing memory.

I squirm, uncomfortable with where the conversation is going but equally thrilled that he's sharing something so personal with me.

'I was a young man of twenty-three, still living in Greece at the time. She was older, in her forties, I think, and very determined to teach me exactly what it is that a woman enjoys.'

I can't help it; I think about my own limited sexual experience. A few casual boyfriends that never hung around more than a couple of months, a single, paltry one-night stand at university, and barely so much as a sniff since. Not for the first time since I met and fell for him, I find myself intimidated by Theo. He's studying me closely now, my obvious unease so at odds with his easy confidence. If only I could learn to be one of those women who reduce men to jelly with just a few teasing phrases. That is never going to happen, though. Not to me, not to Hannah Hodges: celibate beanpole.

I never get to find out what Theo was about to say next, because Claudette arrives back at the table and immediately starts bemoaning the fact that she's burnt her nipples while we've been eating.

'Put some ice on them,' Theo instructs, standing up and slipping his tattered paperback into his pocket. 'We've got work to do.'

7

Elaine's house is nestled at the very top of the Old Town, along a cobbled street decorated with trailing bougainvillea and jacaranda trees, their respective pink and lilac petals carpeting the pathway like confetti. Her front door is painted a bright, cheerful yellow, while the shutters on each of the front windows are a deep turquoise, with flowers painted around the edges on the white stone.

'Did you do these?' I ask, enchanted, as she readies her keys.

Elaine smiles. 'I did. I do new ones at the beginning of each summer.'

'They're beautiful,' I tell her. 'You have a real talent.'

Once we've crossed the threshold, I realise that the painted flowers outside were merely a cherry on Elaine's huge trifle of talent. There's barely a space between all the exquisite landscapes cluttering the walls, and she's covered the entire back door leading out to a small courtyard garden with an intricate image of twisted foliage. Taking a step closer to examine it in more detail, I can see the individual brush strokes where she's added veins to the leaves.

'This is amazing,' I murmur, genuinely at a loss for anything more articulate to say. 'It looks so real that I can almost smell it.'

Elaine, who is busying herself preparing a large glass

jug of iced tea for the two of us to share, merely nods some thanks at me over her shoulder. Trying to look like the professional camerawoman that I most definitely am not, I unfold Tom's tripod and start fiddling with the bag containing the camera.

'I thought we could sit outside, if that's okay?' Elaine says, opening her beautiful painted door. There's a small table and chairs in the yard, along with a number of flowerpots of various shapes and sizes. A strip of sunlight bunting is stretched across the outer wall, and a large blue-and-white clay Indalo Man hangs by the kitchen window.

'I spend a lot of time out here,' Elaine explains, bending down to remove a weed from one of her many pots and dropping it over the wall. 'It's a great place to paint or read, or simply sit and listen to the birds singing.'

'The birds in Mojácar really do like a song,' I reply, thinking back to the wake-up call of my first morning here.

'I like to think it's because they're happy,' she says, smiling at me as she sits down. She's wearing a long green dress today and her hair is once again pulled back off her face. The bangles are still in situ on her wrist, and I notice that she's added a hint of rouge to her lips.

I really should have made more effort with my appearance, but I didn't leave myself enough time to get ready after my early morning swim at the beach. Denim shorts and a light pink vest top were the closest items to hand, and I've pulled my wet hair back into a small ponytail at the nape of my neck. I'm still getting used to not wearing jeans every day and actually being able to see the bare skin of my arms and legs. Being blonde, I'm naturally quite pale, and next to Elaine I look even fairer.

'So,' she says, twisting her fingers together in her lap, 'how is this going to work?'

'I think it's best if we just switch on the camera and then talk,' I tell her, remembering what both Tom and Claudette told me the day before. 'That way we can just try to forget it's even there.'

'I don't know if I'll be able to forget,' she admits. 'But I'll give it a good go.'

The iced tea tastes mildly bitter, but delicious, and I tell Elaine how much I like it as I finish setting everything up. Once I'm happy with the frame and the camera is switched on, I return to my chair opposite hers and begin my questions.

Elaine tells me that she was born in London in 1956, but moved to Mojácar as soon as she turned eighteen, which was in the year 1974. She says she didn't have the place in mind before she found it, but rather stumbled across it after meeting another artist in the South of France.

'And you've never been back to England since?' I ask.

Elaine shakes her head, keeping her eyes on me rather than the camera. They're very dark brown, almost black, and it's hard to look away.

'There's never seemed much point.' She brings up her shoulders in a shrug. 'I didn't have any family, so there was nothing to go back for.'

I open my mouth to ask what happened, but then change my mind. We're here to talk about her life in Mojácar, after all. What took place before that time doesn't really matter.

'I suppose I was a bit of a hippy back then,' Elaine

recalls. 'I believed that I was a citizen of the world, and the people I met while I was travelling were the same. We convinced ourselves that we would be able to change the universe if only we could experience more of life. Of course, that may have been the drugs talking.'

'Drugs?' I fail to hide my shock.

'Afraid so.' Elaine looks more bemused than shame-faced. 'It wasn't such an unusual thing back in those days, and I was only eighteen. I was very happy to follow the pathway to oblivion without worrying about the consequences.'

I've always been too much of a chicken to try drugs. Tom ate some hash cakes once when we were at university, and they must have been seriously strong, because the whole night he kept telling me that my face had turned into a potato and that he had a brother who was a jelly worm.

'What was Mojácar like when you arrived?' I ask now, and Elaine closes her eyes.

'I'll never forget how it felt to look up at the Old Town for the very first time,' she says, taking a deep breath before lifting her eyelids once again. 'Mojácar is unique in that the view looking up from the Playa towards the village is actually better than the one from up here looking back down to the sea. The splendour here is the opposite of most places.'

'That's so true,' I agree, wondering why I hadn't ever thought of it in that way before. 'I constantly have to remind myself to turn around and look back when I'm walking down to the beach.'

'I just felt at peace as soon as I got here,' Elaine

continues. 'I'd been on the road for a few months by that point, and I was weary. Mojácar offered me something that I had failed to find anywhere else.'

She goes on to describe the village as it was then, which surprisingly wasn't all that different to now. Obviously there have been small improvements made over the years, and there are far more gift shops and restaurants than there used to be before the tourists became a regular fixture, but the essence of the village has never really altered.

'What about the Indalo symbol?' I ask gently. 'Was that on every building in the same way as it is today?'

'Oh, yes,' Elaine confirms. 'The symbol dates back to prehistoric times, as you know, and the artists here were quick to adopt it as an emblem.'

'Do you believe in it?' I can't help but ask.

Elaine pauses for a moment to consider this, crossing her legs and showing off the same pair of gold sandals that she was wearing down at La Fuente when we first met.

'I believe that it offers many people a lot of comfort.'

It's a careful answer, and I don't believe I'm getting the full story. Instead of pushing her, I simply sit in silence and wait. Sure enough, Elaine soon begins to talk again.

'Whether you believe in the legend or not doesn't matter,' she says. 'The fact is that the symbol was definitely found in a cave not far from here back in the 1860s, and experts say the area dates to 2500 BC. Ever since the discovery, the Indalo Man has been associated with good luck. And do I believe in magic? Sometimes I do. Don't you?'

I shake my head, almost sad to be letting her down. 'I don't know. I want to. I do love the Indalo and what it stands for, though, and I think that's enough.'

She nods at that. 'I think you could be right.'

'What happened to the artists you came here with?' I ask now. I'm conscious of time passing, and wonder if the battery is holding out on the camera. Theo had advised me to take my time with Elaine. We still had another three and a half weeks left to get all the footage we needed and, as he quite rightly pointed out, Elaine wasn't about to tell me her entire life story in just one session.

'Some left, some stayed,' she says, sipping her glass of iced tea. 'A few are still here, in fact.'

'I read that Mojácar has one of the highest expatriate populations in the whole of Spain,' I tell her. 'Can't say I blame them. I'd happily live here, too.'

'Maybe you will one day.' Elaine smiles.

We finish the iced tea and she tells me more about her painting, which is mostly self-taught. Every autumn she hosts a small exhibition, and for years now she's scraped together a living by having postcards and prints made of her work and selling them through the Old Town's many gift shops. Luckily, she tells me, Mojácar is an area that attracts many appreciators of both art and beauty, so she's never had any trouble selling her wares.

'I could sit here chatting to you all day,' I tell her as the church bells begin to chime for the second time since I arrived. I feel like I love and understand Mojácar even more than I had just a few hours ago, and as much as I'm loath to leave this idyllic little courtyard and my new friend behind, I also can't wait to tell the others all the new things I've learned.

'Shall we say the same time on Friday?' I ask, packing away the last of the equipment.

She nods. 'That would be lovely. I'll take you to my studio next time, if you like?'

There's another Indalo Man hanging on the wall by the front door, this time just made from simple twisted black metal, and seeing it there suddenly reminds me of something.

'Just one more thing before I go,' I say, turning back to her.

'Yes?'

'You said earlier that Mojácar offered you something you had failed to find anywhere else. What was it?'

Elaine draws in a breath, then reaches across and puts a hand in the crook of my arm.

'Hope,' she says.

8

The next few days pass by in a blur of productive activity. We spend the afternoons up in Mojácar Pueblo, collecting footage of the village fortress and conducting interviews with a number of bemused local inhabitants, so my mornings are always packed full of tasks from Theo ahead of that day's filming.

I'm relishing being busy, though there's just one dicey moment on the second day when I turn a cobbled corner in the Jewish Quarter and walk literally right into Diego, who is coming the other way with a large box of tomatoes in his hands.

'*Hola, Hannah – qué tal?*' he's quick to ask.

'*Bueno – gracias,*' I reply, scuttling away in the other direction without bothering to ask him how he is in return. It's so strange to remember how besotted I was with him, even if some of the emotions are still acute. The way I behaved around him as a teenager seared me with a humiliating pain that has never really dimmed, and I hate the way I feel when I'm around him – small and insignificant.

We've been working such long hours that by the time evening arrives, Claudette is content simply to sit on our balcony with her feet up on the wall, sipping a glass of wine and reading over her script notes for the following day. Theo, meanwhile, has taken to vanishing back down to his villa to review and edit the day's recordings, leaving Tom and me to explore the many quirky little restaurants and bars nestled amongst the cube-shaped houses of the village. Mojácar is well and truly under my skin again, and I'm already dreading the thought of having to leave behind the wonderful sleepy atmosphere and the veritable kaleidoscope of greens, blues, whites and sunshine-yellows that I see every time I let myself stop and look around.

Today is Wednesday, and we are all packed into Theo's car heading out of Mojácar on the Carboneras Road towards Macenas, where there are two centuries-old watchtowers – the Perulico and the Castillo de Macenas – that he's keen to include in our film. If we get everything done by lunchtime, then Theo's promised us the treat of an afternoon off, so there's a definite buzz in the air.

'I cannot wait to work on my tan,' Claudette is now saying. She's slipped off her shoes in the back seat next to me and has stretched out her legs so that her toes are poking through the gap between Tom and Theo.

'Can anyone else smell cheese?' Tom jokes, earning himself a poke from Claudette's big toe.

As usual I'm splitting my time between staring out of the window at the unfolding landscape and gazing at the back of Theo's head. Every now and again, he glances in the rear-view mirror and catches my eye. We haven't had a moment alone together since the other day at lunch, so our conversation about his older lady lover has not been continued. Not that I want to hear all about how great some other woman was in the sack, anyway.

For something that was built in the eighteenth century, the Castillo de Macenas is in pretty good nick, and I say as much as we sweep into the nearby parking area in a cloud of dust.

'Spoken like a true intellectual,' remarks Tom, winking at me as he clambers out of the car.

Almost like a small castle in shape and design, the Castillo is constructed from brown and gold stone, its cylindrical edges drawing my eyes up and around. I find it bizarre to think of guards sitting up on the battlements all those years ago, looking out across the vast expanse of sea in search of any vessels that could herald a potential attack or invasion. Then again, what a view they must have had. There's something about being close to a large body of water that makes me feel more invincible, as if the usual limitations of everyday life have slipped away and the possibilities have multiplied tenfold. Perhaps that's why London can feel so relentless and stifling – it's because my mind is subconsciously trapped between all those ugly man-made structures.

Having already coached Claudette through her lines and helped Tom set up the camera, I stroll a few metres away from the group so that I won't be in the way. Today, clouds have joined us for the first time since we arrived, and they add a pleasing new dimension to the dense blue veil of the sky. The scenery in this area is far more rugged than the coast a few miles behind us, with craggy cliffs leaning over the water and clusters of dried plants rotting in the heat. The dust is still here, though, blowing up around me and working its way into my nostrils, ears and probably even my belly button. It never ceases to amaze me just how much dirt I manage to pick up throughout the course of a single day.

Claudette is talking to the camera now, her light French accent sounding mellifluous yet authoritative. Usually she would still be faffing around at this stage, demanding to check how she looks on screen and how she's been framed in the shot, but today she is determined to get the job done. As she remarked to me this morning on our way up the steps outside our apartment, she's planning to spend the few hours we have to ourselves hunting the beach bars for a man, telling me quite brazenly, 'If I don't have sex soon, someone will be murdered.'

I actually don't doubt her for one second.

'Can we try that again, but with a little less haste, please?' Theo is now saying, and as he turns his back I see Claudette stamp her foot with frustration. Tom is quiet when he's working, ever the professional, but I know he must secretly be gritting his teeth at her histrionics.

Leaving my colleagues to it, I wander across the makeshift car park to where the derelict shell of a building is just about still standing. Surrounded by dead shrubbery and tagged with lots of rather artistic graffiti, it's oddly alluring, and I slip my phone out of my pocket to take a few pictures.

What's this? Another missed call from Nancy. Bloody hell – when is that girl going to take a hint? I stubbornly ignore the small voice in my head, which whispers to me that it might be important, that Nancy hardly ever calls me these days and surely she only would if something bad had happened. I refuse to believe that, though. If anything had happened to my parents, then someone else would have been in touch by now. All the same, I fire off a quick text to my mum just to check in.

I was only six when Nancy was born, but I've never forgotten it. She arrived so fast that my dad's new wife Susie didn't even make it as far as the hospital and Nancy, ever the drama queen, was born on the back seat of a taxi halfway there. My dad took me to visit her a week later, and apparently I was enchanted at first. I thought of her as a doll, I suppose, so I was very miffed when I was told in no uncertain terms that she wasn't, and that I was not allowed to swing her around my head by one arm like I did with all my other dolls. Babies may look cute, but they aren't half boring to hang out with, and I hated the way that my dad cooed over Nancy. It was as if now he had her, he no longer needed me, and that feeling has never really left me. As if it wasn't bad enough that he didn't love Mum any more, now it felt like he didn't love me, either.

To make matters worse, Nancy was a very clingy toddler and hugely attached to our dad. She would muscle in on any games the two of us might be playing and cry if she wasn't allowed to join in; she would pick up the pieces of my beloved jigsaws and chew them until the cardboard shapes warped and no longer fitted together properly. When I was nine, I was given the much-coveted role of Mary in the school nativity play, but on the day of the performance, Nancy threw a colossal tantrum and screamed herself sick. My dad was so worried about her that he stayed at home instead of coming to watch me on the assembly hall stage, and I have never forgotten how it felt to look down and see an empty chair where he was supposed to be sitting.

Nancy desperately wanted me to pay her attention, but

even as a child I knew that ignoring her was the best way to punish her. She had this need to be watched, adored and idolised by everyone, and I simply refused to go along with it. She had everyone wrapped around her chubby little finger except me, and I know it drove her mad. Why she was suddenly so keen to talk to me now was a mystery, but it was one that I didn't have time to deal with at the moment.

Angry with myself for letting my corrosive resentment affect my mood yet again, I take aim and kick a stone through the tumbledown doorway of the building, only to leap about fifteen feet into the air with a scream so loud that several birds fly up from the undergrowth.

'Hannah – are you okay?' Theo is beside me in under a minute, out of breath and palpably concerned.

'A snake,' I say, my voice still quivering with shock, as I point to the clear patch of ground where the stone once sat.

'There, there,' Theo says, pulling me against him and sending my senses reeling. 'It's gone now. It cannot hurt you.'

'Sorry,' I mumble against his shirt, my arms dangling down by my sides like laundered tights. 'It just gave me a fright.'

'I won't let it get you,' Theo soothes.

Bloody hell – he's even started stroking my hair. He smells so good, and his chest feels so firm against my cheek. Now I can hear his heart beating. Oh my God, I think I'm going to faint.

Theo gently pushes me away so that he can look into my eyes.

'Are you all right?' he asks, so quietly that I almost don't hear him. 'It didn't bite you, did it?'

I shake my head. 'No.'

'Thank God,' he mutters, releasing my shoulders so that my cheek can again press against the buttons of his shirt. His hands are working their way down my back, his fingers rubbing small circles as they go, leaving me burning with such an overwhelming need that I almost whimper.

'What the hell is going on over here?'

Claudette has marched over and is glaring at us, a graceful hand on her hip and an expression on her face that's easily explosive enough to topple what's left of the ramshackle reptile hotel behind me.

'There was a snake,' I mumble, forcing myself to take a step backwards out of Theo's embrace. 'It just startled me, that's all.'

For the briefest of seconds, I see a shudder pass through Claudette, but she quickly recovers herself.

'Can we get a move on, please? It's almost lunchtime.'

'Come on,' Theo says, turning to me with a smile. 'You can help me direct.'

Somehow I make it through the next hour without melting into a puddle of lustful goo all over the floor, and we're soon back at Theo's villa having dropped Claudette off at a beach bar on the way.

'Fancy a swim before we head back?' Tom asks me.

I hesitate, looking over at Theo who has just returned from taking some equipment inside. I can't stop thinking about how his hands felt, and I absurdly don't want to wash away the sensation of him in the sea.

'You go ahead,' I tell Tom. 'I'll wait on the beach and watch the bags.'

We walk along until we reach a beachside bar offering sun loungers – or *hamacas*, as the Spanish call them – for five euros, then Tom whips his T-shirt off over his head and lollops away across the sand.

I watch until he's happily splashing about in the water, then lie back against my towel and release an audible sigh of contentment. I can hear the wind making the beach umbrellas creak with the effort of standing upright, and somewhere a child is giggling. Music filters down from the bar, a Spanish song that I've never heard but which sounds familiar all the same, and I smile as the notes hover around my ears like a persistent bee.

I've already applied sun cream on all my exposed areas, but I realise now that I didn't remind Tom that he should, too. He won't be feeling the heat in the water, but it's definitely at its peak at this time of day. Just as I'm contemplating getting up and calling him back in to shore, a shadow falls across me.

'A drink for the lady?'

Theo is smiling down at me, his eyes obscured by his sunglasses but his smile as clear as the sky above his head. The clouds from this morning are long gone.

'Hi,' I say, shuffling up into a sitting position.

He's holding a jug of sangria in one hand and three small glasses in the other, and has a rolled-up towel clamped under one arm. He's also changed into shorts and – be still, my throbbing loins – taken off his shirt.

'You can't very well have an afternoon off without some sangria,' he says, sitting down on Tom's vacated sun lounger and slipping his feet out of his flip-flops.

'You're the boss,' I joke lamely, holding out my hand to accept a glass. The sangria is packed with slices of orange, strawberry and lemon, and there's a wooden spoon poking out from the top of the jug.

Until today, I have never been physically close to Theo and he has never seen me in a state of undress. Now the two things have happened in the space of a few hours, and it's a wonder that I'm managing to remain so calm. Thank goodness I chose my one bikini with the padded bra top this morning. Not that a few centimetres of foam are going to convince anyone – let alone Theo – that I've got much up there to show off. Tall, skinny girls just aren't made that way.

'Thanks again for earlier,' I say now, taking a sip of my drink. It's delicious – fruity and sweet and dangerously non-alcoholic-tasting – and I quickly chase the first gulp down with another.

'You're welcome.' Theo regards me for a few seconds. 'I feel responsible for you,' he admits. 'For all of you, really. You are my team and it's up to me to make sure you're well looked after while we're over here.'

I feel myself deflate a fraction at his words. How foolish I'd been to assume that he'd wanted to put his arms around me and comfort me. Of course he was just being nice, like a concerned older brother or something. Or worse, like a dad.

'You always look as if you are lost in thought,' Theo says now, laughing when I immediately go bright red. 'You do! What is going on inside that head of yours, Miss Hodges?'

What it would be like to kiss you, I think, but obviously don't say.

'I was just thinking how much more fun the beach is when you're a child,' I say, which is a half-truth because I was thinking that exact thing a few days ago.

'How so?' Theo has settled himself on Tom's lounger now, his legs stretched out and his glass of sangria balanced against the soft nest of hair on his chest. I wish I could run my fingers through it.

'Well, when you're a kid you build sandcastles and collect shells. Play chase with the waves and eat ice cream until you're sick,' I tell him.

'You could do all those things now, if you really wanted to,' he says, clearly amused.

'You could,' I allow. 'But it's not the same now, is it? When I was a child, the shells I collected at the beach were my most prized possessions. And just digging a hole would keep me entertained for hours.'

I go on to tell him about Chewy, and how my scruffy dog friend used to help me in my hole-digging endeavours, but then end up getting told off for flicking wet sand in everyone's faces. It turns out that Theo had a pet dog when he was growing up in Greece, too, and again I'm struck with how similar we are.

'Would you ever get another one?' I ask, as he tops up both our glasses for the third time.

'I always said that I would if I had a family,' he says. 'But that didn't happen for me.'

'There's still time,' I reply, probably with a little bit too much enthusiasm. 'You're a young man.'

Theo laughs at this and brings a foot across to nudge my leg.

'You are very sweet,' he says, shaking his head. 'But

forty is not that young. I think if children were going to happen, then they would have by now.'

'Perhaps you just haven't met the right person yet,' I say, astounded at my own boldness. 'You know, the right person to have a child with, I mean.'

He smiles. 'Perhaps.'

I would have all your babies tomorrow, I tell him internally, watching as a plucky sparrow comes to rest right next to my bare feet.

'What about you, Hannah?' Theo keeps his voice low so as not to scare away the bird.

'What about me?' I play dumb.

'Do you want to have children one day?'

'Start with an easy one,' I joke, but turning I see that his eyes are serious. 'I guess so, but I wouldn't want to end up raising a child alone, like my mum did.'

'Your father?' he asks, waiting while I drain my glass. This sangria is going straight to my head. I really shouldn't be over-sharing like this, even if it is Theo asking the questions.

'Buggered off before I was two,' I say, trying and failing to keep the edge out of my voice.

'Sorry to hear that.' Theo has reached across again, but this time with his hand, which is now resting gently on my arm. I look down at it, then up at his expression, which is all concern.

'It's okay, you didn't do it,' I say stupidly. 'He met someone else and that was that. At least he didn't leave her, too, though – they're still together now.'

'A small comfort, I imagine,' Theo guesses, spot on as always.

'All my earliest memories are of my mum crying,' I say now, the sangria sweeping over my carefully constructed floodgates. 'She would always pretend she'd been chopping onions or that she'd seen something sad on TV, but I knew it was because she missed my dad. Even now I don't really understand what happened.'

'Love is a very complicated thing,' Theo says. His hand is still on my arm, and he's increasing the pressure. I know it's wrong to be totally aroused while having a conversation about your darkest childhood memories, but I can't help it. There are so few items of clothing between us, and he's being so kind, so attentive. He's actually interested in what I'm telling him, and he's sympathetic, too.

'I loved a girl for a long time, and we broke up,' he says now. 'Like your mother, I found it very difficult.'

'That girl must have been an idiot,' I fail to stop myself blurting, and Theo laughs, removing his hand at last and picking up the almost empty sangria jug.

'Maybe.' He raises an eyebrow. 'Or maybe she is the opposite.'

'What do you me—?' I begin, but at that moment my phone starts ringing.

'Bloody hell,' I swear. 'Sorry, I better just check who it— Oh, it's my mum. Hang on.'

I stagger awkwardly to my feet and move away from the loungers, immediately burning my feet on the hot sand and lunging across to a patch of shade.

'Mum – are you okay?'

'Of course I am. How are you, darling? How is Mojácar? Is it as beautiful as before? Are you remembering to put sun cream on? Have you been bitten yet? You know mosquitoes can be dangerous.'

'MUM!'

'Yes?'

'Stop talking for a moment, will you?'

'Sorry. But you know me. I can't stop being your mother just because you're all grown up now.'

'I know. And thank you. But Mum?'

'Yes, darling?'

'Why did you call?'

'I got your message earlier.'

Of course she did. I had completely forgotten that I even sent it.

'Has Nancy been in touch?' she asks now.

How the hell does she know that?

'I had a missed call from her a few days ago,' I say carefully, omitting to mention the other six or so calls I've ignored. 'Why?'

'She rang me,' Mum says. 'Wanted to know where you were staying and how long you'd be away. She sounded very impressed when I told her you were on your first location shoot. That's what you call it, isn't it? A shoot.'

'Yes, Mum.'

Why the hell was Nancy suddenly so interested in my life, and what I was doing? She never usually bothers to ask.

'She said that your dad had no idea you'd even left the country, so I told her she must be mistaken about that, because you'd said you were going to text him.'

Busted.

'Umm . . . I might have forgotten,' I admit, silently

cursing my half-sister and her huge stupid mouth. Now I'll have to endure a lecture from Dad when I get home about how disappointed he is in me. Just what I need.

'Oh, Hannah.' My mum is clearly disappointed, too, but at least she doesn't dwell on it. Instead, she tells me a long story about how she and Beryl went clay-pot painting for the afternoon and ended up drinking two bottles of Prosecco.

'I was that merry, I had to ask Bill from next door to show me which key to use when I got home,' she trills. 'I hope he didn't think I was coming on to him. No offence to the man, but he does rather remind me of a toad.'

It's another five minutes before I get her off the phone, and by the time I've hung up, taken a very deep breath and turned back around, Theo has been replaced by a soaking wet, very pink-shouldered Tom. I knew I should have reminded him to put on more sun cream.

'That your mum?' he guesses, as I sit back down.

'She's mental,' I say, before adding casually, 'did Theo go to get more sangria?'

'He said he had to go.' Tom shrugs, yanking his towel out from under himself and rubbing it over his dripping hair. 'Wants to start editing.'

I resist the urge to lie on the sand and weep.

'Why the face?' Tom has reappeared from beneath his towel, but even his new Boris Johnson-style hairdo doesn't cheer me up.

'We can't exactly get pissed with the boss watching over us,' he says, jabbing me with a big foot. 'And look – I found you a present while I was swimming.'

Beaming with pride, he presents me with an enormous and very beautiful conch shell.

'I trod on it,' he adds happily. 'So there might be some blood.'

'Lovely,' I deadpan, but I have to hand it to the big goon – he's got me smiling again.

9

I don't know who I offended so badly in a past life, but karma is definitely out to get me today. First a snake tries to attack me — okay, so that's a slight exaggeration, but it easily could have — then my mum calls right in the middle of the best conversation I've ever had with the love of my life, and then I arrive back at the apartment at the same time as Claudette, who is not alone.

'This is Carlos,' she announces, vanishing into the bathroom and shutting the door behind her, leaving the two of us standing mutely in the hallway. Carlos is short and stocky, with masses of light brown curly hair and a grinning, impish face.

'*Hola,*' I say, peering down at him, as a woman of five feet and nine inches can at a man who is clearly not much over five feet.

A flood of Spanish is his reply, and I have to hold my hand up to stop him.

'Sorry,' I mumble. 'I don't speak much Spanish.'

Now he just looks confused, the poor little hobbit, so I go to the kitchen, thrust some bottled water at him, and hurry out on to the balcony to hang up my towel. I should have taken Tom up on his offer to stroll back up the hill stopping at bars along the way, but I was feeling tired when he suggested it and the bus rolled up at just the right moment.

'Are you going out?' I ask hopefully when Claudette reappears, wafting toothpaste and what smells suspiciously like my perfume.

She looks at me as if that's the stupidest question anyone could ever ask another human.

'I think not,' she says, reaching for Carlos. He's been back into the fridge since my back was turned and the two of them are now toasting each other with my bottles of *cerveza*.

'Right,' I say, averting my eyes as Claudette slides a hand around and rests it on Carlos's bottom. 'I'll just. I'll leave you to it, er, leave you alone, then.'

I doubt they even hear me over the sound of their tongues thrusting together, and a few minutes after I've shut the door to my bedroom, I hear Claudette dragging her visitor into her room. Oh, now they're giggling. And now? Yep, that was definitely the sound of bedsprings.

'Oh baby!'

Oh hell.

'Baise-moi,' I hear Claudette say. I know that term, I'm sure I do. It means . . .

There's a crash, followed by more laughter.

Pretty sure it means 'kiss me'. Of course it does.

'Mmmm . . .'

That's definitely not Spanish.

'Oooh!'

I need to get out of here.

A loud slapping noise and a shriek.

Kill me now.

'Yes! Yes! Oh yes! Oh baby!'

That's *it*!

I don't even bother to change out of my beach clothes before slamming the front door of the apartment shut behind me and legging it up the steps as fast as I can. It's depressing enough not having any sex yourself without being forced to listen to other people having it through a wall. Still, it is pretty impressive all the same. Claudette certainly knows how to get what she wants.

The sun is just beginning to droop down behind the honeycomb mosaic of the village as I make my weary way up the hill. During siesta time, it's almost eerily quiet up here, with only a few cafés staying open to welcome exploring tourists, but now that it's nearing seven thirty, the place is beginning to wake once again. There's a natural disarray to Mojácar that I love: the way that plants spill out from window sills and houses sit one atop another, as if they've been balanced there by a child playing with bricks. Ordered chaos reigns supreme here, and it's the very haphazard yet perfect design of the Old Town that makes it so endlessly fascinating.

I reach the Plaza Nueva and take the steps up to the viewing platform. There's no Theo here this time, but there are plenty of empty tables and chairs in front of the café-cum-bar, so I choose one close to the outer railings and order myself a *cerveza*. A gentle breeze is chasing a scatter of twigs and dry leaves around in a circle on the ground, and I can detect the aroma of paella drifting down from one of the open windows above the square.

The waitress brings over a bowl of complimentary nuts, and I mindlessly begin to post them into my mouth, realising as I do just how hungry I am. There are ingredients for pasta or salad back at the apartment, but there's no way I'm risking going back there yet. I think about sending Tom a message and telling him to come and meet me, but I don't. It's actually quite nice to have an impromptu evening to myself, and to have the freedom to explore all the charming twists and turns of Mojácar that I have yet to rediscover.

The beer is tangy and tastes fresh, the perfect accompaniment to the salty nuts, and I let myself enjoy the sensation of it slipping over my taste buds. Drinking here is so different to how it is back at home, where everything always feels so rushed and urgent. The very reason you get a free snack with your beer in Mojácar is to encourage you to linger at your table and take your time. I watch as an older couple sit down a few tables away and study their menus. They both look dressed for dinner, and the woman has clearly spent some time getting her hair just so. The man leans across and points to something he's just read, and his wife chuckles in appreciation.

I want that one day, I think. I want someone to love that I can trust. It's okay to admit it to myself, even though I wouldn't dream of confessing such a thing to Tom or Claudette. Nowadays everyone seems afraid to admit that finding someone to love is a desirable goal. It marks you out as weak and uncool. Young women should be independent, focusing on their careers and becoming happy in themselves before entering into a serious relationship. But regardless of what other people might think, if I'm being brutally honest with myself I'm more worried about getting hurt. This infatuation I have with Theo might be fruitless, but at least it's safe.

Am I just being silly about Theo? I don't let myself

think about it in a serious way very often, because in the past the idea of Theo ever showing an interest in me has seemed so remote – ludicrous even. But over the past few days – and especially this afternoon – I feel as if something has changed between us. He looks at me differently, and keeps touching me. Could it be that he's simply getting to know me better at last, or could he genuinely be flirting with me? I don't think I'd recognise what flirting was if it skipped over wearing a rainbow tutu and slapped me over the head with a wet fish, so I don't have the faintest hope of ever knowing if that's what Theo has been doing. I can hope, though. There's nothing wrong with hoping.

I finish my first *cerveza* and ask for another, along with some grilled sardines, which arrive blackened and swimming in olive oil. I developed a real taste for these slippery little blighters after that first lunch at the beach, and now I can't seem to get enough of them. Pulling apart some bread that's still warm from the oven, I mop up a generous helping of the oil and smile as some of it dribbles down my chin.

The view from up here continues to awe me, and as I eat my dinner I let my eyes sweep lazily across the horizon, taking in the mountains, the greenery, those strange desert-like patches of earth, scattered houses and orchards. The sea has changed colour in the approaching dusk, a navy curtain outlined by the deep golden sand of the beach, and I can see pockets of birds coasting through the warm evening air, their wings outstretched as they dip, dive and spin. What a magical unison of nature it all is, I think, emotion temporarily getting the better of me, and I use a napkin to dab away the rogue tears that have appeared on either cheek. I think of Elaine, who still seems to love this place as much as she did forty years ago, and I wonder what it really was that drove her out of England. People don't just up and leave their homes behind for no reason, do they? I have the feeling that there's a lot more to Elaine's story than she's letting on.

A text comes through on my phone, making the small metal table shudder in protest. It's a group message from Theo, telling us that he's planning to drive out of Mojácar the following morning and that we should feel free to have a lie-in. I wait for the inevitable reply of delight from Tom, which comes through shortly afterwards, and then I try to work out what I can say. Before I have time to tap out my response, however, another message comes through from Theo – and this time it's just to me.

> Do you want to come with me in the morning?
> Yes, please! I immediately text back.

Nice one, Hannah. Way to play it cool.

> Excellent. Meet me at the villa at 8.30 x

He's added a kiss!

Okay, I type back, delight making my fingers shake. See you then! x

Two can play at that kisses game.

Hugely cheered to have been singled out for a special trip and practically cartwheeling with pleasure at the thought of even more alone-time with Theo, I pay my bill and head across the square into one of the many gift shops. I've been meaning to buy Rachel a new Indalo

Man since I arrived. After all, she needs all the good luck and protection she can get now that she's let awful Paul move in with her.

One day I vow I will have a nice house with a much nicer man living in it with me. And maybe, just maybe, his name will be Theo.

10

I can hear Claudette snoring as I slip out of the apartment early the next morning. I had feared that she and Carlos would still be bumping uglies when I arrived home the previous night, but either she kicked him out or he left of his own accord once his new girlfriend started snuffling away like a rhinoceros with a heavy cold, because there's no sign of the shoes and bag that he'd abandoned by the sofa.

I agonised over whether or not to leave a note for Claudette in case she woke up and wondered where I was, but then I figured she probably won't care. In fact, given the green light to sleep in, I imagine she won't actually get up until her belly wakes her at around lunchtime. I did text Tom, however, in as casual a manner as I could, and all I got back was one of those emoji faces with the shocked mouth and the big staring eyes. It's not so unusual, is it – the idea of Theo wanting to spend time with me? Maybe it is.

Deciding what to wear was near impossible, which is frustrating because I usually just throw on whatever's closest. I tried to picture Theo looking down at my thighs from his position in the driver's seat. Would shorts show my legs off best, or was it better to opt for a dress? And should I wear a bikini underneath or just underwear? And if it's the latter, then should I go for it and pull on the lacy satin set that I bought once after a bad date to cheer myself up and haven't worn since? In the end, I opt for denim shorts and a plain green vest over my padded bikini, but throw the sexy undies in my bag just in case. A girl should be prepared is something my mother is always saying, although I'm guessing she means condoms in the handbag rather than a thong and push-up bra.

I leave myself an hour to stroll down the hill to Mojácar Playa, telling myself it's because I want to saunter and not end up sweating all over myself, but of course my eagerness gets the better of me and I'm soon propelling around corners like a lustful Road Runner. There's a café open just inside the shopping centre by the roundabout, so I buy a bag of churros and two takeaway hot chocolates, then cross the road and knock tentatively on Theo's bright blue front door.

'It's open,' he calls, and I reach for the handle, almost dropping my bag of sugary treats in the process.

Theo's scent assails me as I cross the threshold, and the hot chocolates are in danger of decorating the tiles. There are signs of him everywhere, from the sunglasses tossed on to the wooden dining table to the discarded shirt thrown over the back of a nearby chair, but the man himself is nowhere to be seen.

'I brought breakfast,' I say, cursing the quiver that I hear in my own voice. I really need to pull myself together. I'm a twenty-eight-year-old professional woman, for heaven's sake. In the office, back in London, I manage to remain cool as a bag of salad leaves around Theo most of the time, so I can totally handle being alone in a villa with him.

'Morning, Hannah.'

Oh bloody hell, he's so sexy. I want to stick a churro in my eye.

'Hey.'

Theo is dressed more casually than I've ever seen him, in grey shorts and a yellow T-shirt. It's a brave colour, yellow, but of course it works on him. There's a folded road map in one of his tanned hands and a large bottle of water in the other, and he's smiling at me with what looks like genuine excitement.

'All set?'

I nod stupidly in reply and thrust the bag of skinny doughnuts in his direction, making a sort of meeping sound as I do so. Maybe I have actually morphed into Road Runner.

Theo opens the bags and sniffs. 'Churros!' he exclaims, beaming at me.

'And hot chocolate to dip them in,' I add, feeling my face heat up. I'm not used to being the reason Theo is happy.

'A woman after my own heart!' he declares, taking one of the foam cups out of my clammy hand and peeling off the lid.

'Do you think you can eat a whole one without licking your lips?' I ask, trying to look anywhere but at his mouth. 'It's actually a lot harder than you think.'

'First one to lick must buy lunch,' Theo says, playing along, and I giggle in agreement in what I hope is a sexy way.

I've never felt jealous of a deep-fried breakfast pastry before, but I guess there's a first time for everything. There's definitely something very sensual about the way in which Theo is devouring his churro, and I want to lick the sugar off his lips even more than I want to tackle my own, which is saying a lot. His technique is to shove as much of the thing in at once as he can manage, but for some reason I don't feel comfortable doing the same thing. If it was Tom standing across from me, I'd have downed it in one.

'It tickles,' he says now, grimacing and still managing to look handsome.

'I don't know what you mean,' I say, shrugging for effect. 'I don't feel a thing.'

He smirks at that, his tongue on the verge of emerging from between his lips. It's becoming impossible not to look at it. Then, very suddenly, it flashes out and across the sugary residue like a beautiful snake.

'Poor effort!' I joke, pretending to be a lady and fishing in my bag for a napkin to wipe my own mouth.

'I would never let you pay for lunch anyway,' Theo says, taking a gulp of hot chocolate, and my insides melt like mozzarella in a pizza oven.

Once in the car, we take the road leading back up towards the Old Town before hooking a right and heading first west, then north along the highway.

'Aren't you going to ask where we're going?' Theo says. I love the way he handles the car, one hand on the wheel and the other flicking the gearstick almost absent-mindedly, his elbow balanced on the open window and his dark brown thighs spread open across the seat.

'I figured I'd find out when we got there,' I remark, at a loss for anything more flirtatious, or indeed intelligent to say.

'Do you know the way to San José?' he asks now.

'I know that song!' I exclaim.

To my mild embarrassment coupled with knicker-elastic-loosening lust, he then starts softly singing 'Do You Know the Way to San Jose', tapping his hand against the edge of my seat as I join in with the 'whoa, whoa, whoa' bits. I didn't realise that I knew all the lyrics, but I do, and the two of us reach quite a pitch by the time we get to the last chorus.

'Bravo!' Theo shouts afterwards, sounding very Greek. 'That is where we are going!'

'To San Jose?' I squeal in surprise. I obviously wandered away from the queue when they were handing out brains.

'Yes!' Theo is flushed from the singing and his smile is infectious. 'It might not be *the* San Jose, in California, but I imagine it's a good runner-up – and I thought you might like to see it, too, seeing as how you love this area of Spain so much.'

He thought about me?

Luckily, Theo is forced to turn away then to overtake yet another truck, so he misses the sight of my face turning into a giant cherry.

By the time we reach San José forty minutes later, I've disloyally told Theo all about Claudette's new Spanish friend, including the part of the story where I was forced to leave the apartment and eat my dinner up at the Plaza Nueva.

'She is French,' was his response, as if that was all the explanation required.

Tom has also tried to call me twice, despite knowing

full well where I am, and when I feel my phone vibrating against my leg from inside my bag for the third time, I reach down and switch it off. This is the first and only occasion that Theo has ever singled me out for some one-to-one time that wasn't a strategy meeting, and I'm not going to let anything ruin it. Surely Tom can find a way to amuse himself for a few hours without me?

San José is, of course, stunningly beautiful, with a tumble of white stone buildings, pristine beaches and a neat handful of cafés, bars and quaint little gift shops. It doesn't have the same quiet sense of history that pervades Mojácar, but the pace of life feels the same. Nobody is in a hurry here, and locals sit in open doorways on plastic chairs, seemingly content to just sip their coffee and watch the day unfold.

Theo parks the car on the road that runs parallel to Tobacco Beach, and the two of us slip off our shoes and bury our feet in the deep sand. I'm glad now that I chose shorts over a dress, because the wind wastes no time in seeking us out. My vest top is tucked in, but Theo's loose yellow T-shirt is promptly blown right up over his face. For a few, brief, exquisite seconds, I'm free to feast my eyes on his conker-brown torso, and then he yanks it back down again with a grunt of embarrassed laughter.

Aside from a scattering of tourists who have set themselves up on a multi-coloured carpet of towels not far from the shoreline, the beach is predominantly deserted, and Theo points to a large black and white bird that has just snatched a fish from the surf.

'That's a sooty tern,' he says, immediately enthralled. 'You don't see them this close to land very often.'

'Must be a very tasty fish,' I reply, wishing I had something more insightful to offer to the conversation. 'I didn't know you were an expert?' I add, watching him instead of the bird.

Theo shrugs. 'My father taught me the names of birds when we used to go out and fish on his boat.'

'In Greece?' I guess.

He nods.

'Do you ever miss it?' I ask now, and he smiles sadly.

'Yes, every day – especially in the winter.'

'Would you ever move back?' I continue, crossing my fingers behind my back in silent prayer.

'I don't think so,' he says, crinkling his brow as if I'm the first person to ever put the question to him. 'The business means everything to me, you understand? And it would be hard to do the same thing in Greece, I think.'

Thank heavens for that, I think, but actually say, 'The business means everything to me, too.'

Theo turns to face me, his eyes dark pools, then extends an arm.

'Shall we?'

We walk across the sand until it feels damp and sticky underfoot, and Theo bends down to pick up a wide, flat pebble, which he tries and fails to make skim over the surface of the water.

'I'm sorry this is the first time I've brought you along for a shoot,' he says. 'It's not because I don't appreciate you – I do very much.'

'Oh, you don't have to explain,' I mutter. 'Honestly, I'm just happy to work with you. I mean, for you.'

'You have really impressed me since we've been here,'

he tells me, lobbing yet another stone. 'And before that, too, of course. I think this is going to be a very special film when it's finished.'

'I think so, too,' I agree, acute joy making my voice squeaky.

'It's been nice getting to see what you are like away from the office, too, Hannah,' he says, matter-of-factly. 'I find it easy to talk to you, and there aren't many people in my life that I can relax with in this way.'

Bloody hell – did he really just say that?

'Thanks,' I mumble, at a loss for what else to say. I'd like to tell him that I feel the same way, but I'm about as relaxed around Theo as I would be around a rattlesnake I'd just poked with a big stick. When he looks at me, just like he is right now, it makes me want to climb inside myself just to hide from him. Thankfully, a particularly rogue wave decides that this is the perfect moment to rush up the shore and soak us, and I'm able to leap up in the air and yelp, which saves me from having to formulate a proper reply.

'Come on,' Theo laughs, wringing sea water out of the bottom of his shorts. 'Let's go and explore the rest of this place.'

11

The sun moves seamlessly up to its highest point, pressing its hot fingers against our bare limbs as we leave the beach and take the main road along to the village. It's been years since I had a proper tan, but I'm beginning to notice my skin gradually changing colour. It feels softer somehow, but looks coarser, and there's a splatter of freckles across my chest. I'm still ridiculously white compared to Theo, of course, whose natural shade seemed to merge from toffee to milk chocolate practically overnight.

I'd love to know what the local Spanish people think of us as we stroll past them. Do they assume we're a couple? It thrills me to think that they might. One thing is for certain: I have never felt as close to Theo as I do right now. We talk to one another all the time at work, of course, but never about personal things. I love my job so much that it distracts me from becoming too flustered, and I'm able to hide my true feelings for Theo behind my scribbled pages of research notes. Liking him as much as I do has probably helped me become better at my job, if I'm honest. It's not just my passion for discovery that drives me to chase a story down until I catch it, it's my need to be noticed by the man I can't seem to stop loving.

Once we reach the sheltered, winding streets of San José village, the temperature drops to a more pleasant level, and I can stop worrying about sweat patches appearing on my clothes. Many of the small boutiques here are packed with trinkets, artwork and gifts, similarly to the shops back in Mojácar, and I wonder if Elaine's prints have made it this far along the coast. She still hasn't told me her surname, so I'm not sure which signature to look out for in the bottom corner of each reproduction, but I do find myself drawn to one image. It's a simple enough painting of Mojácar that's been printed on to a large postcard, but in this one the artist has added a double rainbow over the clutter of white houses.

'You like this?' Theo asks. He's just been inside the shop to buy us both a bottle of water, and he unscrews the lid of mine before handing it to me.

'I do,' I say. 'I've never seen two rainbows like this before. I didn't know you could get more than one at once.'

'Of course you can.' Theo is surprised. 'I have seen this many times in Greece.'

'Lucky you,' I reply with a smile, only just managing not to tell him how much the rainbows remind me of my childhood Care Bears obsession.

'They must be quite rare in Mojácar,' I add. 'My friend Elaine told me that it hardly ever rains there – even in the winter months.'

'I will buy this for you,' he says, taking the picture out of my hand and heading to the till for the second time.

'No!' I argue, running after him. 'You already bought me water.'

'And you bought me churros,' he replies, grinning with satisfaction as I accept the little paper bag. It's only a postcard, but I feel so happy that it may as well have been an engagement ring.

We carry on exploring until our rumbling stomachs draw us through the open doorway of a small traditional restaurant, which is tucked away in a shady corner on the edge of the village. Wicker chairs creak as we pull them out from beneath a square wooden table, and Theo almost knocks over a small vase of cheerful red flowers as he sits down.

'You like paella?' he checks, before launching into an effortlessly sexy flow of Spanish. The waitress, who is petite, dark-haired and pretty in the delicate way that I could never be, hangs around the table for far too long after she's taken our order, fussing over the arrangement of a paper cloth and sets of cutlery wrapped in napkins.

'Get in line, love,' I feel like saying. It's a bit unfair to dislike the poor girl on first sight, but she reminds me unnervingly of Nancy.

The bread arrives and with it the little birds that I've grown so accustomed to over the past few days. Hopping across the caramel-and-cream floor tiles, their inquisitive little heads tilted and their beaks open to reveal bright pink mouths, they line up around the table legs like a tiny army, waiting for the crumbs to drop.

'You asked me about Greece earlier,' Theo says, his head also on one side. 'But where is your home?'

'Do you mean where I grew up?' I ask, and he nods. 'To be honest, I don't really think of that place as home any more – I don't think I have for a long time.'

'Is London home, then?' he guesses, but I shake my head.

'Not really. Sorry, I'm not making much sense, am I?'

'You believe that, what is the saying? Ah yes, that your home is where your heart is?'

He looks so pleased with himself that I have to agree, and I suppose that is what I think. I'd just never thought about it in that way before.

'I grew up in Cambridge,' I explain. 'Well, in a small village on the outskirts, really.'

'And Tom, too?' Theo says, tearing apart a slice of bread.

'Tom?' I repeat blankly, my mind whirring in confusion.

'I thought you grew up together as children?' he states, breaking up his crust and tossing it down to the waiting birds.

'Oh, well no,' I mutter, uncomfortable at having to correct him. 'We met at university in West London.'

'You seem like brother and sister to me,' Theo says then. 'You even look the same, the two of you.'

He's right about that – Tom and I are both skinny, pale-skinned giants. It's hardly a compliment, though.

'I don't mean that in a bad way,' he adds, freakishly reading my mind, and then he laughs. 'Your face!'

'What?' I bring my hands up to hide behind.

Is my face really so amusing? Does he look at me and just see Tom in a wig? Oh my God. I bet he bloody does!

'You are funny, Hannah,' he says, and when I glance at him through my splayed fingers, he's smiling at me not in amusement, but something else, and I'm aware of my heart rate beginning to quicken.

'The two of you are lucky,' he goes on, throwing down more morsels to a grateful chorus of chirping. 'It is rare to have a friend of the opposite sex that you can be close to without the other thing getting in the way.'

'The other thing?' I ask, deliberately nonchalant.

He looks at me directly. 'Sex.'

Oh God, why did I make him say it? Now my face is the same colour as a stop sign.

'Unless, that is, you and Tom are friends with benefits?'

'NO!' I shriek, scaring away all the birds.

Theo refuses to play along. 'It is not so shocking,' he chides. 'Tom is a very handsome man, and you are a very pretty girl. Of course you have thought about it.'

'I have *not*!' I lie, moving my napkin aside so the waitress can put plates down in front of us. I'm not about to confess that I did, once upon a time, develop a serious but short-lived crush on Tom.

'Come on, Hannah.' He's definitely trying to goad me now. 'You are telling me that nothing like this has ever happened between you and Tom?'

I think about lying again, but I know he'll only ask Tom the same question. In fact, he probably already has.

'We kissed once,' I reply grudgingly. 'Years ago, about two hours after we met. It was nothing.'

'Nothing to you, maybe – but don't you think it was different for Tom?'

I really don't like where this conversation is going.

'We agreed it was a mistake,' I tell him honestly. 'We were drunk and it was stupid. I didn't even remember it the next day, and nothing has ever happened since.'

I want him to know that there's absolutely nothing standing in the way of him and me. Not that he's interested in me like that, but, you know, just in case.

'But you do care about him,' Theo says, not bothering to keep his voice down even though the paella has arrived. It's vast, with bright yellow rice, big shiny chunks of red pepper and a scatter of huge, pink langoustines, and it smells absolutely divine.

I picture my best friend – his adorable sticking-out ears and ridiculous floral shorts, the clumsy way he walks like a three-legged donkey, his straw-like hair and big, generous smile – and I can't help but feel affection.

'I guess I do,' I admit, picking up my knife and fork. 'But only when he's not being a big goof.'

Thankfully, the paella is delicious enough to rapidly distract Theo from the subject of Tom and me. There's so much of it that it's almost overwhelming, and I manage two helpings before my stomach begins to press unpleasantly against the waistband of my shorts. Theo eats with gusto, one hand reaching constantly for bread and nimble fingers ripping open the miniature lobsters. I'm doing my best to be ladylike, but when I try to ease the shells off my own little sea dwellers using my knife, Theo makes a tutting sound and insists on teaching me how to do it using just my hands. He also keeps licking his fingers, which is making it very hard not to slither underneath the table and curl up on his feet like a clingy pet dog.

A companionable silence falls between us once the bill is paid and we're meandering back through the village. Theo has pushed his sunglasses up into his thick, dark hair, and it's sticking up at all angles. How he manages to still look so sexy, despite resembling a pineapple, is a mystery only my lustful loins can answer.

'Ice cream?' he offers, as we pass a stall not far from the beach, but I groan and rub my belly.

'I can't. I'm stuffed.'

'Wimp!' he declares, but he means it in a nice way.

I have no idea what the time is, having switched off my phone and forgotten to put on my watch, but it feels even hotter than it did when we arrived. I should probably reapply my sun cream, but I don't want to start lathering up in front of Theo. He doesn't seem to need any SPF, the lucky thing. Eventually he nips into another small gift shop and I seize my chance, propping my foot up on a low wall and squeezing a generous puddle of lotion on to my exposed thigh. Sunburn is my biggest fear. Well, you know, after nuclear war and fatal disease, obviously. Oh, and maybe Claudette when she's in a bad mood.

'Ready to go?'

Theo is back, his brown eyes glistening and his beautiful lips parted in a smile.

Suddenly I don't want to go back to Mojácar. I want to stay here in this strange sleepy little town and have him peel my prawns and teach me about the birds. I hate the idea that this closeness that I'm feeling now, this sense of being inside the Theo bubble with him, rather than peering in through the sides, will vanish as soon as we have to go back to work.

We've almost reached the car now – I can see the reflective windscreen shade gleaming in the distance – so I hang back on purpose, pretending to be entranced by a cluster of trees set back from the road. Noticing me slow down, Theo turns and claps his hands with pleasure.

'Ah, lemon trees.'

'Are they?' I ask eagerly, following him down from the tarmac on to the dusty, dry earth.

'Can't you smell them?' he exclaims, creases appearing like sheets of music across his forehead.

I sniff the air like a hunting dog. 'Mmmm, yes. They smell amazing.'

'I bet they taste even better,' he tells me, brazenly plucking one of the plump yellow fruits from a low branch and sticking a finger through the waxy skin.

'Isn't that really bitter?' I say, wincing as I watch him chewing.

'Hannah,' he admonishes, sounding very Greek. 'Please do not tell me that you have never eaten a proper lemon before.'

'Of course I have!' I argue. 'I've had lemon cake plenty of times – and I always eat the slice that they give you in a gin and tonic.'

He pulls a face at me. 'That is not real.'

My cheeks are burning now. I hate it when he tells me off.

'Come here.' He beckons me with a finger, and I obediently shuffle towards him through the dirt.

'Now, open your mouth,' he instructs, his voice low and gentle.

I do as I'm told, feeling a tug of desire from somewhere deep in the pit of my gut. He's so close to me now that I almost close my eyes, but instead I force myself to look into his. They're so deeply brown, like melted dark chocolate, and I feel my tongue darting out to moisten my lips.

'This,' he says, lifting a chunk of juicy lemon up to my mouth and waiting while I tentatively lean forwards to accept it, 'is how a lemon should really taste.'

I brace myself for the eye-squinting bitterness that will make me recoil and grimace, but it never comes. Theo's right – this lemon is sweet, almost like an orange, with a tang that is all pleasure and no pain at all – and I grin at him in wonder.

'It's delicious.'

He hasn't moved backwards away from me yet, and is now using the same fingers that came so close to my lips to feed himself another chunk of the lemon, all the while maintaining that eye contact which is making my knees tremble. He looks thoughtful, almost as if he's trying to work out a tricky sum in his head, and I dare myself to believe that he could even be thinking the same thing that I am – that a kiss could taste even better than the fruit.

Alas, just as the thought tiptoes into my head, Theo seems to snap out of whatever trance he was in, and looks over my shoulder in the direction of the car. He doesn't need to tell me; I know that it's time for us to leave.

There's no singing on the drive back to Mojácar, and instead of asking me more questions about my life or even teasing me about Tom, Theo sticks resolutely to the subject of work, telling me his frustrations over the fact that he hasn't yet been given permission to film inside the cave at Los Vélez, where the painting of the Indalo symbol was first discovered.

'It feels important to me to see it,' he admits. 'Even if I cannot film there, I want to visit the area. Perhaps next week I will go.'

I try my best to ignore the crashing disappointment that hits me like a bolting horse when I realise he's not going to invite me along to go with him, and instead try my hardest to remember some of the things I researched about the Indalo legend before we came out here. Theo is polite enough and nods along to my carefully considered words, but his attention seems elsewhere. By the time we're pulling in to the parking space beside his villa back in Mojácar, our conversation has trickled away like sand through a sieve.

'Do you need a lift back to the apartment?' he asks, pausing halfway out of his seat as though the idea has only just occurred to him.

'Oh no!' I hold up a hand. 'I'm fine. I need to go to the shop anyway.'

'If you're sure?' Theo shuts the car door and waits while I collect my bag from the back seat.

'Thank you for today,' I say, my quiet voice reflecting the shyness I'm feeling. 'It was a real treat.'

Theo smiles at me over the roof of the car.

'See you tomorrow, Hannah,' he says, and then he's off, shutting the blue door behind him before I've even had a chance to reply.

Did that day just happen? I think, crossing the road and watching the sprinklers that have just come on in the middle of the lawns by the shopping centre. Thin patches of glistening rainbows appear almost immediately in the spray, and I'm reminded of the postcard Theo bought me today. He was so attentive, so playful, and so interested in me, but now all I feel is hollow. It's as if I climbed all the way to the top of a mountain only to discover that the amazing view I'd been promised when I set off is completely obscured by fog. Now all I feel is lost. Lost and a bit weary.

It only occurs to me to switch my phone on when I'm almost back up the hill, sweaty from the walk, irritable from the disappointment, and desperately craving a cool shower and a drink with an alcoholic content. To my surprise, I have over fifteen missed calls from Tom, two from my dad and five from a mobile number I don't recognise. There's a text from Tom, too, but as soon as I open it up my battery promptly dies on me.

Feeling more than a bit perturbed, I race up the last stretch of hill as fast as my gangly legs can carry me and hurry down to the apartment.

'Hello?' I call, shutting the door behind me and sending up a silent prayer that Claudette hasn't brought home another young Spaniard.

'Out here,' comes the reply, and I follow the sound to the balcony.

Claudette is indeed alone, stretched out on her towel in the one remaining corner of sunlight, a thong made from what looks a lot like dental floss decorating her neat, round bottom.

'Have you seen Tom?' I ask, averting my eyes as she props herself up on one elbow. There's a French novel folded open in front of her on the tiles, and a cigarette sits smouldering in an ashtray.

'Yes, he was here about an hour ago,' she says, eyeing me up and down. 'Where have you been?'

'Just out,' I reply. I don't want her to know about my day with Theo. She'd only ask questions, and I'm not ready to answer any of them. I want to keep the whole thing to myself, and I'm already regretting that I told Tom about it.

'He was looking for you,' she adds, taking a drag and blowing smoke up into the air between us. 'He was with a girl.'

'A girl? What girl?'

Claudette deliberately takes her time replying, sitting up first and taking a long drink of water. Even her nipples look angry, I think, all red and indignant.

'Small, pretty, dark hair.' Claudette takes another drag. 'Big boobs.'

My stomach drops like a snooker ball into a sock.

'Do you know where they went?'

'Are those beers?' Claudette asks, looking at the carrier bag in my hand.

'What? Um, yes.'

'Can I have one?'

'Oh, for God's sake,' I mutter, heading to the kitchen and finding the bottle opener. Of course she wouldn't have thought to replace all the beers she and Carlos drank together – oh no. That would just be too obvious.

'Here.' I thrust one into her outstretched hand. 'Now will you tell me where they went, please?'

Mon dieu! Claudette jokes, getting herself back into a horizontal position. 'Somebody has got their bikini bottoms in a twist.'

'Just tell me!' I plead.

'He mentioned something about pizza,' she says lazily, picking up her bottle of sun cream. 'But before you go, can you ju—?'

It's too late, I'm already slamming the apartment door shut behind me.

12

It can't be her. It just can't be.

It wouldn't even make sense. How would she know where I was? And even if she did, why would she come? No, Tom must have genuinely managed to get lucky.

And yet ... Pretty? Big boobs? There's no way Tom could have scored with a girl that Claudette would describe as 'pretty', not in the short time that I've been away. That's even more unlikely than the alternative. But I refuse to believe that it could be true – it's just too awful a thought to comprehend. It just cannot be her, and that's that.

By the time I've rounded the final corner in my dash through the village and am faced once again with the decorative wrought-iron gates of Diego's pizza restaurant, I'm so wound up that my insides must resemble a treble clef.

Peering through the gaps in the fence, my worst fears are confirmed. There at one of the tables, looking typically smug, annoyingly attractive, and infuriatingly full of herself, is my half-sister Nancy. And she's not alone, either – Tom is gazing adoringly at her from a neighbouring chair, while Diego is in another. I can't see his expression from here, but his body language tells me all I need to know.

What the effing hell is she effing well doing here?

'Hannah!'

Oh bugger, Tom's just spotted me.

His long legs propel him over at an alarming speed – far too quickly for me to have anything ready to say to him except expletives.

'Steady on!' he exclaims, hurt all over his big face.

'What the hell is she doing here?' I seethe, clamping my teeth together like an angry velociraptor.

Nancy has turned her head now and is smiling and waving at me. Not actually coming over here, oh no. She'd rather make me go to her. God forbid the little princess has to get out of her chair. I wave stiffly back.

'I've been trying to call you all day,' Tom says now, careful to keep his voice low. 'Nancy has been, too, but you didn't pick up.'

'That doesn't answer my question of what the hell she's doing here,' I rant, watching Diego put his hand on my sister's arm and shuddering. 'I mean, what the hell does she think she's doing? Nobody invited her.'

Tom shrugs at this, which is obviously very helpful.

'Tom! I mean it,' I hiss, slapping him on the arm in frustration.

'Ow!' he grumbles, rubbing the spot. 'It's not my fault. I'm the one who had to hire a car and drive all the way to the airport to collect her.'

'You should have left her there,' I say, mutinous. 'Hang on – how did she have your number?'

Tom looks at the floor. 'We may have chatted on Facebook a few times.'

'TOM!'

'What? I didn't tell you before because I knew you'd react like this, but she's really not that bad, you know. If you just gave her a chance—'

'Pah!' I snort – and I mean actually snort, like a pig over its dinner.

'She's here because she wants to see you, not me,' he adds. 'She told me that she can't wait to spend some time with you.'

'She's lying,' I snarl.

'Hannah, you need to stop this,' Tom says then, picking up both of my clenched fists. 'You don't hate your own sister – you know you don't. *I* know you don't. You're a kind person and you're my best friend, so I know you're not evil.'

'Thanks a lot,' I mutter, but I can feel my rage subsiding a fraction.

'Just hear her out,' he urges. 'Like you say, she's obviously here for a reason. Why not let her explain it before you go over there and bite her head off like some sort of angry praying mantis?'

Is Tom right? Am I being unreasonable? Is Nancy a demon only because I have made her that way in my head? Is she, in actual fact, a total sweetheart and all this time I've just been coerced into loathing her because of what our father has done?

'Hello, Nancy.'

I've made it as far as the table, Tom's hand a solid force of encouragement in the small of my back and a smile plastered across my face. Nancy glances up at me. Her glossy dark hair is catching the light and there's a flush of colour across her cheeks. There's no way anyone would ever guess we're related, and I've often wondered in the past whether it would be easier for me to like her if she looked like a smaller version of myself. As it is, she's managed to swerve the bits about me that I'm not so keen on – the above-average height, the canoe-shaped chin, the too-large feet – and picked up a whole other host of delightful attributes from her mother's side of the family. Her nose is neat and upturned slightly, like a doll's, and her hands and feet are petite and feminine. She's also got those full lips that so many people pay someone to create for them with disgusting chemical fillers, only hers are natural. She seems to get prettier as she gets older, too, which certainly cannot be said for me. I'm not even thirty yet, but I found my first grey hair the other day. A grey hair!

'Hannah,' she says, smiling at me. 'There you are at last.'

My rictus grin is starting to hurt.

'You arrived just the right time, too,' she adds, dropping her eyes from mine. 'Diego here was just telling Tom and me about that time years ago when you declared your undying love to him and then threw up all over his shoes.'

No, I was right, she is a demon. If the humiliation wasn't coursing through me like lava at this very moment, I'd even feel smug in the knowledge that I was correct about her.

'Oh,' is all I manage, and I feel Tom shift uncomfortably behind me.

'Don't worry,' she prattles, her earlier confidence dissolving as she takes in the expression on my face. 'It was a long time ago, right? I'm sure I've done much worse things.'

'Have you?' I ask, and she looks towards Diego.

'Well . . . Okay, I haven't done that exact thing, but

that's only because I was never allowed on holiday without Mum and Dad when I was growing up.'

She's making a dig at me now. Of course she is.

'It was very sweet,' Diego pipes up, patting me on my rigid arm.

I snatch it away.

'Drink, anyone?' Tom says then, his tone betraying his discomfort. I don't answer him, because I'm too busy wondering what to do first: cry or be sick.

When it becomes apparent that nobody is actually going to move or say anything, Diego stands up and promises to return with drinks for everyone. The shame of my besotted teenage secret being out is so acute that I can't even look at him. I feel like I'm seventeen again, babbling about first love while cupping his face in my hands, trying to make him kiss me. Of course he hasn't forgotten that – I just didn't think Nancy of all people would be the one to make him recount it.

'He's a bit hot for an oldie, isn't he?' Nancy says, parroting Claudette from a few nights ago, as Tom ushers me gently into the vacated chair. I'm so tense that I fear I won't be able to bend in the middle, and will have to lie rigidly against the seat like an ironing board.

Instead of replying, I just cough.

Tom, who can usually be relied upon to fill awkward silences with inoffensive chat, has fallen treacherously quiet beside me. I think about the day he must have had, driving all the way to Almería airport and back in the knowledge that he was collecting the one person I could not stand. As cross as I am about the situation, I feel my heart go out to him. While I was off eating paella and being fed chunks of lemon by Theo, Tom was most likely freaking out.

'Why are you here?' I ask Nancy, deciding not to bother with more small talk.

She giggles and sips her water, looking at me in apparent amusement. How she can find anything in this situation amusing is beyond me.

'I fancied a holiday,' she says, draining her plastic bottle. Diego has returned with a jug of sangria and an extra glass for me, but luckily he's astute enough not to sit back down and join us, which makes Nancy pout at him in disappointment.

'Where's your boyfriend?' I ask pointedly, deliberately making sure that Diego hears me.

For the briefest of seconds, Nancy's eyes narrow, but she recovers quickly.

'We broke up,' she says, shaking her head as Tom offers her the sangria first. 'It's no big deal. He was a loser anyway.'

So, all those hundreds of photos of the two of them that I've seen on Facebook must have been simply for show. I'll give the girl credit – she sure does a good impression of someone utterly besotted.

'You do realise that I'm not on holiday,' I tell her. 'I'm here to work.'

'Is that what you've been doing today?' she asks, and I glare immediately at Tom.

'What?' he exclaims. 'All I said was that you'd gone out for the day with Theo, which is true, isn't it?'

'We were researching other possible locations for the film.' This is directed at Nancy, but she's not even listening.

Diego has reappeared to take the order from another table and she's trying to catch his eye, all the while smiling like a wolf wearing a sheep's overcoat.

'I don't think you'll be able to stay with me,' I add, glancing at Tom to gauge his reaction, and feeling dismayed when I see the corners of his mouth turn down.

Nancy looks at me in surprise. 'What? Why not?'

'There's no room,' I tell her firmly. 'And anyway, like I said, I have to work. I don't have time to look after you.'

'Look after me?' Nancy repeats. 'I am twenty-two, you know. I don't need anyone to look after me.'

'You can stay with me,' Tom offers, and I'm forced to swallow a yelp of indignation.

'No, she can't,' I counter, just as Nancy is thanking him. The only thing worse than Nancy staying with me is Nancy staying with Tom. I can't bear the thought of that. He's my best friend, not hers, and I don't like the way he keeps gazing at her.

'You can stay with me tonight,' I tell her. 'But tomorrow we're booking you a flight home.'

'Oh, come on, Han,' Tom begins, but I raise a hand in warning.

'Claudette said earlier that I was welcome at your place for as long as I like,' Nancy simpers. 'She's really nice, isn't she?'

'It's not up to her,' I argue, kicking Tom under the table accidentally as I cross and uncross my ankles. 'It's up to Theo – he's the one paying for the place.'

'Is he your boss?' Nancy asks. 'The hot one? I've seen photos of him on Facebook.'

'I don't think he'll appreciate you turning up and

sponging off him,' I continue, cursing the colour that's just flooded into my cheeks at the mention of Theo's name. The truth is, I'm more worried about Theo falling under Nancy's spell than him being cross with me about her arrival. Clearly she's already wriggled herself into the affections of Tom, Diego and even Claudette, like the grubby little worm that she is, and I simply could not bear it if Theo started mooning over her as well.

'I'll talk to him in the morning,' I mutter, thinking that it's wise for me to get to him first and explain the situation. If I tell him how awful she is, perhaps he'll back me up and encourage her to leave.

'Oh no!' I suddenly cry, and Tom chokes on his sangria.

'What?'

'I'd forgotten I've got my second session with Elaine in the morning,' I wail. 'I can't cancel on her – I don't even have her phone number.'

'Don't worry,' Tom is quick to reassure. 'I'll talk to Theo. I'm sure he'll be fine about it, as long as nothing gets in the way of the schedule. It's not as if it's going to cost anything for Nancy to sleep on the sofa, is it?'

'The sofa?' Nancy is pouting. 'Isn't there a spare bed?'

'No.' I throw her a thunderous look.

'You know how bad my back can get,' she says, making a face that I'm sure even the most Christian of pacifists would happily punch.

'I used to do dance and gymnastics when I was younger,' she explains to Tom. 'I got to competitive level, but then had a nasty fall off the beam and had to wear a neck brace for weeks.'

'Oh no, you poor thing,' he cries.

I roll my eyes.

'My neck healed fine, but my back still plays up sometimes,' she goes on, rubbing it to illustrate her point.

I can still remember the Saturday that Nancy had her tumble, because it was the exact same day that I needed our dad to give me a lift to Rachel's birthday party. As it was her sixteenth, her parents had splashed out and hired a stately home in the countryside, and everyone from our school year had been invited – including my unobtainable crush at the time, Greg, who was planning to perform live with his band, the Frazzle Rockers. I had been plotting for months about how to seduce him, and was more than willing to relinquish my virginity to him in one of those grand stately bedrooms. Dad assured me that he'd pick me up by six, but he never showed up. My mum didn't have a car then, and it was too far away for me to go by taxi, so I simply sat in the living room of our house in my party dress, crying my eyes out until ten o'clock, when my dad finally called and explained that he'd had to rush to hospital, as Nancy had injured herself. It was later that I discovered she hadn't broken anything, just badly strained some muscles, and that she only actually spent an hour in the accident and emergency department. My dad could have easily still taken me to the party, only Nancy wouldn't let him leave the house, and in his worry for her, he simply forgot all about the promise he'd made to me. Even in a neck brace, drugged up to the eyeballs with painkillers, she'd still taken the opportunity to get one over on me, and I've never forgiven her for being the reason I missed that party. It was so good that people were still talking about it when we did our A-levels.

'You can have my bed,' Tom is now telling Nancy gallantly. He's being so obvious that I'm beginning to feel sorry for him.

'Oh, for God's sake,' I interrupt, before he can dig himself into an even bigger embarrassment hole. 'I'll sleep on the bloody sofa, okay?'

We stay until the jug of sangria is empty, and then Nancy excuses herself on the pretext of needing the toilet, only to slip inside the restaurant to where the bar used to be.

Tom glances at me sheepishly. His hair is a mess today, as if he's been running his hands through it constantly, but he's starting to get a nice tan now. Freckles have appeared on his nose, and the hair on his forearms is bleached white.

'So,' I begin, using my straw to destroy the soggy pieces of fruit in the bottom of my glass. 'How long have you been stalking my sister on Facebook?'

'Hardly stalking!' he argues, but I detect colour in his cheeks. 'It's not like we talk all the time. It's only been three or four times since the last time we met, which was over a year ago.'

'Why didn't you tell me?' I can't help but ask. I'm not sure why the idea of them talking bothers me so much, but it emphatically does. It feels like a betrayal.

'You know why,' he says simply. 'You have to admit; you are a bit mental when it comes to Nancy.'

This is true, but it's very hard to own up to.

'What do you talk about?' I ask instead, abandoning my straw and tapping my fingers on the table top.

Tom lifts his shoulders. 'Oh, nothing much. Just work and stuff.'

'Stuff?' I enquire.

'She wants to go travelling, same as me, so we talked about that.'

'I wish she'd travelled somewhere other than here,' I say grumpily.

Tom takes a deep breath and rests both his elbows on the table, bringing down his hands until they're less than an inch from mine.

'You're going to bite my head off for saying this,' he says. 'But how about you use this time with Nancy to try and build some bridges?'

'Come closer,' I beckon him with a finger.

Tom is bemused. 'Why?'

'Because I am going to bite off your head,' I inform him, refusing to join in when he laughs. 'Seriously, Tom – I know in your world everyone has rainbows and sunbeams coming out of every orifice, but sometimes things are too broken to be fixed. I honestly don't know what Nancy's doing here, but it can't be to see me. She hasn't shown a single bit of interest in me and my life since she was about six years old – why would she suddenly start now?'

Tom leans back in his chair and folds his arms. 'She asks me about you when we chat,' he says. 'She always wants to know how you're doing, what we're both working on, whether you're seeing anyone.'

'Tchuh,' is all I manage, and he frowns at me.

'I'm not saying be her best friend,' he continues. 'Just that you try to draw a line under past events and give her a chance. I like both of you, and I know you're both good people.'

'Pah,' I say this time, but his words are working their way through the rhino-like hide of my resistance.

'Please try,' he says. 'For me.'

Wow. He's resorting to emotional blackmail now.

I grit my teeth. 'Fine. I'll try. That's if she ever comes back from the toilet.'

We give Nancy another five minutes, then my patience runs out and I stomp up the steps into the restaurant, only to be confronted by the sight of Diego's hands clamped around Nancy's bottom and her face turned up towards his. The two of them are kissing each other as if it's in danger of going out of fashion, and bile rises up in my throat. All of a sudden, I'm a rejected seventeen-year-old again, and it feels horrible.

'Nancy, we're leaving,' I announce loudly, and tumble back out into the courtyard. Tom, who is counting out some euros for the waitress, looks at me in concern.

'Are you all right?'

'No, Tom, I'm not all right. My stupid half-sister is inside, eating the face off a man who thinks I'm a total moron.'

'Nancy's snogging Diego?' Tom looks far more upset than I'm comfortable with.

'Focus on me, please!' I demand, but he can't quite wipe the look of potent disappointment off his face.

'Now do you see?' I rant. 'This is exactly the kind of thing she always does. She's a nightmare.'

Tom looks as if he might reply, but before he gets the chance Nancy totters down the steps next to us, her skirt pulled around the wrong way and all her lipstick kissed off her face.

'Sorry,' she says dreamily. 'I took a wrong turn on the way to the ladies.'

*

While Nancy and Tom stroll ahead of me through the darkening streets of the village, her chatting and him laughing nervously along, I mooch behind them doing my best not to breathe actual fire. I know that alcohol is the absolute worst fuel that you can pour on to a bad temper, but at the moment it's all I want. What I need is obliteration. I want to drink so much booze that the pain of Nancy being here is washed away. I want to forget what I just saw back at the restaurant – the sight of my little sister being devoured by my teenage crush – and most of all I want Tom to stop being so nice to her. He should be on my side, so why is he on hers?

Just a few hours ago, everything seemed so perfect. I was sharing such a special day with Theo, listening as he talked about his time growing up in Greece, about his father's love of the ocean and how he'd struggled when he first moved to England. It had felt in those moments as if it was finally my turn to be happy, as if all the dreaming I'd been doing might actually have been the foundation of something real between the two of us. But now, with Nancy turning up like this and ruining everything, that glimmer of hope has been trodden unceremoniously into the dirt, and not even the mystical sight of the cobbled streets bathed in moonlight can lift my spirits.

There's only one thing for it – I need to get Nancy the hell out of Mojácar, and I need to do it fast.

13

Elaine is waiting for me in the courtyard of La Fuente the next morning, a bunch of yellow flowers hanging limply in one of her hands. I take a deep breath before approaching her, trying my hardest to expel all the hurt, anger and confusion that are simmering away in my gut like emotion stew, and her smile as she sees me is so enchanting that I almost cry with gratitude.

'I picked these for you on the way down,' she says, kissing each of my cheeks in turn and handing over the bouquet. 'But I'm afraid they've already started to wilt. It's so hot today, isn't it?'

She's not wrong. I was woken by the sunlight streaming in through the balcony doors of the apartment a few hours ago. There are no curtains in the main living space, and of course I had banished myself to the sofa all night.

'They're beautiful,' I say, genuinely touched, but Elaine looks immediately concerned.

'Are you feeling okay, Hannah?' she asks.

No, I'm not. I've got a bad case of sister hatred coupled with a raging hangover.

'Of course, I'm fine.'

'You look a bit peaky,' she says, peering into my no doubt bloodshot eyes. 'We can reschedule if you like?'

I think about going back up to the apartment to face

Nancy and her latest number one fan, also known as Claudette, and hurriedly shake my head.

'No,' I tell her, smiling with what I hope is enthusiasm. 'I'd honestly rather spend my morning with you than with anyone else.'

And it's true, I would. Even the thought of Theo's company is not as alluring now that Nancy's here. He's bound to say that she can stay, but he'll inevitably also think it's highly unprofessional, and all the steps I've taken with him since we arrived in Mojácar will be forgotten. I'll go back to being the lowly researcher that he has to leave in the office rather than take on location. It's so horribly unfair that I feel like throwing myself down on to the dusty tiles and wailing like a toddler in a tantrum, but instead I let Elaine lead me away towards the road.

'Do you still want to go over to the artists' studio?' she asks, pausing by the crossing.

I nod, and she points ahead of us down the hill.

'We'll need to get the bus,' she says, and I see the stop in the distance.

'Fine by me.'

Luckily we don't have a long wait, and it's actually a relief to clamber into the air-conditioned vehicle and put the heavy camera bag on the floor. The bus moves away and I close my eyes, resting my hot head against the cool glass of the window.

'Beer or wine?' Elaine asks, and I have to smile.

'Both – and some sangria.'

'Never a good combination,' she says, patting my arm. 'We should stop off at the beach so you can swim – everyone says that's the best cure.'

'I've never heard that,' I manage weakly.

'And I've never tried it,' she admits. 'You know,' Elaine says, lowering her voice conspiratorially. 'The people from around this area often refer to Mojácar as "the village of witches".'

'Do you know why?' I ask, wishing I was recording our conversation.

'There used to be a lot of healers living here,' she explains, leaning into me as the bus veers around a corner. 'When I first arrived, people used to come and ask them to make cures for all sorts of things.'

'Did you?' I want to know, but Elaine laughs and shakes her head.

'Not me, no. I never really believed in witchcraft and spells.'

'So, these healers were witches?'

'I think probably they were simply good at listening,' Elaine replies. 'But people will always believe what they want to believe. If, for example, you visited one of these healers and asked for a spell that would make a man fall in love with you, then perhaps you would be given a set of instructions that sounded magical, but were in fact just good sense. Is that, then, real magic? Or is the simple belief that you will get what you want the real trick to it?'

Naturally, as she's been talking, my mind has switched on Channel Theo, and now I'm imagining myself casting a spell on him in his sleep, only for him to wake up and find himself in love with me. There's probably more likelihood of that happening than him coming to such a realisation on his own.

'I like that idea,' I tell her. 'The idea of a spell, I mean. It would be a lot easier than actually having to go on loads of dates with someone.'

'Ah, but with true love there are no short cuts,' Elaine sighs. 'Love has to be planted like a seed in the earth, then nurtured and tended over time. All the conditions must be perfect, or it will wither and eventually die. But if you do this, if you look after your love every single day, then eventually it will bloom.'

I glance out through the window at the straggly palm trees lining the road. They're all still standing after so many years, but they're hardly in a condition that I would describe as perfect.

'I know what you're thinking,' Elaine says, pressing the bell and getting ready to stand up. 'You're thinking that there is not much love in Mojácar.'

'Oh no, I wasn't. I was just . . . Oh, I don't know what I was thinking.'

'Love isn't always sitting in plain sight,' she says, while I heave the camera bag up on to my shoulder. 'Love is in every place and at every time – it is then, it is now, and it is always – but you can never snap your fingers and simply conjure it up.'

I think about her words as we clamber off the bus. Aside from my mum, who I know must love me in that everlasting way, nobody else can claim my love to that degree. I loved my dad once, but now? And have I ever loved Nancy? I suppose I must have as a child. And in my head, I love Theo, but will I love him forever? Is that what I've been building up to since we met?

'Hannah,' Elaine says, gently breaking apart the

complicated web of emotion that I've become entangled in. 'We're here.'

The next two hours pass by in a blissful blur of relaxed chatter, as Elaine tells me more about the Mojácar of old. She talks about why it's become such a Mecca for artists, who are drawn by the history and then stay for the natural palette of the place, the many hues of white in the Old Town and the vibrant blues of the sea and sky above it. The light here is unlike any other, she explains, telling me that even the sunshine of Mojácar is no match for the burning whiteness of the Moorish architecture, and it's this canvas – this pure, crystal whiteness – that provides such a stunning counterpart to the Spanish greens, pinks and reds.

'I could never get tired of painting this place,' she says simply, and I realise that I understand exactly why.

I wish I hadn't waited so many years to come back to Mojácar. The magic of the place, which I let under my skin as a teenager, could have been so much more powerful a feeling if I'd gone through with the promise Rachel and I made to each other about coming back here every single summer. Now that I'm here again, it's as if my senses have memories – my eyes are looking at things in more detail, my nose is working extra hard to pick up the strange and alluring scents, and all the while I'm straining to hear the waves and the persistent breeze. I had been starting to relax and feel more confident – even in front of Theo – but now that Nancy has arrived it's as if a dark cloud is overshadowing everything.

It's with a heavy sense of impending doom that I gather

myself up to go. We arrange to meet again in a few days, at La Fuente. I say my goodbyes and leave Elaine happily tucked in behind an easel at the studio. The heat wallops me like a wrestler, and I'm glad that I selected a dress this morning instead of my habitual denim shorts.

After fishing my shades out of my bag and putting them on to shield my eyes from the mighty sun, I switch on my phone. A message comes through immediately from Rachel:

Tom told me about Nancy. Call me!!! xx

If anyone knows how much I can't stand my half-sister, it's Rachel. During those teenage years of friendship, where we spent literally hours of our time just talking to each other about everything and anything, I tried my best to explain why I had such a problem with her. Rachel has always been a pragmatist, and generous with her sympathy, but even she eventually began to appreciate where I was coming from in relation to Nancy. Tom had never really understood it, but I always felt that Rachel did.

Despite all this, however, I can't quite face calling her yet. My hours spent with Elaine have calmed my frantic misery down to a dull ache, and speaking to Rachel now will only bring everything to the surface again. Instead, I settle for a text message, telling her what happened and promising her that I'll call later in the evening.

I get about three metres along the pavement before a reply pings back through:

She snogged Diego? TROLL!

It's accompanied by a winking emoji face, which makes

me smile. It's easier for her to see the funny side of the situation, what with being in London and having a serious boyfriend. What happened between Diego and Nancy last night reminded me of just how bad it felt to be rejected by him all those years ago. And, unlike me, Rachel no longer has to worry about dying alone on a dusty shelf with all the other spinsters. Then again, I think I'd rather that than end up with Paul.

It's been tough watching her fall for him, and it's not just because I think he's the biggest plonker to walk the earth. Rachel has always been the one I tell my biggest secrets to, the one who has seen me at my very worst but still loves me anyway, and who comforted me every time I fell head over heels for a boy that wasn't interested in me.

Since she met Paul, however, there's less room in her life for me. Rachel will allow me to gabble on about Theo for ages, but not once has she ever disagreed with my protestations that it will never happen. She says it's because he's not good enough for me, but that's just what people say, isn't it? I'd say the same thing to her if Paul dumped her, only I would actually mean it.

I picture the two of us as teenagers now, sitting side by side in our shared bedroom here in Mojácar. I'm sobbing because Diego has just very gently, but very firmly, told me to 'go home and sober up'. This was after I garbled something about seeing our shared future in the stars and promptly vomited on his feet. Now, in between tears, I'm bemoaning the unfairness of it all and demanding to know why he doesn't fancy me.

To her credit, Rachel is managing not to laugh at me,

and is instead drawing devil horns and fangs on to the crumpled photo of Diego that I had taped up next to the bed, and telling me loyally that he's 'probably got wrinkles on his bum skin anyway – he's at least thirty'. I can remember how devastated I was, even in the face of such brilliant support, and it's silly really, because in every other respect I'm pretty tough. I don't cry at sad films, I'm stoic in the face of injury and I shout right back at anyone who attempts to ruin my day by getting pushy on the bus. Rejection, however. Well, that is my kryptonite.

The undergrowth is twitching with life as I make my slow way back up the hill. It would have been quicker to get the bus, but I have no desire to hurry, which is unlike me. Tom's camera bag is imprinting a welt on my shoulder blade and I can feel my feet rubbing inside my sweaty shoes, but still I keep trudging. My mood may be in the gutter, but I feel my spirits lifting as the uphill path curves around and Mojácar appears above me. It doesn't matter what time of day I make this journey, be it dawn or dusk, the view is always just as enticing, and I realise in that moment how very fortunate I am to be here.

Okay, so Nancy is like a bee sting in the behind of my plans, but I can be mature about this. I didn't want her here, but I can't get rid of her now that she is. I have two options: either I can ignore her completely and make her life hell, or I can try my best to rise above her spoilt behaviour and remain calm and professional. I ponder this as I reach the steepest part of the hill, the sun no longer the only thing causing my legs to burn, and decide that yes, I can rise above it all. I am the older sister, after all, and Theo is here. I want him to see just how measured and mature I can be – and the best way to do that is to throw myself into this project with even more enthusiasm.

As I fish my keys out of my bag and prepare to open the apartment door, however, I hear a high-pitched squeal of laughter coming from inside and shudder with irritation. Nancy is not going to make this easy for me.

'Hannah!' she trills, leaping up from where she's been lounging on the sofa. The very same sofa she claimed was too uncomfortable for her to lie on. Oh dear, up go my hackles.

'Hello,' I say carefully, putting down my bags and heading into the kitchen, where I find a small vase and fill it with water from the tap.

'Those are, um, nice,' Nancy says, eyeing Elaine's tired-looking bouquet of yellow blooms as I do my best to make it look attractive.

'Have you had breakfast?' I ask.

She shakes her head. 'No. I don't feel the best, to be honest. Probably the sangria.'

And the Spanish tongue, I think, but don't say.

'Well, help yourself to whatever's in the fridge,' I tell her. 'It's all mine, anyway – except the nail varnishes. Those are Claudette's.'

'Thanks,' she says, then hesitates. 'Hannah?'

'Yes?'

'I'm sorry for just showing up like this.'

Bloody hell – has she had a lobotomy?

'Right . . .'

'I did honestly want to see you, like I told Tom.'

I've screwed my face up so much now that I must look like a sat-on Chelsea bun.

'And I'm sorry about Diego.'

'Oh, don't worry.' I manage a snuffle of laughter. 'It's not as if I like him any more. That was about a hundred years ago.'

'Even so,' she says, fiddling with the frayed bottom of her denim shorts. 'It wasn't cool.'

She's definitely had a lobotomy. Or perhaps a personality transplant. Are they offering those on the NHS these days?

'It's fine,' I reassure her, checking the time. We really have to go soon, or we'll be late to meet Theo. 'It was just a bit of a shock, that's all. I honestly don't care.'

I don't hear her reply, because I'm shouting Claudette's name over the sound of the bathroom taps running. There's an irritated snarling noise, and then she yells back to 'give her a bloody minute'. A minute is all I'll give her, I think ruthlessly.

'We have to go to work now,' I tell Nancy, collecting my notebook from the table and packing it into my bag. 'If you walk out with us, I can point you in the direction of the beach?'

Nancy looks at her feet. 'Well, I, erm . . .'

'She's coming with us,' announces Claudette, who has just emerged from a fog of hairspray and perfume.

'No, she isn't,' I say, feeling my earlier resolve to be mature crack like a dropped egg.

'I told Claudette about my plan to become a TV presenter,' Nancy says, her voice small. 'And she very kindly said I could come along and observe. You know, see a real professional at work.'

'She may as well learn from the best,' puts in Claudette, modest as ever.

'Wouldn't you rather go to the beach?' I plead, thinking of the look on Theo's face when we turn up with an interloper.

'We can do that later.' Claudette is adamant. 'Now come on, Hannah – I don't want to be late.'

I wish Mojácar was a village of witches, I think darkly, closing the door behind the three of us a minute later and shooting an evil look at the back of Claudette's legs as she starts up the steps. If it was, I'd hunt one down and buy a spell that would turn a certain small French person into an actual frog.

14

'The original Indalo Man symbol is believed to date back some four thousand five hundred years, and some believe that it represents a god holding a rainbow above his head, as part of a protection pact with mankind. Others, however, believe that the true meaning has been lost over time, and that now it is purely a symbol meaning good luck, or a charm to ward away evil.'

'Cut there,' calls Theo, strolling across the cobbled square to speak to Claudette. I already know what he's going to say, that she needs to inject a bit more enthusiasm into her words. The symbol is what the documentary is all about, and it won't work if we don't get our viewers excited about it.

We're filming at Plaza Iglesia today, which sits in the heart of the Old Town and is home to the Mojaquera – a marble statue of a woman carrying a large clay pot of water on her head – as well as the imposing Church of Santa María. Once a fortress, it's constructed from vast slabs of brown stone, and dominates the area like a bullish big brother, one that looks all the more unmistakable next to the sugar-cube-like buildings that cower beneath it. While it's not my favourite spot, I do like the sense of history that comes from being close to something that was first built as far back as 1560. There's also a huge and fully blooming bougainvillea, which has dropped its beautiful magenta petals all over the tables and chairs of a tapas restaurant on the edge of the square.

Claudette has now repeated her opening spiel and moved on to the more recent history of the area, and as I listen to her words, I'm reminded again of Elaine.

'The Almerian artist Jesús de Perceval moved to Mojácar in the 1940s,' Claudette says, her voice full of authority. 'Ten years later, he founded the Movimiento Indaliano, which chose the Indalo figure as its official emblem. This group attracted many painters, artists, writers, poets and musicians, and their work has assured the passage of the Indalo from simply a cave painting to a symbol that is recognised all over the world. As well as good luck and protection, the Indalo is also associated with rejuvenation, rebirth and hope.'

Was that why Elaine found what she was looking for when she arrived here? I wondered. That hope she told me about, which is linked to the Indalo. When I had my little tattoo done all those years ago, it was more to do with my love of Mojácar than my belief in what the symbol actually meant, but since coming back here it feels as if it's taken on a whole new layer of importance. I like the idea that it's been protecting me over the past ten years, and I love how much myth surrounds it.

Nancy has taken advantage of a break in filming to go over and chat to Claudette, who infuriatingly seems just as enamoured with her as Tom and Diego. Thank God for Theo, I think, staring adoringly at the back of his dark head. Aside from a polite handshake of greeting when we first arrived this morning, he's barely said three words to her. Then again, he's only said about four to me. The pressure of the tight deadline is clearly getting to him, and as such his concentration is absolute.

A large patch of sweat has appeared on the back of Tom's blue T-shirt, and I cringe in sympathy as I watch him setting up his camera for the next shot. Claudette has moved from the shade of the bougainvillea to the vast arched doorway of the church, and is now making a fuss about being in the direct sunlight. The fact that she was sunbathing topless all day on the balcony of our apartment yesterday seems to have conveniently been forgotten, as she complains to Theo about wrinkles and the risk of skin cancer.

'Come along now,' he soothes, keeping his tone conciliatory. 'Your skin looks fabulous in this light, I promise you.'

Oh, he's good. He's really good.

Claudette happily stares straight into the camera and begins charting the history of the church behind her, going into ecstasies over its unique pastel mural, but before she can reach the end of her final sentence, a mobile phone starts ringing.

'CUT!' yells Theo, immediately swinging around to locate the source of the interruption.

'I'm so sorry,' mutters Nancy, fumbling in her bag and finding the offending phone.

'It's okay,' Theo says, glaring not at Nancy but somehow, horribly, directly at me. 'You weren't to know. Hannah, you should have told her.'

'I did!' I squeal, even though I know it's not true. I hate the way Theo's looking at me, like I'm nothing more to him than an irritating fly that keeps landing on his ankle.

'Hannah,' he says, a warning note in his voice. 'Please do not shout at me.'

'I'm not!' I say again, far too loudly. But it's just not fair. Nancy is the one at fault here, and I'm being made to take the blame. It's exactly the same as it was when we were little kids. I would go to visit my dad and we would be encouraged to play together, then Nancy would cry for absolutely no reason and I would be told off. Well, I'm not having that happen again – not here, no way.

Before I work myself up enough to say anything more damaging, Tom steps in and suggests that I go and film some more vox-pop interviews down by the beach. We've only managed to collect a few that are useable so far, and Theo is keen to start and end each segment of the film with local people talking about what Mojácar and the Indalo symbol mean to them.

'You have the hand-held camera, right?' Tom says, his expression conveying far more than his words. He's doing me a favour, I know he is, but that isn't enough to douse the hot coals of resentment smouldering inside me.

'I think Tom is right,' Theo agrees. 'I don't really need you here today, Hannah. I have all your notes and Claudette knows the script.'

I hate them. I hate all of them.

'Fine,' I say, giving up with a sigh. 'Come on, Nancy.'

'Oh, Nancy can stay,' Theo adds, and I swear I feel a knife go right through my heart. Looking up, I see that Tom is just as surprised as me.

'We'll bring her down to the beach later and meet you,' puts in Claudette, who I'm convinced is enjoying all the drama. 'There is live music at Carlos's bar tonight – we can make a night of it.'

'Fine,' I say again, apparently unable to locate any other words from inside my angry hive of a brain.

Snatching up my stuff without looking at a single one of them, I glance once more at the beautiful bougainvillea and head off across the cobbles, using every fibre of self-control I have left not to stomp. It takes me another five minutes to reach the bus stop just below the Plaza Nueva, and by that time I've put a call through to Rachel.

'I hate her, I hate her, I hate her!' I moan, before my friend has even finished saying hello.

'Erm, hello Hannah, so nice to hear from you. I'm fine, thanks – nice of you to ask.'

'Sorry,' I mumble, kicking at the kerb. 'But I hate her.'

'I got that part.' Rachel is smiling at the other end of the line, I can tell, but by the time I fill her in on the latest instalment of the 'Nancy ruins Hannah's life' story, her mood has changed.

'I'm so sorry, Han – that does sound a bit unfair.'

'A *bit*?'

'Okay, it's a lot unfair. Theo is clearly an idiot.'

'Oh, but he's such a gorgeous idiot,' I sigh, quickly updating her on what happened yesterday between the two of us in San José, before Nancy arrived on the scene.

'Wow,' she says, exhaling with the sort of pride you only ever get from your very closest friends. 'It sounds to me as if Theo has got the mega-hots for you.'

'I wish he did,' I grumble, paying the bus driver and choosing a seat right at the back. 'But of course he doesn't.'

'Why do you say that?' Rachel presses. Bless her, trying

to be supportive. I wish she had flown out here to join me instead of Nancy.

'Because he's far too good for me,' I begin, ignoring her protestations. 'And because he thinks I'm an idiot that looks like Tom in a wig.'

'What?' Rachel is understandably confused.

'He said that we looked like brother and sister.'

'That is not the same thing as saying that you look like Tom in a wig,' she states, and I find myself giggling despite my despair.

'What am I going to do?' I wail, watching a group of Spanish teenagers board the bus carrying beach towels and a football.

'About Theo or Nancy?'

'Both!' I exclaim.

There's a pause as Rachel thinks through her answers, and I picture her pretty green eyes slanted in concentration.

'Theo just lost his temper because he's hot and stressed and because Claudette winds him up,' she replies, wise as always. 'He will have forgotten all about it by this evening, so my advice is to just do as he says today and get some amazing interviews, then never mention it again.'

I do like that idea, but I don't know if she's right about him forgetting. Still, me showing him just how well I can work under my own steam will definitely help me get back into his good books.

'And Nancy?' I ask, a scowl appearing on my face as soon as I utter her name.

'I know you don't want to hear this,' Rachel begins, and I groan loudly. 'But she hasn't done anything all that bad yet. I know it's annoying that she's hanging around and getting you into trouble, but that was more Theo's fault than hers. You have to be the good cop with Nancy, or she'll just play up more.'

'How did you get to be so smart?' I ask, affectionately begrudging.

'I've met Nancy, don't forget,' she points out. 'Men can't see through the little-girl-lost act in the same way that we can. They're just not made that way. All they see are her boobs.'

I laugh out loud at that, but then in the next breath I'm overcome with a new panic.

'What if that's why Theo wanted her to stay – because of her boobs?'

'Then he's a pig and disgusting,' Rachel says crisply. 'And you'd be better off without him.'

Her use of the word 'pig' has just reminded me of Paul, and I climb off the bus with the guilty realisation that I haven't even asked how her life is going. I am a terrible friend.

'How's living with a boy, then?' I say now, bending to scoop up a bright green cricket from the pavement and put it safely into the grass.

'Oh, you know, smellier than it used to be,' she laughs. 'But no, it's fine. In fact, it's lovely. He's even cooked me dinner a few times.'

'And it's edible?' I reply, struggling with the mental image of Paul dressed in a pinny, serving fajitas.

Rachel giggles again. 'Not really,' she admits. 'But at least he's trying.'

'I'll have to come over and sample some when I'm back,' I promise, even though we both know I won't.

'You know, one day all this will seem so funny,' Rachel says. 'Life has a way of doing that, I always find. Of showing you just how okay you really are.'

'I hope you're right,' I tell her, meaning it. 'Because at the moment, it feels like there's hardly anything left for me to laugh about.'

15

For someone who only started interviewing people face-to-face a few days ago, I think I'm pretty good at it. In my role as researcher, I'm often trusted to chat to sources over the phone, or send out questions via email, but this trip is the first time I've been permitted to hold the camera and think on the spot.

With every vox-pop interview I collect, I can feel my confidence growing, and after a few hours I realise just how silly I was to be angry with Theo. Okay, so he sent me away from the shoot, but he also had no qualms in letting me work by myself, without any of the constant direction that Claudette seems to require from him. If anything, I should be flattered, not pissed off.

And this bit is so much fun, too. If I'd stayed up in the village with the others, I'd have been standing around like a spare limb, but instead I've spent the entire afternoon chatting to local people and admiring the rugged coastline down at the beach. There is something about this place that stops it feeling like just another holiday resort. Rather than catering for British holidaymakers by opening ghastly English-themed pubs and serving baked beans on toast, the people of Mojácar have stuck steadfastly to their own personal tastes, and the result is quirky, alternative and refreshingly unique. When Tom and I were in our second year of university, we and a group of our mates booked a week-long trip to Magaluf, and I couldn't believe how touristy it was. Not surprising, really, when you consider that Mojácar was my first taste of Spain – in that regard, I was spoilt. I had got on the plane back then expecting a similar vibe to the one I had grown accustomed to, but the reality had been anything but. And that was also the holiday where I'd developed a random, week-long crush on Tom.

There was no real reason for it that I could understand, other than the heat and the copious amounts of alcohol we were pouring into ourselves on an almost daily basis, and I never acted on it or told anyone how I felt – not even Rachel. My friendship with Tom was simply too dear to me to risk messing it up, and so I held my tongue – quite literally – and waited for the feelings to pass. And they did. As soon as we were back on UK tarmac, he went back to just being my lanky mate, and that's the way it's been ever since.

Dusk is falling by the time I catch up with the others at the beach bar where Carlos works, and I feel much better than I did this morning. In fact, it feels as if the silly disagreement with Theo was days ago, and now I'm more than ready to forget it ever happened. I'm also more than ready for a cold beer, so I'm thrilled to find one sitting waiting on the table, courtesy of Tom.

The beach bar is split-level, with a lower seating area leading out on to the sand and an orderly arrangement of sun loungers set in rows between us and the sea. Inside everything seems to be made of wood, from the polished bar top to the furniture. Green, blue and yellow sheets are strung across the beams above our heads like a canopy, keeping off the dipping sunlight and providing the perfect trampoline for a number of tiny birds. I can see the shapes of their delicate little bodies casting shadows across the material.

'Good day?' Nancy asks, the first person to speak as I take my seat.

'Great, thanks,' I chirp, taking a huge slug of beer. 'You guys get everything done that you needed to?'

'Just about,' says Tom, clinking his beer against mine with a knowing look.

'It was a very frustrating day,' Theo cuts in, his tone slicing through my upbeat mood like cheese wire.

'Oh?' I enquire, looking over to where Claudette is stubbornly ignoring all of us, her feet up on a spare chair and her eyes closed.

'Tomorrow is another day,' he says with a sigh. 'That is what I have to remember.'

Gosh, it's unlike him to be this despondent. I try to catch Tom's eye, but of course he's looking at Nancy. Not surprising, really, given that the floaty top she's wearing is struggling to keep her boobs in check. Nancy herself is staring down at her phone, which I can see is logged into Facebook. Trust her to choose social media over a setting as glorious as this one.

'Are you okay?' I ask Theo quietly, touching his hand with a finger. He glances down and moves it away, picking up his own beer and taking an even larger sip than I did.

'I think I will go now,' he announces, standing up so abruptly that Tom's drink is almost a casualty. I watch him weave through people at the bar and then I can't bear it, I have to follow him.

'Theo!' I catch up with him just as he's about to climb up the steps leading to the road.

He lifts an eyebrow.

'I'm sorry,' I babble. 'About this morning. I shouldn't have snapped at you. And I'm sorry about my sister being here. I didn't invite her – I have no idea why she's even here and I don't want you to think badly of me.'

'Hush.' To my surprise, Theo steps forwards and puts a single finger across my lips. I can feel a trace of his pulse and my body surges with pleasure.

'I should not have sent you away, Hannah, but you are the only one here that I can trust to work by herself.'

I really am?

'Claudette is so . . .' He tugs at his hair. 'Particular.' He smiles sadly. 'I feel like her father sometimes, and it is very tiring.'

'Poor you,' I tell him, rubbing the top of his arm awkwardly.

'I am sorry not to stay with you and have a drink,' he says, sounding genuinely regretful. 'But if I sit here with her, I will end up . . . you know? And we cannot have that.'

I nod. 'Of course.' And then, as he turns to leave, something makes me say, 'I could come with you?'

'To the villa?' Theo asks. He's looking at me with a new directness now, and it's as exciting as it is unnerving.

'Only if you want some company,' I say, inwardly cursing my hopeless reserve. If only I knew the words to use that would make it clear to him how I feel. Instead I sound clumsy and shy and annoyingly coy.

After what feels like an age, but is probably less than a single minute, Theo shakes his head.

'I think tonight, it's not such a good idea,' he says, and before I can respond he has taken a step forwards and kissed me lightly in the soft part of my cheek, just beside my mouth.

'Maybe another time, yes?'

'Okay,' I hear myself say, although I have no idea how I managed to say anything given the fact that I'm no longer human and am in fact a puddle of drool on the concrete bar floor.

I watch him go and then drift dreamily back to the table, sinking into my chair with my fingers still touching the spot on my face that Theo kissed. A band has set up on a makeshift wooden stage a few tables away, and a red-faced bass player is tuning his instrument, the deep sound making the hairs stand up on my arms.

'I thought you weren't coming back,' says Tom, pointing to my now-empty bottle. 'I'll go and get another round in.'

'Thanks,' I croon in a sing-song voice, smiling up at his bemused expression.

'Are you drunk?' asks Claudette, who is smoking a cigarette and drinking red wine.

On love, I think, grinning at her across the table.

Carlos hurries past with a tray of drinks, giving Claudette a wink as she flicks ash on to the floor.

'Not yet,' I reply, then, motioning to Carlos, 'How's your boyfriend?'

'Pfft,' is her response, and Nancy starts giggling.

'Did I miss something?' I ask.

'That one will never be my boyfriend,' sneers Claudette.

'Your buddy, then?' I reply, making sure she knows what I'm getting at.

Claudette sighs. 'He kisses like a wet sponge,' she declares, stubbing out her cigarette with aggression, and Nancy bursts out laughing.

'Oh.' I search the bar for the man in question. He seems so self-assured to me, so much like a small peacock strutting around in front of the hens.

'That is what I said,' Claudette drawls, exasperated rather than amused. 'Now, I must teach him.'

Nancy is still laughing when Tom comes back with drinks for everyone, so I quickly fill him in on our conversation. Not surprisingly, he's nowhere near as amused as Nancy.

'If he's such a disappointment, then why come back here at all?' he asks Claudette.

'He is good in other ways,' she informs us. 'He has nice hands.'

Tom turns puce.

'Claudette!' I admonish. 'TMI!'

'Oh, don't be such a prude,' she scolds. 'You should try him sometime. I don't mind.'

'Gross!' I yelp, picking up my beer. 'Sloppy seconds is not something I'm into, thanks very much.'

'Oh, really?' Claudette lowers her sunglasses. 'What a shame.'

'Why a shame?' I ask, immediately feeling uneasy.

Just as she's about to reply, the band starts up and the music is so loud that we all jump – even the ultra-cool Claudette. The atmosphere in the bar switches from laid-back and lazy to buzzing with energy, and a few people even get up and begin to dance.

'This is brilliant!' yells Tom, tapping his big foot along to the music.

'Come and dance with me!' Nancy says, leaping to her feet and reaching for his hand. I watch them start to wiggle away together in front of the stage, Tom all arms and legs and Nancy all shimmies and hair flicks.

'She is adorable, your sister,' Claudette informs me, waving at Nancy as she looks over in our direction.

'Half-sister,' I correct automatically.

'It's no wonder Tom has fallen for her,' she adds casually.

Usually I would bat away her comments and tell her she's mistaken, but there's no denying what the two of us can see happening right in front of us. That is, the look of delight and adoration on Tom's face as he spins an exuberant Nancy around in a circle, and the way he watches her every move as she dances away from him and then back, picking up his hands and laughing at something he's said. It doesn't make me feel angry exactly, more resigned – but I'm not about to admit that to Claudette.

'He's not her type,' I say instead, picturing the gym-buffed Adonis I'd seen with Nancy in her Facebook photos. 'And anyway, she was snogging Diego last night.'

'Lucky Diego,' breathes Claudette, and I snap my head around to glare at her.

'What?' she says, innocence personified, pouting at me over the rim of her wine glass. 'Your sister is a very attractive girl. I don't care what sex a person is – if I fancy them, then that is that.'

'But she's my sister,' I point out, unable to quite believe what I'm hearing. As if it's not bad enough that Tom is salivating all over Nancy; now she's reeled in Claudette, too. In less than forty-eight hours, Nancy is very firmly nestled in the cosy nook of her friendship – a place where I've been trying to get for years. It's not that I want Claudette to fancy me, but it would be nice to at least be considered a possibility.

'Your half-sister,' Claudette reminds me, and I understand exactly why Theo had to leave the bar earlier.

'I don't think you're her type either,' I retort with a grin, swigging my beer. There's no way I'm going to let my guard down and make it obvious how fed up I am.

'Maybe not.' Claudette shrugs, leaning back to run a casual hand up the inside of Carlos's shorts as he passes her chair. 'But if I'm not allowed to make a move on her, then Tom can't either.'

'Oh, don't worry,' I say grimly. 'I plan on having this exact same conversation with him, too.'

In the end, I don't manage to corner Tom for long enough to warn him away from Nancy, but it doesn't matter anyway, because as soon as Carlos finishes his shift, he brings over one of his Spanish mates and my sister is invited up to dance yet again – and this time her partner is far less gentlemanly than Tom.

It's easier to watch her when it's not my best friend she's wrapping her arms around, and I even start clapping along to the music as the night wears on. Tom has been steadily drowning his sorrows ever since Ignacio the dancer's arrival, and he's now very drunk indeed. So drunk, in fact, that he's resting his forehead on the table.

'Imbecile,' remarks Claudette affectionately, the next time she comes up for air from her snogging marathon with Carlos the wet sponge.

Meanwhile, I can't stop thinking about the kiss Theo gave me, and the way he looked at me when I offered to accompany him home. I know he was tempted – I could feel it – and this knowledge is making me feel lighter than air. If I allow myself to open another door in my fantasy, however, into a bedroom containing the two of us, I immediately feel clammy with nerves. Theo is far older, far sexier and far more experienced than me, and my biggest fear right now is that I won't be able to satisfy him even if I were ever to get the chance. What Claudette and, apparently, my own younger sister find so easy does not come naturally to me – and it doesn't help that I've barely been near a man in years.

Nancy and Ignacio return to the table and he pulls her down on to his lap, running his hands up across her face and into her glossy dark hair. Her cheeks are pink with exertion and outwardly she looks happy, but something a little awkward in the way she's holding herself makes me take notice.

'Nancy, do you want to go?' I ask, deciding to give her an out. Ignacio is staring at his friend, who in turn is still kissing Claudette, and I'm not sure I like the look on his face very much.

She turns to me, flushed and bleary-eyed.

'Already?' she whines. 'It's still early.'

'Well, it is almost ten,' I say, looking at my watch. 'And most of us have to be up for work in the morning.'

'I don't have to be,' she points out, but I can tell her

heart's not in it. I don't care what Rachel said, I'm going to have to play bad cop this time.

'Well, I've got the keys,' I say, standing up and rubbing Tom's shoulder until he stirs. 'So, no arguments.'

'Party pooper,' she grumbles half-heartedly, but I'm gratified to see her wriggle out from Ignacio's clutches and collect her bag from the floor.

'I'll come back tomorrow,' she promises the Spaniard, but he's already on his feet, moving away back to the bar.

'Are you coming, Claudette?' I say loudly, but she shakes her head. I really hope she doesn't come crashing back into the apartment with Carlos in the middle of the night – especially now that I'm on the sofa.

The three of us leave the beach bar and walk along the main road towards the taxi rank, which is situated under some trees opposite the shopping centre. Tom is stumbling with his head down and Nancy has her arms wrapped around herself in a hug, both of them silenced by the throbbing hum of cicadas.

You can see so many stars down by the water at this time of night, and it never ceases to amaze me just how many of the sparkly little blighters there actually are in the sky. If you'd lived in London all your life, you'd be forgiven for assuming there are merely a handful, but of course there are billions. As if Mojácar wasn't magical enough with its fairy-tale village and mythical history, when the sun goes down you also get this added layer of spellbinding beauty – a tapestry of twinkling wonderment. It's enough to bring a person to their knees in awe.

As our taxi heads up the hill and I see the lights of the

old town blinking above us, I allow myself to picture Theo sitting on the deck of his villa, looking at those very same stars. And for a brief, delirious second I imagine that while he's gazing up at them, he's also thinking about me.

16

Dawn has just broken when I slip quietly out of the front door and tiptoe up the steps, taking the steep slope opposite the apartment that will lead me into the depths of Mojácar Pueblo. There are jacaranda trees hugging the sides of the small white houses all the way along this hill, and the lilac petals of their flowers are a near-match for the light lavender tint in the fresh morning sky.

I can feel the familiar burn in my calves already, but it's almost a welcome sensation, one that I've become so accustomed to in the eight days we've been here. I like to think my legs don't hurt as much as they did on that first weary afternoon, but perhaps they do and I've simply got used to the pain. I'm wearing a new floral dress that I picked up from one of the boutiques in the village, which is shorter than I usually go for and tighter, too, but I don't mind showing off a bit more leg now that I have some colour. Claudette always looks impeccable and Nancy so effortlessly feminine, and my tatty shorts and vest ensembles were making me feel like a poor third.

Claudette did, of course, as I had grimly predicted, bring Carlos back to the apartment last night – but not until at least three a.m. Given that I was on the sofa again having deposited a bleary-eyed and oddly quiet Nancy into my bed, there wasn't much I could do to avoid being rudely awoken. There was no sign of his handsy mate Ignacio, though, so I could at least be thankful for that.

It's a puzzling feeling, this protectiveness I seem to have developed over my half-sister. I can barely remember a time, not even when we were children, where I felt the need to step in and look after her. That was how it felt last night, though. Something deep in my gut signalled to me that Nancy was in distress, and I acted accordingly, removing her from the clutches of that Spanish boy and taking her somewhere safe. Well, relatively safe. We are staying in an apartment clinging to the side of a vast hill after all.

But this morning I want some time alone. Hell, I need it. I want to work through the script and see where we will be filming over the next few days, and I'm also craving space in order to devour each morsel of memory about the kiss that Theo gave me. It wasn't just the softness of his lips as he pressed them against my cheek, it was the way he looked at me before he did it. Something passed between us by those steps into the beach bar and I'm convinced that it came from a place way beyond simple friendship.

I've reached the top of the slope at last, and pause to catch my breath. The houses in this part of the village are packed together so tightly that the people living in them are probably able to visit their neighbours for dinner without ever leaving their front rooms. Perhaps this is why so many Mojácar residents grow miniature forests on their balconies, the pots full of flowers and twisted leaves providing a barrier to prying eyes. Whatever the reason, I'm glad they do, because every time my eyes travel upwards they are greeted with a veritable rainbow of blooms. The reds, yellows, pinks and purples look all the more vivid set against the sheer white backdrop of the buildings, and the smell is heavenly, too. While the walk down to Mojácar Playa is scented heavily with earthy pine and lemon, up here the aroma is overwhelmingly floral. In the midday heat it can become close to cloying, but at this time of day I'm happy to inhale deeply and let the fragrant perfume wake up my senses.

What a place, I think, as I always do, urging my eyes to seek out every dusty corner and roam across even the smallest details. Glancing upwards as I turn a cobbled corner, I see from the street sign that I'm on Calle Indalo, not far from Plaza Nueva. I'm not drawn to the viewing platform today, though, because I'm craving a bit more solitude, so after a pause I cross the wide, flat stones that make up the floor of the square and head uphill again.

There was a bar up here, once upon a time – Rachel and I used to head there on the nights that Diego's place was shut – but I discover that it's long since closed down. The outside still looks the same, though, and I experience a flutter of amused déjà vu as I make my way past the dusty blue shutters and the faded paintwork on the sign outside. La Barra de la Vela, it was called, which I remember translates as the Candle Bar, and it used to be full of candles, too. They were set in little glass jars, which were strung up in the interior and around the outside seating area, and there was one in the centre of each table. In hindsight, I imagine each and every one of them was a citronella candle to keep the mosquitoes away from the customers, but the two of us had found the whole set-up charming and sophisticated; something that Rachel and I – at that age and with those levels of alcohol in us – were definitely anything but.

We would turn up after midnight, dressed in cheap Lycra miniskirts and brightly coloured boob tubes that showed off our strap marks in stark detail, and clatter up to the bar in our high heels. The barmen, who were only a few years older than us, would lean over the polished wood to kiss us on either cheek, then look us up and down and make loud exclamations in Spanish. At the time, we assumed they were admiring us, but in truth they were more likely just amused. The flirting that would go back and forth was all very genuine, though, and Rachel would always be the one to step in if she thought one of the boys was getting a bit too amorous. The bar would close at three or four in the morning, and we would take off our painful shoes and walk arm in arm back down the hill, whispering to each other about the night we'd just had. I had felt invincible in those days. Well, I did until the night I threw up on Diego's feet.

Leaving the sad shell of La Barra de la Vela behind, I use the final bit of strength in my legs to make my way up the steps to the Mirador del Castillo – the highest point in Mojácar. There's a large, square-shaped veranda up here offering uninterrupted views out towards the sea, and in the corner furthest from where I'm standing, a café is nestled under a tall wooden shade. Feeling extremely cheeky, I hurry across and extract one of the stacked metal chairs from outside, hooking it over an arm and making my rapid way over to the outer wall. My plan is to sit for a while, taking in the view, and I tell myself that the café owner wouldn't begrudge me the use of his chair for such a simple pleasure.

The sky is a soft cornflower blue now, and the wedge of Mediterranean in the distance a sapphire scribble streaked with white. The sea is never calm and flat in Mojácar – something I had forgotten in the years since I'd last been here. It is stirred perpetually into a shifting unease by the persistent wind.

Despite being up so high, the breeze in this part of the village is more a gentle caress than a battering, but I know it must be different on the coast. Is Theo woken each day by the sound of waves crashing against the shore? The romantic side of my brain likes to think so, even if the dry-as-a-cracker side thinks it's being a soppy idiot.

Oh Theo, Theo, Theo – had he wanted that kiss to lead to more last night? Had he felt the weight of it as I did, a metaphorical anvil sitting right on my heart? An anvil would not be a good thing to be lumbered with in Mojácar, I decide, idly doodling a picture of myself lying crushed underneath one in my notebook and chuckling to myself – not with all these hills.

Taking one long, luxurious last look at the view of the horizon, I fold open the script we're using for today's filming and wait for inspiration to strike. My boss may be a meticulous planner, who always knows exactly where he wants to shoot every single scene, but I know this place better than he does. I want to make sure that I have something to contribute, even if he dismisses me. What was it my teacher at primary school always used to say? Ah, yes – always be part of the discussion, and don't be afraid to put yourself forward. Show willingness. To be fair, I doubt Mrs Wilson with her childlike voice and grey beehive was thinking of the same sort of willingness I was when I offered to accompany Theo home to his villa last night, but she's never going to know.

Whilst almost everything in Mojácar feels like it was built in a bygone age, in fact much of the architecture was constructed in the 1960s. A combination of the Spanish Civil War, which ended in 1939, and a severe drought in the area, had decimated the population. Numbers of Mojácar residents had dropped from over eight thousand to just a single thousand, and many of those people were living hand-to-mouth in extreme poverty. The Indalo symbol may have been protecting them from earthquakes and the evil eye, but apparently it couldn't turn the dry earth soft enough for crops. Mojácar was in danger of crumbling in on itself and being forgotten, and in the end it was the actions of one man that changed the future of Mojácar and helped make it thrive again. Theo has written a huge spiel about him in the script, and I read it again now, allowing myself to hear the words in his deep, accented voice.

'In 1960, the Mayor of Mojácar, who was a man named Jacinto Alarcón, joined forces with a group of artists led by Jesús de Perceval, and he and this Movimiento Indaliano, as they were known, set about publicising to the wider world just how beautiful and unique Mojácar was. Jacinto promised that he would give land away free to those willing to move into the area and build a dwelling. It worked, and folk came from all across Europe and the world to settle in Mojácar. They dug wells for water and built homes and businesses that were in keeping with the

Moorish style that set the place apart – and everything was overseen by Jacinto. By 1966, Mojácar had been awarded the prize of "Most beautiful and improved village in Spain" by the Ministry of Tourism and Information, and of course people began to visit.'

I bet every mother who lives in Mojácar calls at least one of her sons Jacinto, I muse, scribbling a note on the script to remind myself to try and find out. Elaine would be a good person to ask, given that she's been here since not long after the tourist boom. In fact, there's a chance she may even have met the original Jacinto, before his death in 2001, and I write myself another reminder in my notebook.

Leaning forwards in my pilfered chair and looking again at the view spread out below me, I find it extraordinary that only fifty years ago the place must have been a jumble of half-finished buildings and rustic scaffolding. There would have been donkeys laden with stones trundling up the hill, their big floppy ears coated in white dust, and bemused locals peering out from behind their curtains at all these strange foreign faces. They were all welcome, though, which is a nice thought. Mojácar is as delectably diverse and welcoming today as it must have been in the sixties, and it's a trait that certainly makes it stand out. I have never felt like an outsider here, which is perhaps why I've been able to take the place into my heart and keep it there for so many years. I've always had this strong sense that Mojácar is a special and unique place, and it feels so good to be proven right.

Just as the church bells in the village below begin to chime the hour, I hear a commotion behind me and realise that the café owner has arrived to open up for the day. When I race back across the veranda with his chair, however, he merely gives me a friendly wave of acknowledgement. Back home, I would probably have been arrested. Not that you could borrow a chair in London anyway – they would all be chained to the floor.

Heading back down the dust-covered steps to the Plaza Nueva in search of strong coffee, I instead bump almost directly into a rather bewildered-looking Tom, who hurriedly looks over my shoulder as I approach him.

'Is Nancy with you?' he asks, before I've even had a chance to rib him about the state of his hair.

'No. Why?' I'm immediately suspicious.

'Oh, thank God,' he says, visibly relaxing. 'I haven't cleaned my teeth yet.'

'Lovely,' I retort, veering deliberately away from the hug of greeting that I had planned to bestow on him.

'Feeling rough?' I guess, taking in his bedraggled hairdon't and his crumpled face. 'You look like a pillow that's been bashed in,' I add, laughing as he scowls at me.

'I woke up and there was no water in the apartment,' he explains. 'It was either venture out and find some, or die from dehydration.'

'Those five extra beers you had probably weren't the best idea,' I tell him, not unsympathetically.

'Did Claudette bring that bloke home again?' Tom asks, as we cross the square and head towards the ice-cream parlour that also sells coffee.

I nod. 'Of course she did. The two of them kept me awake half the bloody night.'

Tom emits a strange coughing sort of laugh. 'Just him?' he asks, ultra casually.

I narrow my eyes. 'Tom, if what you're asking is did my sister get it on with that Ignacio bloke, then the answer is no, she did not.'

He looks sheepish at this, but I detect relief in his eyes.

'You don't actually fancy her, do you?' I'm saying it in a jokey way in the hope that he'll laugh along with me and deny it, but he doesn't. Horrifically, he looks utterly contrite, as if he knows I'm about to tell him off.

'We get on well,' he says carefully.

'You barely know her.'

'Dos cafés, por favor,' Tom tells the man behind the counter. I notice that he's wearing a 'Jacinto' name badge and smile to myself.

'I know her well enough to be sure I fancy her a bit,' he replies, counting out some euros.

'It's just a bit weird, I suppose,' I tell him, wishing he wasn't making me point it out. 'Because she's my sister. I told Claudette the same thing.'

'Don't you trust me?' Tom looks hurt as he passes me my coffee. 'I'm not one of those arseholes that picks women up and drops them for no reason.'

'I know you're not,' I sigh. 'But Nancy's only just broken up with her boyfriend, remember? She's probably on the rebound, hence her getting off with Diego – and that's not something you want to get tangled up in.'

'Hmmm,' says Tom, sipping his hot drink.

'And anyway, you're practically my brother,' I add, keen to lighten the mood and sound less like I'm telling him what to do. 'It would be like a weird kind of incest if you two got together.'

We've crossed the square again now and climbed the steps to the viewing platform. All around us, Mojácar is coming to life – shops are opening and café chairs are being scraped across the stone floor as tourists settle down for breakfast. The sun is steadily making its way upwards like a fiery kite, and a sentry line of tiny birds are perched on the railings ahead of us, warming their feathers in the dappled light streaking through the trees.

'Is that really how you think of me?' Tom asks now, turning to look at me instead of the view. 'As a brother?'

'Sometimes I do,' I admit. 'Theo said to me the other day that he thinks of us in that way.'

'Does he?' Tom is surprised.

I nod, tasting my coffee for the first time. It's rich and thickly layered with flavour, and the bitterness immediately makes me feel more alert.

'So, you two talked about me on your little date?'

'It wasn't a date!' I correct, although the colour of my face is in danger of betraying my real feelings.

'He took you for a day out, just the two of you,' Tom replies. 'Sounds a lot like a date to me.'

'I don't think he saw it that way,' I admit, sounding like a grumpy teenager. 'I honestly think he was just trying to be nice.'

Tom looks at me without speaking, his concerned expression filling in the gap.

'Just be careful,' he says eventually, keeping his eyes fixed on the flat-topped hill in the middle distance. 'I know how much you like him.'

'Don't be silly!' I reply, but it's obvious Tom suspects me. For a beat, I consider telling him about the kiss Theo gave me, the buzz of electricity that I felt in the air as he looked at me, but the words grind to a halt in the back of my throat. If it were any other man, I probably would, but this feels different somehow. Theo is Tom's boss, too, and the thought of confessing makes me feel mildly sick. The more people who know about my crush on Theo, the harder it will become to conceal, and I take so much comfort from keeping it as my own little secret. If it gets out, it could end up hurting me, and I can't risk that.

'You don't need to worry about me,' I say instead, finishing my coffee and looking around for a bin. 'I'm a big girl.'

'If you say so.' Tom shrugs as we make our way back down the steps. 'But promise me you'll tread carefully around Theo?'

The way he's saying it, you'd think Theo was an irritable alligator rather than the sexiest man to ever walk the Earth, but I promise anyway just to cheer him up. Privately, however, my mind is taking a very different path, and as I send Tom off to clean his teeth and brush his ridiculous hair, I let myself relive that kiss one more glorious time.

17

'There is no way that Walt Disney was born here.'

I open one eye and use it to shoot scorn in Tom's direction.

'He was.'

'According to who?'

'According to this book,' I point out, holding up the tattered paperback that Theo has very kindly lent me. The man himself isn't here, sadly. He had some incredibly boring permit paperwork that needed to be sorted out, so he's given us the afternoon off while he drives back to Almería. Because we were filming at the beach all morning, we decided to stay here, and now Tom and I are lying side by side on a pair of sun loungers, two empty *cerveza* bottles nestled in the sand between us.

'It says here that the young Walt – whose real name is José Guirao, by the way – used to help his father, who worked at the docks in Villaricos. When his dad passed away, a ship captain took pity on the man's widow and her young son, and agreed to take them to America to start a new life.'

'I don't buy it,' Tom sniffs. 'If it was true, why wouldn't there be a statue up or something?'

'Shush,' I scold, eager to finish telling him the story. 'Once in America, the same captain found José and his mother a job on a farm in California—'

'Convenient,' interrupts Tom.

'Oi! And the farm owner was called Walt Disney. When José's mum eventually died a few years later, the farm owner adopted the boy.'

'Of course he did.' Tom is starting to annoy me.

'And then,' I continue, gritting my teeth as Tom laughs, 'about thirty-odd years later, Walt Disney's secretaries turned up in Mojácar saying they'd come for his birth certificate so he could get married.'

'Why isn't it common knowledge, then?' Tom wants to know.

'Walt Disney never confirmed it,' I tell him, putting the book down and closing my eyes. 'Whenever he was asked the question, he would shrug and say, *"Chi lo sa,"* which means, "Who knows?"'

'A man of mystery,' croons Tom, but I can tell that he doesn't believe anything I've just said. The way I see it, the truth isn't the part that really matters anyway – it's a good story, and Theo agrees with me that it needs to be in our film.

'Where do you think Nancy got to?' Tom asks now, twisting his long, lean body around so he can see into the bar. We're back at the place where Carlos works again, more out of habit than anything, and Nancy went inside a while ago to get herself a drink. She's not keen on sunbathing, preferring to keep her pale skin covered beneath a garish flowing kaftan covered in pink sequins, which I think looks like fairy vomit, but Tom pretends to find enchanting.

'Probably just sitting in the shade with Claudette,' I reply, not bothering to move. Unlike my half-sibling, I've become a big fan of lying out in the sun – especially now that I definitely have a sort-of tan. It may be pale gold rather than mahogany like Theo's, but it's still better than the milk-bottle white that I was twelve days ago.

'I can't see her,' bleats Tom.

I take a deep breath in through my nose and sit up, clamping my undone bikini top to my chest with my hand.

There is no sign of Nancy or Claudette at any of the tables within my eyeline, or up at the bar, and I wrinkle up my nose and squint in an effort to see right back to the cluster of smaller tables furthest away.

'Maybe they went to the shop?' I suggest, resuming my sun-worshipping position and trying my best to quell the unfathomable unease that has just crept through me. What is it about Nancy that makes me feel so on edge? It doesn't make sense.

'I'm going to check,' decides Tom, snatching up the empty bottles and swinging his discarded T-shirt over one shoulder. I listen to his flip-flops as they flap up the wooden walkway between the loungers, then I hear his voice as he asks after Nancy and Claudette at the bar. The couple who run this place – Sofia and Camila – are quite taken with our French friend, and the three of them have started to drink together occasionally.

'Camila says they left with Carlos about ten minutes ago,' Tom announces, passing me a fresh *cerveza* as he sits back down.

I feel my skin prickle despite the heat.

'Did she say where they were going?'

'Probably to meet that idiot, Ignacio,' mutters Tom,

taking a swig of his drink only to have it bubble over the lip of the bottle and dribble down his chin.

'I'm sure they'll be back in a bit,' I tell him, but I'm saying it more to reassure myself than him. There's no real reason for me to worry, I know that, but for some reason I don't like the idea of Nancy being with Claudette. She may pretend to be street-smart, my sister, but I can tell that she's in awe of the older and far more worldly Claudette. Hell, before this trip, I felt the same way. I don't like the idea of Nancy being led astray, or being persuaded to do something just to impress her new idol.

'I'll give them half an hour, and then I'll call,' I say out loud, and Tom nods in agreement. Is he worried for the same reason as me, I wonder, or is it purely because he doesn't want her getting off with Ignacio?

I try to close my eyes and be lulled by the sound of the wind stirring up the surface of the sea, the waves crashing against the shore and the music drifting down from the bar behind us. It's some sort of jazz singer, and the lyrics are Spanish and soothing in tone. It makes me think of glamorous ladies in wide-brimmed hats and navy bathing suits, a cigarette nestled in one of those fancy holders in their hands and a tall glass of Pimm's in the other. I should be more relaxed than I have been in months, but I'm not. Thanks to Nancy and Claudette buggering off without telling me, I'm now starting to feel nauseous with anxiety.

To kill some time, I scoop up my sarong and knot it across my front, leaving Tom to guard our stuff while I head to the toilet and throw cold water across my face. The sun has coaxed out a scatter of freckles across my cheeks and nose, but my eyes look sore, with large bags beneath them. Spending each night on the sofa is definitely not a long-term solution. If I don't get some decent sleep soon, it will start to affect my ability to work, and I'm damned if I'm going to allow that to happen. Why did Nancy have to turn up like this? I hate feeling sorry for myself, I really do, but I keep coming back to the same conclusion: things would be so much easier if she wasn't here.

I pull my hairband off and rake my fingers through my messy mop. It feels coarse, and I attempt to flatten it with water, but that does little to improve its appearance. I must buy myself one of those conditioning treatments and actually remember to use it. Salt water coupled with hours of exposure to the sun every day has bleached it even blonder and sucked out everything that used to make it shine. I think enviously of Nancy's glossy shoulder-length locks. Her hair shines so much that you can almost see your face in it, and it's a huge injustice that she inherited Dad's fabulous barnet, while I got stuck with his big ears and long toes.

'It's been twenty minutes,' Tom announces, as soon as I return to the loungers, and I sit down and take a deep breath.

'Fine, I'll call her now, then. Pass my bag, could you?'

I know it's going to go straight to voicemail before I even press the buttons. Call it half-sisterly intuition.

'I'll try Claudette,' Tom says, immediately extracting his own phone from inside my bag and frowning a few seconds later.

'Voicemail.' He holds it up to show me. 'What the hell are they playing at?'

'I don't know,' I say grimly. 'But I wish whatever it is they would stop.'

We hang around on the loungers until the wind picks up and the sun begins to sink, eventually moving from the beach up to a table and ordering an array of tapas, which we pick at rather than eat. Neither Claudette nor Nancy has returned or switched on their phones, and Camila can't get hold of Carlos either. As I keep telling Tom, we really shouldn't be worrying, because they're both grown-ups, and for all her faults, Claudette is responsible enough not to let anything bad happen to Nancy. Of course, I am still fretting, though, and with every hour that passes and we hear nothing, my mood is worsening. Nancy's not even here with us and she's still managed to sabotage my day. It's absolutely bloody typical.

'We should head up to the village after this and check the bars,' Tom says, spearing a chunk of patatas bravas and dunking it in the oil surrounding the chorizo.

'I don't see why we should run around looking for them when they clearly don't want to be found,' I say with a sniff, using my fork to scrape the creamy feta filling out from a plump Peppadew pepper and then pushing it around my plate. Privately, I'm half hoping that Theo will arrive at the bar looking for me after his return from Almería, but I'm not about to tell Tom that. I know that if we're down here by the beach, then there's far more chance of bumping into him than there will be up in the pueblo, and I'm loath to put any unnecessary distance between the two of us.

'Hang on a minute,' Tom says, standing up and dropping his knife on the table. 'There's Carlos. CARLOS!'

'*Hola,*' the curly-haired Spaniard says as he approaches us, horizontally casual in the face of Tom's obvious impatience.

'Where's Claudette?' I ask, not even bothering to greet him properly first. If Carlos is bemused by this, he doesn't show it; he merely yawns and stretches his short arms above his head.

'Sleeping,' he says, smirking. 'I leave her at your place.'

'What about Nancy?' Tom puts in, and Carlos looks a little less sure of himself.

'She is . . . Er.' He pauses, looking from Tom's concerned features to mine, which I hurriedly arrange into a smile.

'It's okay,' I assure him. 'She's not in trouble – I just need to know where she is.'

Carlos looks uneasily at Tom. 'Ignacio, he take her for a drive,' he admits, his eyes widening at Tom's grunt of disapproval.

'Where?' I ask. '*Dónde?*'

'Around. Not very far. I don't know, but it will be okay.' Carlos smiles at the two of us in encouragement. 'Ignacio, he is my best friend for many years. He is a good boy – you understand?'

I picture Nancy's face the other night, her eyes secretly pleading with me to rescue her from the over-familiar arms of her Spanish admirer. Why the hell would she agree to go off in a car with a strange man in a strange country? It was stupid behaviour, even for her.

Carlos looks crestfallen that his admission has gone down so badly with us, and starts walking backwards away from the table, muttering something about going back to work.

Tom and I exchange a look.

'I told you she was selfish,' I mutter, pushing my plate away.

Tom sits back down and reaches for his drink. He doesn't look angry so much as upset, which only serves to make me even more furious with my errant sister.

'She's just young,' he begins, but stops when he sees the venom in my eyes.

'That's no excuse!' I rage, reaching for my phone and then swearing as it yet again goes straight through to Nancy's voicemail. 'If she ends up mangled at the bottom of a cliff then it will be all her own fault.'

'You don't mean that,' Tom argues.

'I do!' I snap right back. 'It will be her fault, but I'll be the one who gets the bloody blame for it, just like I always have for anything that Nancy has ever done wrong in her entire life. I didn't ask her to come out here to Spain, I didn't want her anywhere near me, and now she's gone and done this. I'm going to wring her bloody neck!'

'Calm down,' soothes Tom, his hand on my shoulder.

I shrug him away.

'Shall we go and talk to Claudette, then?' he suggests, having also given up on his food. 'Or I can ask Carlos to call Ignacio and tell him to bring Nancy back?'

'NO!' I growl, then feel contrite when I see his bruised expression. 'Sorry, I don't mean to have a go at you. I'm just pissed off with her for vanishing like this, that's all.'

'I see that.'

'Please, Tom – just be on my side for once.'

'I'm always on your side, Han.'

He looks mutinous now and I swallow my next

comment, washing it away with the last dregs from my water glass.

'Come on,' I tell him, standing up. 'Let's go and interrogate Claudette. I'll enjoy being the one to wake her up for a change.'

By the time we get all the way back to the apartment and I've given Claudette the third, fourth and fifth degree, it's almost nine o'clock and there's still no sign of Nancy. We don't find her in any of the bars in the Old Town, and I'm so worried that I even force myself to pay a visit to Diego's pizza restaurant in the hope that she's somehow ended up back there again.

To Diego's credit, he's very nice to me, and promises to call me if Nancy does show up. I refuse his offer of a drink, however, telling him honestly that I have to meet Tom, but as I leave, I file it with all the other reasons I have to be fed up with my half-sister. It would have been nice to sit and chat with Diego. Now that I'm able to face him again without turning into a radish, I'd like him to get to know the Hannah that I am now, as opposed to the one he rejected all those years ago. He would be such a good person to interview for the film, too, I realise. As well as being incredibly handsome, he has an impressive command of English. If I was channel-flicking and came across his bronzed features and dark, almond-shaped eyes, I'd be drooling all over my sofa cushions.

I find Tom at our pre-arranged meeting spot near the main square and we search the local bars again, subdued into silence by our mutual concern. I'm starting to feel guilty for ever mentioning the idea of Nancy being in an accident, because now it's all I can picture in my head – twisted metal and angry flames, the *policía* turning up at the door of the apartment in the early hours to break the news, and me having to call my dad and tell him, admit that it happened on my watch. For the first time in a very long while, I feel dangerously close to crying.

'Are you okay?' Tom asks, taking in my trembling bottom lip and shining eyes.

Unable to reply, I just shake my head, and he pulls me against him. We always hug so awkwardly, Tom and I, like two stalks of corn leaning against each other.

'Will you walk me back to the apartment?' I murmur into his ear.

'Of course.'

We walk down the hill without speaking, Tom's long left arm wrapped around my shoulders, and I watch the shape of our conjoined shadows bending in the light from the street lamps. There's a flicker as a bat passes in front of one, and the tinny sound of moped engines as a convoy of teenagers zip past us. We reach the steps leading down to the apartment in what feels like barely minutes, and I'm suddenly anxious at the thought of Tom leaving.

I move out of his embrace and turn to face him, waiting until he looks down and our eyes meet in the half-darkness. This is usually the point at which one of us would make a joke or say something stupid, but neither of us do. Instead, Tom just looks at me as if he's seeing me properly for the first time in years, his frown of concern merging slowly into a reassuring smile. I'm scared and he's here for me, just as he always is, but this time it feels different. This time it feels as if there are unsaid words in the air between us, and I have no idea what to say to him. I close my eyes for a fraction of a second and lift my chin higher, but just as Tom is moving a hand towards my face, we hear a loud giggling sound.

'Nancy?'

I swivel around in the direction of the road to find that it is, indeed, my sister who was laughing. She's swaying slightly on her high-heeled sandals and her hair looks messed up, as if somebody's been running their hands through it. I can't tell from where I'm standing, but it looks to me as if she's also very drunk.

'Where the bloody hell have you been all day?' I demand.

Now that I know she isn't lying dead in a ditch, the relief has instantly turned into anger, and I storm along the pavement towards her.

'I said, where have you been?' I ask again, coming to a halt just in front of her.

'Don't mind me,' Nancy chirps, pointing at Tom. 'I didn't mean to interrupt you.'

'You weren't,' Tom is quick to tell her, and the red mist around me swells even thicker.

'I thought you were dead!' I exclaim. 'You can't just disappear like that, Nancy. It's not fair. I've been worried sick all bloody day!'

'Chill,' she says, stumbling forwards in her stupid shoes and stepping on my exposed big toe.

'For God's sake!' I yelp, hopping around and clutching my foot.

'Sorry,' Nancy sniggers, sounding anything but as she strolls over to Tom and leans against him.

'You can't just take off with random Spanish men whenever you feel like it,' I inform her, wincing as I put my flip-flop back on. 'Not when you're staying with me.'

Infuriatingly, Nancy doesn't even reply; she just laughs again.

'It's *not* funny!' I yell, finally losing my temper with her completely.

I see Tom wince at the volume of my voice, but Nancy merely stares at me, her eyes glassy and her mouth set in a hard line.

'Slut,' I add. It's a barely more than a whisper, but Nancy hears it.

'Take that back,' she hisses, and Tom clamps his arm around her a little tighter.

'Why should I?' I retort. 'It's the truth. First you're all over Diego and a few days later you're off doing God knows what with Ignacio. You want to be careful, or you'll get a reputation.'

'Bitch!' Nancy storms, and this time Tom has to hold her back.

'Takes one to know one,' I snap back, feeling the adrenalin surge through me. My heart is racing now and I'm shaking with rage. How dare she not apologise? How bloody dare she call *me* a bitch?

'Will you two stop it?' Tom orders, his voice annoyingly stern and teacher-like. 'Say sorry to each other.'

'Pah!' I snarl, just as Nancy scoffs.

There's a beat of silence as the two of us just glare at one another, and then Nancy starts to cry. Of course she bloody does. And Tom, being the utter twerp that he is, seems to believe her tears are genuine and starts to comfort her, nestling her head against his chest in a far more protective way than he did with me a few minutes ago.

'I think it's best if Nancy stays at mine tonight,' he tells me, glancing at me over the top of her head. 'There's no point in you having a go at her, Hannah. She's back safe and that's all that matters.'

I hate him. I hate her. I hate them both.

'Fine,' I say, storming past them and heading down the steps. 'You two are welcome to each other.'

18

Despite having my bed back for the night, I still don't manage to get much sleep. Even when I do, I'm plagued by dreams of Tom and Nancy whispering horrible things about me, and about my dad, too, telling me how disappointed he is in me, and asking why I can't be more like his other daughter. His favourite daughter.

Claudette is up before me for once, because she and Theo have a script meeting at his villa before we commence filming for the day. The jealousy I feel about this fact has been steadily barbecuing my small intestines since I woke up, and if it wasn't for the pre-arranged meeting with Elaine that I have at La Fuente this morning, I'd insist on going with her. And anyway, I remind myself as I listen to Claudette crashing around in first the bathroom and then the kitchen, I know I don't have anything to worry about when it comes to her and Theo. After what he admitted to me at the beach the other evening, I know he sees her as more of a necessary evil than a desirable vixen.

I wonder how Nancy is feeling this morning, if she's even woken up yet. From the state of her last night, I'd guess she's facing a humdinger of a hangover today, although the thought of her having a crashing headache and feeling sick is only a small comfort. I don't allow myself to even entertain the image of her in Tom's bed, or him beside her, and the two of them snuggled up together. I just can't. I won't.

Elaine has brought me coffee today instead of flowers, and it's so nice to be welcomed by someone friendly and kind that I almost give in to the tears that have been threatening since yesterday.

'Are you okay?' she asks without hesitation, her soft, lined face full of concern. She's wearing her hair down for the first time this morning and it makes her look gentler somehow, and younger. She's dressed in a long, flowing red skirt and a white crocheted blouse that she's knotted at the waist, and there's a thin strip of brown flesh just visible between the two. I'm back in my shorts and vest combo today, too tired and fed up to make any sort of effort.

I think about lying and telling her that I'm fine, that there's nothing to worry about, but this time I don't. This time I simply shake my head from side to side. Instead of leading me away from La Fuente, Elaine motions for us to sit down on the steps, and she waits while I compose myself, her eyes trained on those floating rainbows that she adores so much. The breeze has dropped this morning and the sun feels heavy and abrasive, and I fidget around trying to find a comfortable position.

After a while, the sound of the water running into the marble basins begins to soothe me, and I take a deep breath, inhaling the droplets of moisture that are dancing in the air all around us. I start by telling her about Nancy, explaining how I've always struggled to get on well with her. Elaine nods along as I describe how my sister turned up here unannounced, then disappeared yesterday, and how worried I was, and finally I recount the argument we had last night, skipping over the details but admitting that what I said to her perhaps wasn't very nice.

For a long time after I've finished talking, Elaine continues to watch her rainbows, and then she turns to face me.

'I don't have any brothers or sisters,' she says, tucking her sweep of dark hair behind one ear. 'It was always just me and my mother.'

'Do you still see her?' I ask, smiling as I picture my own mother, so scatty and warm and full of love for me.

Elaine shakes her head. 'Not for a long time now.'

'That's a shame,' I reply, before I've really had time to think it through. 'Well, unless she's not very nice, that is.'

Elaine emits a low chuckle at this. 'Oh, she's not a monster. Just not very good at being a parent.'

'Sounds like my dad,' I tell her, stretching my legs out in front of me. There's a bruise starting to emerge on the big toe that Nancy stepped on.

'What did he do?' Elaine asks.

'It's more what he didn't do,' I reply, watching a little boy in blue shorts carry his empty water bottle over to one of the spouts. His mum is trying to help him fill it up, but it's obvious he wants to do it all by himself.

'He didn't stick around. He was gone before I was even two years old.'

'That must have been hard for your mother,' Elaine guesses.

'It was,' I agree. 'I never had any idea how hard until I was a bit older. She was always very careful to protect me from any sort of upset, so she didn't let me know what my dad had done to her for quite a long time. She always told me that they still loved each other, but it wasn't true. Well, not in his case at least.'

'I don't think my father ever knew I existed,' Elaine tells me now, sounding wistful. 'I certainly never met him.'

I picture my own father, his broad shoulders that he used to let me ride on and his wide smile. I used to do just about anything to get him to bestow that smile on me. Then later, once I hit puberty, I did anything I could to make him cross. I don't even remember now why I behaved that way, because I never did it with my mum. It was always just him.

'I'm sorry,' I say, unsure of how else to reply.

'Don't be,' Elaine says. 'You can't miss someone you've never met, after all.'

'I suppose.'

The boy is now trying to screw the cap back on the top of his bottle, and the look of concentration on his adorable little face is making me smile. I wonder if I'll ever bring my own child here to this fountain one day, and see his or her expression light up at the sight of the flowers in their pots. At the moment, it seems totally surreal to imagine myself as a mum, but I do like to think that I'll always come here to Mojácar. Now that I'm back after such a long time away, I can't believe I waited so many years.

'Have you ever spoken to your dad about what happened?' Elaine asks now.

'Not really,' I admit, shifting my shoes through the dust. 'I know that he met Susie – that's Nancy's mum – a few months after I was born, and I've overheard him tell people that it was love at first sight.'

'Do you believe in that?' she wants to know, and I reply with a bitter laugh.

'Even if it was true, I don't think it's a good enough reason to leave your wife and baby daughter,' I say simply. 'He should have at least tried to make things work.'

Elaine is silent for a few minutes before replying.

'I can understand why you're angry with him,' she says gently. 'It must feel as if he abandoned you.'

'He did!' I reply, failing to stop the hostility creeping into my voice. Talking about my dad always tips me over the edge.

'But he's still in your life,' she points out. 'It may not be in the same house, but he is still there.'

I know she's right, but it doesn't make me any less resentful towards him. Aside from the odd boyfriend here or there over the years, my mum has never really recovered from having her heart broken. I know she secretly still carries a little love in her heart for my dad, even if she won't admit it, and I wish she wouldn't. He doesn't deserve it. I remember what Elaine said to me before about the nature of love, and how true love lasts for always. Is that why my mum has never moved on properly, because she can't stop loving my dad?

'I think I'm horrible to him because my mum never is,' I blurt, realising as I say it that it's absolutely the truth. 'She wants to keep the peace and I just want to snipe at him.'

'And your half-sister?' Elaine asks.

'She's just spoilt,' I grumble. 'Nancy can do no wrong,

as far as my dad is concerned. She's his baby with the love of his life, so of course she means more to him than I do.'

'Do you really believe that?' Elaine sounds genuinely interested.

'Yes,' I insist, getting to my feet and brushing the white dust off the back of my shorts. 'I really do.'

Tom is waiting for me on the apartment steps when I get back from seeing Elaine, his eyes narrow from lack of sleep and a half-empty bottle of water clamped between his knees.

'All right?' I ask, looking anywhere but at his face. How extraordinary that just last night he felt like the closest person in the whole world to me, and now we can barely acknowledge each other.

'Yeah. You?'

'I'm okay. Just been with Elaine. She remembers Jacinto the mayor – you know the one I was telling you about?'

Tom nods.

'Apparently he was quite a character, and knew the names of everyone in the whole of Mojácar.'

'That's impressive.' Tom braves a look at me, but I drop my eyes.

'I think Theo will love it,' I tell him. 'It will be great to have that level of detail.'

'Listen, Han,' he begins, but I carry on talking across him.

'I don't want to talk about it.'

'Nancy feels really bad,' he goes on, apparently choosing to ignore me. 'She was crying half the night.'

'The truth hurts,' I mutter, and he looks at me

reproachfully. 'What?' I cry, throwing up my hands in exasperation. 'What the hell do you want me to say, Tom? You know how worried I was. What she did was totally selfish.'

'I want you to tell Nancy that you overreacted because you were concerned. I know you don't really think she's a slut.'

'Oh, I definitely meant it,' I argue, even though it's not strictly true. I have been feeling guilty all morning about saying that particular thing to her, but I don't appreciate Tom telling me off about it. If I had been contemplating apologising, which I genuinely was, I certainly won't be now.

Tom takes a deep breath, seemingly more exhausted than irritated, and glares at me.

'She's your sister, Hannah.'

'So you keep telling me.'

'You're older than her – so you should be the one to make the effort here.'

I can't actually believe he's still talking.

'Why should I?' I reply. 'Nancy has always got every single little thing that she's ever wanted, and I'd rather cartwheel over hot coals than give her the satisfaction of an apology.'

Tom is getting fed up with me now; I can tell because the tops of his ears are bright red.

'She's not the person you make her out to be,' he says then. 'She made a mistake yesterday and she's sorry, but the two of you are as bad as each other when it comes to backing down. The thing is, Han, what she really wants is your approval – that's all she's ever wanted.'

'Since when do you know so much about it?' I demand.

'Since we sat up talking half the night,' he replies. 'And since—' He stops abruptly, catching the end of his sentence on the tip of his own tongue.

'Since what?' I prompt, dread wrapping itself around my throat like a clammy hand.

Tom looks at the floor.

'Talking isn't all you did last night, is it?' I say, already knowing the answer.

There's a loaded beat of silence, then he looks right into my eyes.

'No,' he says.

19

The Indalo Man on my wrist may be driving away storms with his magical rainbow shield, but he's failed to protect me from the whirlwind force of Nancy. She's been in Mojácar for a week now, which is all it's taken for her to steal first my sanity, then my bed, then my best friend.

By forcing myself to focus solely on work yesterday afternoon and refusing unequivocally to speak to Tom about anything not relating to the documentary, I somehow made it through to the end of the day. Theo could tell something was wrong, and asked me at least four times if I was okay, but I was so dumbfounded by what Tom had confessed that I couldn't even feel comforted by his attention. Uncharacteristically for me, I made my excuses to leave as soon as we wrapped for the day and took the bus right to the other end of the beach. I needed time alone to stew, and to call Rachel and fill her in on what had happened. She was naturally as appalled as I was at the idea of Nancy and Tom together, and it made me feel a lot better about the fact that I was almost mute with anger. I didn't even know how I'd react if I set eyes on Nancy, so I waited until after eleven before heading back to the apartment, only to find no sign of her. Claudette, who was wrapped around Carlos on the sofa clad in just a bra and shorts, informed me cheerily that my sister had, in fact, gone to stay the night at Tom's place.

Waking early on Saturday morning with a full day off stretching ahead of me, I pulled my new favourite flower-patterned dress on over my bikini and came straight down to the beach, hoping that I could somehow swim away the turmoil raging inside.

As it turns out, the turbulent Mediterranean does little to calm my disgruntlement. First, I stand heavily on the sharp edge of a stone on the way in, only to lurch sideways and get unceremoniously smashed in the face by a wave. There's a whole seventeen kilometres of beach to choose from in Mojácar, but I appear to have waded into the section with the most seaweed, and it insists on wrapping its slimy tentacles around my legs and arms as I do my best to front-crawl through the surf.

I've just given up and am staggering back into shore when I see Theo jogging along the sand towards me, his dark, muscular arms glistening with sweat and the white wire of his headphones bouncing off the front of his black vest.

I think he's going to run right past me, but at the last second he turns and almost trips over in surprise.

'Hannah!'

'Morning, boss.'

'Good swim?' he enquires, looking over my shoulder at the frothy swirl of the sea.

'It was actually awful.' I grin at him. It feels nice to be smiling again – moodiness really doesn't suit me. 'Good run?'

'Hard run,' he admits, wiping his brow. 'I'm glad that I have seen you – now I have an excuse to stop.'

He's glad to see me. I let those sweet words settle over me like jam atop a crumpet.

'It's very hot,' he adds, lifting the bottom of his vest and using it to remove the sweat from his top lip. My nostrils are assailed by a mixture of limes and delicious man-smell, and it's all I can do not to leap open-legged into his arms.

'Can I offer you some breakfast?' he asks, and I accept wholeheartedly, running back to the lounger where I left my towel and bag. I deliberately avoided the patch of beach close to his villa because I wanted to be by myself, but now that I've bumped into Theo all the way down here, it feels like fate.

I assume that he means breakfast at one of the many beachside cafés, but Theo leads me past each of them in turn, chatting all the while about the time he ran the London Marathon and how it was 'the most painful experience of my life'. I laugh politely and exclaim in awe at his impressive finishing time of three hours fifteen minutes, but inside I'm a tangled mess of lust.

Theo is taking me back to his villa.

'I don't have churros, I'm afraid,' he says, retrieving his key from a little hidden pocket in the back of his running shorts and slipping it into the lock. 'But I do have eggs.'

'Eggs sound perfect,' I assure him, wondering how I'll force any food at all past the wedge of adoration that is stuck fast to the inside of my throat.

'Take off your dress, if you like.'

'WHAT?'

Theo turns at the sound of my surprised yelp and laughs.

'Your bikini is still wet,' he says, and we both look down at the two circular wet patches on the front of my dress.

'Oh. Right. Of course. I will in a minute, after . . .' I give up speaking and shut my mouth, but Theo is smiling. He's pushed his sunglasses up into his hair, which is plastered flat from sweat.

'You can have a shower, if you prefer,' he offers, peeling off his vest only for it to get caught in his headphones.

'Here,' I say, desire propelling me forwards through the shyness. 'Let me help you out.'

It's impossible to rescue him from the tangle of damp material and twisted wire without touching his bare torso, and my hands immediately turn clammy with longing. His stomach is firm and taut, his chest hair wet, and his face when it finally emerges is lit up with a genuine smile. Sometimes he looks so gorgeous that I can't even comprehend how he can be real.

'Thank you,' he says, balling up the vest with both his hands. 'Now I must shower, but help yourself to a towel or a drink – whatever you like.'

What I'd like most is to help myself to you, I think, but instead I thank him and cross to the pile of fresh towels that are stacked on a chair by the bathroom door. I wait until Theo has disappeared into what I assume is his bedroom before yanking off my dress, which has, rather embarrassingly, got a large wet patch across the bottom as well as on the front. Sliding open the patio doors and crossing the smooth wood of the decking, I toss the part-soaked garment over the balcony railings. Bikinis really should be better designed, I think, wrapping one of Theo's dark-blue towels around my body and knotting it across my chest – I appear to have brought back half the Mediterranean in mine.

I hear the shower start to run and allow myself to imagine Theo standing under the water, his eyes closed as the soapy residue from his shampoo runs down across his face and chest, then lower down, into the dark cleft of his buttocks and along the length of his— Bugger, my phone's ringing.

'Mum, this really isn't a good time.'

There's a tut at the other end of the line.

'Why? What are you doing? You told me you had a day off.'

Since when did my mother turn into Miss Marple?

'I do,' I hiss, cupping my hand around the phone so Theo won't hear me and tiptoeing away from where I'd been lurking next to the bathroom door. 'But I bumped into my boss and we're having a, erm, very important meeting.'

'Do you mean Theo?' my mum asks loudly. She's never really picked up on the fact that you don't need to shout when you're having a telephone conversation. 'He's so dishy.'

I should never, *ever* have shown my mum those photos I'd covertly taken of Theo at last year's Christmas party.

'Like I said, Mum, it's not the best time to chat,' I repeat, wondering why I even answered in the first place.

'I was just calling to ask you about Nancy.'

'What about her?' I reply, my tone instantly cold.

'You didn't tell me she was there with you,' says Mum, trying and failing to sound disinterested. I didn't tell her, it's true, but only because I don't like discussing Nancy with her. Talk of my half-sister inevitably leads to a conversation about my dad, and I hate having one of those with Mum.

'I didn't think she would be for long,' I tell her honestly. 'I certainly didn't invite her out here.'

'I thought that you probably hadn't,' Mum muses. 'That's what I told your dad when he called.'

Oh God, here we go.

'What does he care?' I mutter, unable to prevent the bitterness creeping into my voice.

'He's relieved that she's with you,' Mum says. 'The thing is, she didn't tell him she was going over to Spain, either. I don't think she told anyone.'

'Well, she always has been selfish,' I retort, and am rewarded with another tut.

'She is okay, isn't she?' Mum says, and I picture her soft, pretty face etched with concern. How does Nancy do this? How does she manage to make herself the centre of attention all the bloody time?

'Oh, you know Nancy,' I drawl, opening Theo's fridge door and closing it again. 'She always gets whatever she wants and to hell with anyone else.'

'Sounds like her mother,' puts in my mum, then immediately begins to chastise herself. 'I shouldn't have said that. Sorry, darling – that was unfair of me. Susie's a very nice woman. You know I like her very much.'

I know full well that she does not.

'Don't worry, Mum – it's not like I'm going to tell on you, is it?'

The shower has stopped now and I can hear Theo cleaning his teeth.

'I really do have to go now,' I tell her, catching sight of my reflection in the mirror on the wall behind the sofa and grimacing. The salt water from my swim has helpfully turned my hair into Shredded Wheat. 'I'll call you tomorrow, I promise.'

'Okay, darling. Love you. Bye!'

I hang up and stare at my phone. While I was talking to Mum, a message has come through from Tom.

Can we talk? it says, very simple, no kiss.

For a few seconds my fingers hover, ready to type back a reply, but then I realise that I don't know what to write. For the first time since I met Tom nine years ago, I have nothing to say to him – and it's all Nancy's fault.

By the time I've nipped into Theo's shower and washed away the remnants of my swim, the man himself has chopped up fresh tomatoes, red onions and green peppers and is whisking eggs in a glass bowl. He's dressed in navy shorts and a crisp white T-shirt, and I watch the muscles in his back moving beneath the material. It's so hot outside now that my dress is almost dry, so I pluck it off the railings and duck back into the bathroom to put it on. My bikini, on the other hand, is still far too wet to wear, so I have no choice but to go commando. Usually this wouldn't freak me out all that much, but then usually I wouldn't be standing beside Theo as he made the two of us a breakfast omelette. I don't think I have ever felt more naked.

'Can you grate?' he asks, reaching into the fridge and handing me a healthy chunk of Manchego.

'Of course,' I babble, happy to be given a task. 'You could say I'm great at it.'

He nods.

'You know – I mean I'm great. At grating,' I add.

Theo gives me a sideways look. 'Yes. I got it.'

Oh. Right.

'Can I taste?' he adds, opening his mouth.

'Um . . .' Does he genuinely want me to feed him cheese?

'My hands are busy,' he says, even though it's not completely true. He could easily put down either the bowl or the whisk, but he's choosing not to. He must actually want me to do it for him.

I use a knife to cut a generous corner off the Manchego and bring it up to his lips, laying it across his pink tongue with tentative fingers.

'Perfect!' he announces, grinning at me. 'Or, as the Spanish would say: *perfecto*!'

'That's an easy one to remember,' I trill, smiling right back at him.

'Do you know what goes very well with this type of cheese?' he asks now, dashing oil into two frying pans and turning down the heat underneath each one.

'Omelettes?' I guess, and he shakes his head.

'Of course omelettes, yes – but also almonds.'

'As in the nuts?'

Of course he means the nuts – why am I such a cretin?

'Yes, but they must be salted.'

'Sounds, er, *perfecto*,' I joke weakly, stepping backwards out of the way as Theo starts cooking the onion and peppers. He's very flamboyant in the kitchen, just as he is at the dinner table, adding dashes of seasoning here and there and picking up bits of grated cheese from the huge pile I've created.

'Do you cook, Hannah?' he asks without turning

around, which is a blessing because it means he can't see my face turn red. I sense that this is an important question, because it's clear to me now that Theo definitely does enjoy cooking. He's a mature, independent, modern man who is good in the kitchen and understands enough about flavours to know that salted almonds go perfectly with Manchego. If I tell him that my culinary expertise is limited to jacket potatoes with tuna and mayonnaise or, if I'm feeling really daring, the odd plate of Welsh rarebit, then I fear he will not be very impressed.

'I'm very keen to learn more,' I say eventually, diplomatic as ever, and he seems to like this answer, as he ushers me forwards to join him by the stove.

'The trick to a good omelette is not to overcook your eggs,' he begins, lifting one of the pans to show me just how far he's turned the heat down. 'And you want your onion and pepper to retain some bite, but not be raw. These two things can make you have some gas in your stomach, you know, if you do not prepare them correctly.'

Gas is something I definitely do *not* want today.

'And when we add the cheese,' he continues, picking up two large heaps of it and sprinkling them on top of the omelettes, 'we must put the pans under the grill, so that it bubbles.'

'Yum,' I say, for want of anything more articulate to contribute.

Theo catches my eye. 'Yum indeed.'

We eat out on the wide balcony, my wet bikini dripping droplets of water on to the wooden decking beside us and the wind doing its best to flash my bare bottom to the chef. In the end, I have no choice but to clamp the cotton skirt between my thighs and then firmly cross my legs, kicking Theo under the table as I do so.

'Sorry!' I cry, reaching down to rub his leg and then veering back up in horror when I realise what I'm doing.

'Do I make you nervous, Hannah?' he asks, regarding me with bemusement.

'No!' I fib, picking up my cutlery with shaking hands.

The omelette is so delicious that I eat the entire thing, plus the two slices of bread that Theo passes me. Thankfully he hasn't gone full Spanish and smeared garlic mayonnaise all over them, but he is very generous with the butter. Everything tastes rich and fresh, the saltiness of the cheese balancing the sweetness of the red onion, and the oil adding an earthy depth to the plump chunks of tomato.

'Perfecto!' I tell Theo when I've finished, making full use of the newest Spanish word in my vocabulary.

He refuses my offer to wash up and takes the empty plates back inside the villa himself, only to re-emerge five minutes later with a huge cafetière of black coffee and a little pot of vanilla yoghurt for each of us.

'This is a real treat,' I tell him, peeling back the foil lid and sticking my teaspoon through the set surface. 'Thank you for inviting me.'

'I told you before,' says Theo, licking his own lid. 'I like spending time with you, Hannah. You are very easy company.'

I blush with joy.

'But I don't want to keep you here if you have plans,' he adds, propping his tanned bare feet up on the seat of a spare chair and wriggling his toes. 'It is your day off, and I'm sure you do not want to spend it with your boss.'

'Oh, I do!' I tell him, probably with a touch too much enthusiasm. 'What I mean is, I didn't have any other plans. I don't have a plan.'

'What about your sister?' Theo asks, and my smile closes up like a clam.

'She's with Tom.'

'Oh?' It's clear what he's asking, but I pretend not to understand. I don't want to say the words – not even to him. But he's not letting me off the hook.

'And they are together?' he queries, raising an eyebrow when I nod in reply. 'Wow. I am surprised to hear that.'

I don't want to talk about Nancy and Tom. I wish he wouldn't. I want to forget that either of them exist for a few hours.

'Do you have any more old-Mojácar stories to tell me?' I say instead, driving us down a new path of conversation – one that I know Theo will like. 'I really loved the one about Mariquita and the wizard.'

He hesitates for a moment before replying, perhaps wondering whether to allow me to change the subject, and then he puts his feet down on the floor and pours the coffee.

'As a matter of fact, I have many.'

20

In all the many fantasies I've had about Theo in the years since I met him, none of them have ever featured what the two of us have been doing today. When I daydream about him, it always involves him kissing me ravenously, tearing my knickers off with his teeth and having his wicked way with me, while some sort of cheesy love-scene soundtrack plays in the background. Don't get me wrong, all those vivid concoctions are pretty amazing, but none of them come close to the simple pleasure of just hanging out with Theo for the day.

Since we finished the delectable omelettes he prepared for us this morning, Theo and I have swapped stories about our childhoods – I told him all about Chewy and he actually bellowed with laughter when I admitted some of the scrapes we used to get ourselves into – played thirteen games of Rummy, seven of which I actually managed to win, and eaten all the rest of the Manchego plus a good portion of the bread.

It's been so nice to be here by the sea all day, watching the waves scurry up the shore gobbling sandcastles and displacing shells. From up here on Theo's wide balcony, the wet pebbles down below us look like scattered gems, the light from the sun making the polished surfaces gleam and sparkle. There's been a steady stream of human traffic passing by, with families, couples, dog walkers, joggers and noisy groups of teenagers all taking their turn on the sand. The mischievous wind provides a comedy element, too, and Theo and I have shared many chuckles as we watch people hurtling along after a rogue beach umbrella or errant napkin. At one point during an extremely intense round of cards, somebody's straw hat blew right up on to the balcony and landed in the plunge pool.

As well as enjoying the view of the world going by coupled with Theo's undivided attention, it's been a relief to get away from Tom and Nancy. For the past few hours, I've allowed myself to pack that particular problem away into a far corner in my head to be dealt with another day. Distraction was all I needed, and I can't think of a better person than Theo to provide it. After touching on the subject of my best mate and my half-sister in the morning, he has been astute enough not to mention it since, and with every hour that passes and I'm still here in the villa, I'm starting to feel more relaxed. I even managed not to collapse into a quivering heap on the floor when Theo took it upon himself to rub sun cream on to my back and shoulders, but I was still tingling all over at least half an hour after it happened.

My bikini dried hours ago, but I still haven't bothered to put it back on, and now that I'm feeling more at ease in Theo's company, I'm even enjoying the fact that I'm going commando. While he hasn't yet said or done anything to make me think he's aware of my almost-naked state, a part of me knows that he is. And it's that same part which is making me feel increasingly hot with desire. When he showed me the editing suite he's set up inside the second bedroom an hour or so ago, the two of us were so close together in front of the screen that I swear he must have been able to hear my heart hammering away lustfully in my chest.

'Can I read you something?' Theo asks now, picking up his notebook from the table in front of us. We've been moving our chairs to match the progress of the sun all day, and his is now only a few inches away from mine. Whenever he brings up his arm, the dark hairs brush against my bare skin, and I feel a tugging sensation from somewhere deep inside.

'Of course,' I tell him, arranging myself into a comfortable position and giving him my full attention.

'It is the introduction for the film,' he explains, resting his ankle on the opposite knee and laying the book across his lap. As he clears his throat in preparation, I get the sense that he's even a little bit nervous – and that's something I've never known him to be before.

'On the south-east coast of Spain, in the foothills of Sierra Cabrera, there is a place both hidden and proud. A village that seems to shimmer as you look upon it, the cluster of white buildings a honeycomb shot through with moonbeams of colour. There is a neat harmony of simplicity here, an exquisite union of nature and creation, and as you take the steep pathway leading into the heart of this architectural utopia, you will feel your very spirit begin to sing. This is a place where time seems not to stand still, but to circulate in the air like the ever-present dust. It is timeless yet magical, flawed yet faultless, but most of all it is unforgettable. It is Mojácar.'

I hadn't even realised that I'd closed my eyes until Theo stops talking, lost as I was in the cobbled streets of the place that he has just described so beautifully.

'Wow,' I breathe, turning to face him and pushing my sunglasses up on to my head. 'That was. Wow.'

'Do you really like it?' Theo asks, his handsome face deadly serious. I love seeing him like this, more vulnerable and human than he usually is. It makes me feel special, as if he is now relaxed enough to let his guard down in my company, that he trusts my opinion and even craves my approval.

'I really, really like it,' I assure him, braving a light touch of his arm. 'You've captured that unique Mojácar essence perfectly. You're so clever.'

'Careful now.' Theo finally smiles. 'You will give me a big head.'

I cough as my dirty mind conjures up the inevitable image, and reach for my water to mask my smirk.

'You deserve to have a big head,' I tell him, longing making my voice sound all gravelly. 'It honestly gave me goosebumps – and it must be thirty degrees out here.'

'I'm glad you like it,' he says, rubbing his thigh absent-mindedly. 'I have found it quite hard to put into words how it feels to look at Mojácar. I want to demonstrate how wonderful it is, but I do not want to sound corny or over the top, you understand?'

'I do – I know exactly what you mean.'

There's a pause while we just look at each other, bonded in the moment by our mutual enthusiasm for the subject, then Theo gets to his feet.

'It's past five now,' he says, looking at his watch and then at me. 'Shall I open a bottle of wine?'

We toast Theo's amazing intro as the gradually dipping sun streaks through the railings and throws patterns of gold across our bare feet. I've never had chilled red wine before, but it's very pleasant, and Theo has added a slice of lemon to each of our glasses.

I watch as a Spanish woman leads her young daughter down to the edge of the water on the beach below us. The girl is at that adorable age where she's just begun to walk, and her chubby little legs are wobbling with glee as she toddles across the wet sand. What a place to grow up, I think, not for the first time. There's so much to be said for stripping back your life and ridding it of clutter – a fact that I know to be true, yet still haven't done anything about. The thing I hate most about my bedroom back in the shared house in Acton is all the stuff I've accumulated over time. There are DVDs I never watch, CDs gathering dust, photo albums I haven't opened for years, clothes I don't wear, jewellery I've never bothered to untangle, ornaments I've had since I was a teenager, books I'll probably never read, shoes with holes, more clothes. We're led to believe that all these material things will make us happy, that they signify success and contentment, when, in actual fact, the opposite is true. All that this clutter does is anchor you to one place. I think all you really need to be happy is what that little girl down on the beach has – the sun on your back, food on the table and someone to love who loves you in return. If it's so simple, though, why do we dither around for so many years looking for something else?

'Hannah.' Theo is peering at me. 'You look miles away.'

'Sorry,' I say, blinking rapidly and putting down my glass. 'I was having an epiphany about the trappings of modern life.'

'Oh?' Theo is leaning towards me. 'Tell me more.'

'Hold that thought,' I say, standing up. 'Nature calls.'

Once in the safety of the bathroom, I turn on both the taps and beam at myself in the mirror. A day sitting out in the sun has given me a warm glow – well, either that or the wine is stronger than it tastes – and my eyes are sparkling with the promise of an evening spent in the company of Theo. It's not my imagination; he is most definitely behaving differently around me. He's been teasing me all day, dropping deliberate innuendos into the conversation and finding excuses to touch me. He could have asked me to leave hours ago, but he hasn't. On the contrary, he's found pretexts for me to stay – and he was nervous about reading that introduction to me. The fact that I'm the first person he's shared it with makes me feel even taller than I already am, and, as I wash my hands and tuck away loose strands of hair behind my ears, I feel sure that for once I'm not grabbing at the wrong end of the rod.

Striding back across the decking and reaching for my wine, I'm about to compose another toast in praise of Mojácar, when Theo's phone starts ringing. He answers it as I sit back in my chair.

'Hello. Yes? Hello, Tom.'

My heart sinks.

'Hannah is here with me, yes.'

Oh no.

'I think so, yes.' He turns towards me. 'Hannah, are you okay?'

I nod, unable to speak.

'She is nodding,' Theo says, but he looks slightly perturbed now.

'Yes, I will tell her. Yes, we're meeting at the old well first thing on Monday. Okay. Right. Bye, Tom.'

Theo puts his phone back on the table.

'Did you two have an argument?' he asks. He doesn't have to say who he means, not now.

'Not really.' I shrug and sip my wine. It suddenly doesn't taste as nice as it did a few minutes ago.

'He wanted me to tell you that he's booked lunch for you both tomorrow, at the place with the barbecue.'

'Right.'

I can't help it, I let go of the heavy sigh that's been building inside me.

'Are you upset with Tom for making a move on your sister?' Theo asks me now.

I know that if I raise my eyes, his will be waiting.

'Yes,' I whisper.

Theo holds my gaze, then abruptly stands up and walks inside with the half-empty wine bottle. He doesn't say anything, so after a few seconds I follow him, taking a seat next to him on the pale grey sofa. The sky outside the glass doors is a rich admiral blue, but it feels dark inside the villa, and more intimate than the seats outside on the decking. I wish he would put on some music, something to soften the energy in the air between us.

'Are you angry because you like Tom?' Theo wants to know. I had forgotten how direct he can be sometimes. I'm not sure if it's his age or his Greekness, but whatever it is, I find it deeply unsettling.

'I don't fancy Tom, if that's what you're asking,' I tell him firmly. 'I just find it a bit weird, that's all.'

What I don't add is that I feel betrayed, because Tom

has sided with Nancy when he should be backing me. I don't tell Theo that the thought of Nancy stealing away one of my closest friends makes me so mad I could sob. It's all too complicated and messy – and I don't want him to think that I'm conflicted when it comes to my feelings. I know who I want, and it isn't Tom.

'Who do you fancy?'

I knew the question was coming, but the words still hit me like tiny metaphorical bullets. I find that I can't look at Theo, so instead I stare hard at a brown glass ashtray on the coffee table in front of us.

'You shouldn't ask me that,' I mumble, and I hear him move a fraction closer to me.

'Why not?'

'Because,' I say, still not looking at him.

Theo waits for a moment before replying, then leans back against the cushions and laces his fingers together behind his head.

'Perhaps you are right,' he concurs. 'Maybe it is best that we remain as we are.'

'What do you mean?' I ask, reeling around to face him.

'I am your boss,' he points out, releasing his hands so he can use them to gesture wildly in the air. 'It would not be fair on you.'

'Yes, it would,' I babble quickly, before my sensible side can lasso my words back into my mouth. Theo is frowning slightly, and I realise it's now or never.

'I'm a grown woman, Theo. I know what I want.'

'Do you?' He's said it so quietly that I instinctively shuffle along the sofa so I'm closer to him. His already impenetrable eyes look like ebony stones in the half-darkness, and my hands go clammy as he scrutinises me. The atmosphere in the small space between the two of us is so intense that I'm surprised it's not making my hair stand on end in static strands.

'If we do this, we cannot let it affect our work,' Theo murmurs.

I widen my eyes and nod my head urgently up and down, all of a sudden so aware of my lips that it feels strange to use them.

'Come here to me.'

Oh. My. God.

I can't help it; I drop my eyes again. The shaky confidence that I dredged up a few minutes ago has fallen away, and now I feel as if I'm floundering in a deep pool of sexual inadequacy. I want Theo, but I'm afraid.

'Hannah,' I hear him say, and when I finally raise my chin and look at him, Theo's already moving towards me, and the next second our lips are touching, then our tongues. His hands travel into my hair, across the small of my back, along my bare thighs, and I let out a low moan of pleasure.

My heart is hammering and there's a pulse beating incessantly from somewhere much lower down, too. I try not to kiss him back too eagerly, keen to prolong the moment and savour the taste and feel of him, but Theo has other ideas. His hands are up on my face now and he's angled my head towards his own, his tongue exploring every crevice of my mouth, then moving down my neck and across my throat. His passion is surprising me, and I try in vain to keep up with the urgency of his kisses and his grasping fingers. My head is beginning to spin.

He mutters something in Greek, then his hand is down the front of my dress, extracting one white breast, and he's bending his head to kiss my exposed nipple. He's not being gentle with me, but the ferocity of his desire is making me almost pant with pleasure. Theo actually wants me; I can feel it. And I want him.

Sliding his hands down around my waist, he hoists me up so I'm sitting astride him, and I flinch a fraction as my dress rides up. It's only a tiny hesitation, but it's enough to snap Theo out of the trance that he was in, and he pauses with his mouth around one breast, looking up at me with a mixture of longing and confliction.

Don't stop! I want to scream at him, but I can't seem to find the words. Instead I hold my body against his, my chest pressed up to his and my hips rocking very slowly backwards and forwards. There's a single layer of clothing now between us, and I can feel how much Theo would like there to be none. Leaning in to tentatively kiss his neck, I walk my fingers down to the waistband of his shorts and search for the button.

'Wait.' He catches my hand in his own.

'What's the matter?' I ask, not daring to look at him.

'I don't have condoms,' he says, his voice laden with lust but unmistakably disappointed. 'Do you?'

'No.' I shake my head sadly and sit back on his knees. 'I didn't think that . . . I never thought . . .'

'It's okay,' Theo says, putting a warm finger against my lips to silence me. 'We still have plenty of time.'

I want him to kiss me again, but instead he eases me back on to the sofa cushion and playfully ruffles my hair, a lopsided smile on his flushed face.

'Hannah, Hannah, Hannah,' he murmurs, tracing a finger around the line of my jaw. 'You are very beautiful.'

'If you say so,' I say with a laugh, but he frowns at me.

'Do not argue with me now – I am your boss.'

'That's true,' I agree, shyly nibbling the tip of his finger as he slides it between my lips. 'And I promise to do whatever you say.'

Theo groans at this, but it's one of desire rather than dismay. We both look down to where the material of his shorts is being strained almost to tearing point, and again he begins to mutter in Greek.

'Perhaps pour us some more wine,' he instructs, standing up and heading towards the bathroom. 'I just need a few moments.'

I know why he needs a moment. I know so well that my face is now the same colour as a London bus that's been set on fire, and I giggle as he closes the door behind him.

Can this really be happening? Have I just been writhing against my sexy Greek boss while he leaves love bites on my boobs? Yes, I absolutely have, and it's the greatest feeling I have ever experienced in my entire life. Tom may think he won the top prize when he somehow convinced Nancy to get off with him, but my finally getting off with Theo is actual next-level stuff. If I wasn't so massively peeved with Tom, I'd be calling him right now to boast about it.

Sod Tom, I think, inserting my boobs back into my now-even-more-favourite dress and topping up both the glasses with more wine. He can hire a plane to sky-write his messages of infatuation with Nancy for all I care.

21

When I woke up this morning, a good five minutes passed when I genuinely believed that I'd simply had a very good, very real dream about hooking up with Theo. But no, it's actually true – there are nibble marks on my chest to prove it, and a text message on my phone from the man himself, thanking me for an 'amazing day'. Theo had an amazing time with me. Me! Hannah Hodges – Queen of the Singletons.

On the very edges of my euphoric happiness, however, a grubby disquiet is steadily creeping its way back into my subconscious. Despite what's happened with Theo and the way it made me feel briefly invincible to pain, I'm still pissed off with Tom and Nancy. In fact, I don't think I've been this riled about anything in a very long time – perhaps since finding out that my dad had run off and left me and my mum. But then that's been a long-standing, festering resentment that I've grown up with – not this white-hot anger that I'm experiencing now. Being ecstatically happy at the same time as being twisted into knots of animosity is a very confusing way to feel, and I keep veering between the two like a spider monkey swinging through a jungle. My brain wants to be happy, but my heart feels brittle – and I'm not sure whether to laugh or cry.

Theo shooed me out of the villa after we'd finished the bottle of wine last night, telling me in no uncertain terms that if I didn't get myself back to the apartment immediately, then he wouldn't be responsible for his actions. Given that those actions would almost certainly involve the two of us naked, sweaty and entwined, it took some serious persuading on his side. When I eventually did get up to leave, he followed me to the door and kissed me for so long and with such tenderness that every single atom in my body was left buzzing with pleasure.

I want to run back to the villa now, knock on his bedroom window and climb under his sheets, but I force myself to stay put. I don't even text him. Playing it cool is never something that I've been very good at, but Theo is far too important to allow anything to go wrong. He's a red-blooded man, and I know that I must leave it up to him to make the next move. And anyway, I can't spend my Sunday in bed with Theo, because I've got to go and meet bloody Tom and at some point will probably have to face even bloodier Nancy. Groaning at the injustice of it all, I reach down and pull the thin sheet back over my head, vaguely thinking that a lie-in might actually be a good idea. Alas, I had forgotten who I was sharing an apartment with.

'Hannah!'

Claudette doesn't wait for me to answer before she opens the door. She's wearing quite a lot of clothes for her this morning, and by that, I mean nothing more than a lacy red bra and denim shorts. Her tan is flawless, of course, as is her sweep of neatly styled dark hair.

'Ah, you're alone,' she says, looking around the room as if she can't quite believe it.

I frown. 'Who did you think I had in here, the Spanish national football team?'

'You wish,' Claudette replies, amusement dancing in her eyes. 'I thought Nancy would be here.'

'She's with Tom,' I inform her, stifling a yawn.

'Are you sure?' She looks puzzled.

'Pretty sure,' I reply. 'They've been attached at the hip since she got off with him the other night.'

'She did what?' Claudette sits down next to me, her expression aghast.

'I don't know the specifics.' I shrug, only just catching my grimace in time. 'But I know something is going on between them. I thought you knew.'

Each of Claudette's eyes is wider than the drum of a washing machine.

'I did not know,' she declares, a scowl adding lines to her forehead.

'I assumed you'd be all for it,' I add. 'You're always nagging Tom to be more confident with girls. Well, now he's finally done it.'

I expect Claudette to pull one of her wry expressions, but instead she shakes her head vehemently. 'But she is . . .' She wrings her hands. 'And he is . . .'

'Tom.' I finish.

'Yes. Tom. An imbecile!'

I should stick up for him, really, tell her she's being a bit mean, but I'm still cross with him so instead I just let out a snort of laughter.

'How the hell did it happen?' she wants to know.

I can feel my face screwing up unpleasantly.

'The other night when she went off with Ignacio, we had a row. I told her off and she went to stay at Tom's.'

It isn't much of an explanation, but it's all I have. I don't know the details of what happened once they got back to Tom's little apartment. I don't want to know them, not ever.

'Tom is a dark fox,' Claudette says now.

'You mean horse,' I correct.

'I mean giraffe.'

This time I really do laugh. Tom is very much like a giraffe, with his long neck, patchy tan and big, appealing eyes.

'I'm meeting him today for lunch,' I tell her. 'Why don't you come?'

Claudette may have been winding me up over the past few days, but I like how anti the idea of Tom and Nancy she is. Plus, her being there might help to ease the inevitable tension.

'I can't,' she says regretfully, standing up and walking over to the full-length mirror to admire herself. 'Carlos has the day off, so we are going to a nudist beach.'

Of course they are.

'Okay . . .'

'You must put a stop to this thing with your sister and Tom,' she instructs, without bothering to turn away from her reflection.

'How can I?' I grumble. 'I'm not a fan of it either, but I can't tell them what to do.'

'She is your sister,' Claudette points out. 'If she knew how you felt, then she wouldn't want to cause a problem.'

I actually scoff at that. All Nancy has ever done is cause problems for me. Her mere existence is a problem.

'You need to tell her how you feel about Tom.'

'What?'

Claudette finally stops examining herself and comes back towards me.

'Come on, I know you like him more than a friend.'

'I really do not!' I reply, half-laughing as I throw off the bedsheet and stand up, hurrying past her into the bathroom. Why does everyone keep accusing me of having lovey-dovey feelings for Tom? I'm getting sick of it.

'I honestly don't,' I say again loudly, so she'll hear me over the sound of the taps running. When I re-emerge, Claudette is in the kitchen making herself tea. It would never occur to her to offer to make one for me.

'It's okay to admit it,' she says. 'The two of you would be perfect together.'

I think about what she said just a few minutes ago, about how Tom was an imbecile, as if he wasn't good enough for Nancy. Aside from it being absolutely not true, it's also pretty damning of me, who she obviously thinks of as being way down the league table compared to my half-sister.

'Theo is the one I like, not Tom,' I blurt, regretting the words as soon as I've said them. I expect Claudette to laugh at me, but instead she just looks at me with an appalled sort of disappointment and shakes her head.

'What's so wrong with that?' I demand, trying to keep my tone nonchalant.

For a second I think she's going to reply, but then she simply drops her spoon into the sink and steps past me.

'Nothing,' she says over her shoulder as she goes towards her bedroom. 'Except everything.'

I'm still replaying Claudette's words in my head three hours later, when I arrive at the beach restaurant to meet Tom. I followed her into her bedroom and asked her what she meant, but she refused to elaborate, telling me to bugger off because she had to get ready for her date with Carlos. How you can really get ready to wear nothing is beyond me, but there's no arguing with Claudette.

I can't shake the feeling that she knows a lot more than she's prepared to tell me, and that none of it will be stuff I want to hear. It doesn't help that I haven't heard from Theo all morning. Despite my resolution to remain aloof and let him do the chasing now, I'm still hurt that he hasn't even sent another text to check up on me. That, coupled with Claudette's cryptic throwaway comment, has left me on edge, and the next person I see is definitely not going to get the best version of me.

'Hi.'

Nancy is sitting alone at one of the tables inside the restaurant, her phone in her lap and her beach bag hanging on the back of her chair. She looks up at my greeting and braves a smile.

'Hi.'

There's an uncomfortable silence, and Nancy looks back down at the screen of her phone. From where I'm standing, it looks like she's going through someone's photo album on Facebook.

'Where's Tom?' I enquire, pulling out the chair furthest from her and sitting down.

She raises her eyes, her expression sheepish, and I immediately understand.

'He's not coming, is he?'

'He thought it would be better if we . . .' She stops, frowning momentarily at something she's seen on her phone. I don't need her to finish the sentence, because I know what Tom thought. I can't believe I didn't realise that this was his plan all along. Normally we know exactly what each other is thinking, but all the confusion of the past few days has clearly had an effect on my already weary brain.

The waiter scurries over to take our order, tapping his pencil against his little pad of paper as I faff around with my own phone and purse. Having not even glanced at the menu, I ask for the same barbecued sardines that I had the last time I was here, plus a large bottle of *agua sin gas*. Nancy mumbles something about a salad and points to the menu, and before long we're alone again. I wonder why she's chosen to sit inside on such a nice day – and with a view as captivating as the one outside on the sand. The napkins on the table are twitching ever so slightly in the breeze coming from the ceiling fan above us, and the silence is punctuated by the sound of pots crashing together and shouts of Spanish coming from the open door of the kitchen.

Clearly Nancy is not going to apologise for getting her claws into my best friend or for disappearing for hours with a strange man, but I'm damned if I'm going to make her feel better by filling the hush that's fallen over the table. The more minutes that pass by, the heavier the silence feels, and soon it's practically gooey. Even if I opened my mouth to say something innocuous now, the words would be swallowed up like a bug into the mouth of a Venus flytrap. There are almost too many things for me to ask Nancy, and now that I'm here facing her, I don't know where to begin.

The bread arrives, and for want of anything better to

do, I break a chunk apart and dip it into the mayonnaise, only remembering about the garlic when it's already in my mouth.

Great. Theo's bound to invite me round again now.

'I think Dad's pissed off with me,' Nancy says suddenly, helping herself to a roll from the basket, but then abandoning it on her plate.

'Welcome to my world,' I reply, and she gives me the hint of a smile.

'He's never cross with you,' she tells me. 'All he ever talks about is how proud he is of you.'

This is news to me, and it sounds so unlike him that I almost cough up my bread.

'Honestly!' Nancy says, plaiting her napkin with nervous fingers. 'He tells everybody that his daughter works in television – he loves boasting about it.'

'I barely speak to him,' I tell her honestly. 'We always end up arguing whenever I do, so I've stopped bothering.'

'You should see him,' she says, picking up her knife and putting it down again. She looks so agitated today, I realise, as if there are not just ants, but beetles, worms and butterflies in her pants. I'm used to her giggling and flirting, being all coy and peering up at people through her thick, dark lashes. This new Nancy feels like a stranger. Perhaps this row she's had with Dad was worse than she's letting on.

'I'm sure Dad's not cross with you,' I tell her now, keen to reassure her despite my displeasure at what else she's been up to. 'You're his favourite, his little angel – there's no way he'd ever get angry with you.'

'I'm definitely *not* his favourite!' Nancy is indignant. 'He thinks I'm stupid, I know he does.'

'Where is all this coming from?' I ask, my voice gentle now. She looks so young sitting there in that silly pink kaftan covered in sequins, her plastic sunglasses tangled up in her black hair. All this time I thought she had the role of Daddy's Girl well and truly in her grasp, but it seems I was mistaken. What was it Mum told me yesterday about Nancy not telling anyone she was coming out here to join me? I'd assumed it was because she was being selfish, but perhaps there was a deeper reason.

She hasn't answered my question, so I ask another.

'Did you and Dad have a fight?'

She shakes her head.

'Well then, what?'

Another shake.

'Nancy,' I say, exasperated. 'I can't help you if you don't tell me what's wrong.'

She looks up at my words, her eyes searching my face, making sure I mean what I say, but her reply is halted by the arrival of our food. By the time the waiter has gone, she's looking back down at her lap again.

'Do you want a sardine?' I ask, trying another tack. I'm trying to remember if I've actually seen her eat anything since she arrived, and I don't think I have. Even now she's merely staring at her plate of salad as if it has teeth.

'I don't like fish,' she mutters.

'We can order something else?'

Another shake of the head.

'Shall I just call Dad now?' I ask, picking up my phone from the table and holding it up.

'No!' It's almost a shout, and a passing waitress eyes us in concern.

'If he's cross, it's only because he's worried about you,' I tell her. 'Like I was the other night.'

She drops her eyes at that, but still doesn't apologise.

'You don't have to stay at Tom's every night,' I continue, my olive branch now so long that it's in danger of taking out her eye. 'You can stay with me and Claudette again.'

'Thank you.' She gives me the smallest of smiles and finally pops a cherry tomato into her mouth. From the expression on her face as she chews it, though, you'd think it was a pellet of dung.

'Do you like Tom?' I ask, looking not at her but at the fish on my plate. It's a fiddly job, getting the blackened meat away from the fragile bones, and I don't want to end up choking. If I'm totally honest, I also don't want to know if her face lights up when she talks about him.

A pause. 'He's really nice,' she says. 'He's funny.'

Both those facts are true, but she hasn't answered my question.

'But do you fancy him?' I prompt, willing her with every ounce of hopefulness in my body to say no.

'I don't know,' she admits. 'He's been so sweet to me, but I . . .'

'But you've been sleeping with him,' I prompt, seeing her cheeks flame.

'No,' she stammers. 'We only kissed. Just once, that night after we . . . When we stayed up talking.'

I hate the mental picture of the two of them – of Tom, especially, going in for a kiss when he knew how I would react. It feels as if it's come out of nowhere, but clearly he's had a thing for Nancy for quite some time.

Nancy seems to read my mind, because the next second she says, 'He didn't take advantage, if that's what you're thinking. It was the next day. In the morning.'

That's even worse.

'Right.'

Suddenly the sardines taste like ash in my mouth.

'Tom's no Diego,' I say then. Why, I have no idea – but Nancy glances up in what looks like amusement.

'No, he's definitely not.'

'And have you heard from him – Diego?'

She looks surprised by the question.

'No, of course not.'

'You looked pretty keen on him when you were eating each other's faces last weekend,' I point out.

'It didn't mean anything.' That shrug again, so nonchalant. Diego just one of many in a line of men that she's chewed up and tossed aside. I think about my dad again, how he so easily discarded my mother as if she and I meant nothing to him. At least I know where Nancy gets it from.

I want to ask her again if anything else happened with Tom, whether or not they've kissed more – or worse. I can't quite seem to get the words out, however, and instead turn my attention back to my lunch. I can just about hear the faint sound of the sea, churning and pounding as it always is in Mojácar, stirred into a frenzy by the wind.

I'm sure Tom's plan when he arranged this lunch was for Nancy and me to have a proper heart-to-heart – after all, he's known for years what I think of her, and how strained our sibling bond has become – and I suppose we have managed it, in a small way. I had no idea that my dad talked about me in glowing terms. In fact, I had no idea he even thought about me that often, let alone brought me up in conversation. It's not quite enough to make me think fondly of him, but I am tempted to get in touch now, mostly because I'm intrigued to know what has happened between him and Nancy to make her distance herself from him. The positive thing is that my anger has eased a bit. Now that I know Nancy is unsure about Tom, I also feel convinced that a kiss is all that has happened. I feel as if I can look him in the eye now and see my friend again, not the horrible boy who hurt me. I'm going to try, at any rate.

The waiter removes our plates, enquiring in broken English if there was anything wrong with Nancy's salad, which is still sitting limp and untouched. I reassure him as best I can, then order myself a bowl of chocolate ice cream out of guilt. Nancy vanishes to the toilet with her phone for so long that I think she's done another disappearing act, but eventually she returns to the table, her eyes all red and squinty.

'What's happened?' I ask.

'Nothing.' A sniff. I watch as she stows her phone in her bag and fights the tears.

'It's clearly not nothing,' I say. I know I should go over to her chair and put an arm around her, but I don't. We've never really been demonstrative with each other. I don't actually think I've laid a finger on her since she was about five, and that was only because she tried to throw herself in the pond when we were taken to feed the ducks.

Watching someone cry always unsettles me, and instead of acting on the compassion I feel, I grow impatient – and it's no different this time. I don't say anything, but I know Nancy can sense my discomfort because she's fighting hard to keep it together. When the waiter passes by a few minutes later, I order a jug of sangria, and Nancy looks up in surprise.

'Nothing that booze can't solve,' I tell her as cheerily as I can manage, my head on one side. 'It's only Dad, you know. He'll come around. Nothing is bad enough to cry about in a place as gorgeous as this, is it?'

Nancy blinks away her fresh tears and looks past me out towards the beach, where children are building sandcastles and decorating them with pebbles and shells, dogs are collecting soggy driftwood and depositing it at the sand-covered feet of their owners, their tails wagging with excitement at the prospect of a game, and the blue of the sea stretches away into the distance, its endless motion so strong yet soothing. She looks to me as if she's taking it all in for the first time, and so I let her, enjoying the feel of the breeze stroking my bare skin. By the time our order arrives, Nancy has stopped crying and has a glazed expression on her face.

'Truce?' I say, holding a spare spoon out to her and pushing my bowl of ice cream across the table.

She hesitates for a second, then takes it from me.

'Truce.'

22

I adore the way the Old Town comes alive at sundown. Locals emerge from their little white homes post-siesta, stretching rested limbs above their heads and taking deep breaths of warm late-afternoon air into their lungs in an attempt to wake themselves up for the evening. For many people living here in Mojácar, this is the time of day when they make most of their living, opening up their shops, bars and restaurants to travellers from all across the world. The smell of paella wafts out from open windows, ordered that morning to be slow-cooked to perfection for families, couples and large groups of friends. Fairy lights that have been hung up like bunting outside boutiques and gift shops twinkle in the fading light, and the sound of contented chatter rises in volume as more people spill into the narrow cobbled streets.

From up here, on the roof terrace of a jazz bar not far from Diego's restaurant, I can see and hear all of this going on below me, and the sounds are interspersed with strains of music – a lone saxophone, a woman singing sleepily in Spanish and the more traditional and upbeat pop songs coming from the bars. The atmosphere feels charged, and I imagine that I can hear the hum of energy in the air.

We're currently filming a segment about Mojácar's Moorish history, and Claudette is standing in front of Tom, whose shoulders are frozen in concentration as he watches her through the camera. Theo is off to one side, taking in every word, his focus fully on the task and a rolled-up script in one of his tanned hands. I think about what his hands were doing to me just a few days ago, and smile to myself. While he hasn't invited me back to the villa since Saturday, he did run a lone finger down my spine earlier today, when he knew the others were distracted, then dropped a single kiss on my bare shoulder. I've been tingling in that same spot – and others – ever since.

Nancy isn't up here with us. Much to Tom's dismay, she agreed to Diego's offer of a drink downstairs in the bar. It was him who convinced the owner of this jazz club to let us in to do some filming before the official opening time, and we're all very glad he did, given the stunning views we've been able to capture. Well, I say all of us, but I'm sure Tom would have preferred it if Diego was not involved. He's still lapping up every word Nancy utters and hanging around her like cling film, but as far as I can tell, she's treating him as just a friend. I know I should simply pull him to one side and ask him to explain the whole truth about what's happened between them, but I'm still unsure whether or not I want to hear it. And anyway, something has shifted in our friendship since Nancy turned up. I feel as if he's judging me every time he looks at me, and I can't relax around him in the way that I once did. I know Tom senses the awkwardness, too, because I keep catching him staring at me with those big, sorrowful eyes of his. It's as if Nancy's arrival has cut a swathe in the very air between us, and now we can't find a way back across to each other.

Claudette has stopped talking, and Tom stands up straight, rubbing his back with a big hand as Theo crosses over to review the footage. A few days ago, he asked to see everything I have recorded with Elaine, too, but I'm yet to get any feedback. If I was bolder, I'd see if he wanted to discuss it over dinner. If I was Claudette, I'd probably suggest a full review in his bed. But I'm neither, so of course I haven't mentioned it since Sunday evening when I handed over the memory sticks.

They're about to commence filming again when a plane comes into view overhead and Theo lifts up a hand to halt proceedings. Looking up at the unblemished blue sky, I grin in delight – there's a large banner stretched out behind the aircraft advertising what looks like melons. Only in Spain, I think, just as the church bells chime in the near-distance.

The image of melons brings back a memory, too, of Rachel and myself sunbathing down at the beach that last summer we visited Mojácar together. There was a man who strolled up and down the sand every day selling little plastic tubs of fruit salad, and each time he came into view we would giggle in unison at his odd bellow.

'Fresh, fresh, fresh fruit. Fresh fruit. Fruit salad!' he would yell, tripping over his own words as he stumbled into a hole near the shoreline.

One day he glanced sideways at us as he passed, noticed our laughter and immediately headed in our direction.

'Oh my God!' Rachel squealed, quickly lying back against her lounger and closing her eyes.

'Pretend to be asleep,' she hissed.

It was too late for me, though, because Fruit Salad Man

was already standing over me, his shadow blocking out the sun.

'*Hola,*' I said politely, somehow managing not to laugh, even though I could see Rachel's body shaking with silent mirth beside me.

A sniff.

'Do you want?' he asked, motioning to the tray balanced up on his shoulder.

'No, thank you. I mean, *gracias*,' I mumbled back at him, trying my best to smile without giggling.

He sighed at this, and crouched down on his haunches next to me. He was older than I'd thought, the lines around his eyes and the flecks of grey in his stubble a contrast to his thick head of dark curls and lurid pink shorts.

'You think me funny,' he said, and although it wasn't a question, I shook my head quickly from side to side.

'No!'

He regarded me for a few seconds, a bead of moisture running down from his forehead to his jaw. I could sense that we'd annoyed him with our giggling, and in that moment, I saw us as he must have: two silly girls with nothing to do all day but lounge around laughing at him.

'Do you want some water?' I offered, taking both of us by surprise. Rachel opened one eye, but didn't move to sit up.

Fruit Salad Man shook his head.

'Is okay. I am okay. *Bueno.*'

I put down my bottle of water and smiled.

'You work, in England?' he wanted to know.

'No,' I admitted, feeling oddly ashamed. 'I'm a student.'

'Good,' he replied, nodding and shifting his weight on to his other foot. 'What will you do, after?'

It was a simple enough question, but I didn't have an answer for him, just as I didn't have one for my teachers, or my parents, or even myself. I'd chosen sociology, history and psychology as my A-level subjects, but didn't feel passionate about a single one of them. It all felt like nonsense, simply box-ticking. Do your A-levels so you can go to university, get a degree so you can get a job, work hard so you can buy a house, create a home so you can have a family. I knew the drill; I just couldn't picture myself being satisfied with any of it.

'I will come back here,' I told the fruit seller instead, laughing as he pulled a face. 'Why is that bad?'

'This place is okay for holidays,' he said, putting his tray down and rearranging the pots of fruit salad needlessly. 'But for work, it's not so good.'

'Do you not enjoy your job?' I asked, even though I knew from his expression that he didn't.

He shrugged. 'I need money. My wife is having a baby, and I don't want her to work.'

'Congratulations,' I replied, surprising him again, and this time he actually grinned, standing up and looking away from me, along the beach.

'Family,' he said then, turning to me once again. 'Family is everything.'

I watched as he strolled away, his cries of 'fresh fruit' beginning again in earnest, and found myself ridiculously close to tears.

'That was weird,' remarked Rachel, sitting back up.

I nodded in agreement, but inside all I could think was,

I know what I want to do. I want to work with people. I want to learn all about them. I never forgot about my encounter with Fruit Salad Man, and he's probably a big part of the reason I ended up in this job. As well as the everyday boring stuff, being a researcher means spending a lot of time with people, and it's this part of my job that I enjoy the most. I always have. Mojácar showed me who I was, and who I wanted to be.

I'm still lost in thought when Theo says 'cut' for the final time and claps his hands together in appreciation that this segment is now complete. We're well ahead of schedule, and with each passing day Theo seems to relax a fraction more, as if he's striking through a mental checklist of things he must remember to do. I'm enormously flattered that he's made any time for me at all, given how hard he works and how much editing he has to do, and I know that must be why he hasn't called me back to continue what we started at the weekend. It will only be a matter of time now until it happens. For such a long time, it was 'if' and now, miraculously, it has become 'when'. I wonder if Tom has worked it out, whether he can tell just by looking at me that something huge has happened. I think he probably suspects, but, like me, is muted by this new barricade of awkwardness that has wedged itself into the very same gap between us that was once filled with laughter and fun. I hope we can get past it. We must.

'Can I buy you all a drink?' Theo asks, patting Tom on the shoulder as he packs away the equipment. Blimey, he must be really happy with our progress.

'Yes, please!' I'm quick to agree, but I notice Tom

pulling a face. He was probably hoping to sneak Nancy away from Diego. Well, he'll just have to lump it.

Claudette is reading a message on her phone. 'I am meeting Carlos in an hour,' she tells us. 'So, let's make it a quick one, *oui*?'

Is it my imagination, or did Theo just catch my eye and wink?

We find Diego downstairs with Nancy, his handsome face just inches away from hers and one of his hairy hands on her thigh. She's wearing cut-off jeans today and a smock-style top with blue and orange patterns embroidered across the front. I'm inwardly reluctant to admit it, but the laid-back look actually suits her. Now if only she'd stop plastering half of Boots across her face . . . I don't know how she can bear all that thick foundation during the daytime hours, when the temperature rockets up to the thirties. I'm amazed it doesn't all melt off her face. She can't believe that she needs all that rubbish to look good, can she? Nancy is a lot of things, but I've never known her to lack self-esteem. Then again, perhaps I don't know her as well as I thought.

Tom is hovering uncertainly behind Nancy's stool, obviously desperate to interrupt but far too polite to actually say anything. Theo, who is seemingly oblivious to the multitude of complications going on around him, has his back to us and is now chatting away to the owner in rapid Spanish. I hear the word 'Indalo' and glance instinctively down at my little tattoo. I used to love it because it reminded me of Mojácar, of how I felt here – but from now on it will forever take my mind to Theo. The realisation makes me treasure it even more.

'Here you are, Hannah,' says the man himself, sliding a cold beer into my waiting hand and letting his fingers brush against my knuckles.

I want him to kiss me. I want him to kiss me so badly that I almost weep.

Nancy has refused Theo's offer of a drink, and I can see a bottle of Diet Coke on the bar in front of her, a bright pink straw poking out of the neck. I'm glad she's not drinking. I don't think my nerves could bear another of her vanishing acts. Claudette who, unlike Tom, is not shy in any way whatsoever, pulls a stool out from under the bar and sits herself down right between Diego and Nancy. I can't help it; I have to smile at her blatant audacity.

'You look happy today.'

Theo is beside me again, his lime aftershave immediately making my heart thud lustfully against the walls of my chest. I think about his finger stroking my spine, his hands pulling down my dress. It would be easy, too, as the one I'm wearing today is short, black and made of Lycra. One tug and he could take it right off over my head.

'I am happy,' I tell him, moistening my lips. 'Are you happy?'

Theo looks at me as he takes a sip of beer. There is so much I know he wants to say, but he won't. Not here, not when the others are in earshot.

'I am happy with the film,' he says, a suggestive twitch lifting one corner of his top lip. He's toying with me. I know it, and I love it.

'Just the film?' I murmur, keeping my eyes on the group over at the bar. Tom is now leaning around Diego in an attempt to get Nancy's attention, but from what I can tell, she appears to be oblivious to both of them.

'There are other things, too,' Theo tells me, deliberately letting his knuckles brush across my knee. If he took one step to the left of my stool, he'd be standing right between my legs and I could pull him against me, slide my hands into the rear pockets of his shorts and knot my ankles around his thighs. He could bend me backwards and kiss my neck, my chest, the hollow of my throat.

'I have looked at your footage.'

I'm not prepared for the sudden change of subject, and I blurt a nonsensical reply. Theo laughs, obviously amused by my incoherence, but when I pull an offended face he grabs my hand.

'Don't be like that, you know that I think you are adorable.'

Sod being adorable, I want to be sexy, sophisticated, wanton, irresistible . . .

'Hannah, are you listening? I said that it's a very good start.'

I really need to get a grip. I can't think straight around Theo lately, not even about something as important as work. Lust is making me blind, deaf and apparently mute.

'The footage, your interviews with Elaine, they contain some great stuff.'

'Oh. Right. Thanks.'

He takes another swig of beer before continuing.

'I have been thinking about what you told me about the healers that Elaine mentioned.'

'You mean on the bus? I didn't record her, sadly.'

'I know.' Theo frowns at the bad news and my heart

breaks. 'But do you think she would say it again? These old stories, about the myths and legends of Mojácar, go to the heart of our subject.'

'I'm sure she would,' I say, smiling with confidence. 'I'm seeing her tomorrow morning, actually, so I'll ask her then.'

'And also,' Theo pauses as two Spanish women make their way over to the bar. Seeing him look them up and down makes my insides churn like angry butter.

'Also?' I prompt.

'Ah, yes. I want you to ask her more about why she came here in the first place. There must have been a reason that she chose Mojácar, out of every place in the world. Can you ask her that?'

'Whatever you want,' I tell him, adding quietly, 'you're the boss.'

He's giving me that look again, the one that makes me want to drag him into the nearest dark cobbled corner and ravish him. When he suddenly puts his bottle of beer down and makes to move away, I think for a thrilling second that he might ask me to go with him – but it's not to be.

'Where's your new boyfriend gone?'

Tom has appeared at my elbow, looking red in the face and uncomfortably sweaty. Of course he can't possibly know about what's happened between me and Theo, but the casual way he refers to him as my boyfriend makes my cheeks burn.

'Men's room,' I say primly. 'And he's not my boyfriend.'

'I know,' Tom replies, squinting at me. 'It was only a joke.'

'Funny,' I reply, but neither of us laughs.

'Diego's a bit annoying, isn't he?' mutters Tom.

I sigh. 'Not if you're female,' I tell him, feeling far less guilty than I should for winding him up. In truth, Nancy doesn't seem very interested in my former crush today. She's crossed her legs so they're facing away from him and has turned all her attention on to Claudette, who in turn has rested her tiny feet on the rungs of Diego's stool.

'Do girls really like that look?' Tom asks. 'You know, foreign sleazebag.'

'Just because he's handsome and happens to be Spanish doesn't make him a sleaze,' I scold, but then I remember that Diego kissed my sister about three minutes after meeting her and change my mind.

'Okay, so he might be a slight sleaze at times – but he's still hot to look at. Sorry, Tom, but it's just true. There will always be girls who fall for a pretty face.'

He's about to answer when we both see Nancy slip off her stool and head towards the toilets. She actually said something this morning about not feeling too great, and I assumed she'd had too much sangria, but perhaps she's been drinking the water out of the taps or something. I made that mistake myself years ago, and Rachel still has my number saved under the name 'Dear Ria' in her phone. She didn't call me that yesterday when I rang to tell her about the Theo hook-up, however – instead she gave me a new nickname: 'legend'.

'I hope she's okay,' Tom says, echoing my own trail of thought, and as soon as Nancy reappears, he hurries over to make sure. Theo is chatting to the club owner again, but he keeps looking over at me through the steadily increasing throng of customers jostling for position at the bar. The music is getting louder, the crash of boisterous jazz making me feel even more jittery, and all I can hear being spoken is Spanish.

When the crowd clears, I see that Claudette has left, presumably to meet Carlos, and Tom has a concerned arm around Nancy's shoulders. Diego is nowhere to be seen, either, but then he probably had to go to work at the restaurant. I'm not even sure where Theo is now – I can't see him at the bar. Tom catches my eye and beckons me over.

'Nancy's not feeling well,' he shouts over the din.

I bend down so I can look into my sister's face. Her skin has the telltale waxy sheen of someone on the verge of sickness, and I take an instinctive step backwards as she opens her mouth.

'What was that?' I ask, as her words are swallowed by a particularly aggressive strum of a double bass.

'She wants to go,' booms Tom, and Nancy nods weakly in agreement.

Now I'm in a quandary. I need to find Theo, at least tell him why I'm leaving. He'll think I'm so rude if I just disappear. Then again, I can't tell Tom that I need to locate Theo without him getting even more suspicious than I know he already must be, and I'm just not ready to share my Theo truth with anyone here in Mojácar. Not yet, anyway. I want to keep it all to myself.

I glance around desperately as yet more people file in, their shrieks of greeting and excited babbling chatter almost deafening. Nancy is really pale now, and Tom is looking at me beseechingly.

'Come on then.' I turn reluctantly towards the exit. I'll just have to message Theo and tell him what happened.

Once outside, Nancy seems to perk up a bit, and the

colour comes back into her cheeks. I'm half-tempted to send her and Tom on their way and head back to the jazz club, but something stops me. As extraordinary as it might be, I realise that I am genuinely concerned about my sister's wellbeing. It's been creeping up on me for days, ever since she went missing and we had that stupid fight. Seeing her so upset at the beach unnerved me, too, as historically Nancy has always been the more confident one. And now she's feeling unwell, that initial fear for her safety that I felt has been exacerbated. I actually care about her.

As we walk through the narrow, dusty streets, the fading light lending a mauve tinge to the white buildings, it doesn't seem possible that we were just in that lively, noisy bar. Mojácar is such a place of contrasts: of history and vitality, of sleepiness and playfulness, of adventure and comfort. I feel so much more alive here than I ever do back in London, and despite the fact we're all heading home, I know I'm not ready to call it a night just yet.

Tom puts a hand on my arm after I've let Nancy into the apartment and waits until we both hear the bathroom door close.

'Will you come out for a drink later?' he asks, keeping his voice low.

'Why not come in and have one?' I offer, but he shakes his head.

'Nancy needs some rest. You should wait until she's asleep, then text me and I'll come to meet you.'

'Okay,' I agree, and he removes his hand.

'Hannah.'

'Yes?'

'I'm sorry.'

'Don't be,' I say too quickly.

'But I am,' he insists. 'I just think that . . . Oh, never mind. We'll talk later. I'll see you in a bit, yeah?'

Nancy doesn't put up a fight when I urge her to get into my bed, and I fuss around her like my mum used to when I was ill as a child, leaving her the option of bottled water or Coke and needlessly plumping up the pillow. Once she's settled down under the sheet, she looks horribly like she might start crying again, so I switch off the light and practically run out to the balcony, stopping at the fridge as I pass to grab myself a beer.

I'm guessing that what Tom wants to talk about is Nancy. He knows as well as I do that her being here is affecting our friendship, and I really hope that he wants to try and move past it. The thing is, I can tell how much he likes her. In fact, anyone with eyes in their head and even the thinnest trace of curiosity would be able to tell. But I can't believe that he would choose a possible romance with Nancy over what we have – that's not the Tom I know. But then love does make people behave selfishly, doesn't it? My dad knows all about that.

I wait half an hour before I sneak back to my room to check on Nancy. Her eyes are closed, her hair a dark fan across the white pillowcase, and I close the door with a soft click. As I take out my phone to message Tom, however, a text comes through from Theo, and I breathe in sharply.

'Come to the villa.'

It's not a question.

23

The first thing I'm aware of when I open my eyes is the light. It's so bright that I have no choice but to scrunch up my face like an empty crisp packet, and for a few seconds I can't make sense of what's happening.

I'm not in my room. I'm not in the apartment.

I blink and bring a hand up to rub away the grotty combination of sleep and dried mascara that is nestled in the corner of each eye. That's better, now I can see. I can see large glass doors looking out over the beach, I can see the sea nibbling away at the shore, I can see a smear of clouds in the sky, and yes – those are my pants on the floor.

MY PANTS!

I manage to catch the excited yelp of delight before it exits my lips, but I have to clamp my hands over my mouth to do so, and it's enough to disturb a blissfully sleeping Theo, who is lying with his back to me about two inches away.

'*Kalimera,*' he mutters, reaching across and finding my thigh.

'Kali-what?' I giggle, putting one of my own hands on top of his.

'*Buenos días,*' he says, his voice even deeper than usual. 'Good morning.'

'Yes, it is,' I say playfully, and am rewarded with a squeeze.

'Sorry I woke you,' I whisper, wondering if it's acceptable to lean over and kiss his shoulders. There's a soft patch on his neck where his hairdresser has forgotten to run the clippers across, and I have an overwhelming urge to nuzzle my lips against the twist of hairs.

'The light woke me,' he says, finally stretching and turning his head towards mine. The tips of our noses touch and he looks right at me, directly into my eyes, not saying anything else because he doesn't need to. My insides hurtle up to my throat like a lust missile and my heart begins to throb against Theo's chest. Instead of kissing me like I think he's going to, Theo simply blows gently on my throat, the warmth of his breath so much like a caress, and walks his fingers across my stomach.

I want to shut my eyes and drink in the sensations, but I'm loath to miss out on even a minute of his gorgeous face, the intensity of his gaze, the way his lips curve and seem to swell with anticipation. I should respond to his fingers, now lower and more insistent, but I feel overcome with nervous trepidation. I have never felt like this before, so scrutinised by desire, and it's as frightening as it is thrilling. I may be out of my depth, but I've never been one to flounder, and as Theo props himself up on one elbow and begins to trail his tongue down my body, I finally find my hands and slide them through the hair on his chest, around and down across his back to his adorably pale bottom, which is sculpted by muscle and dusted with more soft, fine hairs.

Last night when I arrived at the villa, he wasn't slow and measured with me like he's being now. He'd barely opened the door before grabbing my shoulders and pinning me against the wall with hot, passionate kisses. I'd responded with enthusiasm, lifting up my legs and wrapping them around his waist as he pulled my underwear to one side. This time he was prepared, and within a few minutes our bodies came together and connected with a unified cry of pleasure. For a man of medium height and build, Theo is a lot stronger than he looks, and when we'd finished in the kitchen he had no trouble scooping me up and carrying me through here, to the bedroom, where we started all over again.

I didn't have time to feel embarrassed about the whiteness of my untanned boobs, all I had room for was Theo – his mouth, his hands, his need for me. My dreams were coming true, and I was relishing every little taste of it.

If anything, though, this morning is better. I like that he's taking his time to kiss every inch of me, that I have time to process what I'm feeling and savour the solidness of him as we move together. He never closes his eyes, either, but he's not smiling. His expression is far weightier as he looks down at me, as if he's trying to work out a puzzle. I grin at him in an attempt to lighten the mood and get him to laugh at the sheer ridiculousness of it all – of us together in this way – but Theo pulls me up and kisses me until I start to see black spots. I can hear my breaths growing shorter and shallower, and then finally, deliciously, I give in to the waves that are flooding over me.

Theo mutters something in Greek as he eases backwards on the mattress and wipes the sweat from his face. He looks flushed and serious, and I find that I can't quite meet his eyes. My body is still tingling and I want him to lie down again and hold me; I want him to kiss me deeply and with feeling, but instead he takes a deep breath and swings his feet around to the tiled floor. Strolling naked to the corner of the room, he picks up a towel and gives me a brief smile, before heading towards the bathroom.

Should I follow him? I wonder, pulling the sheet up and across my naked body as I hear the shower begin to run. Or should I get up and make us coffee, fetch some water? It feels so surreal to be here with him, to have shared myself with him so entirely, and now that my heart rate is slowing and the metaphorical dust is settling, I find myself anchored to the bed with indecision.

I should get up and make the bed at least, put some clothes on. Maybe one of his shirts? That's what girls do, right? Men love that. But what if he's annoyed? What if he'd rather I didn't put my sweaty beanpole limbs into his no-doubt expensive shirt sleeves?

The shower has stopped.

Rearing up out of the bed at speed, I've only just managed to yank my little black dress back on when Theo reappears, dripping water and looking good enough to eat off a cracker.

'Help yourself to a shower,' he says, bending over and picking up my bra from the floor.

'Thanks.' I snatch it out of his hand and ball it up with my pants. 'But it's okay. I'll grab one back at the apartment before I go to meet Elaine.'

'Whatever you prefer,' Theo says, turning his back on me to rummage in his drawers for some clothes.

'I should leave you to . . . I mean, I'll make us coffee. If that's okay? Shall I? Or should I go?'

He pauses and eyes me with amusement.

'Hannah,' he says, beckoning me to him with a finger.

I cross the room shyly, and he strokes my cheek with one hand.

'You don't have to be nervous. I am not, how do you say it, going to eat your head.'

I giggle at that.

'Now,' he instructs, giving me a quick peck on the lips. 'Run along and do your interview. I will see you later, yes?'

I nod. 'Of course.'

As soon as I'm a safe distance from the villa, I switch on my phone and predictably find two missed calls and a text from Tom. Understandably, he's pretty pissed off with me for ditching our plan to have a drink last night – not least because I didn't even tell him that I was. I thought about it, I really did, but I didn't know what to say. All I could think when I got that message from Theo was how best and how fast I could get down to the villa. In my excitement, poor Tom became an afterthought – and now I do feel genuinely guilty. But what choice did I have? I've been waiting years for Theo to summon me over for sex, whereas Tom and I can go for a drink anytime.

I send him a quick message now apologising, explaining that I fell asleep on the sofa and failed to hear the phone. It's utterly lame, but I don't want to share the Theo news via text. If I do decide to tell Tom what's just happened, I want it to be face-to-face.

It's still early, but the sky is a solid sweep of blue, and the red pavement tiles feel warm beneath my shoes. I cross the road and stroll past the immaculate lawns outside the shopping centre, enjoying the feel of the mellow breeze against my skin and the scent of pine in the air. Everything here is so clean and well cared for – there is no litter or graffiti, and the colours seem to sing. I think of Acton High Street back in London, with its muted palette of greys and browns, its overflowing bins and complicated pattern of black chewing gum trodden into the paving slabs. The faces of the people I pass here are sun-warmed and open, which is such a contrast to the downcast and occasionally even hostile locals back home. If only London had a beach, or sunshine, or the sea. If only people could learn to love their city again and respect their neighbours. I must try to be a better citizen, I think to myself, as I start the long trudge up the hill. I need to remember this Mojácar feeling and take it with me when I leave. I don't ever want to forget how it feels to be here.

My buoyant post-coital mood lasts right up until I reach the apartment door, only to have it yanked open by Claudette before I've even had time to get the key in.

'There you are!' she cries. 'About time.'

'What's going on?' I ask, utterly mystified by her sudden concern for my whereabouts.

'We didn't know where you were,' she exclaims, leading me through into the main living space where Nancy, Carlos and – oh, wow – Ignacio are all waiting. My sister is obviously feeling better, because she's snuggled so tightly against her Spanish admirer that she's in danger of being swallowed whole.

Poor Tom, I think fleetingly.

'I was out,' I say, trying not to think about the

underwear in my handbag and the trace of Theo all over my skin.

'So, it's not okay if Nancy wants a night out, but when you bugger off it's fine?'

I frown at Claudette. She's clearly just repeating what Nancy has said to her. So much for a sisterly truce.

'And we know you weren't with Tom,' Claudette interrupts as I open my mouth. 'He's been just as worried as we were.'

'You're all being silly,' I say, laughing gently to try and lift the mood. I look first at Nancy and then back to Claudette. 'As you can see, I'm absolutely fine.'

I'm acting as if all this third-degree nonsense isn't bothering me, but it is. Claudette must have been the one who let Ignacio into the apartment, and I don't like the way he's pawing at Nancy, even if right now she appears not to mind.

'It looks as if you've all been enjoying your own cosy sleepover anyway,' I mutter, going to the fridge and extracting a cold bottle of water.

I think I see Nancy wince at my words, but I don't care. I don't see why I'm the one in the wrong all of a sudden. I left her tucked up asleep in my bed – it's not as if she was in any danger.

'Who were you with?' Claudette asks then, her tone ultra-casual.

I pause on my way to the bedroom.

'Nobody you know.'

I shuffle my feet against the tiles. She's seen straight through my lie as if it's made of glass.

'You're making a mistake getting involved with him,'

she replies, giving me a look that has more sharp edges than the contents of a toolbox. Carlos reaches up from his seat to hold her hand, but she bats him away.

'I'm not saying this to be unkind, Hannah. I think you need to be careful.'

'I have no idea what you're on about,' I tell her honestly. She's being absolutely mental – more insane than usual, which is really saying something. And as for Nancy, she can forget about that phone call I was going to make to Dad today to help smooth things over between them. If she's going to sit there and let Claudette moan at me without saying a word, well then, I don't see why I should go out of my way for her.

'Listen, I'm sorry that you were worried about me,' I tell the four of them. 'But I'm fine, really. I can look after myself.'

I see Nancy sit up and open her mouth as if she's going to say something, but before she has a chance I turn away and go into the bedroom, closing the door firmly behind me.

24

I'm still feeling mildly indignant forty minutes later when I knock tentatively on Elaine's front door, but as soon as she opens it and welcomes me inside, some of the tension leaves my rigid body. I love this place, filled as it is with trinkets and paintings – the colourful clutter of a lifetime spent in Mojácar. Elaine herself is decorated today, too, in a beige smock covered in paint splatters.

'I lost track of time,' she explains, crossing to the kitchen sink to wash her hands. Peering through the window into the little courtyard garden, I see the beginnings of a painting propped up on an easel.

'Is that La Fuente?' I ask, accepting a glass of fresh orange juice.

'Very good.' She looks pleased, and I return her smile.

'Are you painting it from memory?'

'I am,' she admits, dropping her eyes bashfully. 'I can see it in my head whenever I close my eyes, so why go to the trouble of carrying my canvas all the way down there?'

'Why indeed?' I agree with a smile.

Elaine pops upstairs to get changed while I set up the camera and tripod, this time choosing an angle that will capture plenty of her artwork in the background. If she's going to appear in the documentary, she may as well use it as an opportunity to advertise her talent. When she reappears, I reach into my bag and extract the print that

Theo bought for me in San José, of Mojácar with the double rainbow.

'Is this one of yours?' I ask, holding it up, and her eyes widen in surprise.

'Yes! How did you know?'

'I didn't,' I admit. 'I was just drawn to it, and then the more I looked at it, the more I thought you must have painted it. Plus, it has the rainbows.'

Elaine has arranged herself on a small red sofa while we've been talking, her bangles clinking together as she tucks away a loose strand of hair.

'You know how much I love those,' she tells me, and I switch on the camera.

'Why two rainbows?' I ask. 'You don't see two like that very often, do you?'

'Hardly ever,' she agrees, crossing and then uncrossing her legs. 'In fact, I've only ever seen it happen once in my life.'

'Was it here?' I guess, but she shakes her head.

'It was in London, actually – not long before I left for the last time.'

I remember what Theo said, about pushing Elaine to tell me the reason why she ended up here, and the beginning is as good a place as any to start.

'Why did you leave?' I ask quietly, and I see her tense up a fraction. I'm just about to apologise for being nosy and move the conversation on, when she starts to talk.

'As I told you before,' she begins, glancing at the camera and then back at me, 'I never knew my father. I was brought up by my mother in a huge house on the outskirts of the city. She always told me that a rich friend had left it to her in their will, but I realised years later that it was more likely to be a squat.'

I risk a sip of juice, not taking my eyes off Elaine as she continues to speak.

'She had an open-door policy, and as long as people donated food, then they were welcome to stay.'

'What about school?' I enquire, but Elaine shakes her head.

'My mother didn't really believe in modern education. She wanted to raise me in her own way, and it was far easier to slip through the system in those days.'

'You poor thing,' I murmur, but Elaine disagrees.

'Oh, don't worry. I thought it was the greatest. I was free to do whatever I wanted, and the older I got, the less my mum kept tabs on me. She was very loving towards people, my mother, just not to me.'

'Is that why you left?' I want to know.

Elaine pauses before answering, a faraway look on her face.

'In the end, I had no reason to stay,' she says simply, but we both know there's more to the story than she's letting on.

'One of the women who passed through and stayed with us at the house for a time was Spanish. She had fallen in love with an Englishman and come back to the UK with him, but their relationship hadn't worked out and she was so sad, so broken. He had left her with very little, and so my mother took her in and held her hand while she cried for this great lost love. Eventually Bonita started to talk about her home, about a village hidden in the mountains where fresh water runs out of the fountains and all of your wishes come true.'

'Mojácar?' I whisper, and her eyes gleam.

'Yes. Mojácar.'

'What happened to her, Bonita?' I ask, half-wondering if she's in a house around the corner even as we speak.

'She died.' Elaine looks almost apologetic. 'Took an overdose while she was living with us. My mum was so angry about it. I remember her saying that she'd ruined everything, and that now the police would be sniffing around.'

She doesn't mention drugs, but it's obvious that there must have been some in that house. I try to picture the scene inside, of human bodies slumped against ragged sofas, ashtrays overflowing with joint stubs and peace signs daubed on the walls. It doesn't seem like a very safe place for a child to be.

'Love can be a dangerous thing,' Elaine says now. 'When you have it and can feel it in return, it's the most wonderful, precious thing in the world, but if you lose it . . . Well, it can be so destructive.'

'Have you ever been in love?' I ask boldly, glancing down at the Indalo Man tattoo on my wrist. Elaine sees me do it and smiles at me with affection.

'Yes,' she says. 'But not in the way in which you are thinking.'

'Are there more ways than one?' I wonder aloud, but I already know the answer. I know because I love my mum, and I love Tom, I guess, but then I think what I feel for Theo is a kind of love, too.

'Each love is different,' Elaine says. 'People talk of great love, but sometimes that is the most precarious of all. When love makes you unsteady and unsure, it can be more of an enemy than something to treasure. Love needs to be strong, to prop you up and make you happy.'

'You seem to know so much about it,' I tell her. 'You must have had a great love to know what it is.'

'Perhaps.' She gives me a sideways look. 'Or perhaps I just notice things. Like you, for example.'

'Me?' I can feel myself starting to blush. 'What do you mean?'

'Something has happened since I saw you last,' she remarks. 'You can't sit still, and there is a new colour in your cheeks.'

'That's probably sunburn,' I joke, but I can feel myself squirming as she gazes at me.

'How are you getting along with your sister?' she asks now, thankfully changing the subject.

'Not much better,' I reply, filling her in briefly on what happened this morning at the apartment.

'Why do you really think she came here?' Elaine asks when I finish, and I find I have no idea how to answer her.

'I don't know,' I tell her honestly. 'She says it's because she wanted a holiday, but then she refuses to sunbathe. And she didn't even tell our dad that she was coming, which is really odd because she's always been his little pet.'

'Perhaps things have changed,' Elaine suggests, and I have to agree.

'It still doesn't make sense for her to come here, though,' I say, realising that until this moment I clearly haven't given the matter enough consideration. 'Even if she has had a row with my dad, she and I aren't exactly best friends.'

'Did you ever get on?' Elaine wants to know.

'I was excited when she was born,' I say, recounting what my mum has told me about that time of my life. 'But she was a clingy baby and hated it when I held her. She's wailing her head off in all the photos of the two of us.'

'Babies do that,' Elaine remarks.

'Well, Nancy did it until she was at least six,' I reply. 'And then she was never fun to play with. She would scream if I didn't let her win at everything, and she would cheat at games, then blame it on me. When we were both teenagers, I was over at my dad's for the weekend and I heard her saying awful things about me to her mum, all this stuff about how I looked like a boy, and that she was embarrassed to be related to me.'

'That's cruel,' Elaine allows. 'But she was still young. Teenagers say lots of things they don't mean.'

'She did mean it,' I argue. 'I know she did. I refused to go back there after that. I told my dad that if he wanted to see me, then he'd have to take me out for the day. Then, of course, Nancy got jealous. She thought I was getting special treatment, but she didn't understand that she got to see my dad every day, she got to live in his house with him. I didn't have that any more because of her and her mother. I had one single day with him every two weeks, and still she wanted more.'

There's a silence as I catch my breath.

'Sorry,' I mutter, taking another sip of juice. 'I shouldn't be ranting at you like this. It's very unprofessional and unreasonable of me.'

'I don't mind,' Elaine assures me. 'I never had a sister – or a dad, for that matter – so I'm not sure how much help I can be.'

'You're lucky,' I mutter. 'Honestly, sometimes I think I would be better off if it was just mum and me. If my dad had simply left and moved to the other side of the world or something. Eventually we would have lost touch, and I wouldn't have to deal with Nancy, and be reminded every time I see her that my dad chose her mum over mine.'

'It must be hard,' Elaine says, but she's frowning as if she doesn't really believe it.

'You think I'm overreacting,' I say, embarrassed. 'Sorry, I really will stop going on about it now.'

'Don't ever be sorry,' Elaine touches my arm. 'I think we're friends now, aren't we?'

I nod. 'Yes.'

'Well then, as your friend I'm always here if you need to talk – and I won't ever judge you, I promise you that.'

'Thank you.' I feel ridiculously like I might start crying.

'You can't choose your family,' she adds. 'And I'm even worse than your dad, in a way, because I really did leave and not go back. I used to tell myself that my mother would have been relieved to see the back of me, but I feel differently now – now that it's too late.'

'Too late for . . .' I begin, but at that moment the camera starts to beep.

'Oh bugger,' I swear, getting up from my seat. 'The battery's about to run out. Hang on.'

A quick search of the bag, however, reveals no cable.

'I must have left the charger plugged in at the apartment,' I groan, again humiliated. 'I'm so sorry. First I start blabbering on about my own problems and now this. You must think I'm awful.'

Elaine stands up and pats me on the back. 'I assure

you, I think nothing of the sort,' she says, heading into the kitchen. 'We can finish the interview another time. But first, will you have some breakfast with me?'

I can already see the fresh bread, cheese and tomato piled up on the worktop, and my stomach rumbles in anticipation. It's been ages since I last ate anything, and I have had quite the workout in the past twelve hours. Plus, the way I'm feeling towards Claudette and Nancy at the moment, I'll use any excuse not to have to spend time with them.

Picking up the postcard with the two rainbows and slipping it back into my bag, I walk across to the kitchen and join my new friend.

25

In my haste to get away from Claudette's judgemental scrutiny in the apartment this morning, I forgot to pick up my copy of the schedule, so as soon as Elaine closes her front door behind me, I take out my phone and text Tom, asking him where they all are.

Instead of replying, he calls.

'Hey,' I say. 'Where are you?'

'At mine,' he says. 'Theo and Claudette have gone to record some voiceover stuff at the villa.'

'Oh,' I reply, the news halting me in my tracks. I watch as a bird comes to land on a nearby balcony, its head turned towards the sun. It's silly to feel jealous, but that doesn't stop it happening.

'What are you up to?' he asks.

I shuffle my feet in the dust. 'Nothing much.'

'Meet me up in the village,' he says, and hangs up before I have a chance to respond.

I find him sitting on a bench in the Plaza Nueva, the light shining through the branches of a nearby tree dappling his face with colour. There's a few days' worth of stubble decorating his jaw, and his hair has been bleached a shade lighter by the sun. He watches me as I approach, a smile lifting one side of his mouth and that Tom kindness which I know so well lighting up his eyes.

'You look tired,' he says, as I come into range.

'Late night,' I reply, remembering a fraction too late that I lied to him. 'I mean, I didn't sleep all that well, you know, being on the sofa.'

Tom sighs. 'I know you weren't at the apartment,' he tells me. 'Claudette called me at about seven this morning demanding to speak to you.'

'Sorry about that.' I brave a look at him as I sit down on the bench. The dress I'm wearing is white, and I like the way the skirt looks against my tanned thighs. The breeze is soft today, like a murmur, and I slip my flip-flops off and stretch my feet out in front of me.

'And sorry for lying, too. Twice.'

'It's okay.' Tom pokes me in the arm. 'I forgive you.'

Unlike Claudette, he doesn't ask where I was or who I was with. Probably because he knows me well enough to recognise when there's something on the tip of my tongue. When we first met each other all those years ago at university, Tom and I were almost immediately the sort of friends who could finish each other's sentences, and a large amount of our chatter consisted of shared laughs or private jokes. I can remember so well the first time I introduced Tom to Rachel, and how astounded she was by just how similar the two of us were. A lesser friend would have been jealous of that closeness, but Rachel was just happy that I'd found someone I could be myself with.

'Are you sure you don't fancy him?' she'd practically pleaded, but I'd simply laughed the suggestion away.

'Tom,' I say now, staring at the cobbled ground rather than him. 'About Nancy . . .'

'Yes?'

'She's just broken up with someone.'

'I know that,' he says. 'She told us, that first night in the bar.'

'Well, I just mean . . .' I stop, searching for words that won't make me sound bossy or condescending.

'You mean she's not looking for a boyfriend,' Tom says.

'I don't know if she is or not,' I admit. 'I'm not sure if she knows what she wants.'

He nods at this, his expression grave.

'Do you know where she is now?' he asks, and I picture Nancy as she was this morning, wrapped around Ignacio on the sofa.

'Probably resting,' I say, as breezily as I can. 'She was feeling ill, remember?'

Now I'm lying to Tom again. This is what Nancy makes me do.

'Probably,' Tom agrees, but his eyes are sad now. As much as I hate the idea of him and my half-sister together, I can't help but feel sorry for him. I know how it feels to crave a person and not be able to have them. Even before Theo, I've had a lifetime of that with my dad, and a good few years of Diego infatuation thrown in for good measure. The fact that I've somehow managed to ensnare Theo after all this time is as astounding to me as it is brilliant, but it's still so precarious. I don't even know if anything will ever happen again.

'I slept with Theo,' I blurt out, swinging my legs aggressively in an attempt to mask my humiliation, as Tom exclaims in shock.

'What?'

'Last night. That's where I was. That's why I didn't meet you.'

'Bloody hell!' I can't tell whether he is impressed or disgusted. The expression on his face is not one I've ever seen before.

'I know,' I say, wincing as I turn to face him. 'It's mental, isn't it?'

'Definitely,' Tom agrees, standing up off the bench and pacing in a small circle. 'How did it . . . ? How did you . . . ?'

'It just happened,' I mutter, standing up and reaching for him so he has no choice but to stand still. 'I don't know if it will again.'

Tom is looking at me as if I'm a stranger, and I feel compelled to keep talking.

'It's not that mental,' I point out. 'I'm single, he's single.'

'But he's old!' Tom proclaims, and I narrow my eyes at him.

'He's barely even forty – hardly old.'

'But he's your boss!' comes the reply. He's peering at me now as if he's worried about me, and I prickle with irritation.

'It's not going to affect work,' I assure him. 'I won't let it.'

'You say that now,' Tom warns, running a hand through his stubble. 'But what if you get hurt?'

He's doing it again, reading my mind and voicing the thoughts that I've been steadfastly ignoring.

'I'm perfectly capable of dating a man I work with,' I inform him, sitting back down on the bench and folding my arms. 'Theo and I are both professionals.'

'Not very professional to shag your employees,' grumbles

Tom, coming to sit beside me and then swerving to the side to avoid my punch.

'Oi!' he mutters. 'Don't hit me for looking out for you.'

'I wanted it to happen,' I tell him. 'It's what I've wanted for so long now that I can't even remember a time that I didn't. Why do you think I haven't dated anyone in years?'

Tom's expression is still unreadable, but I watch his eyes flickering as he scans back over time, picturing the two of us in the London office with Theo, trying to remember if there were any signs that he missed. I can tell he wants to warn me off, but he manages to stay quiet, instead picking up one of my hands and squeezing it between his own.

'Just promise me one thing,' he says, looking right into my eyes.

'Just one?' I joke, but he shakes his head.

'Promise me you'll take care of yourself.'

I chuckle at that and try to extract my hand.

'We used protection, if that's what you mean,' I say, but he just looks sad again and squeezes my hand even tighter.

'That's not what I meant.'

Thankfully, at that moment, the wind picks up an unanchored stack of napkins and blows them right into our faces, causing me to laugh and eventually Tom joins in. By the time we've picked them all up and deposited them in the nearest recycling bin, the mood between us has lifted. Tom shrugs off his concerns and changes the subject away from both Theo and Nancy, suggesting instead that we walk down to the beach and get some lunch.

'I've got a better idea,' I say, smiling as a plan comes into shape in my mind. 'But it would mean hiring a car.'

It takes Tom and me over an hour to reach the rugged Sierra Maria mountains, which are situated in the north of Almería, and it takes all my not-very-extensive map-reading capabilities to get us there at all. I insisted that the two of us change from flip-flops into trainers before we left Mojácar, and looking at the rugged terrain ahead, I'm very glad we did. I also had the foresight to swap my beautiful white dress for my faithful old denim shorts, and I yanked on a sleeveless T-shirt, too.

Tom was mostly quiet on the drive, and we kept the radio on to fill the silence, occasionally singing along when a song came on that we recognised. I told him more about my progress with Elaine, and how I suspected that there was more to the story than she was prepared to share.

'She'll tell you,' Tom was quick to assure me. 'You're a very good listener, you know. I don't think you realise how good.'

He was right; it wasn't anything I'd ever considered before. But it comforted me to know that he believed in me, even if he was obviously worried about me hooking up with Theo.

'How far away is this cave?' Tom asks me now. We've parked up between the Vélez-Rubio and Vélez-Blanco areas of the park, and the Sierra Maimon mountain is looming above us, its jagged peak the darkest of browns against the impenetrable blue of the sky.

'About half an hour,' I say, wrinkling up my nose as I

peer at the map we picked up from the kiosk by the park entrance. 'It should be straight ahead of us, up that path.'

'You mean up the side of that massive mountain?' exclaims Tom, blanching beneath his tan.

'What's the matter, old man?' I lean over to do some exaggerated stretches against the bonnet of the car only to burn both my hands on the hot metal.

'Ouch!'

'Idiot,' deadpans Tom, but he's smiling at least.

We set off full of enthusiasm, but soon begin to flag. The path up the side of the mountain is not only incredibly steep, it's also littered with loose gravel and crusty dead plants. The sun is relentless, too, and I'm very glad that I'm here with Tom and not Theo. There's no way I'd want him to see me looking this sweaty and red-faced. Well, not unless I was out of breath for a very different reason.

There doesn't appear to be anyone else on the mountain today but the two of us, and it would feel almost eerie if it wasn't so stunning. The view as we climb higher gets all the more impressive, with distant hilltops dancing in the throbbing heat and the emerald clusters of forests stretching far away to a horizon streaked navy by the sea. In contrast to the clean whites, pinks and blues of Mojácar, the palette here is made up from earthy browns, golds and greens, and I keep getting left behind because I'm stopping to take photos. Tom, who has brought his proper big camera along with him, has so far resisted the urge to capture the scene, and is steadfastly plodding up towards the cave like a man on a mission. It's only when I catch him up that I see how much he's struggling with the combination of the heat and the weight of his bag.

'Here.' I hand him my bottle of water. 'Drink this before you keel over and I'm forced to carry you back down to the car.'

'Thanks,' he manages, unscrewing the top and glugging it down.

I think he's going to give up altogether when we reach a sign that cheerily informs us it's another twenty minutes up to the entrance, but he grits his teeth and keeps going, and eventually we reach our destination.

The Cueva de los Letreros – Cave of the Signs – doesn't look like much from the outside, but as soon as Tom and I cross the threshold and enter the dark, musty interior, I can sense the buzz of energy in the air. I know from my research that historians believe the cave was used for rituals or ceremonies, but my interest is focused on something else: the symbol painted on the far wall.

'Do you see it?' I whisper, pointing past Tom to an assortment of dark red drawings. There are shapes that look like animals, and others that may be flames, but at the top there is the unmistakable figure of a man, his arms outstretched and a semi-circle connected to each of his hands: the Indalo Man.

'I see it,' he replies, and for a few minutes we simply stand in silence taking it in. Inside the cave, away from the pestering wind, the only sound comes from the two of us as we breathe, and I relish the silence. This moment feels important, and I know I won't ever forget it.

Tom begins to wriggle his bag off his back, keen to capture everything we're seeing on camera, but I doubt that even he will be able to record this feeling. I don't believe in real magic, but in here it feels possible. More than that, it feels probable. My eyes move across once again to the figure, the talisman that I've carried with me every day for the past ten years, the symbol that means so much to so many, and I'm assaulted by a wave of emotion.

'I'll be outside,' I mutter through my unshed tears, turning away so rapidly that I stumble into Tom's bag. He catches me, his hand hot and heavy on my arm.

'Thank you,' he says, his fingers trailing against mine as he lets me go.

'What for?' I ask, mystified.

'For bringing me here.'

I shrug and take a step backwards.

'It's okay.'

'It's a very special place,' he adds, still looking at me as I reach the cave opening.

'I know.' I smile at him. 'And I wouldn't have wanted to be here with anyone else. I mean that.'

And it's true. I do.

26

'I can't believe it's only a week until we fly home.'

Theo squints against the light as he smiles at me in sympathy. We're sitting in his bed drinking strong black coffee, and as always the blinds are drawn so the sun can light up the room. He likes to be woken this way, as I have discovered.

'I know,' he says, moving his arm so I can nestle up against his shoulder. 'But we have to finish editing the film. I am excited to package it together now, as I'm sure you are too?'

'Of course.' I wriggle my bottom and turn to face him, but he's looking away in search of his book. Since finding that battered paperback here in the villa, Theo's barely put it down. This is the fifth time I've stayed over here now, and our secret is well and truly out. Since confessing all to Tom, I've stopped being so careful around Theo while we're out filming, and it didn't take Claudette long to notice. While she hasn't actually come out and said anything, her scorn has felt almost palpable at times, and I'd be lying if I said she hadn't hurt my feelings.

I can tell that Tom still isn't thrilled about the situation, either, but at least we're back to being proper friends again. It's been nice hanging out with him in the evenings while Theo is editing, even if he would rather be with Nancy. Whatever happened between those two is definitely over now, because my sister is spending all of her time with Ignacio. He's over at the apartment pretty much every day now, along with Carlos, but I have no idea if he's actually staying the night, because I'm always down here at the villa.

'Shall I tell you another story?' Theo asks now, and I agree happily. Being read to is such a nice thing, and I could listen to his voice all day.

Theo clears his throat. 'As you are aware, Mojácar has a Moorish history, and was once inhabited by Arabs.'

'I do know that,' I beam, but he hushes me.

'During those times, and indeed until the beginning of this century, there was no such thing as dating in Mojácar. If you wanted to ask a girl out, there was a rather complicated way of going about it.'

'Oh?' I enquire, running my fingers through the nest of hair on his chest.

'The old custom I'm talking about is called "club inside, club outside" – shall I tell you the Spanish?'

'Go on, then, I might learn something.'

Theo glances at me over the top of the book. 'Cheeky,' he says, but he's smiling. 'The translation is *porra adentro, porra afuera*, and it involved the entire family of a young couple. You see, the Arabs did not really believe in courtship, or even getting to know the person you would end up marrying. Instead, when a young man's parents had selected the girl they thought would make a suitable match for their son, the father would walk up to her family's house and bang loudly on the door with a club, before shouting "*porra adentro* – club inside", and would then throw the club into the hallway.'

I feel my brow furrow up at his words. 'What?'

Theo grins. 'I know, but listen. This club throwing was considered a proposal of marriage, so if the girl's family accepted, they would leave the club on the floor and preparations would be made.'

'What if they weren't keen?' I want to know.

'Well, in that case the girl's father would pick up the club and bang it on the inside of the door, before yelling, "*Porra afuera*" and throwing it back through the window into the street.'

'That is so bizarre,' I tell him, and Theo nods, shutting the book and regarding me with amusement as he sips his rapidly cooling coffee.

'You know what is an even better story?' I whisper.

'Go on.'

'It's one where a very handsome and clever Greek director lets his lowly researcher go with him to film in Turre today . . .'

Theo frowns at me. 'Hannah,' he begins, shifting himself away. 'We've been over this already.'

'It's not fair,' I moan, hating how teenage I sound. 'Claudette and Tom get to go, but not me. I can help, I've been reading up about the place.'

'There isn't enough room in the car,' he says, finishing his coffee. 'And anyway, you will only distract me.'

I must have pouted at this, because the next second he's pinned me down on the mattress and is kissing my neck and my face over and over until I squirm with delight.

'You are a very naughty girl, making me feel guilty,' he murmurs, his teeth closing around the soft part of my ear.

'Sorry,' I breathe, not meaning it one bit.

Just when I think he's going to move his mouth around

until it covers mine, Theo bends his head instead and blows a huge raspberry in my armpit.

'Get off me!' I shriek, half-heartedly wriggling underneath him, but I can sense that I've lost his attention as he looks past me towards the clock on the bedside table.

'I have to get up,' he groans, levering himself off me and rolling away. I have to fight the temptation to clamber on his back and pull him down on to the sheets, and instead settle for admiring his toned bottom as he strolls around the room fetching his clothes.

'You should spend the day with Nancy,' he tells me as he heads to the bathroom, shutting the door before I can reply. To Theo, my sister is family and that should be enough to bond the two of us – but of course he has no idea how complicated things are. While we've been perfectly civil to each other over the past week, there haven't been any occasions where the two of us have been alone. As far as I can tell, she's no longer ill or crying for no reason, so I don't feel too guilty about spending time away from her.

I have no desire to get up, but the idea of still being here at the villa when Claudette and Tom arrive makes me uncomfortable, and by the time Theo is back from the shower – looking sexy as hell with droplets of water all over his tanned chest – I'm dressed and ready to leave.

'I like this,' he says, picking up the hem of my red sundress and rubbing the cotton between his fingers. 'Why do you never wear dresses like this in England?'

'Because it's cold,' I reply. 'And because I love my jeans.'

'I like this new Hannah,' he states. 'She is more womanly than the old Hannah.'

I know he means it as a compliment, but for some reason his words sting a bit.

'Be good today,' he tells me when I don't reply, dropping a kiss on my shoulder then patting me on the bottom as I turn to go. He says that to me all the time, but I have no idea what he thinks I might be getting up to in his absence. It's not as if I'm working my way through the men of Mojácar when his back is turned.

I make my way along the main road at an aimless pace, reluctant to head back to the apartment but not tempted by the bank of shops on the corner by the roundabout. It's getting hotter with every passing day, and the heat is so intense this morning that I feel as if I can see it vibrating in the air around me. A persistent wind is bothering the very tops of the palm trees and chasing dirt in circles around my ankles. Theo persuaded me to accompany him on a late-night swim before we retired to bed, and my hair feels hard and knotted from the dried-in traces of salt. It's funny to think that I used to spend so long painstakingly applying my make-up every morning back in London, just in case he deigned to look in my direction at the office, and now he's seen me laid bare and washed clean. I feel so much closer to him now, but more wary of him at the same time. Neither of us has broached the subject of what will happen when this trip is over and we have to go back to normality, and I know why I haven't. The mental image of Theo in my tatty bedroom in the big shared house in Acton just doesn't work. More than that, it's actually laughable. What would he make of my stuffed toy collection and wall of drunken photos? I'd need a month and a two-grand IKEA gift card to get that place looking anywhere near good enough to let Theo into it – and even then, he'd have to run the gauntlet of my housemates.

No, we'll just have to stay at his. He must have a gloriously modern bachelor pad just crying out for some female energy. I wonder if he'll take me out to dinner at one of those swanky places along the Thames? Or up the Shard? He probably has membership at a club with a swimming pool on the roof – the sort of places Tom and I used to say we'd rather die than be seen at. But that was before. I'm seeing an older man now, so I need to be sophisticated. Perhaps I should start wearing pencil skirts and stilettos? Then again, I'd definitely be taller than Theo in heels, and I wouldn't want to make him feel emasculated . . .

I've been strolling along while mulling all this over and suddenly realise that I'm only five minutes away from the beach bar where Carlos works. There's a low white-stone wall up ahead that has baked to a crisp in the sun, and the top of it always reminds me of the lemon meringue pie my mum used to make when I was little. I feel a bit guilty because I've been ducking her messages for days now, unable to face all her questions about Nancy. The only person I have answered calls from is Rachel, but even she seems distracted. Now that the initial excitement about Theo and me getting it on has passed, she isn't as keen to discuss him, and keeps turning the conversation around to the subject of Paul, who can apparently do no wrong.

Camila greets me at the bar with two kisses and a warm smile, and I'm gratified to see that Carlos has got the morning off. What I want is a few undisturbed hours in the sunshine – time to switch off and relax. We've been working such long days; I think I've earned it. And anyway, I won't get the chance for much longer. Whenever I think about going home, I feel punched with sorrow. Mojácar feels like more of a home to me now than London. The pace of life suits me, and I love the people. Elaine, especially, has become such a good friend over the past three weeks, but as she has no phone at home and no email address, I'm starting to worry that we'll quickly lose touch after I'm gone. I must talk to her about it. Perhaps she'd even consider coming back to the UK if she had a friend to visit?

'Agua sin gas, por favor,' I tell Camila, returning her smile as she hands me a bottle of still water, but when I hand her some euros to pay for a sunbed, she shakes her head.

'Nancy is already there,' she explains, pointing down the beach. Sure enough, I can just see the garish pink of my half-sister's kaftan underneath one of the bright green umbrellas.

For a good minute, I seriously consider abandoning my plan and sneaking off before she spots me, but then I think about what Theo said this morning. If I can prove to him that I can be mature enough to make nice with Nancy, then maybe he'll think I'm even more womanly than he does already. It will also mean I can finally call my mum back and tell her what she wants to hear: that Nancy and I are fine and that there's nothing to worry about.

Taking a deep breath and flicking my sunglasses down over my eyes, I make my way along the makeshift wooden jetty between the sunbeds and come to a halt beside her.

27

My dad told my mum he was leaving her on a Sunday. Obviously I was too young at the time to know what day of the week it was, but I know it was that particular day because my mum told me years later that it happened just after she'd cooked a joint of roast beef, and she only ever does that on a Sunday.

She said he was quiet all through the meal, and that at first she simply put it down to tiredness. I wasn't a very good sleeper, and at that time I was regularly getting the pair of them up at four a.m. on an almost daily basis. On reflection, I'm surprised my mum even managed to prepare an entire roast dinner. If it had been me, he'd have been having macaroni cheese out of a tin and that would have been that. But my mum was trying to be a good wife to him and a good mother to me. In hindsight, she admitted to me once, the whole roast beef thing was her attempt to keep things normal. She had sensed that my dad was growing distant, and she was terrified to ask him the question why. As it turned out, my mum was far more astute than even she realised.

I've decided to tell Nancy the story now, as my mum always told it to me. Not because I want to goad her, but because I want her to understand just how hurtful it was, and has always been. My mother pretends to be okay about it now, but I know she's never really forgiven my father for leaving. As for me, I've just grown up always knowing that he did something bad, and that resentment has sat like a huge, murky puddle in the meadow of my affection for him. I'm not sure if I'll ever completely get over it, but I am starting to realise that I have to try.

Nancy has been listening quietly, but her large, dark eyes widen with sympathy as I explain how shocked my mum was to find out that my dad had already made the decision to go.

'He didn't even give her the chance to fight her corner,' I say now, sniffing in disgust. 'She begged him to reconsider, but he wouldn't. He gave us up without so much as a discussion.'

'Had he already met my mum?' Nancy wants to know, and looking at her now I realise that she's angry. It's not directed at me, though. For the first time ever, it's aimed at Dad.

'Yes,' I say simply. 'He told my mum that he'd tried to ignore his feelings, but that he couldn't do so any longer. He didn't want to have to pretend any more. Imagine that. Imagine the person you love, the father of your child, admitting to you that they'd only been pretending to love you all along.'

'It would be horrible,' Nancy agrees, and I think she really means it. She looks more serious and intense than I've ever known her to be, and despite the heat I look down to see goosebumps on my arms.

'I always thought it was a mutual thing,' she tells me. 'Mum's always told me that she met Dad when he was single.'

I shake my head. 'That's not true.'

Nancy is fiddling furiously with a loose thread on her

beach towel and wraps it around her finger before snapping it in half.

'I guess I never really thought about it from your mum's point of view before,' she says then, and I glance up in surprise. It's not like Nancy to be contrite or admit that she could have been in the wrong, and for a moment I'm too taken aback to respond.

'I suppose it suited me to believe what Mum told me,' she adds, baffling me yet again with her new self-awareness. 'I didn't like the idea of Dad being with anyone else. I guess I still don't.'

'I don't either,' I agree. 'But I had to grow up with it.'

There's a beat of silence as Nancy absorbs this, and then she looks up at me. Her refusal to sit in the sun, coupled with all the late nights hanging out with Claudette and the Spanish boys, has lent her skin a greyish pallor, and there's a bruise of colour under each of her eyes. She looks as if she hasn't slept for days.

'Do you think . . . ?' she begins, but then seems unable to continue.

'That he cheated on my mum?' I guess, and she nods. 'I don't know. I really hope that he didn't, but then I guess that's just wishful thinking. I mean, he must have been sure about Susie. Sure enough to leave us behind.'

'I hate people that cheat,' Nancy snaps, and there's genuine vitriol in her tone.

'Is that why you broke up with your boyfriend?' I ask her gently now, the idea only just occurring to me. I think back to the photos I'd seen of the two of them on Facebook – they looked so sickeningly happy with each other that I'd even remarked on it to Tom at the time. It had struck me as odd that they'd broken up so abruptly, but then Nancy had brushed aside my questions about him when she first arrived and I, distracted fool that I am, hadn't bothered to delve any deeper. Now that I've thought of it, I realise that it would explain a lot – the tears, the random kissing of strangers, the look of contempt on her face right this second . . .

'No,' she grunts, looking away to where two tiny birds are picking at a discarded paper napkin. 'He didn't cheat on me.'

'Well, I'm glad,' I say, puffing out my chest. 'If he had, then he'd have an angry big sister to contend with!'

It's a bit of a feeble gesture, but I can see that Nancy appreciates the effort. I don't think we've ever had such a measured conversation before, and it feels weird, as if I'm only just getting to know her, and she me.

'It's seriously hot – shall I get us a drink?' I ask, standing up and reaching for my dress, but when I return a few minutes later with a water for me and a Diet Coke for her, Nancy is crying.

'What's the matter?' I ask, digging a quick hole in the sand with my foot so I can put down the drinks without them toppling over sideways.

'Nothing.' She shakes her head.

This is my fault. I shouldn't have told her the truth about Dad. I should have let her continue on through life thinking that he was infallible. He's always been her hero, and now I've gone and tainted him. Then again, isn't it always better to know the truth? Once you have all the pieces, then surely you stand a greater chance of putting them all back together – even if the puzzle does take half a lifetime to solve.

'Don't be upset about Dad,' I say gently, awkwardly patting her shoulder. 'It was all such a long time ago. I shouldn't have brought it up.'

Nancy is still sobbing, but there's no sound. There are just tears running like two minuscule streams down her cheeks. At a loss of what else to say, I remain silent, my hand on her back.

'Have you ever been in love?' she suddenly asks, and I laugh in surprise.

'I think so. No, I mean I have. Well, I think I have.'

Classic Hannah Hodges response to a simple question: mumble incoherently like a toothless Womble.

'Theo?' she guesses, and I blush.

'Is he good to you?' is her next question, and I smile in relief that it's one I can actually provide an answer to.

'Oh, yes – he's great.'

'I'm glad.' She smiles weakly at me through her tears, and I get a sudden urge to cross over to her sunbed and put both my arms around her. If she's surprised by this outpouring of affection after a good twenty years of solid scowling, then she doesn't mention it. Instead she just cries a bit more, and I feel overwhelmed by helplessness.

'Shall we call Dad?'

A vicious shake of the head.

'Do you want to call your mum, then?'

Again, a fierce rebuttal.

'Some food?' I try, groping through the limited options open to us.

'Just a drink,' she says, sniffling like a hamster, and I reach down and fetch her glass.

All the ice has melted in the sun, and she stares down

at it for a few seconds as if contemplating what to do next. Then, before I have the chance to propose a toast to sisterhood, she's grabbed the straw between her fingers and necked the entire thing in one go.

'Thirsty?' I enquire, smiling as she raises a hand to her mouth to disguise a belch, nodding at me in amusement.

'Then let's get a real drink.'

'Salud!'

We cheer the word so loudly in unison that a family on the next table actually recoil in alarm, but that only makes us laugh all the harder.

'I am drunk!' I declare, bashing my beer bottle against the side of Nancy's cocktail. 'Drunkety, drunken, drunkola!'

'I'll drink to that,' she giggles, sucking on her straw and smiling at me through half-closed eyes.

We've been at the beach for hours now, and I've lost track of how many drinks I've had, which I'm mildly aware should be a worrying fact, but can't be bothered to care too much about. It feels so nice to be merry like this and – best and most oddly of all – it's actually really fun getting drunk with Nancy. Who would have thought it? Not me, that's for sure.

Since our heart-to-heart this morning, we've been making up for lost time and filling in the gaps we've missed over the years of refusing to talk to each other. Well, I say we, but I've been doing most of the talking. I had no idea that my sister was such a good listener, but she really is. I've told her all about Theo and about Rachel and oafish Paul, and now I'm explaining how great Elaine is. In fact, I've even decided that the two of them should meet.

Like I said: drunk, drunkety, drunken, drunkola.

Having skipped breakfast and forgone lunch in favour of yet more alcohol, by the time the sun is setting I'm feeling more than a little worse for wear. Staggering back from the little shack that comprises the ladies' toilet, I collide with Carlos, who is carrying two plates of food, and almost fall over sideways from laughing.

'*Idiota,*' he mutters with a frown, and I stick my tongue out at him.

'Look at the sunset!' I slur at Nancy when I'm back in my seat, but she already is. The view of it from here is even more beautiful than it is from up in the village, the smudged pastel pinks and yellows turning the surface of the sea into molten gold. I try to focus my eyes on the dark patches of gently shifting water, but everything is swimming in and out of focus.

Nancy is sending someone a message on her phone, but I can't see who it is from here. She hasn't cried for at least three hours now, which is a huge improvement on the earlier part of the day. I'm vaguely aware of the fact that I should get us both some food, or at least a taxi home, but both tasks feel impossible. What it would be nice to do is have a quick nap. Yes, that would help, I think blearily. And the top of the table is so comfortable now that my head is on it.

'Hannah!'

I sit up so fast that I almost smack the top of my head on Tom's chin, and he has to swerve out of the way.

'Bloody hell, Hannah!'

I start laughing, I can't help it, and Nancy joins in, although she definitely looks more sheepish than amused. She can certainly hold her booze, too, I'll give her that. She's been matching each of my beers with a variety of colourful cocktails, but she doesn't seem anywhere near as wasted as I am.

'Thomas!' I declare, grabbing his hand and steering him into a vacant chair. 'Have a drink!'

'I think you've had enough for everyone in here,' he mutters, not unkindly.

'Where's Theo?' is my predictable next question, and Tom shakes his head.

'Gone back to the villa to celebrate.'

'Celebrate what?' I demand, fear snaking its way through the reeds of drunkenness in my brain like a pike.

'The filming went really well today,' he says, and I get the sense that there's a 'but' he isn't adding.

Before I can press him, though, Tom has a question of his own.

'How long have you two been drinking?'

Nancy giggles again at this and gives him the benefit of those huge, dark eyes of hers.

'A few hours,' she simpers, her eyes not leaving his as she sucks on her straw. It would usually piss me off, but today I'm impressed. If only I could learn how to flirt so openly and with such confidence. Then again, I remind myself happily, I've already managed to get my man.

'I miss Theo,' I sigh out loud, and Tom rolls his eyes.

'I think it's best if he doesn't see you in this state,' he points out, but that just makes me grumpy.

'No!' I cry, loud enough to cause a few heads to turn in

our direction. 'I'm going to go to the villa – and you can't stop me!'

'Au contraire,' Tom says, putting a big hand on my arm and gently forcing me to sit back down.

'Trust me, Hannah,' he says. 'You don't want to go there, not tonight.'

'Maybe I'm a little drunk – so what?' I grumble, putting my head back down on the table. It really is very comfortable.

The next thing I'm aware of is Tom helping me up the steps of the bar to the street, where by some miracle there's a taxi waiting. Nancy gets in first and leans her head against the window, and Tom sits between us, giving the driver instructions in very bad broken Spanish. I want to take the mickey out of him, but for some reason talking has become an enormous effort. Once at the apartment, Tom makes me wait at the top of the stairs while he helps Nancy down to the door first, then comes back and orders me to climb on his back.

'You'll kill yourself on these stairs one day,' he warns as we make our way down, but this just makes me laugh all over again.

'Let's have another beer,' I say as soon as we're inside, heading to the fridge only to begin swearing in earnest. Claudette has drunk my entire stash. Of course she has.

'Bloody Claudette!' I rage, slamming the fridge door and seeing Tom wince as all the items inside fall over.

'I need to be sick,' announces Nancy, and vanishes into the bathroom.

'Don't make that face,' I scold, as Tom does a

convincing impression of a wounded ferret. 'Nancy and me are friends now! Sisters! Isn't that what you wanted?'

He eyes me with distrust.

'Why now? Why today?'

It's a good question, and I think about answering until I spy a packet of crisps on the coffee table.

'Cheese and onion!' I cry, falling on the bag and stuffing a handful into my mouth. 'My favourite.'

I can't understand why Tom looks so upset. We've been drunk together too many times to recount, and he knows how much I love crisps. Why isn't he happy for me?

'She'll be okay,' I tell him as I chew. 'Nancy, I mean. She's just had a few too many.'

'She's not as bad as you,' he says grimly, and I narrow my eyes at him.

'You're no fun these days,' I reply, kicking off my flip-flop only to have it fly straight up in the air and hit me in the face. Tom doesn't even laugh.

'What happened to my fun friend, Tom?' I ask him. 'Where did he go? Go and get him. I miss him.'

Tom sighs at this and sits down beside me.

'I'm right here,' he says, searching my face with his eyes. He's wearing a blue polo shirt today that makes him look very handsome, and he's even swapped those terrible floral shorts for a plain black pair. He must have gone shopping by himself, because I certainly didn't take him. Wonders will never cease.

'I miss you,' I say again, not entirely sure where the words are coming from, then pick up his nearest hand in both of mine.

'You don't have to miss me, I'm right here,' he says, so

quietly that I almost don't hear him, and for a second I wish I could kiss him. It would be easier than trying to find all the words I want to say to him – words which are, at the moment, lingering hidden at the bottom of a well filled with beer in my head.

'Hannah . . .' he begins, but the sound of the toilet flushing distracts him. Nancy appears in the bathroom doorway looking even more ill than she did this morning, and in a moment Tom is beside her, ushering her towards the bedroom. I should go and help him really, check that Nancy is okay and tell her how glad I am that we spent the day together, but the sofa is so darn comfortable.

I'll just lie down here for a few minutes, I think. Just until Tom comes back, and then I'll tell him how sorry I am for being so hammered, and how happy I am that we're best friends again, just as we've always been, like we're supposed to be. The thought is enough to comfort me, and before long my eyes close and everything dissolves into sleep.

Alas, as is always the case when you drink like Oliver Reed with an unquenchable thirst all day long and forget to alternate your beers with water, I wake up a few hours later with an achingly full bladder and a throat like knotted old rope. Claudette's bedroom door is shut, but my own is ajar, and I'm definitely not prepared for what I see when I peer through the crack into the gloom.

There on my bed, his arms wrapped around her and contented expressions of slumber on both their faces, are Nancy and Tom. I'm not sure whether it's the result of suddenly sobering up or if I'm just still very drunk, but when I tiptoe back to the sofa and pull a blanket over myself, I find that I cannot stop crying.

28

I wake abruptly to the sound of very loud and very insistent knocking.

'What the hell?' I grumble, staggering up and immediately squinting as a shaft of sunlight rattles through my hungover brain like a circular saw.

'OKAY!' I yell through the wooden door, pushing my hair off my face. The banging is so loud that it's scaring me, which in turn is making me angry. Sliding the security chain across first, I inch open the door and arrange my features into a glare.

'Oh, it's you.'

Carlos looks mutinous out on the steps, his curly mop pushed back with a plastic hairband and a bottle of beer dangling from one hand. It doesn't take a genius to realise that he's been up all night, and the smell of alcohol on his breath makes me take a step backwards.

'Can I come inside, Hannah?' he says slowly, but it doesn't sound like a question.

'What do you want, Carlos?' I ask. His eyes are bloodshot as he looks at me, and I can sense a quiet disgruntlement radiating off him. He takes a deep breath before replying, and as he moves slightly to the left I catch sight of Ignacio behind him. He is also holding a half-empty bottle of beer and – rather more worryingly – a motorcycle helmet.

'Where is Claudette?' Carlos demands, pushing in vain against the door. Thank God he's one of the small Spanish men, and not a great hairy beast like Diego.

'In bed, I assume,' I tell him, but he doesn't seem to understand and shakes his head.

'No! Where is she?'

'Hang on,' I say, slamming the door shut in his face and heading straight to Claudette's room. She can blooming well deal with her own drunk Spanish boyfriend.

The empty bed stares back at me vacantly, unmade but not slept in recently either. I suddenly feel very sick indeed.

'She's not here,' I say through the gap a few moments later.

Carlos throws his hands up in the air and begins to recite what I can only assume are some very bad words indeed in Spanish. While he's taken up with his tantrum, Ignacio steps forward and smiles at me beseechingly.

'Nancy?' he asks hopefully.

I shake my head. 'She's ill,' I tell him, then resort to miming someone puking when he looks puzzled. There's no way I'm letting either one of these leathered idiots across the threshold.

'NANCY!' Ignacio shouts over the top of my head, and I glare at him until my head starts to throb.

'Shhhh! She needs to sleep – and you two are drunk. Go away and sober up.'

'Shut up! Shut up!' Carlos mocks, putting on a stupid girly voice. I think about Tom asleep in the bedroom with Nancy and contemplate calling for him to come and help me – but that would only exacerbate the problem. If Ignacio thinks that Tom has been spooning with his beloved, Lord only knows how he'll react. At the moment, the two of them are just being idiots, but there's an edge with drunkenness that can very quickly descend into something nasty, and I'm not keen on finding out just how bad things could get.

'I'm going to shut the door now,' I tell them, trying my best to sound authoritative, but Ignacio sticks his arm through the gap and tries to reach for the chain.

'Get off!' I demand, slapping his hand until he pulls it back.

'I love her!' he cries, just as I push the door shut for the second time. 'Nancy! I love you more than nothing in the world!'

Nothing in the world? Wow. What a compliment, I think, amused by Ignacio's declaration despite my hammering heart. I can hear the two of them talking on the other side of the door, but I have no idea what they're saying. In the end, thankfully, I hear the sound of their trainers heading back up the stone steps, and a few minutes later the splutter of a moped engine firing up.

'Have they gone?'

Wheeling around, I find Nancy standing a few feet behind me. Her hair is a mess and she's clutching one of the apartment's scratchy brown blankets around herself.

'Yes, I think so,' I tell her. 'How are you feeling?'

'Awful.' She gives me a half-smile. 'You?'

'Like my head's been used as a bongo.'

'I've got some paracetamol in my bag,' she offers, and I nod a thanks, following her back down the hallway and heading into the kitchen to get us both a glass of water.

'Are you not having any?' I ask when she comes back with just two tablets, but Nancy shakes her head.

'I'm okay.'

'Must have been that tactical chunder you had,' I say, then regret it immediately because the mere thought makes me want to hurl too.

'Is Tom not up yet?' I enquire casually, and Nancy wraps the blanket around her shoulders a fraction tighter.

'He went to get breakfast about half an hour ago.'

Just as she says it, we hear the sound of the key in the lock and a grunt as the chain prevents the door from opening. I hurry across to let Tom in, immediately clocking a paper bag in one of his hands.

'Oh good, you're up,' he says to me. 'Put the kettle on, would you?'

I do as I'm told, not because I would ever let Tom tell me what to do or even because I remotely want a cup of tea, but just because I've slipped into a sort of numb trance. The same question keeps repeating itself over and over in my mind: where is Claudette?

Nancy goes into the bedroom to get dressed, and Tom joins me in the kitchen, his kindly face a picture of concern.

'I'm worried about Nancy,' he whispers, passing me the sugar.

'She's just hungover,' I hiss back.

If Claudette didn't stay with Carlos last night, and she wasn't here, then where was she?

'What were you talking about yesterday?' Tom asks, and I squint at him in confusion.

'Oh, you mean Nancy,' I say, the events of the previous day swimming to the front of my mind with regretful clarity. 'I told her the truth about my dad. She, er . . . She didn't know the whole story, you know, about him leaving my mum for hers.'

I assume Tom will condemn me for this, but instead he just looks wistful.

'I think it's a good thing that the two of you talked it out,' he says eventually, stirring the tea when it becomes apparent that I'm not going to. 'You needed a good heart-to-heart.'

I suppose he's right about that, but I can't muster up enough energy to say anything in response.

'Though I suppose it could have stirred things up, unsettled her,' he adds, and I nod slowly.

Where the hell is Claudette? She can't be where I think she is. She just can't be.

'Like I said, she's always been my dad's little princess,' I tell him quietly, leaving him in the kitchen while I wander away to find my phone. There's only six per cent battery left, but I don't have any messages waiting for me – not from Theo or from our absent French friend. My guts are now churning so much that I have to sit down.

'But she's been out of sorts since she arrived,' Tom persists, sitting down beside me on the sofa. 'Since before she found out that your dad behaved like an arse.'

I force myself to stop thinking about Claudette.

'She was snogging Diego a few hours after she landed,' I point out, not unkindly, but I still notice the hurt on Tom's face.

'But is that out of character?' he demands.

I should have the answer. Nancy is my half-sister after all, but in truth I have no idea. My opinion of her is based on how she was when we were teenagers and what I've seen during my secret social-media stakeouts. I haven't actually spent any quality time with her since I started university, which was ten whole years ago. Aside from birthdays and that awful graduation lunch my dad made us all go on, I've barely seen her.

'I honestly don't know,' I admit then, turning my eyes to Tom. 'I've been such a terrible sister, haven't I?'

'Oh Han.' Tom pulls me against him as the tears threaten. It's really not like me to cry all over him, not ever. Well, not unless they're tears of laughter, which they so often are when the two of us are together.

'Don't be so hard on yourself,' he soothes, squeezing me until I have to pull back in order to breathe. 'It's not been easy for either of you.'

'When did you get to be so wise?' I grumble, and he laughs gently.

'A compliment from Hannah Hodges – bloody hell, girl, you must have drunk a lot last night.'

'Shut up,' I mutter, but he's got me smiling again.

The bedroom door opens and Tom lets go of me before Nancy reappears. I try not to be offended, but my insides are twisting like honeysuckle around a trellis. An image of Claudette at Theo's villa assaults me – the two of them toasting the success of the day's filming, drinking a whole bottle of wine then opening another. But she wouldn't have stayed over with him, would she? He would never have let her, not now he's with me.

Tom has picked up a bag of magdalena cakes for breakfast, and I break one into pieces now and absent-mindedly post it into my mouth. They're incredibly sweet and moist, but light, too. It's just a shame that everything tastes like old feet on my hungover, bitter tongue.

Nancy seems to be struggling with hers, too, and is now folding the paper case into quarters rather than eating the actual cake. Tom, who wolfed his own down in three mouthfuls, is looking at the two of us like a concerned parent.

'Come on, eat up!' he chivvies, and I smile weakly at him over the rim of my mug. 'We have to be up in the square to begin filming in half an hour,' he reminds me, and I groan in dismay.

'I think I'll stay here today,' Nancy puts in, bringing her knees up to her chest and wrapping her arms around them. 'I'm not really feeling up to it.'

'Can I get you anything?' Tom is quick to ask. 'Something different to eat, or some painkillers?'

She smiles. 'No, thank you. I'll be fine. Just need to sleep it off.'

'Well, don't answer the door if those idiots come back,' I say, and then explain to Tom what happened with Carlos and Ignacio.

'Nothing in the world?' he asks when I'm through, clearly amused.

'I know,' I agree, traipsing to the kitchen to dump my empty cup in the sink. 'His English isn't the greatest. But he was trying, to be fair to him.'

'I'll be back to check on you in a few hours,' I tell Nancy twenty minutes later. A shower and change of clothes has gone some way towards making me feel less of a slug, but a solid fist of dread is still clamped over my heart.

The door has barely shut behind us before Tom starts up again.

'She's not eating either,' he says, refusing my offer of help in carrying the camera bag. 'She's definitely been sick more than once, too. I think she might be bulimic.'

'She's not bulimic!' I argue. 'She's just hungover.'

'But last night, when we got back here, she said, "I need to be sick,"' Tom persists. 'Not "I think" or "I feel", she used the word "need".'

'Don't you think you could be reading too much into it because you fancy her?' I reply, careful not to sound too accusatory. 'Isn't it more likely that she's a bit of a lightweight who suffers from bad hangovers?'

'I suppose.' He's grumpy with me now, but I'm too tired and wobbly to appease him. In truth, I'm getting a bit fed up of him fussing around my sister as if she's a complicated sculpture made out of playing cards.

Neither of us mention Claudette. I don't because I'm too scared of Tom confirming my fears, and Tom is presumably too scared to be the one to confirm them. He doesn't need to, though, because when we reach the square ten minutes later, everything becomes horribly, gut-wrenchingly clear.

29

'The archway of the original Arabic door into the city was rebuilt in the sixteenth century, and it has remained unchanged ever since. Once upon a time, this was the spot at which visitors would be stopped by guards and asked to pay in order to enter, and the Mojácar village shield is still here on the brickwork above us.' Claudette turns slightly and points upwards to where the gold and pale blue crest is clearly visible against the white stone. Below it, just above the curve of the arch, is a small wooden door giving on to a tiny balcony. In true Mojácar tradition, this narrow ledge is decorated with a sprawl of bougainvillea, the dark pink petals so bright that they appear almost artificial.

The scene is so perfect, so epic in terms of its history and important to the narrative of our story, but I can't appreciate a single thing about it. I'm seething with unspent rage, my throat welded shut by the glue of unsaid words, and my body twitching with palpable unease.

Claudette stayed the night at the villa. She spent the night with Theo.

The most infuriating aspect of the entire situation is that neither of them seem to be remotely guilt-ridden. On the contrary, Claudette started moaning about the fact she was having to wear one of Theo's shirts almost as soon as Tom and I arrived, while the man himself simply strolled over and kissed me on the cheek as if nothing was awry.

AS IF NOTHING WAS AWRY!

As we made our way through the Old Town streets to the archway, Tom kept glancing nervously at each of us in turn, as though waiting for something to erupt, but I'm damned if I'm going to say anything. I know Claudette well enough now to realise when she's enjoying herself, and that's exactly what she's been doing all morning. She knows full well that I'm upset with her – with both her and Theo – and I can tell she's going to do her best to tease me for the rest of the day. Well, she can try. I'm going to rise above it. I'm not going to make a fool of myself.

'Hannah?'

From Theo's tone of voice, I suspect it's not the first time he's tried to get my attention.

'Yes?'

'The script. Can you help Claudette, please?'

'Of course.' I smile sweetly at him and step forward, ignoring Claudette's smarmy expression and waiting while she repeats the next few sentences back to me. It's not like her to need this much help with her lines, so I can only assume she's doing this on purpose to rile me. The next time it happens, I catch her unawares.

'Your boyfriend was over this morning looking for you,' I tell her, the smile never leaving my face. 'He seemed very upset when I told him you weren't in.'

Claudette narrows her eyes, but only loses her cool for a split second.

'Poor little boy,' she says dreamily. 'I will cheer him up later, don't you worry.'

I want to yell in her face that she's a vile cowpat, but instead I smile back demurely.

In the end, thanks to Claudette stalling on her lines and tourists wandering into shot, it takes far longer than Theo had planned to get the archway scene finished, and he doesn't let us stop for a proper lunch break. I'm not sure whether he's ignoring me on purpose or whether he's just totally caught up with the filming, but either way I don't get to talk to him until much later that afternoon, when we've changed location and are down by La Fuente at a pop-up table-top sale. The owner of the jazz club where we filmed the other day tipped Theo off about this place, as it's a favourite haunt for many of the ex-pats who have made Mojácar their home. I look around in the hope of seeing Elaine but there's no sign of her, so instead I approach the customers browsing through the goods, striking up a conversation and then inviting them to talk a bit about Mojácar on camera. I love this part of my job the most, meeting new people and hearing their stories, and today more than ever it feels important to be able to lean on my job for support. I seem to be failing at other key aspects of my life at the moment, so it's reassuring when these strangers respond well to me. Theo seems happy, too, if a little distracted, and I wish I could go over and kiss him, perhaps rub his shoulders or his neck. I can't, though – and not just because we're in public. I can't shake off the image of him and Claudette alone together in his villa, and now I'm back to being struck virtually mute whenever I'm near him.

There's so much available to buy here, from antiques to clothing to jewellery and even furniture. I suppose it's the Spanish equivalent of a UK car boot sale, and I regret not bringing my purse out with me when I see how many nice little gifts I could have picked up. I'm particularly drawn to a gold necklace with an Indalo Man charm, and I pick it up and finger it in wonder.

'He will bring you luck,' the stall owner tells me, but as I put the necklace back down he notices my tattoo.

'Ah, I see that you know the Indalo.'

'Yes,' I smile at him. 'I do indeed.'

'And has he brought you luck?' the man wants to know. 'Has he kept you safe?'

I think about how happy I was waking up in Theo's arms yesterday, and how wretched I feel today, knowing that he let Claudette stay with him, and almost shake my head. But he looks so hopeful and sincere, that instead I tell him yes.

'What have you discovered?'

I turn to find Tom at my elbow, and point to the necklace.

'Why don't you get it?'

'It doesn't work like that,' I explain. 'You can only give the Indalo as a gift, you can't buy one for yourself.'

'Then I'll get it for you,' Tom offers immediately, and the man behind the table claps his hands in delight.

'No, no,' I say, stopping him before he can fish out his wallet. 'I already have my tattoo, remember? I don't need another Indalo.'

'Oh.' I'm not sure who's more crestfallen, the man who wants the sale or Tom, who has pushed his sunglasses up into his hair to give me the benefit of his sad eyes.

'Come on.' I lead him away, apologising to the man over my shoulder as we head back towards the other two.

'Are you okay?' Tom asks, and I feel tears welling up yet again.

I can't answer, so instead I just nod, biting down on my bottom lip to steady myself. Claudette, meanwhile, has charmed another local and Tom is called away to film the interview. Theo and I are finally alone, but I have no idea what to say to him.

'You are very quiet today, Hannah,' he says after a time, not turning to look at me. There's a trail of clouds crossing the sky today, and every few minutes, one will pass in front of the sun, dappling the grey tarmac of the car park we're in and turning Theo's eyes from dark brown to jet black.

'I'm okay,' I tell him, staring hard at a really ugly bronze model of a donkey on a nearby table.

'You are not yourself,' he says, stating it as a fact rather than asking me.

'I am,' I lie, shaking my head. 'I'm fine.'

'Somebody has upset you,' he replies, his tone inching towards playful. 'Shall I guess who?'

Why is he doing this? Why is he being deliberately cruel?

I shrug, and he blows air out through his nostrils as if he's exasperated.

'It is not like you to be this way,' he tells me, running a finger along my bare arm, which causes me to quiver with pleasure. My body is betraying me, but I can't help it. I'm putty around those long, tanned fingers of his – he knows it just as well as I do.

'I'm just tired,' I murmur, my voice more conciliatory now that he's touching me again. 'Claudette's boyfriend turned up banging on the door first thing this morning looking for her.'

'Oh dear.' Theo is clearly amused by this little nugget of information, which isn't the response I was after. He should be alarmed or at the very least sympathetic, but he's neither.

'So I hear Claudette stayed with you last night. Did you two just get drunk and pass out?' I ask him then, hating myself for needing to know, and loathing the way my question sounds so full of hope.

Theo doesn't answer straight away, and I fear I may have stepped over the line into inappropriate, but then he reaches for my hand.

'Hannah, you don't need to worry,' he assures me. 'I did not invite Claudette over for the same reasons that I ask you.'

He sounds genuine, and when I look into his eyes, I find that I believe him. So Claudette stayed over at his – so what? They go on these shoots abroad together all the time, and it stands to reason that they would be friends. She's just winding me up by letting me believe something more happened. This is my darling Theo – the man I have loved for as long as I can remember. I don't really believe that he's capable of sleeping with Claudette right under my nose – he's just not that person. She very easily might be, but he isn't.

I return the pressure of his grasp, and he leans across and gives me the briefest kiss on the side of my mouth before letting go and heading over to where the others have just finished.

I was so silly to freak out. Theo's right, I don't have anything to worry about – he's still just as into me as he was yesterday, and nothing's changed between us. But if that really is the case, then why won't this creeping sense of impending doom go away? No matter how many times I tell myself that everything is all right, my body refuses to settle down. Perhaps I should have let Tom buy me that Indalo necklace after all, because something in the very depths of my churning guts is telling me that I'm going to need all the good luck and protection I can possibly get.

By the time five p.m. arrives and the Old Town shutters begin to close around us for siesta, I'm so shattered that I can barely stand up straight. Clearly I can't handle the booze as well as I once could, because my hangover has been getting steadily worse throughout the day rather than better. As we're so close to the apartment, I use the excuse of needing to check on Nancy to head back and get my thoughts in order. I know that Theo is likely to summon me to the villa in a few hours, but I feel slightly reluctant to go. It's not that I don't trust Theo or believe that anything happened between him and Claudette, it just feels almost as if the villa is the scene of a crime, and I know I won't be able to shake off that feeling for a while. I can't risk behaving in a way that might put Theo off, not when I've done so well getting him to like me.

I'm still mulling it all over when I reach the front door, but as I raise the key to the lock I hear shouting coming from inside. It's Nancy, and she sounds angry. Very angry indeed.

'I know he's there!' she yells, her voice high and accusatory. 'I'm not going to stop calling – he can't hide from me forever!'

What the hell is going on? Has she called Dad and he's refusing to speak to her?

There's a pause, presumably while whoever it is on the other end of the phone is talking, and then Nancy starts up again.

'No, I'm not! No, it's his fault. How dare you say that to me?'

Should I go in there? I don't know what to do.

'Oh, so that's the way it is now, is it? You and him? Oh, I might have guessed. You've always been after him. I've seen you looking at him.'

She's definitely not talking about Dad. At least, I really hope she's not . . .

'Don't you dare hang up on me!' she rages now, and I wince at the menace in her voice. So much for Nancy being a quiet little earwig over the past few days. Clearly she's been saving up all her energy for this.

'BITCH!' I hear her cry, followed by the sound of something smashing, and it's this that propels me through the door. Nancy is standing out on the balcony amidst the remains of what was once a coffee mug, her arms folded and her shoulders shaking.

'What the hell's going on?' I ask, and she swings around in surprise.

'Hannah! Hi, sorry, I just dropped a mug. Sorry, I'll pay for it.'

'I don't care about the bloody mug,' I tell her. 'I heard you shouting at someone.'

'That was just my friend Amy,' she says, wiping the tears angrily off her cheeks. 'Well, she's not my friend any more.'

I open my mouth to ask what Amy's done, but before I can get a word out Nancy cuts across me.

'Where's Tom?'

'He's . . . Er, I think he's gone home.'

'Can we go there?'

'Yeah, I guess so. If you want to.'

She flashes her teeth at me, but it's about as convincing a smile as the ones I've been giving Claudette all day.

'I need to get changed,' she says, and stomps past me.

There is something very odd going on, I realise, fetching the dustpan and brush and sweeping up the shards of china. Maybe Tom has been right all this time and there is more to Nancy's slightly weird behaviour than simply a few heavy nights. As much as I hate the idea of calling Dad, I fear it might be time. If he's the reason behind all this, then I need to know.

When I take out my phone, however, it immediately starts to ring in my hand.

Theo.

I stare at his name on the screen, flicking off the ringer and waiting until he gives up and ends the call. As predicted, a message arrives a few seconds later.

'Come to the villa. Now.'

I could weep with the longing I feel for him, and the desire to be close to him again is almost enough to break down my resolve, but then I remember Nancy. I can't leave her alone, not now, not after what I've just witnessed. It's not Tom's job to look after her, I know that now. It's mine.

With trembling fingers and a frantically hammering heart, I quickly type back a reply.

Nancy still not well, sorry. See you tomorrow, I promise. H xxx

I press send and watch while the message registers as delivered. After what feels like an age, Theo responds.

Ok.

No kisses, no concern for my sister, no nothing. I've blown it, haven't I? After years of waiting for my dream man to notice me, I've gone and fallen at the first hurdle. How could I have let this happen? And how the hell am I going to fix it?

'Shall we go?'

Nancy is standing ready behind me, her make-up immaculate and a flowing duck-egg blue dress making her eyes gleam. She looks beautiful, and for the first time in my entire life, I tell her so.

30

'I'm going to miss seeing these mountains every day.'

'Hampstead Heath isn't quite the same, is it?' Tom agrees, gazing out across the water to where the dark brown masses of centuries-old earth stand like sentries along the coastline.

'The colours, too,' I add, lifting my sunglasses so I can fully appreciate the fresh cobalt of the Mediterranean sweeping against the golden shore. The sky above us is the same piercing shade of blue that Disney animators choose for their princesses' eyes, and so ever-reaching that it makes me feel dizzy to behold it.

We've been sitting on the sand for about half an hour now, having dropped Nancy off at the beach bar on the way down here, but both Claudette and Theo are running behind schedule. While I fully expect it of her, it's not like our boss to be tardy, and I've been driving Tom mad by checking my phone every few minutes. I'm desperate to see him, but terrified at the same time. Will he even be speaking to me after I rejected his offer last night?

Claudette has obviously made up with Carlos, because a few minutes later she arrives on the back of his moped and kisses him goodbye for long enough to earn herself some puking noises from Tom and me. She's also very clearly chosen to forget about the frostiness between the two of us yesterday, because after flinging her bag down on to the sand, she greets me with an enthusiastic kiss on each cheek.

'Good night?' guesses Tom, and she smiles knowingly.

'That stinks,' I remark, holding my nose as Carlos speeds away in a cloud of dust and petrol fumes, but Claudette doesn't hear me because she's too busy pulling off her dress over her head.

'What?' she demands, looking at Tom and me as we exchange a glance. 'I need to make the most of this weather while we are still here. There is as much chance of proper sunshine in England as there is of Tom having sex again before he is forty.'

'Nice,' Tom deadpans, and I chuckle at the two of them, grateful that some of the past week's tension seems to have finally eased. I'm still not entirely happy with Claudette for a number of reasons, but I just can't muster up the energy to be annoyed with her today. My mind keeps straying back to Nancy and the phone call I overheard last night. She refused to talk about it on the walk up to Tom's apartment, and then proceeded to persuade him and me to go to Diego's restaurant for dinner. The cynical part of my mind suspected that, not content with spooning and doing heaven knows what else with Tom and fooling around with Ignacio, Nancy was now planning to have some more fun with my teenage amour. However, when we got there, she barely spoke two words to Diego all night. In fact, she was so despondent in her responses to his over-the-top flirting that I ended up feeling sorry for the guy.

'Where is Nancy?' is Claudette's predictable next question.

'At the beach bar,' I tell her, pulling my vest top away

from my back before it adheres itself to the sweat. The temperature is rising by the minute, and it's so hot now that I've had to dig little holes in the sand for my feet to sit in because the top layer is burning my skin.

'Where is our esteemed leader?' Tom asks Claudette, but she's now lying flat on her towel and so ignores him.

'Should I call him?' I say out loud, but not to anyone in particular. 'I should, shouldn't I? Just to check that everything's okay.'

'Whatever you think.' Tom is dismissive. He's wearing a cap today to keep the sun out of his eyes, and his hair is sticking out above his ears. I reach up to tuck it in for him as I press the button to call, but as soon as I do, a ringing sound comes from directly behind us, causing both Tom and me to jump round in surprise. Claudette, of course, hasn't even flinched.

'That was me, sorry!' I tell Theo, getting to my feet so quickly that I don't notice the fact that my skirt is stuck inside my bikini bottoms.

'She was worried about you,' puts in Tom, yanking it back out for me.

'Worried? Why?' Theo looks distracted, and steps past us before I have a chance to answer.

'Tom!' he barks.

'Boss?'

'Get the camera set up. We should capture these fishermen here.'

That's Theo all over, noticing the human element of the setting while the rest of us are merely hypnotised by the view of the landscape. Well, I say the rest of us – Claudette has had her eyes resolutely shut since she arrived.

The fishermen are, in fact, fisher-boys, judging by their skinny little limbs and unlined faces, which break open in wide grins as I make my way along the concrete jetty to ask if it's okay to include them in our film.

'*Sí, sí, sí!*' they trumpet happily, taking it in turns to flex their non-existent muscles and swing their rods into the air.

'You'll scare the fish!' I tell them, but this only causes even more laughter, and I can sense Theo's irritation burning a hole in the back of my skull. By the time I've managed to explain that all we want them to do for us is to sit or stand still, exactly as they were doing before, and quelled the inevitable demonstrative outpouring of argument that they all put up, a good fifteen minutes have passed. Add that to the forty-five or so that we were already behind schedule this morning and you've got yourself one grumpy Greek director.

'Someone got out of bed on the wrong side,' mutters Tom under his breath as we eventually break for lunch. Theo has grudgingly agreed to stop for a quick bite to eat at a bakery-cum-café on the opposite side of the road to the beach, but not even the smell of freshly deep-fried churros seems able to rouse him from his melancholy. I wish I could cheer him up with a kiss, but I know it's a bad idea. It's as if his ill temper is holding up a hand, telling the three of us not to come any closer under any circumstances. Could it all be down to the fact that I refused his offer last night? I don't have enough of an ego to believe it. So what, then?

Tom has apparently forgotten that he ate a pizza the size of a tractor wheel for dinner last night and has ordered himself another slice for lunch. I find that I can't face food, which is very unlike me, so I order a fruit salad in a panic and then have to endure Claudette talking at length about how fortunate she is that she never has to diet.

'I just don't gain weight,' she says breezily, and I'm sure I can hear the sound of twenty thousand or so women gritting their teeth in unison.

Theo ignores her and rubs his temples with two long, tanned fingers.

'Are you okay?' I ask at last, being sure to keep my voice at a murmur level.

Theo stops rubbing and sighs.

'I'm sorry,' I whisper, but he shakes his head a fraction.

The waitress arrives with our second round of drinks and a bowl of salted almonds to go with them, which Tom dives into despite the fact he's still chewing on a mouthful of his main course.

'Ah, almonds,' Claudette cries, clapping her hands together. 'Theo, shall we ask for some Manchego to go with them?'

There's a loud crash as my spoon hits the bowl of fruit salad.

'If you want,' Theo says, eyeing his coffee but not picking it up, and Claudette lifts an arm to attract attention.

Manchego and almonds! my brain shouts at me, stamping its feet for effect.

'Man . . .' I begin, but the word withers and dies before it's out of my mouth. Tom stops tackling the large, stringy lump of mozzarella that he was attempting to swallow and frowns at me.

She knows about the Manchego and almonds, my memory

pipes up, this time settling for a large metaphorical elbow in the ribs. I haven't picked up my spoon from where I dropped it, and now my cheeks have turned the same colour as the watermelon chunks in my salad.

'Oh yum,' Claudette says happily as the waitress returns with the cheese. 'Cumin seeds as well – *très bon*!'

I watch in horrified awe as she snatches up Theo's side plate and spoons a selection of nuts and Manchego on to it, before returning to her own lunch.

How does she know about this odd flavour sensation? Theo only told me – that night at the villa, the night that we kissed for the very first time.

But she knows about it, too. Claudette knows and either Theo told her, or she taught him. I'm not sure which is worse, but at this moment the idea of either explanation is making me feel like I want to throw up the few pieces of orange I managed to eat.

'Hannah?'

I glance in Tom's direction.

'Are you okay? You look like you've seen a ghost.'

'I'm fine,' I parrot automatically, reminding myself acutely of Nancy.

Why do people always say that? Is it just the inbred nature of all British people to tell another person that they're fine when in reality they're absolutely anything but? You could be in an ambulance with your torso on one stretcher and your legs on another, and you'd still try to persuade the bloke driving the thing to hospital that you were 'fine to walk there'. Lunacy.

The thing is, Tom knows me far better than Theo or Claudette do, and therefore he knows that for some reason the bottom has just fallen out of my world, and now he's trying to communicate with me across the table through the medium of mime.

'Why are you flapping your arms?' Claudette enquires, her words seasoned with a large spoonful of disdain.

Tom stops doing an impression of an injured pigeon and looks at me knowingly. What does he want me to do, stand up and announce loudly that I think Theo and Claudette have been having it off in between feeding each other nuts and cheese? That she knows things that he shared with me in an intimate setting?

In the end, I don't get to say or do anything, because Claudette is suddenly up on her feet and is rushing towards the door.

'Mon dieu!' she exclaims, turning back to face us. 'It is raining.'

'It hardly ever rains here,' I say stupidly, echoing what Elaine told me by La Fuente the very first time we met. It is raining, though. I can hear it. And now that Claudette has pushed open the doors, I can smell it, too.

'There's nothing like rain in a hot country to remind you just how hot it really is,' marvels Tom, pointing down at the steaming pavement tiles on the other side of the glass. I have a sudden and utterly ridiculous urge to run out and start dancing in it, but of course I don't. Not here, not when Theo is watching.

'Shall we film it?' Claudette wants to know, but our director shakes his handsome head.

'No, I don't think so. I think the magic of the rain here is as Tom says, in the smell and the feel. It will be difficult to translate that into film. I fear that it will simply look like rain, and the audience will associate it with the coldness they are used to in England. I don't want that.'

It's the most Theo's said all day, and both Tom and I look at him in surprise.

I'm torn between reaching across the table to hold his hand and upending the bloody Manchego cheese with cumin seeds on his head. In the end, I settle for neither, which it turns out is a good decision because as soon as it becomes clear that this rain isn't going anywhere fast, Theo looks me in the eye for the first time all day and tells me he'll drive me over to Elaine's studio for my next interview.

'Oh no, I'll be fine,' I say. Predictable as ever.

He fixes me with one of those no-nonsense gazes of his.

'I insist.'

31

Theo wraps his arm around my shoulders as we leave the cover of the café and head out into the rain. He's managed to conjure up a newspaper from somewhere and holds it up over our heads like a makeshift umbrella. It's a noble gesture, but totally ineffectual against the onslaught, and by the time we've slipped and slid across the road to where the car is parked, the two of us are drenched.

'Bloody hell!' I exclaim as soon as the doors are shut behind us, laughing as I wring out my hair. The rain is crashing down on the roof of the car so loudly that Theo has to shout his reply.

'Crazy!'

We look at each other, and finally, blissfully, Theo cracks a smile. His wet fringe is plastered to his forehead and the shoulders of his pale blue shirt are navy where they got soaked. Feeling all of a sudden very brave and totally unlike myself, I launch my body across the space between us and kiss him, gratified when he responds with an enthusiasm that I had feared he was no longer feeling.

'Hannah,' he says, when we pull apart for air, but I don't let him finish. I kiss him again and again until the windows turn white with condensation and the two of us are clawing at each other.

Take me back to the villa! I want to scream at him, but I don't. I may be brave enough to kiss him, but I draw the line at telling him what to do. He is a proud Greek man, and I get the impression he wouldn't appreciate me issuing him with instructions. In the moment, though, I don't care about the fact that Elaine is waiting for me or that Tom and Claudette can probably see us from over the road – I'm simply consumed by what I'm feeling. I needed this kiss as a reassurance from him that everything is okay, and that it's just pure coincidence that the day after Claudette crashed out at his villa she started talking about almonds and Manchego. I can't bear to consider the alternative – I'm just not ready for my idyllic Theo bubble to be burst yet.

'Hannah,' he tries again, and this time I drop my hands down from the sides of his face into my lap.

'Yes?'

'We have to go.'

Really? He's really going to make me go and sit with Elaine when all I want him to do is tear off my clothes and ravage me?

'Hannah.'

'Yes, okay. Let's go.' I don't mean to sound peeved, but my mouth betrays my brain as usual and Theo puts his head on one side and frowns at me.

'You need to tell me where I am going,' he points out, his hands on the steering wheel. 'I don't know which way to drive.'

Of course he doesn't. Why would he? I'm such an idiot.

'Sorry, sorry!' I tell him, braving a squeeze of his slightly damp thigh.

He doesn't say anything this time, and so I begin issuing directions, trying not to feel upset by the abrupt way he's distanced himself from me. When I'm kissing Theo, or when I'm in bed with him, I get these flashes where I feel as if he's devouring me, that I'm the only thing he's thinking about and that together the two of us are invincible. It never translates into the everyday, though, because as soon as his hands or mouth aren't on me and there are other people around, that closeness evaporates and I'm left trying desperately to scrabble it back.

I think about what Elaine said on the bus all those weeks ago, about the nature of love – isn't love by its very essence all-consuming and mutually passionate? How can I be in love with Theo when I'm constantly having to reach for that feeling, only to find it always just out of my grasp?

I mull this over as we drive, Theo being extra-cautious on the roads because of the still-pounding rain. It's ridiculous for me to think that he shares my feelings. I may have been lusting after him for years, but clearly he's only caught up with me since we've been here in Mojácar and he's got to know the Spain version of me. Plus, he's Theo and I'm me. He could take his pick from all the women in the world, so why would he settle for someone like me, with hardly any sophistication and even less sexual prowess?

'Is this it?' Theo asks, snapping me back to the present moment.

The entrance to Elaine's studio is just ahead of us on the right, and I try not to groan as Theo indicates and turns the car. I just want a few more minutes alone with him. I need to feel that he wants me again, that he cares about me.

'I will see you later?' he says as I unbuckle, and relief floods over me even more powerfully than the rain that's still hammering the roof of the car.

'Yes, please,' I say, and he smiles at that.

As I hurry towards the studio, however, I realise that he didn't say when or what time, and I almost run back to flag him down. It's never occurred to me to feel annoyed about the fact that Theo is always the one in charge, but at this particular moment it does rankle a little bit. Now I know that I'll spend the rest of the afternoon and this evening checking my phone for a text from him, and that I can't make dinner plans, go shopping or even take a nice long shower without worrying that I'll miss it. As much as I want to be the person that Theo desires, I can't help but feel miffed about the unfairness of it all.

'You're soaked!' is the first thing Elaine says to me as she opens the door, and she hurries off in search of a towel while I begin unpacking the equipment. Luckily, Tom had the foresight to order a waterproof bag for his camera – not that any of us ever expected this sort of weather to descend.

'Here.' Elaine has returned and hands me a bright pink beach towel with a picture of Barbie on it.

'It's not mine,' she adds, as I raise an eyebrow, and the two of us exchange a smile. She seems slightly subdued today, though – not her usual warm self – and answers my flurry of polite questions with monosyllables. I hope she hasn't changed her mind about allowing us to use the footage. Elaine's story is the human glue keeping the unique dynamic of this film together, and it won't be as good without her input. Claudette may be beautiful, but even the most dedicated admirer needs more than one voice of authority in a documentary like ours.

'Sorry,' she apologises, as yet another of my probing questions fails to elicit more than a few words from her. 'It's the rain, it always makes me feel out of sorts.'

'Good thing you no longer live in England, then,' I joke, but she merely pulls a face.

'Are you okay, Elaine?' I ask, shoving thoughts of Theo aside so I can concentrate fully on her. 'Shall I switch off the camera and we can just talk?'

She shakes her head. 'No, leave it on.'

'There's no pressure on you to say anything you're not comfortable with,' I remind her. 'I would never put anything into this film that you haven't agreed on beforehand.'

'Oh, I know you wouldn't.' She gives me a watery smile. 'You're a good girl.'

I notice now that there's no easel set up in this part of the studio today, and that Elaine herself isn't dressed in her usual paint-splattered smock. Instead she is wearing a shapeless black dress, and it makes her look older somehow.

'Why does the rain make you sad?' I ask gently, and she sighs. For a short time, we simply sit in a companionable silence, and I'm just about to offer to make us both a cup of tea when she starts talking.

'The last summer that I spent in England, it rained almost every day,' she says, looking at the camera rather than me. 'At first people complained about it, but then it seemed to unify everyone. There was a kind of Blitz spirit in and around London – that uniquely British "we're all in it together" feeling. Do you know what I mean?'

I nod. 'I do.'

'I used to walk around in it all day long,' she continues. 'I would arrive home in the evening, drenched right through and shivering, and my mother would barely notice.'

Again, I picture the house that Elaine described to me, graffiti daubed on the walls and the strung-out bodies of random strangers piled up on old furniture.

'He was still there,' she says then, and I feel the hairs on the back of my neck stand up to attention.

'Who's he?' I ask, my tone light.

Elaine sighs again and closes her eyes, her internal struggle clear as it distorts her features.

'I told you, didn't I, how it was for me growing up?' she says, and there's an urgency in her voice that I haven't heard before.

'Yes, you told me,' I soothe. 'You said people were always passing through, and that your mother had an open-door policy to waifs and strays.'

She nods feverishly. 'Yes. And I think that sometimes, these people thought of me as . . .' She stops again and wrings her hands in her lap, her nails digging at the soft flesh between her thumb and forefinger. I hate seeing her like this, so obviously in distress as she digs up the past.

'I'm going to make us both some tea,' I announce, standing up before she can argue. I assume that she'll follow me out into the corridor and along to the little kitchen, but she doesn't, and when I return she takes the hot mug from me with a grateful smile.

'Sorry,' she says again, shaking her head as I tell her not to worry. 'It's just that I haven't talked about what happened for a long time. Not since it happened, in fact.'

I know now that she's going to tell me something bad, and I get the same sensation that I used to as a child, when I'd sit peeling scabs off my knees. I was a clumsy kid and forever falling over, but I was also impatient. I would pick at the edges of my scabs and wince as the skin began to bleed, but that would never be enough to stop me. I'd pick and pick until I could see the wet pink flesh beneath the scab, by which time it would be too late, and the whole process would begin all over again.

'His name was Robert,' Elaine recounts, more matter-of-fact now than emotional. She obviously used the time that I was making tea to get her thoughts in order. 'He was a lot older than even my mother, but he was almost like a child in the way that he talked and behaved. He started following me around the house like I imagine a puppy would, and I was happy to let him tag along in the beginning.'

There's something about the word 'beginning' that makes me shiver.

'My mother was always surrounded by men,' she adds, and I think fleetingly of Claudette. 'She was happy to let them into her house and into her bed, but none of them had ever shown an interest in me. Not until Robert.'

I want to hear what happened, but I also have to sit on my hands to stop myself from clamping them over my ears.

Elaine sips her tea before she continues, the steam wisping off the top mingling with the loose hair around her face. I can still hear the rain, and find that I'm taking comfort from the familiar sound.

'When Robert arrived, it was as if my mother finally

remembered that I was there,' Elaine explains. 'I was seventeen, and like most teenagers I suppose I resented my mother as much as I was desperate for her to love me.'

'You should never feel desperate for a parent to love you,' I say then, an image of my father flashing uninvited into my mind.

'You're right,' Elaine agrees. 'But I don't think my mother knew how to love me then. Perhaps she never did. She was so good at caring for strangers, but she had this strange disconnection when it came to me.'

'And Robert?' I prompt gently.

Elaine sips her tea again. 'He noticed me,' she says simply. 'At that time, it was enough to keep him in my favour. I knew he was too old for me and actually I was quite repulsed by him, but I relished the way that my mother would watch the two of us, as if she couldn't understand why this man would choose to spend his time pursuing me rather than her.'

I feel like I already know how the story is going to end, but I still need Elaine to tell me, even though I know how much it will hurt to hear the words.

'I thought that I was in control of the situation,' she says then, and I can hear the sadness and regret laced in between her words. 'But Robert was a grown man; he was a lot bigger and stronger than me, and . . .'

She stops, a haunted look on her face, and I instinctively reach for her hand to reassure her. There's a silence as we each fill in the gaps in her story in our own minds, and I shake my head to chase away the rogue tears that are threatening.

'Afterwards, he seemed disgusted by me,' Elaine says,

again with that chillingly matter-of-fact tone. 'Perhaps he was disgusted by what he'd allowed himself to do, but I think he blamed me. I think rapists often do blame their victims, as a way of coping with their own guilt.'

The casual way in which she's just mentioned rape shocks me, and I feel an immediate and very strong surge of rage on her behalf.

'Did you go to the police?' I want to know, but she shakes her head.

'No, I went to my mother, which was of course the worst thing that I could have done.'

'Why?' I demand. I can't believe, even after taking into account what Elaine has told me about her free-spirited parent, that a mother would ever do anything other than support her own daughter.

'She told me it was my own fault,' Elaine says, a nonchalant shrug disguising how I know she must really feel. 'She said that I'd led him on, and that this is what happens when you pretend to be a grown woman when you're really still a child.'

'That's horrible!' I cry, and she smiles at me gratefully.

'Yes.'

The rain is falling even harder now, and it's beginning to sound like white noise.

'After that Robert transferred his affections over to another woman in the house, and nothing more was ever said about it. I was supposed to just carry on living my life as if nothing had happened, but how could I?'

'I hate him,' I mutter, vitriol turning my voice into a growl, but I can sense that there is more of the story to come.

'When I found out about the baby, I didn't dare tell my mother,' Elaine says, and I turn to her in alarm.

'A baby?'

She nods, her mouth set in a very thin and firm line.

'I managed to keep it a secret for months, just by wearing loose clothes. I had a part-time job at a market, and I confided in one of the other girls who worked there, but she was the only person I told. I knew that I had to take folic acid and avoid certain foods, so I did all that, but I never visited a doctor or anything. I was too worried about the news getting back to my mum – or even worse, to Robert.'

'He was still there?' I ask, surprised.

Elaine grimaces and wraps her fingers around her mug a little tighter.

'He left before I really started to show,' she says. 'I was relieved, of course, but I was also angry with him. I wanted more than anything for him to be punished, but then at the same time I couldn't bring myself to hate him entirely because I had begun to really love our child. The bond was strong before she even arrived, and I was determined to give her a better childhood than the one I'd had. I wanted to protect her.'

Her voice has grown shaky again as she drags up all these long-buried emotions, and I swear I can feel my heart breaking in sympathy.

'In the end, my mother must have grown suspicious, because she hid in my bedroom while I was taking a bath and caught me getting dressed.'

I must have gasped at this, because Elaine turns to me in concern.

'She wasn't very impressed, as I'm sure you can imagine, which even then I knew was ironic given how she made believe to the rest of the world that she was some sort of earth mother.'

'Unbelievable,' I mutter darkly, and Elaine narrows her eyes in agreement.

'She dragged me along to a doctor and told this man that I was unstable, that I could not be trusted with a baby and that she wasn't prepared to look after it. There was a big argument and I ran out into the street – it was all very dramatic.' She looks almost apologetic as she tells me this part of the story.

'Of course it was – how could it not be?' I rant. 'I'm sorry, Elaine, but your mum sounds like a right piece of work to me.'

Again, that quiet nod of the head.

'My mother was adamant that I put the baby up for adoption,' she says, turning to face me before continuing. 'But I didn't come to that decision because of her; I did it to give my daughter the chance of a better life. I could have kept her, but that would have been selfish. We would have struggled for money and there was no father in the picture. I wanted her to have the life I hadn't had.'

It all makes sense when she puts it like that, but I still can't imagine giving up my own child. Then again, isn't that exactly what my father did when he left my mum? Poor Elaine didn't feel like she had a choice, and she'd been put into that position against her own will – but he didn't have either of her excuses for behaving so utterly reprehensibly.

'You poor thing,' I say with feeling, noticing the tears on her cheeks.

'Afterwards,' she continues, suppressing a sob, 'I couldn't even bear to look my mother in the eye. I had a few months to wait until I turned eighteen, and as soon as I did, I got hold of my passport, packed a bag and left. I can remember that day so clearly. It had been raining and the air smelt just like it does today. I sat in Trafalgar Square in the centre of London watching the water fountains and tried to decide what I was going to do, where I was going to go, and then I looked up and saw these two rainbows and it suddenly came back to me, that story Bonita, the broken-hearted Spanish girl, had told me about Mojácar and the Indalo Man with his protective rainbow. I don't know why, but I felt in that moment that if I could make it here, then I would be safe. Safe from my mother and from Robert, but also safe from my own memories and sadness. I was half right, too, because I never have seen my mother or that man again. They could be dead for all I know. Sometimes I hope that they are.'

They're harsh words, but absolutely warranted, and again I feel that protective swell of anger on Elaine's behalf. I want to storm back through the passages of time to rescue the teenage version of this woman, who in just a few weeks has become such an important person to me. I simply cannot bear to even imagine her turmoil, yet here it is in front of me. She has spent the past forty-two years mourning the loss of a child she loved and a mother who never really loved her. It's heartbreaking.

There are so many more questions on the tip of my tongue, so many doors to her story that still remain closed to me, but I can sense that Elaine has finished for the day. She's sitting back on her chair now, her eyes closed and a serene expression on her face. Instead of filling the silence with unnecessary words, I reach across to gently pat her clasped fingers, only for her to slide her hand into mine. For a time, we simply stay as we are, the only sounds our shared breathing and the patter of the still-falling rain.

As I lift my gaze from my lap to the camera, I can see the two of us reflected in the lens – small, warped figures in the domed glass – and realise in that moment just how brave my new friend has been today.

32

The rain continues in earnest for the rest of the afternoon, a low rumble of thunder always threatening but never quite making it as far south as Mojácar. Despite the downpour, I choose to walk back up the hill to the Old Town, enjoying the fragrant aromas coming from the undergrowth as the dry earth turns from a dusty tan to a deep chocolate brown.

Elaine's story has settled into my subconscious, and I feel numbed by it. I'm not sure if I feel sad or angry or just a deep sense of shock, but whatever it is has stilled me. Do I tell Theo what happened? I know instinctively that he will be quietly thrilled that I have extracted such a remarkable story from Elaine, but at the moment I feel uncomfortable about sharing it with him. Obviously Elaine needed to unburden herself, but she may yet change her mind about wanting the story to be included in the documentary, and the least I can do is give her a few days to mull it over. If Theo becomes involved, he will want me to persuade her to give us the green light, and the idea of that makes me itch with discomfort.

I've got as far as the turning to La Fuente when my phone starts vibrating in my pocket. I pull it out, expecting to see Theo's name, but it's Rachel.

'Hey,' I say, my voice slightly crackly. It's an odd time of day for her to call me, given that it's the middle of the afternoon back in the UK and by rights she should be at work. Rachel does some sort of exciting marketing job that I don't really understand, but I know it keeps her extremely busy.

'Are you okay?' she immediately wants to know, and I smile. I forget how long Rachel's known me sometimes. Clearly she can tell from my uneven tone that something is up.

'I'm fine,' I assure her. 'Just been a weird day, and it's raining here.'

'Rain? In Mojácar?' Rachel exclaims.

'I know,' I tell her, ducking under the awning of a gift shop to take shelter. 'I kind of like it, to be honest.'

'Spoken like a true Brit!' she jokes, but her delivery is weak.

'What's up, Rach?' I decide to cut straight through the polite chit-chat.

There's a pause, and I picture my friend at the other end of the line. Her dark red curls and her shining green eyes, the way her neat little nose is peppered with freckles and her nails are bitten down to the quick. I used to tap her hand with my plastic ruler at school whenever I saw her fingers heading towards her mouth, but to be fair to her, nail-biting is probably her only vice. Well, that and Paul.

'I've got some news,' she says, and again I can sense her hesitancy.

'Stop biting your nails,' I order, and she laughs.

'How did you know I was doing that?'

'I'm an oracle. I know everything.'

'If you know everything, then you must know what I'm going to say next.'

I take a deep breath and watch as a tiny lake of rainwater snakes down the road and vanishes into a drain.

'You've dumped Paul?' I guess, failing to keep the hopefulness out of my tone.

'Oi!' she squeals.

'Okay, I'm sorry. But I thought now that you know Diego is available again, you might have decided to ditch Paul and try your luck with him.'

'Very funny,' she deadpans, but I don't hear what she says next because there's yet another rumble of thunder.

'What was that?' I ask loudly, putting my spare hand over my uncovered ear.

'I said, it's actually quite the opposite.'

Oh no.

'Hannah?'

She hasn't.

'Are you still there?'

'Mmm-hmm.'

I know what she's going to say, but I don't want to hear it.

'Paul proposed!'

Of course he did.

'Yay,' I manage, the word trailing out like air out of a sad balloon.

'I'm getting married!'

She's not giving up the gusto.

'That's . . . It's great.' I can feel myself frowning, and force my mouth into the shape of a smile.

'You will be my chief bridesmaid, won't you?' she rushes on. 'Paul has got a younger sister and a niece that I have to include, but I want you in charge.'

'Are you sure you don't want me to have a word with Diego?' I ask hopefully, but she doesn't laugh.

'Come on, Han – at least try to be happy for me. I know you and Paul aren't the best of friends, but he makes me happy. I need you to try harder to get along. I'm going to marry him, so there's no avoiding it.'

I can't help it, I sigh.

'I am happy for you,' I tell her, trying my best to sound convincing. 'It just seems to have happened really fast, that's all.'

'Not that fast,' she argues. 'I live with him, Hannah. I love him. What's the point in waiting?'

'It's such a big decision,' I say grudgingly. 'You could change your mind about him in a year or so.'

Now it's Rachel's turn to sigh.

'Hannah, I know your mum and dad's marriage didn't work out, but that's no reason to assume that mine won't.'

Ouch.

'I know that,' I grumble, feeling like a sulky teenager.

'Do you?' she demands. 'I mean, do you really?'

'Of course I do!' I tell her, but I know I don't believe what I'm saying. I don't really have a great opinion of marriage, do I? I've been cynical about the entire concept since I was a child. Am I upset because I think Paul is a bit of a tool and Rachel can do better, or am I just scared by how rapidly I'm being left behind? My best friend is in a boat heading along marriage river, and I'm still splashing around in the baby pool of dating. Soon she'll become one of those smug wedded people who only ever socialise with other couples, and she'll forget all about me.

'You know, I don't want to be cruel, Hannah,' Rachel

says now, and I automatically brace myself for another blow. 'But you're not really in any position to judge anyone else's relationship, having never had a real one yourself.'

I open my mouth to argue, but I have no defence.

'Paul and I may seem silly to you, looking in from the outside, but to me he's everything. I want to be his wife and I feel ready to take the next step. We're staring thirty in the face now, Han, and I want to start a family.'

'So you're settling!' I interrupt triumphantly, even though I know it's unfair, and I hear her gasp with exasperation.

'No, you idiot, I'm not settling. If you could just make more effort with Paul instead of doing your best to intimidate him, then you'd see how perfect he is for me. As far as I'm concerned, I'm marrying the man I love. What could be better than that?'

My brain helpfully lines up a list of things better than the prospect of marrying Paul, such as licking a stinging nettle or strolling naked through a busy shopping centre. When it becomes apparent that I'm not going to reply, Rachel resorts to her killer bombshell.

'Tom warned me you'd be like this.'

That reignites my mouth.

'What?'

'He warned me not to expect a fanfare, but I don't think even he thought you'd be this horrible about it.'

I wince at this accusation, because I'm not trying to be horrible or intimidate anyone. I'm just being realistic. Marriages fall apart every day; people fall out of love with the person they've promised to cherish for no apparent reason. I know what I should do at this stage is apologise – tell Rachel I'm just scared of losing her, admit defeat and ask her what she's planning for the hen do – but the comment about Tom has rankled me, so instead I go on the attack.

'Why did you tell Tom before me?' I ask, anger muddying my voice and making me sound disgruntled.

I imagine Rachel shrugging as she answers. 'I've been talking to him loads over the past few weeks, and because I knew *he* at least would be happy for me.'

I ignore the second dig.

'Talking to him loads?' I repeat. Tom hasn't mentioned as much to me, which strikes me as odd considering how honest the two of us have been with one another lately.

'He's needed someone to talk to,' she informs me stiffly, her meaning clear – that I haven't been there for him.

I hate the idea of Rachel and Tom discussing me behind my back. I hate it almost as much as the prospect of this bloody wedding that I'll be forced to attend. I want to ask her what he's been saying, but my pride sticks a big foot in my gob and stops me.

'What's wrong with Tom?' I demand instead. 'What has he got to complain about?'

I can hear the sound of voices at Rachel's end of the line, and she puts her hand over the receiver as she replies to whoever it is.

'Hannah?'

'What?'

'I have to go; I have a meeting.'

'Fine.'

She lets out another long sigh. 'Don't you have anything else to say?'

I think about her harsh comments, the accusation that I'm in some way warped and damaged by the failure of my parents' marriage, and the fact that she went behind my back and told Tom her engagement news first.

'Nope.'

Another sigh.

'Right. Well, take care of yourself over there. I guess I'll see you when you get back.'

I open my mouth to start saying something smart back, but she's already hung up and I'm answered by the silence of a dead line. Without really thinking, I immediately locate Tom's number and press call, drumming my fingers against the wall of the gift shop as I wait for him to answer.

'Hello?'

'It's Hannah.'

'I guessed that much when your name flashed up on my phone,' he jokes, but I'm not in the mood for laughing.

'I suppose you were expecting it to be Rachel, given how tight the two of you have become,' I retort acidly.

'Oh,' is Tom's response. 'She told you her news, then?'

'Her happy news? Oh yes. I'm thrilled, as I'm sure you know. She said the two of you have been talking almost every day,' I tell him, my voice sounding high.

'Not every day,' he argues.

'And talking about me!' I add, kicking the wall for good measure.

Now it's Tom's turn to sigh. I'm sick of people sighing at me, like I'm some sort of nuisance.

'Where are you?' he asks.

'Why?' I bark, my bad mood making me reluctant to tell him anything he wants to know.

'I'll come and meet you, so we can talk properly.'

I pause as Elaine's story floods back over me, and I think how nice it would be to sit down with Tom and tell him about it, get his advice on how best to handle it and what I can do to help my new friend, but my stupid pride is still sitting with its huge size-nine boot firmly wedged in the way.

'I don't want to talk,' I tell him grumpily, and he braves a small laugh.

'Then why did you call me?'

'Oh, shut up!' I rage, realising as I turn around that the rain has stopped at last. The apartment is only ten minutes' walk up the hill, but the thought of being in there is becoming less alluring by the second. I can't face being cooped up, not while I'm in this mood, not while there's so much to process.

'Go back to yours,' Tom instructs gently. 'I'll meet you there in a bit and we'll talk it out, okay?'

'Fine,' I snap, then end the call before he has time to reply.

What Tom doesn't know, however, is that I have absolutely no intention of going back to the apartment. What I need now is a sympathetic ear, a strong drink and the opportunity to forget everything that's happened over the past few hours – and I know just the place I can get the whole package.

33

There's no sound coming from inside the villa when I reach the blue front door, but I barely hesitate before I begin hammering on it. When Theo eventually opens it with an aggravated jerk, the look of annoyance on his face almost makes me run away.

'Hannah!' he says at once, pulling me in through the gap. 'What is the matter? You scared me with the banging.'

'Sorry,' I mumble, my heart crashing against my chest. Once I decided that I was coming here, I practically ran down the hill and along the beach, which was pretty treacherous given all the rapidly evaporating puddles. The rain has done little to dim the soaring temperature, and the sun is now merrily causing steam to rise off from every visible surface.

'You are soaked,' he declares, looking me up and down. He doesn't rush off to fetch me a towel like Elaine did, though. Instead he just stands in front of me, one of his hands on each of my wrists, staring at me like I'm a curious object he just dug up on the beach.

'Sorry for startling you,' I mumble, embarrassed now as I always seem to be whenever he fixes me with one of his stares.

'I am glad you are here,' he says, relaxing his grip a notch. 'I was going to message you and ask you to come.'

He was? Relief courses through me.

'We need to have a talk, I think,' he says then, but I shake my head and he gazes at me, surprised.

'No?'

'Can we just . . . ?' I begin, faltering when he doesn't immediately understand what I'm getting at.

'Something is the matter,' he guesses, lifting my chin with a finger as soon as I drop my eyes.

So many things are the matter, I think. One of my best friends thinks I'm a bitch, and the other is infatuated with my sister, who in turn is acting like a mad person. Then there's the small matter of Elaine's confession, not to mention the tumble of confused feelings I have for Theo himself. I don't want to talk about any of it, though – what I want is to forget.

'Hannah,' he says again, and I take a step closer to him. I don't know how to tell him what I want, so I let the need I'm feeling take over, and bend forwards to kiss his neck. At first he doesn't move, but when my lips reach the underside of his jaw and I let the tip of my tongue tickle the rough of his stubble, I hear his breath start to quicken.

'Is this what you want?' he murmurs, pushing himself against me so I can feel how aroused he is.

'Yes,' I whisper, kissing the lobe of his ear and the soft, warm groove just beneath it.

The next second, we're pulling at each other's clothes, mine far trickier to remove than his because they're still so wet. Theo guides me over to the sofa and turns me around, but for the first time ever I push back against his hands. I want him to look at me this time, and I make that point clear as he tries and fails to bend me over. He looks almost angry, so I take his hand and start to kiss his fingers one by one, walking towards the bedroom door as I do so, urging him to follow me.

'You want to play games,' he states, and I feel a thrill trickle through me. I wish he would laugh with me, or cup my face in his hands and kiss me gently and with care. That's not Theo's style, though – especially not today – and it's only a matter of minutes later that we're entwined on the top of his sheets, his hands pulling at my damp hair as he kisses his way roughly down across my chest and stomach. I keep waiting for the jumble of emotions I'm feeling to be washed away by what he's doing to me, but instead they just seem to swell in my mind with renewed clarity.

I close my eyes and try to concentrate on the sensation of Theo's tongue against my inner thigh, of his teeth as he nibbles at me, but all I actually feel is discomfort, and reflexively I squirm away from him.

'Oh no you don't,' he growls playfully, clamping his hands across my bare bottom and squeezing the flesh between his fingers. I can feel how much he wants me now – hell, I can see how much – but it doesn't offer me the comfort I'm craving. I wriggle out of his grasp again and try to coax him down on to the bed next to me so I can kiss him. What I want to feel is cherished, not desired. I want him to hold me like a fragile little bird, not manhandle me like a bolting ox. Theo goes along with my tentative kisses for a few minutes, but his hands are still roaming all over me, prodding and pinching until eventually I can't take it any more and stop him by sitting up.

Misinterpreting what I'm doing, Theo props himself up on one knee and angles himself by my mouth, but I can't. Just like that, I simply cannot do it.

'Sorry,' I mumble, turning my face away until he kneels back down beside me. His eyes look black with lust and there's a sheen of sweat across his face.

'What is the matter?' he asks, trailing a single finger over my exposed breasts then abruptly removing it when he sees me shift uncomfortably away.

'How does Claudette know about the almonds and Manchego?' I ask breathlessly. I knew the question was at the forefront of my brain, but I never imagined that I'd have the guts to actually come out with it.

Theo frowns for a moment before answering.

'Because I told her,' he replies, letting each word out slowly and deliberately.

'When?' I want to know, but Theo gives me an exaggerated shrug.

'I don't know, Hannah – maybe last year, maybe before then? Why does it matter?'

His Greek accent has become more pronounced now that he's pissed off with the line of questioning, and in any other circumstance I would probably find it amusing. In this case, however, it simply aggravates me that he's not taking my queries seriously.

'Have you and Claudette ever slept together?' I demand, flushing crimson at my own daring.

Theo sits down then and pulls the sheet over the lower half of his body with an irritated mutter of indecipherable Greek.

'Of course.'

Whatever I was expecting him to say, it wasn't that, and I roughly wipe away indignant tears.

'What is the matter?' he demands, glaring at me from beneath his stupid sheet. 'You ask a question that you are not ready to hear the answer to, then don't blame me for telling the truth.'

This cannot be happening.

'When?'

I've instinctively bent my knees so they're facing away from him, and now I cross my arms across my chest to hide my nudity.

Theo looks exasperated and not a little angry, and for a moment I think he might get up and storm out. Then again, we're in his bed, in his own villa. I've got him cornered, so to speak, and after staring at the doorway for a few beats, presumably contemplating an escape, he turns again to face me, his expression challenging.

'The first time, or the most recent time?'

'Both,' I say calmly, ignoring the actual physical pain that his words have just caused me to feel.

Infuriatingly, he shrugs again, as if this information is the most blasé piece of news he's ever imparted.

'The first time was three years ago, not long after Claudette worked with me on the film we did in Vancouver,' he says. 'The last time was at Christmas, after the office party.'

Gross, I think. What a bloody cliché.

'What about the other night?' I want to know, but my voice has lost some of its edge, and I now sound more defeated than defiant.

'The other night, nothing,' he states, and I do believe

him. After all, there's no reason for him to lie about that when he's been so brutally honest about everything else.

'You should have told me,' I whisper, too scared to look at him but too caught up in the moment not to let the words out. I know this is the last chance I'll get to talk to him like this. After what I've done today, there won't be any going back.

'Hannah, Hannah, Hannah,' he says, his tone now conciliatory. 'Why did you ask me these things? I would never lie to you, but you should have trusted me. There is no reason for anyone to know about Claudette except for me and for her.'

'I think Tom has guessed,' I mumble in response, knowing as I say it that he must have. He tried to warn me off Theo, after all. Come to think of it, so did Claudette.

'Perhaps.' He shrugs, obviously not bothered either way.

The tears that I've been trying my best not to unleash are now making a determined bid for freedom, and Theo notices them, too, reaching around to the bedside table for a tissue.

'Don't be so silly,' he croons. 'I am not with Claudette now.'

'But you have been,' I point out. 'Don't you see – that changes everything?'

'Why?' he asks, and I dare myself to look at him.

'Because it's just too complicated,' I tell him. 'And it makes me feel as if I was second choice.'

Theo places a hand on my bare shoulder, squeezes it gently.

'You must understand, Hannah,' he begins. 'Until we

came here to Mojácar, I did not really know you. Of course we would talk sometimes, and I knew that you were good at your job, reliable and smart.'

He did? I look up, mollified slightly.

'But I did not know the real you – the Hannah that has come alive before my eyes in this place. She is fearless and funny and warm.'

'I'm not fearless,' I argue. 'I'm scared of everything – especially you.'

Theo takes back his hand.

'You are not scared of me,' he says. 'What scares you is who you are with me. I have seen the change in you. When we came out to Mojácar, you were a girl, but now you are a woman. You are relaxed and happy – you hold up your head high.'

'Do I?' I'm now more intrigued than upset, and also astounded that Theo has been paying so much close attention to me. And I suppose he's right, in a way – I do feel different here, more focused and grown up. Mojácar has enchanted me again, as it did all those years ago when it shaped me into the person I am now, and softened my heart. Being here has made me question how I feel about my father and about Nancy, and made me realise what it is I want from my life. All this time I thought it was just Theo, but now I'm beginning to realise that the whole concept of myself and him is a fantasy. Just as I used to daydream about Diego, a man I knew deep down that I could never be with, so I have created this make-believe relationship with Theo. No wonder I've been feeling so jittery over the past few weeks; it's because my fantasy became a reality, and for the first time in my adult life, my heart was in serious danger of getting broken. Fantasies are safe, I see that now. Reality is very different.

'Hannah, can I tell you something?' Theo says, stirring me out of my train of thought and arranging the sheet so that it's covering both of us.

I nod.

'Do you remember what I told you before, about the girl that I loved?'

'Yes,' I croak.

'I met her when I was thirty-two,' he says. 'And for a time, I was the happiest I had ever been. She was the first girl I had ever been myself with, you understand? And together we travelled around the world. It was she who inspired me to start my business, so I could tell the hidden stories of these places we had explored.'

'What happened to her?' I ask, the softness of my voice reflecting the calmness I feel inside.

'I broke her heart,' he says simply, staring past me out towards the beach. I know the view so well that I can imagine what he's gazing at without having to turn my head. I want to ask him why, but I can tell that he's struggling with what to say next.

'I was a *malaka*,' he says then, attempting a smile. 'An idiot. I mistook our closeness for simple friendship, believed that our intimacy and the easiness I felt around her had killed our passion. There were moments where I felt like I loved her, but then others when I thought she was wrong, that we were wrong. But, of course, I was the one who was wrong.'

'You poor thing,' I say, groping for his hand, but Theo moves it away and runs his fingers through his dark curls.

'I am not the one who deserves sympathy,' he sighs. 'I broke her heart and my punishment has been to never get over it. I cannot forgive myself, and so now my heart is closed to anyone but her. I have tried to move on, but I cannot forget her.'

'Why don't you find her?' I ask, his stricken expression enough to make me forget myself for a moment. 'Tell her how you feel.'

'It is too late.' He turns to me, his eyes heavy with regret. 'She is happy now, and it is not my place.'

Theo may be older than me, he may have more experience and more sophistication, but he's just as lost as I am. Just as I have let fear steer me down a safe path all my life, so he has allowed heartbreak to direct his own. I may be terrified of rejection, but Theo's scared of being the one who rejects. Despite everything that's happened, all I honestly feel in this moment is pity. Not just for Theo, but for both of us.

'I am sorry,' he says then, taking my hand and lacing his fingers through mine. 'I should have told you in the beginning that I could not offer you anything serious. I assumed that you were thinking the same thing as me.'

'I thought . . .' I begin, hesitating as I ponder how to put what I'm feeling into words.

'You thought more?' he probes softly, and all I can do is look at him. How can I admit that I didn't think at all? That I never planned past the point of that first kiss, because I didn't think I would ever achieve it. I had convinced myself that I was in love with a man who I barely even knew outside of work, but I never stopped to question what love really is. If I had, I would have realised long ago that Theo and I were never going to amount to anything.

'You are a very special girl, Hannah,' Theo says, increasing the pressure on my hand. 'You deserve better than anything I could offer.'

'But I don't know what I want,' I reply, exasperated with myself.

'That is okay.' Theo uses a finger to lift my chin. 'You don't have to know yet. There is so much time. You are still young, and there is a whole world out there.'

There's a beautiful logic to his words, and now that he's being so nice to me, I find that I'm no longer even upset about the Claudette situation. Theo isn't rejecting me so much as letting me go, and it's obvious to me now that we never had a future past these few glorious weeks. And that's okay – it really is.

'I thought I was in love with you,' I say honestly, looking down at my lap rather than at him. 'You are all I wanted for as long as I can remember.'

'Me?' Theo sounds genuinely surprised.

'Of course,' I reply, braving a smile. 'I thought you knew.'

He laughs at this, grateful to have the tension fall away a fraction, and shakes his head in bewilderment.

'I definitely did not know,' he assures me. 'But I am flattered, of course. And I am glad that this happened, because now we are friends – real friends.'

I smile against his chest as he hugs me, acutely aware that the two of us are still naked beneath the sheet. Whatever I hoped to achieve by coming here to see Theo, I would never have guessed that this would be the outcome, but now that everything is out in the open, it feels as if I can breathe properly again. Finding out that Theo had indeed, as I suspected, slept with Claudette has been my greatest fear over the past few days, and now that it's happened and I've survived – well, better than that, I feel relieved – I can take my foot off the emotion throttle at last.

Theo must sense the shift in my mood, because he lets go of me and brings his fingers up to my cheek, turning my face towards his and kissing me lightly on the lips. It's the kiss I've been waiting for him to give me since I first laid eyes on him, and for a few delicious seconds I give in to what I'm feeling and simply allow myself to be in the moment, enjoying the taste and feel of him, relishing the tenderness and revelling in the whispers of pleasure that are creeping through my insides.

Theo pulls away gently and our eyes meet.

'Will you stay here with me tonight?' he asks, posing it as a question for once.

It would be so nice, I think, to simply lie in the comfort of his embrace and enjoy more of those kisses, but the fact is I have somewhere more important to be.

'I wish I could,' I tell him, giving him one final and lingering kiss. 'But I have some amends I really need to make.'

He grins in bemusement as I wriggle back into my still-damp dress and brazenly pinch one of his shirts from the wardrobe to wear over the top, rolling up the cuffs as I button it up.

'They are lucky to have you, Hannah,' he tells me. 'I hope you know that.'

I pause at the door.

'Who?' I ask, allowing myself one last look at those broad, tanned shoulders, that tangle of black curls.

He smiles at me then, and I know that I'll never forget this exact moment.

'All of them,' he says. 'Every single one.'

34

I know something is wrong before I even reach the apartment. There's a stillness to the air that hints at disquiet, as if a huge amount of noise has just occurred and stirred the dust up until it's hanging limply in the darkness.

Silence can be so loud. Until this moment, I had no idea just how much comfort I'd been taking from all those familiar little noises – the sound of my sandals on the warm paving stones, the hum of the cicadas nestled in the surrounding plants, and the faint buzz of the mopeds driving along the coastal road below. Even the distant throb of music drifting down from the bars far above me was soothing. Everything was as it should have been as I made my way up the hill; nothing out of the ordinary was happening.

Inside the apartment, however, it's a completely different story.

There are no lights on, and the first thing I see is the broken pieces of the large hallway mirror – actually, I feel them, crunching unpleasantly between the bottom of my shoes and the tiled floor.

I want to call out her name, but a halting hand of fear prevents me, so instead I take a deep breath and edge forwards over the shards of glass as quietly as possible. It's dark, but the moon must be shining through the front windows, because the patterned tiles ahead of me are dappled with smudges of grey.

'Hannah?'

It's barely a whisper, but it startles me so much that I scream. Scanning the floor in the half-darkness, I make out the huddled shape of a small person in the far corner. There's a blanket wrapped around her shoulders, which are shaking, and her knees are pulled up under her chin.

'What the hell is going on?' I croak. My voice sounds unfamiliar, as if the top layer has been scraped off.

Silence.

Stepping carefully over what was once a mobile phone, I make my way over to the tightly folded shape and crouch down slowly on to my haunches.

'What happened, Nancy?' I whisper. 'Why are you sitting like this in the dark?'

A muffled squeak comes out from beneath the blanket.

'Did Carlos or Ignacio turn up uninvited again?' I ask, my hands on her shoulders, but my eyes up and alert.

'No.' It's barely audible.

'Is there anyone else in the apartment?' I whisper, trying to make my voice as quiet as it can go. I can't detect the sound of anyone else, but I'm confused as to what could have happened that was bad enough to make her end up down here on the floor.

Nancy's head under the blanket turns from side to side.

That means we're safe, at least. Resting backwards on my heels, I finally let out a breath and cough away the petrification that's lodged itself in my throat.

'I'm going to turn the lights on.'

'No!' Two hands shoot out and grab my wrists.

The heart-thumping anxiety I experienced in the hallway is refusing to let go.

'Who broke the mirror?' I ask, folding back the blanket with my still-anchored hands. Nancy's face is a mess of tears and wet strands of hair are stuck all over her forehead.

'It was—' She stops, giving in to more tears.

'Come on.' I gently peel away her fingers from around my wrists and put a stiff arm around her. 'I won't be angry, I promise – I just need to know.'

'Tom.'

'What about Tom?'

There is no way that Tom did this.

'Talk to Tom,' she says, her voice muffled by my shoulder. 'Tom was here. He was here with me and . . .'

'Why the hell would Tom throw his phone at the mirror?' I ask, my voice sounding high and strange. Before I'm really aware of what I'm doing, I'm back up on my feet and heading towards the exit.

'Please don't go!' Nancy cries, sounding horribly like some sort of animal caught in a trap. For some reason, though, I can't turn back to her. I don't want to look at her, to see the state she's in. If Tom was really involved, then I need to know how.

As I stumble back across the broken glass and out of the still-open front door, I catch sight of the painted Indalo Man symbol on the wall beside the door. He was supposed to protect her, I think, tears causing the dome of his rainbow shield to distort in front of my eyes. He was supposed to protect all of us.

'Tom!'

The hard mass of unarticulated rage that had wedged itself into my throat abruptly comes free as I reach the door of Tom's studio flat, and I bring my fist up to pummel the wood.

'TOM!'

The door opens.

Without waiting to be invited, I barge past him and storm into the middle of the room, my eyes flickering from the glass of what looks like whisky on the coffee table to the strange expression on my friend's face. My brow knots up as I stare back at him, trying to fathom what it is that I can't quite read in his eyes. He's not angry, or amused or even upset. No, Tom is frightened, and that is worse than anything else could have been.

'You'd better sit down,' he says eventually, so quietly that I take an involuntary step towards him in order to hear.

Our eyes meet yet again, but he drops his first, gesturing towards the sofa with a hand.

'I'm fine standing,' I say tightly, thinking privately that I couldn't sit still even if I wanted to. The nervous energy hurtling through my body is making me jittery, and I can't seem to stop moving from one foot to the other.

Tom hesitates for a moment, then crosses the room and sits back down facing his tumbler of what I assume must be medicinal alcohol. I watch as he picks up the glass and swills the amber liquid inside, his hand moving to disguise the tremble in his fingers.

'You've seen Nancy?' he asks, looking up towards but not at me.

I nod. 'She's in a right state, crying all over herself in the dark, but she wouldn't tell me why. She said you were there. What's going on, Tom? Did you smash the mirror?'

Tom doesn't answer me immediately, instead bringing his drink up to his lips and taking a hearty slug, only to begin coughing as the fiery liquid hits his throat.

I fold my arms across my chest while I wait for him to regain his composure, noticing as I do so the pile of discarded T-shirts littering one of the chairs, the carton of milk left out on the kitchen counter, the stack of dirty mugs in the sink.

'I didn't touch the mirror. I went over there to meet you,' he says now, his tone faintly accusatory. 'Where were you?'

'I went to see Theo,' I say, fixing my eyes on the clock above the front door. 'I was upset after I spoke to Rachel and I just wanted to see a friendly face.'

'How did that go?' Tom asks, and I take a deep breath.

'It was fine,' I reply, staring straight at him. 'But it's over between him and me.'

'I'm sorry,' he says, taking another sip and wincing, although whether it's because of what I've just said or the alcohol, I can't tell.

'What happened with Nancy?' I prompt, closing a firm door on my eventful few hours with Theo. 'Did you say something to upset her?'

'No!' Tom looks up, his eyes beseeching.

'She's borderline catatonic,' I snap. 'And there's broken glass all over the floor – I thought Ignacio had turned up at first and they'd had a row or something, but then Nancy kept on saying your name, and so—'

'Hannah!' he interrupts, his misery radiating off him.

'What?' I demand, narrowing my eyes as I stare at him. His odd demeanour is scaring me, and I don't understand why he won't just give me a straight answer.

'What do you mean, "what"?' he says, one of his fingers bothering the ice in his now empty glass. 'I don't know anything about the mirror being broken.'

'But Nancy said—' I begin, but stop when Tom abruptly gets up from the sofa and walks towards me.

'Look at me,' he pleads, and I raise my eyes until I can see them reflected in his own. 'You know I'm telling you the truth.'

'But I don't understand,' I say, still reluctant to let him near me. 'Nancy has got no reason to start smashing things.'

There's a pause, and unwillingly I think back to the previous evening, and Nancy hurling the mug to the floor.

'Perhaps she has,' he counters. 'Have you not noticed what's been going on with her?' He crosses to the small kitchen area to fetch his bottle of whisky.

'Do you want one?' he asks, but I shake my head, already thinking that I must get back to my sister.

'That she's been a bit erratic?' I ask, and he nods impatiently. 'Well, yes – but I think it's just because she's had a row with her best friend or something. And she's angry at Dad . . .'

Tom is sitting back down again, and this time I join him, picking the spot on the sofa that's furthest away.

'As soon as I got there today, Nancy was . . .' He pauses, his eyes darting up and then off to the side. 'Well, she was all over me,' he mutters.

My heart thumps horribly against my chest.

'And?'

'I mean, like, she was really all over me,' he says again, and this time my hands turn cold and clammy. 'She didn't even let me speak, she just started kissing me straight away and pulled me into the bedroom.'

My mind conjures up an image of myself and Theo, the two of us ripping at each other's clothes just as Nancy and Tom must have been doing at exactly the same time. I hadn't let him get a word in, either, and I imagine now what it must have felt like to be Theo, to have me so obviously unhinged in his arms. Of course, Theo being the red-blooded – albeit emotionally damaged – man that he is, he was more than willing to comply, but I find it hard to picture Tom having the same response.

'And?' I prompt again, and Tom glances at me sheepishly.

'And nothing,' he groans. 'I kissed her back at first, okay? I'm only human.'

'Debatable,' I snap, and he closes his eyes briefly before continuing.

'I ... Er, we ...' He's clearly struggling to get his words out, but I wish he would just get on with it. The thought of him and Nancy together is making me feel as if my limbs are being pulled off my body without anaesthetic. Whether it's because it's him in my mental image or her, I can't tell.

'You had sex,' I state, unable to bear his babbling any longer, but Tom immediately shakes his head.

'No! Absolutely not. We didn't. I mean, I thought that she wanted to, but then as soon as I stopped her ...' He pauses again and picks up his whisky.

'What happened, Tom?' I cry, standing up and sitting right back down beside him. I'm angry and fearful, but my overwhelming instinct now is to comfort him. He looks utterly wretched.

'She just flipped,' he mutters. 'She slapped me off her and started screaming at me to get out and leave her alone. But you know I would never do anything to hurt her, Hannah. You know I wouldn't.'

There are tears in his voice now and I want to pull him against my chest and console him, but I find that I'm frozen – rooted to the spot by the vile image that he's describing.

'Then what happened?' I ask.

Tom sits back and runs his hands through his hair.

'Then I left,' he says. 'I came back here and started drinking.'

'Why didn't you call me?' I want to know, but he looks at me as if it's the most stupid question he's ever heard.

'Because I was embarrassed,' he says, incredulous. 'Because a girl that I thought liked me had just thrown me out, and because you're her sister, Hannah. Forgive me if this sounds obvious, but I didn't think you'd want to hear from me, to be honest.'

He's right, of course, I wouldn't have wanted to hear it. Yet here we are anyway.

'I can't believe you would think that badly of me,' he says now, and I can tell just how hurt he is.

'I didn't – I thought it was Ignacio who had kicked off and upset her. But then Nancy said—' I babble, but he cuts across me.

'I know she's your sister, Hannah, but I'm supposed to be your best friend.'

'I could say the same thing to you!' I retort. 'You're my best friend and she's my sister, and yet that didn't stop you trying it on with her, did it? It didn't stop you going along with her advances tonight. As far as you knew, I was on my way back and could have walked in and found the pair of you at it.'

He has the grace to look slightly sheepish at this, but I haven't finished.

'And you went behind my back and slagged me off to Rachel!' I add, standing up and walking away from him. 'I suppose you knew all about Theo and Claudette, too, and just let me make a fool of myself anyway.'

To my horror, Tom barely reacts at the mention of their names.

'So, it is true,' he mutters, downing the remainder of his drink and fixing his mouth into a hard, straight line. 'I thought as much.'

'Why the hell didn't you tell me?' I cry, the sound making us both flinch.

'I didn't think it was my place,' he says, refusing to raise his voice. 'And because I didn't think for a moment that—' He stops, shaking his head.

'That what?' I ask, hearing the words tremble.

He sighs before replying, and I'm sure I detect what looks an awful lot like pity in his expression.

'That you and he would become a thing.'

'And why is that?' I snarl, my mouth now completely adrift from my brain.

'Because you're you,' he exclaims. 'And he's him.'

'Oh, I get it,' I rage, digging my fingernails into the fleshy tops of my arms to stop myself from crying. 'Claudette is good enough for him, but I'm not. He's Theo the great and powerful and I'm just a joke. Well, thanks a lot.'

Tom stands up. 'Hannah, come on.'

'Stay away from me!' I growl, so menacingly that Tom actually recoils. By the time I reach the front door, he's sitting back down again, his big stupid head in his big stupid hands. He looks defeated, beaten, weary and bereft, but I'm too upset to care.

'And stay away from Nancy, too,' I throw in as a parting shot, just as he looks up. I know the pain in his eyes would have made my legs buckle at the knee, but I don't see it. I have already slammed the door shut behind me and am heading back home to my sister.

35

I find Nancy exactly where I left her, although she's no longer sitting upright but has rolled over on to her side, her knees pulled up to her chest and her hands knotted together across her shins. Instead of trying to move her, I simply sit down on the tiles by her head and gently run my fingers through her hair, just as my mum used to do to me when I had a nightmare or a tummy bug. It seems to soothe her, and it's helping me to stay calm, too. There are so many things I need to ask her, but for now it's enough just to be here for her, and I'm surprised at how good it feels to be her big sister.

That fear I experienced earlier tonight when I found her curled up in that sobbing ball will stay with me forever. It cut through all the other feelings I had towards Nancy and gripped me with an urgent yet simple realisation: I love my sister. I care about her wellbeing and I don't want anything bad to happen to her. Just knowing those things for a fact is a comfort, and for the first time ever I can picture a future relationship between us. Not just one of sibling rivalry, either, but one founded on real friendship.

Nancy used to try to cuddle up to me when we were still kids. My dad would put a film on and wrap us up together under a blanket on the sofa, one on each side of him. Nancy would always wriggle free, though, and come across to me. I can remember now how her sticky little hand felt as she slipped it into mine, and how I'd rest my cheek against the top of her glossy black head as she nodded off to sleep. It was all so simple then, but over time I'd let my resentments rule my heart. Nancy wasn't the one who had changed her behaviour – I was.

I switched on the hallway light when I came back, but the main part of the apartment is still shrouded in darkness. I can see the white chocolate button of the moon through the glass doors of the balcony, the sky now so clear after the earlier rain. The crickets have fallen silent, so I know it must be late, and I pass the time by counting the scatter of stars thrown out like gems across velvet. I think about Elaine, and of Theo and fleetingly of Tom, although I don't let my mind dwell there for very long. I think of Rachel, and wonder if my idiotic words are causing her to have a sleepless night. I hope they aren't, and that she knows me well enough to realise how much of a fool I am. It was only a few hours ago that we spoke, but I feel as though a decade has passed. Everything that has happened has added years of wisdom and understanding to my weary mind, and I let those things percolate inside me as I sit on the floor.

It's time, I think. It's time for me to change and to grow up a bit. I'll be leaving Mojácar a different person, and I'm thankful for that, even if the road up to this point has been a tough one. Whatever has happened to make Nancy react in such an erratic way, we'll get to the bottom of it. There's nothing we can't deal with, nothing I'm not fully prepared to hear, and nothing that could possibly shock me more than the other things I've heard over the past twelve hours.

'Hannah.' It's barely a whisper, and I blink before turning away from the stars.

'Yes?'

Nancy lifts her head and rests it on my lap.

'I need to tell you something.'

'It can wait,' I soothe, tucking her hair behind her ear so I can see her face. She's stopped crying now, but her wet cheek gleams blue in the light from the moon. 'You don't have to worry. I spoke to Tom; I know what happened between you two and it's okay.'

A tear snakes out.

'No, it's not.'

'Nancy, it's okay,' I try again, lifting my knees until she has no choice but to sit up. 'Whatever it is, we'll deal with it. Nothing is worth all this,' I say, gesturing towards the chaos all around us.

She makes a small noise, but doesn't sound convinced or even comforted.

'Come on,' I say softly, getting to my feet and wincing slightly as all the blood rushes back into my legs. Reaching for her hand, I help her up and catch her as she staggers into me.

'Steady on!' I joke, my attempt to lighten the mood falling flatter than a pancake.

'Sorry,' she mumbles, her eyes wide beneath the dark sweep of her matted fringe as she takes in the smashed pieces of mirror.

'It's okay,' I repeat, steering her firmly towards the bathroom. 'Go and wash your face, then you're going to get some sleep and we'll talk in the morning, okay?'

She nods but doesn't smile, and a few seconds later I

hear the water running. By the time she joins me in the bedroom, I've remade the bed and have fetched her a glass of water.

'Why are you being so nice to me?' she murmurs as I pull the sheet up around her. She's changed into a huge, baggy grey T-shirt with her university coat of arms printed on the front, and I wonder if it belongs to her ex-boyfriend.

'I'm making up for lost time,' I tell her, sitting down on the edge of the bed. 'I'm sorry I've been such a crap sister.'

'Half-sister,' she replies with a hint of humour, and I laugh, relieved.

She closes her eyes but I don't leave for a while, instead preferring to wait until I'm sure she's asleep. Her eyelashes are thick and cast spiky shadows across her cheeks, and her breathing is slow and measured. Just as I'm about to tiptoe away, Nancy sneaks out a hand and grasps my wrist.

'Thank you,' she whispers, not opening her eyes. 'Thank you for looking after us.'

'It's my pleasure,' I say, bending down to kiss her shiny head. 'Now go to sleep.'

I spend the next few hours pottering around aimlessly and cleaning up the mess in the apartment as quietly as I can. Other than the big mirror and Nancy's poor mobile phone, nothing else is actually broken. It's a good thing I do pay a pittance for my shared room in the Acton house, though, because the bill for the ornate mirror isn't going to be a small one. Still, I scold myself as I empty a dustpan full of broken glass into the kitchen bin, what matters is that Nancy is safe. Everything else can be sorted out with a polite apology and a generous PayPal transaction.

Every time I hear even the smallest sound, I fear it's Claudette returning with Carlos, but thankfully the hours pass and there's no sign of her. For someone who pretends to be so blasé about her Spanish holiday fling, she doesn't half spend a lot of time with him – and I'm glad, too. If a broken hairdryer can cause her to erupt like a tiny volcano, then God knows how she'll react when she sees what's happened in here.

I'm in the bathroom washing my face in preparation for bed when the nagging thought that's been lingering in my mind since Nancy went to sleep suddenly crashes through my subconscious like a drum kit down a metal stairway.

What. The. Hell?

'Looking after *us*,' Nancy said to me. 'Us!' Who the hell is 'us'?

'Nancy! Nancy, wake up!'

There's a groan from under the sheet.

'Come on, up you get!' I order, switching on the overhead light. She must sense my urgency through all those heavy layers of sleep, because I feel her shoulders tense up under my hands.

She sighs then, defeated.

'Give me a minute to get dressed.'

'I've wanted to tell you so many times.'

Nancy is looking down at the ground as she speaks, pushing the soles of her trainers through the jumble of sand and dust at her feet. After she got up, I hardly said a word to her, instead just gathered up my bag and led her out of the door and down the hill to the beach. I knew she would need the walk to get her thoughts in order, and I needed the air.

'I know we haven't been the best of friends, but as soon as I found out about the baby, I thought of you straight away – I was too scared to tell Mum and Dad and I thought you'd know what to do. I kept promising myself that I would just come out and say it,' she continues. 'But every day it got harder. After a while, I think I started to believe that if I ignored it, if I just kept quiet and tried to forget it was happening . . . Well, that it might just vanish, you know?'

I nod.

There's a thin shaft of light appearing now from behind the thick carpet of sea.

Dawn. A new day, a fresh start.

'So, you hadn't fallen out with Dad?' I guess, and she shakes her head.

'No, not at all – but I have been ignoring his messages and calls since I got here.'

'That makes two of us,' I tell her, and we share a small smile.

'Does your ex know you're pregnant?' I ask her.

She moves her head a fraction and looks up to show me fresh tears.

'I told James as soon as I'd had it confirmed by the doctor.'

'And he didn't take it too well?' I guess, feeling a wave of fresh pity.

Nancy's nodding now, through her tears. She takes a deep breath and gets her sobs back under control.

'He accused me of doing it on purpose,' she says,

disbelief in her voice. 'I'll never forget it. He went so pale, like I'd told him I was dying or something.' She shrugs and turns to look at me, to gauge my reaction.

'It must have been a shock,' I allow, careful not to give in to the torrent of disdain that is sitting like barbed wire in my mouth, ready to curse this stupid boy, this wimp who was supposed to love my sister.

'I thought he would calm down after a few days, once he'd got over the initial shock,' Nancy continues. 'But he just seemed to get worse. He was ignoring all my calls and messages, and none of his friends would tell me where he was.'

My blood is definitely boiling now and I reach across and place my hand on top of hers. The Mojácar wind chooses that moment to sneak up alongside us and blow sand across our bare legs, but neither one of us reacts.

'Eventually, he turned up,' she says, her words weighted with sadness. 'It was a week after I had first told him.'

She's starting to struggle again, and I close my eyes in preparation to hear the next part of the story.

'He was so cold, Han. I tried to hug him and he was just rigid. He wouldn't even look at me. It was as if he'd prepared a stupid speech, because he just stood there and recited words at me like a robot. He said we were too young, that he would borrow some money from his parents and that we would deal with it.'

'Arsehole,' I mutter.

'I knew what would happen, though,' Nancy says, gazing straight ahead to where the sun is now rearing the top of its fiery head. 'I knew he didn't want me any more. I could feel it. I used to be able to feel how much he loved me, you know, but that day there was nothing. I guess I thought . . .' She stops again, steeling herself, and I squeeze her shoulder encouragingly.

'I thought that if I kept the baby, then at least I would always have a connection to him. He would have to see me, and perhaps in time he would love me again.'

It makes sense, of course, but it's also completely nonsensical. I think of my own parents, and how my arrival clearly did nothing to change the way my dad felt about my mum.

'It doesn't always work that way,' I tell Nancy now, and I know she understands why I've said it.

'I know.' She shakes her head sadly. 'But it's all I have. I know you think James is horrible, but I still love him. I can't help it.'

'And Tom?' I enquire, unable to help myself.

She looks uncomfortable, and I almost tell her that it's okay, but she starts talking again before I get the chance.

'He was kind to me,' she says simply, and I'm immediately shamed. 'I was getting no replies from James, and I suppose I just needed to feel wanted by someone. Does that sound pathetic?'

'No,' I assure her, thinking of myself turning up at Theo's front door. 'It really doesn't.'

'Diego, Ignacio, Tom – they were all just about me feeling better for a few hours. I wanted to feel desirable in the way I used to with James, and I knew that Tom liked me. When I was with him, it helped me to forget. I'm so sorry,' she says, her face crumpling. 'I'm such a stupid cow. All those men deserve better than me.'

I watch as a napkin dances up to us on the breeze,

executes a strange sort of wiggly performance by our feet, then hurries off again.

'I don't think you need to worry about Diego,' I say lightly. 'I think you made his summer with that kiss.'

'I can't believe I did that,' she mutters, but there's a hint of a smile on her face.

'Ignacio clearly thinks you're more than desirable,' I add, putting on my best male Spanish voice and declaring, 'I love her more than nothing in the world!'

'Oh stop!' she laughs, and I give her a gentle nudge with my elbow.

'And Tom will be fine,' I add. 'Once he knows about . . . Well, the whole story, then he'll understand.'

'I can't bear what I did to him last night,' she says then, putting her face in her hands. 'He was so sweet to me and I just went wild. I don't even know what set me off, I just all of a sudden couldn't deal with what was happening. After he left, I caught sight of myself in the mirror and hated what I saw. I tried to call James again and he didn't answer, so I just threw my phone. I didn't even think about what I was doing until I'd done it.'

'It's okay,' I say again. 'It's only a mirror, and we can arrange another phone. And don't fret about Tom, either. He's a good person – he cares about you.'

'I can't stop thinking about the baby,' Nancy admits. 'Turns out that being pregnant is quite a hard thing to ignore.'

'Have you been getting sick?' I ask. 'Or was the other night really because of the booze?'

'No,' she says, digging her trainer in a little deeper. 'That day we got drunk together at the beach, I was actually drinking non-alcoholic cocktails. I felt like we were getting on for the first time in forever and I didn't want you to think I was a bore.'

'Well, you convinced me,' I exclaim, and she gives me the benefit of a smile. How stupid and self-involved I've been. I simply didn't notice all these clues staring me in the face – the reluctance to wear a bikini, the floaty clothes and her almost constant state of nausea. What Tom had taken to be an eating disorder and I had assumed was merely attention-seeking was, in fact, symptoms of another life beginning.

'How far along are you?' I ask.

'I think about four months,' she says, her hand instinctively going to her belly. She's still wearing the oversized T-shirt that she wore to sleep in, and it's so baggy that it's impossible to see if there's any bump at all.

'I'm barely even showing yet,' she says then, reading my mind. 'But in my head, I am. I feel so bloated and tired all the time. I know I should be eating more, but everything seems to smell like old socks. This baby is clearly going to be a very picky eater, unlike me.'

There's renewed colour in her cheeks when she talks about the baby which makes me feel warm, and the beginnings of an idea start to take shape in my mind.

'Who else have you told?' I want to know, but she shakes her head.

'Aside from James and the GP, nobody knows. You're the first person I've told. Well, in fact, you guessed.'

'I'm a bit slow on the uptake,' I admit, and am gratified to see the corners of her mouth go up.

'In my head, I planned to walk straight up to you and

tell you the minute I got here,' she says now, and again I'm aware of that creep of shame. I'd been so obviously annoyed when Nancy turned up – no wonder she'd retreated inside herself. She'd come here to me looking for help and support, and all I'd offered her was hostility. I have never been more ashamed of myself.

'But then I just couldn't tell you,' she finishes. 'You seemed so cool and together, and I didn't want you to be disgusted with me like James was.'

'Cool and together?' I repeat, laughing out loud. 'Are we talking about the same person?'

'You are!' she insists, refusing to play along. 'You have no idea how much I've always wanted to be just like you. I hate that you look like a supermodel and I look like a pug.'

'What?' I cry, still spluttering with mirth. 'I think pregnancy has addled your brain!'

She looks momentarily hurt, and I quickly apologise.

'Too soon?' I guess, and she nods.

'Sorry. I guess I'm still getting my head around the idea. This is the first time it's actually felt real – you know?'

'It's amazing,' I tell her, realising as I do so that I should have said it ages ago. Because it is, isn't it? The idea of a new life, a new member of our strange little family, is amazing. Rather than being appalled, I'm really excited, and I tell Nancy so.

'You think I should keep it, then?' she asks.

'That's your decision,' I assure her. 'But I want you to know that whatever you choose to do, I'll support you. I plan on being a far better sister from now on.'

'I've always thought you were a great sister,' she argues. 'I was just jealous of you – I always have been.'

'Me, too!' I exclaim, and then we're both laughing. How silly we've both been, and for so long, too. Now that I have Nancy back, I can't believe I ever let her go.

'What do we do next?' she says eventually, and I pause to watch another wave scatter polished pebbles across the shore. There are so many things we need to do, and boxes we need to tick, but before all that I want to go through with the plan that has been formulating in my mind.

'I think there's a few calls we have to make,' I tell her, picking up a stone and throwing it into the surf. 'But first there's someone that I'd really like you to meet.'

36

The sun has clambered like an adventurer to the top edge of the sky while we've been walking, and the buildings of the Old Town glow bright white around us. Yesterday's rain has scattered bougainvillea petals across the light grey cobbles and the sky is a freshly laundered blue. The dust is for once settled, and the air seems cleaner somehow, the tangy scent of lemons and wild herbs tickling at our nostrils as we make our slow way through the streets.

Now that I know Nancy is pregnant, I find myself aware of every uneven surface and steep path, the urge to keep my arms wrapped safely around her a difficult one to quell. Everywhere I look, an Indalo Man seems to gaze back at me, more relevant and poignant now than it has ever been. All this time I selfishly assumed that it existed to keep me safe and comforted, but of course what it really represents is the need within ourselves to look after others. Perhaps when you feel safe, you are more able to tend to the protection of others? Or maybe it's a whole lot simpler than that, and you just naturally look after the people you care the most about. I don't intend to ever forget that fundamental lesson.

The bells in the church begin to chime just as we reach our destination, stilling the pair of us into a reverent silence, and I wait until I cannot detect even the vibration of their sound before bringing up my hand and tapping my knuckles against the wood.

She's at home, just as I knew she would be.

Elaine makes a pot of tea and listens while I explain why we're there. As soon as she hears Nancy's news, a smile spreads across her face and I know then that I did the right thing by introducing the two of them. Once I'm finished, Elaine recounts her own story once again, this time with fewer punctuations of pain, but it's still enough to move Nancy to tears.

'Did you ever see your daughter again?' she asks, dabbing at her eyes with a tissue from the box that Elaine has just thrust in her direction.

Elaine shakes her head. 'No. But I think about her every day.'

'Do you regret having her in the first place?' Nancy wants to know, which seems like an odd question to me, but Elaine doesn't seem to mind.

'Of course not,' she smiles, her eyes flickering down to where Nancy is again resting her hand on the tiny swell of her stomach. 'I love her just as much now as I did then – and I always will love her, just the same.'

I interrupt them to tell Nancy about the rainbows, and how Elaine had ended up here in Mojácar. My sister's eyes are wide, and she starts to look properly at all the artwork on the surrounding walls.

'When I found out I was pregnant, I felt sick,' Nancy says. 'I couldn't help but feel angry at the baby, which is so unfair, I know. The thing is, I wanted to be a TV presenter. It sounds silly, but I even had an internship set up this summer at ITV – and now I have to give it all up.'

'No, you don't,' I say, incredulous. 'You can still do whatever you want with your life even if you do keep the baby. It's a baby, not a ball and chain.'

'Do you really think so?' Nancy asks, and I assure her that I do.

'It doesn't matter anyway,' she says then. 'Because I've always known deep down that I'm going to keep it. I'm so scared, though – what if I'm a terrible mother?'

I see a single tear slide down Elaine's cheek.

'You won't be,' she says, smiling at me for confirmation, and I nod.

'She's right, you won't.'

'I'm scared,' Nancy says again, and I fear my heart might split open inside my chest.

'I know you are,' I tell her, my voice choked. 'But you won't have to do it alone. You have me, and you have your mum and dad – and my mum.'

'Your mum?' Nancy is surprised, but I laugh and wipe my eyes.

'Oh yes – she's going to be over the bloody moon, trust me.'

'What about James?' Nancy insists, and I wish I had an answer for her that would fix that broken smile she keeps bravely trying to wear.

'I don't know,' I tell her truthfully. 'But at least now you won't have to face him on your own.'

'My friend Amy is after him,' she says then, her voice faraway as she presumably detaches herself from the misery of those words. 'I called her the other day and he was there, I could just tell.'

'Perhaps he was reaching out?' I suggest, attempting to

soothe. 'Try not to worry about him just yet, okay? We can deal with him later.'

It's easier said than put into action, though, and I'm relieved when Elaine takes over.

'Can I paint you both?' she asks, and we turn to her in surprise at the abrupt change of subject. 'Don't look so alarmed,' Elaine chuckles, picking up her mug of tea. 'I am an artist, you know.'

'But you do landscapes,' I say stupidly, and she grins.

'Only because I've never found a human subject worth doing. Come on, it will be fun. We can go down to La Fuente before anyone else is up.'

'You mean paint us now?' Nancy is aghast. Even in her strange catatonic state, she's realised that a grotty old T-shirt probably isn't the best garment to be painted in, whereas I, in an even grittier twist of fate, am still wearing the shirt that I pinched from Theo's wardrobe.

'I can lend you a dress each?' Elaine adds, taking in our anxious expressions, and to my surprise Nancy is the first to agree.

'Go on, then,' she says, reaching across to shake Elaine's proffered hand. 'It will be fun.'

My initial confusion over Elaine's motivations for painting us slips away about ten minutes after she's positioned us down at La Fuente, and I watch as the tension seems to evaporate from my sister just like the water from the marble basins around us. What Elaine realised that I didn't was that Nancy needed some quiet time to simply sit and think. I know, because I needed it, too, and there's something about being down here in this particular spot, with the sound of the water running and the innate sense of history trickling through the very stone upon which we're now sitting, that makes it perfect for contemplation. The story about Elaine's baby, the confrontation with Theo, finding Nancy at the apartment, the argument with Tom and even the news that I'm going to be an auntie all take a quiet back seat in my mind, each problem patiently waiting its turn to come up and be examined in more detail. Some are more troubling than others, of course, and for Nancy there is only really one to consider. I imagine I can see the cogs whirring behind her eyes now as she gazes up towards where Elaine has set up her easel, the sound of her pencil against the sketch pad indecipherable behind the constantly trickling water.

Rainbows dance in the air around us, and I see Nancy's expression flicker as she notices them for the first time. How must it feel, I wonder, to know that you have another life inside you, one that you made? I'd always thought that it must seem alien and uncomfortable, but now it simply feels magical. Then again, Mojácar has a knack of doing that, of dusting those who discover it with its bewitching sense of mysticism and beauty. There has always been magic here, and now, finally, I have seen it in action.

37

It's the final day of the shoot, so after an hour at La Fuente, I gently signal to Elaine that I need to go. After everything that's happened, it doesn't seem possible that normal life is continuing, but I know Theo — and nothing is likely to stand in the way of that man and his schedule. As far as he's aware, everything between the two of us is absolutely fine, and I suppose it is, really. In fact, it feels like a relief not to have those raving butterflies in my gut at the thought of seeing him. He's just a man, after all, a person that I shared an experience with and cared for — he's not some sort of god.

Elaine rolls up her paper before Nancy and I have the chance to check on her progress, and promises that she has enough to be going on with.

'I can fill the rest in from memory,' she assures us. 'Believe it or not, mine is pretty good.'

I don't doubt that fact, but I wonder if it isn't as much of a curse to her sometimes as a gift. There must be much that Elaine would rather forget, but she's spent decades now remembering every small detail. That's the way life works, though — some things stay with you always, while others are lost in the folds of time. There's absolutely no doubt in my mind that this trip is one I will never forget, for so many reasons.

Elaine pulls Nancy into her arms and gives her a hug,

smiling at me over her shoulder as I suppress a yawn. It's been a very long night, and I would give anything to be allowed to just lie down and sleep. Alas, there is work to be done.

'Can I come and see you again before we leave?' I ask Elaine.

'And me,' adds Nancy, rubbing her eyes.

'Girls, you will always be welcome at my home – whenever you like,' says Elaine, her kindness radiating off her like steam off a pudding. I'm just about to answer when I feel my phone begin to vibrate in my bag. Taking it out, I examine the screen and let out a little groan.

'Hello.'

'Hannah – where are you? Someone has broken the mirror in the apartment!'

Claudette sounds genuinely concerned, and I let myself enjoy her discomfort for just a nanosecond before setting her straight. I may have forgiven her for Theo, but she does still owe me about twenty bottles of pilfered beer.

'There's nothing to worry about, Claudette,' I tell her. 'I'll explain everything when we get back.'

'Well, hurry up,' she bosses. 'We have to meet Theo in an hour.'

Theo can wait for once, I think, but instead I promise her we'll be ten minutes. When I hang up, Nancy is looking at me fearfully.

'You won't tell her, will you?' She hesitates. 'About the baby, I mean.'

I shake my head. 'Of course not. Nobody needs to know. I won't even tell Tom, I promise.'

We walk with Elaine to the midway point of the hill

where the road forks up and away into the depths of the Old Town, then continue up the sloping pathway in companionable silence. It's a beautiful day, and I can hear birds singing to each other as we head down the stone steps to the apartment. The bushes bristle with life as the crickets and cicadas begin their daily chorus, and a light breeze ruffles the topmost leaves of the surrounding trees. Nancy is so exhausted that she can barely keep her eyes open, and again I feel that protective pull to look after her and keep her safe. Tom must have sensed it as soon as he laid eyes on Nancy, I realise now, although he'd ended up misinterpreting her feelings.

'Mon dieu!' exclaims Claudette, taking in the two of us as we shuffle into the hallway of the apartment. We must look quite a sight, I allow, each of us wearing one of Elaine's tie-dye dresses and with eye bags that you'd have to pay extra to stow at the airport check-in desk.

'Later,' I tell her, throwing a pleading glance as she comes towards us. Then, turning to Nancy, 'Will you be okay staying here and getting some sleep?'

She nods, too beaten down by the events of the past few hours to even utter so much as a murmur. Claudette's eyes are on stalks so long that I fear I'll trip over them. I thought I'd feel weird when I saw her, but I find that I don't feel much of anything. Hadn't Theo treated her in the exact same way as he'd treated me, after all? Okay, so Claudette was probably more savvy and therefore knew the score before she jumped into bed with him, but she didn't actually do it as a slight to me, did she? I'd rather just draw a line under the whole sorry mess.

Claudette, however, is clearly in the mood to talk, and

I quickly use the excuse of forgetting to pick up groceries in order to escape back out of the apartment. Any other person would probably have come after me, but Claudette is a big fan of a well-stocked fridge, so she lets me go on the assurance that I'll be back within half an hour.

As soon as I'm a safe distance away, I reach for my phone.

'Darling!' The sound of my mum's voice almost brings me to tears.

'Hi, Mum.'

'What is it? What's happened? Are you okay?'

How does she do that?

'Not really,' I begin, lowering myself wearily down on to the sun-warmed top of a low wall. 'Nancy's pregnant.'

Silence.

'Mum — are you there?'

'Yes.'

'Well then, say something.'

I hear her take a deep sigh. 'You'd better start at the beginning,' she says.

It doesn't take long to fill her in on the facts, but I leave out the details about Nancy smashing up the apartment, instead explaining diplomatically that she has had some trouble dealing with the news. When I tell her about James's reaction, she scoffs in disgust as I guessed she would. I assure her that Nancy is okay, that she's mostly just relieved to have it out in the open and that I'm going to call Dad with her later and break the news to him and Susie. My mum listens to all of it, and then she says something that really does bring tears to my eyes.

'I'm proud of you, Hannah.'

'I didn't do anything,' I protest. 'I've been a shit to her, Mum. She came to me for help and I turned my back on her.'

Another sigh.

'This is all my fault,' she says.

'What are you talking about?' I chide. 'You aren't even here.'

'I'm the reason you've struggled so much with Nancy,' she tells me.

I open my mouth to argue, but she cuts across me.

'I know you've always been cross at your dad because of what he did to me,' she admits, stunning me into silence. 'But I shouldn't have let you. I selfishly wanted you on my side, but I never considered how much damage it would do to your relationship with him.'

'It didn't,' I begin lamely, but she continues in earnest.

'Your dad did break my heart, it's true, but he's always loved you. I've never been able to get over him, you see? Not really. I tried for a long time, but eventually I realised that it was less painful to just carry on loving him as much as I always had. He gave me you, after all, and I love you more than anything in the whole world.'

'Mum,' I manage through my tears.

'You should talk to him,' she says now. 'Ask him to tell you his version of what happened, of why he left.'

'I don't want to,' I reply, taking a juddering breath. 'I'm so angry with him, Mum.'

'And that's my fault,' she says again, and I wish we were having this conversation face-to-face so I could hug her.

'You have to forgive him,' she continues, more resolute now than upset. 'You don't have to agree with what he did, but you can try to understand. Being angry about it will eat you up – trust me, I know.'

'Do you think he'll be cross, about Nancy and the baby?'

There's a pause while my mum considers the question.

'No,' she says. 'I think he knows just as well as I do that being a parent is the greatest gift you can receive. I think he'll be absolutely fine.'

I remember what Elaine said to me and Nancy just a few hours ago, about the way she loved her own child: then, now and always.

'Mum?'

'Yes, darling?'

'I love you.'

I sense her smile at the other end, and then her voice cracks as she says, 'Love you too.'

I sit for a moment after hanging up, listening to the distant whisper of the sea and letting the glow of the sun warm my tired limbs. The dusty landscape is spread out below me, folded down like the sides of a cardboard box, and everything feels open and inviting.

The shop, I remember, getting slowly to my feet. If I don't get a move on, we really will be late to meet Theo.

I fill a paper bag with tomatoes as if in a daze, then reach for a second and top it up with peaches. I'm just staring sleepily at the cheese selection when I feel a light touch on my elbow.

'*Hola,* Hannah.'

Diego is grinning at me in his usual mischievous way, and I humour him as he points out which yoghurts I should be buying and how he likes my new dress. I'm still wearing Elaine's bright purple tie-dye number, so I roll my eyes at him in disbelief. The difference in how I feel around him now to how I did on that first night in the restaurant is so huge that I find it difficult to believe that nervous girl was even me. In the same way as Theo has gone from being a demi-god to a normal bloke in my eyes, Diego is now just someone I can look at with affection. He looks downcast when I tell him we will be gone in a few days' time.

'It has been nice to see you again,' he tells me, following me to the till and waiting while I pay.

'You too,' I agree, coming to a halt outside the shop.

'You know, I tried to look after you and your friend before,' he says. My face must register confusion, because he adds, 'Your dad, he came to ask me to look out for you.'

'He did?'

He means Rachel's dad, obviously, and the realisation of what must have happened makes me chuckle.

'Yes.' Diego is nodding. 'I say to you, "No alcohol, nothing alcohol", but still you were sick.'

'I was,' I agree, amused by the memory for the first time.

'You were very young, you and your friend – always so happy,' he adds wistfully. 'And now you are a woman. Different, but still the same happy face.'

What is it with men suddenly realising that I'm a woman on this trip, I think, but I smile at Diego as he kisses me farewell on each cheek. For so many years, I've been tormented by the memory of this man rejecting me, when in reality he was simply trying to look out for me. To him,

Rachel and I were two teenagers who had drunk too much – totally harmless but absolutely untouchable. Far from being the sleaze that Tom was so quick to brand him, Diego is actually a decent man – and, what's more, I no longer have to feel like an idiot in front of him.

'You look happy,' remarks Claudette, as we make our way up the hill to the village twenty minutes later.

'Just exhausted,' I reply. And it's true. I'm starting to feel very strange indeed.

'Are you going to tell me what happened last night?' she demands, pulling a tube of sun cream out of her bag and massaging a blob into each of her bare shoulders. She is wearing a strapless dress today that is so tight that it would look cheap on anyone else, but of course Claudette gets away with it.

I shrug nonchalantly. 'I was pissed and fell over – that's how the mirror got broken.'

She eyes me with distrust.

'Honestly, Claudette, you know how clumsy I am when I've had a few.'

Thankfully, she decides to let the matter drop, but only because she has another topic she wants to discuss.

'Did you have a fight with Theo?' she asks, direct as ever.

'Why would you say that?' I reply, refusing to make it easy for her. She knows full well why – she made sure that I knew about the two of them.

'I know that you and he have been sleeping together,' she remarks.

'So?'

'So, I know how he can be.'

I don't want to discuss Theo with her. There's literally no point.

'It's over,' I tell her, shutting the conversation down, and she stops walking. 'What?' I enquire, unable to keep the exasperation from creeping into my voice.

'Are you okay?' she says. Am I imagining it, or does she look a little bit guilty?

'Fine,' I assure her. 'Honestly, there's no reason to worry.'

'And we are okay?' she adds, still not moving.

I take a breath. 'Of course we are.'

'You know,' she says, as we carry on up the hill, 'Theo is not a bad man – he is just set in his ways.'

'I know that,' I say, keeping my tone neutral.

'It's a shame, really, that he is the way he is,' she muses. 'One day he will not be so good-looking, and then he will find himself very lonely.'

I find that hard to believe, and tell her so.

'I think he has been through a great heartbreak,' she continues, squinting as the sun emerges from behind a large cloud and reaching for the sunglasses that are balanced on her head. 'And now he is scared of committing himself.'

'Maybe,' I say, hiding my surprise behind a veil of disinterest. I had assumed Theo would have told Claudette the same story he told me, about losing the woman he loved, but apparently, he hadn't – and I didn't really think it was my place to share his secrets.

'Wow,' Claudette looks at me in bemusement. 'You really are over him, aren't you? Good, now you can stop messing around and get together with Tom.'

We've almost reached the square now, and sounds of life are filtering down as the cafés and gift shops open their doors for the morning trade. The smooth pavement tiles feel hot beneath my sandals, and a trickle of sweat is making its way down my spine. I just had time to pull on my favourite dress before we left, the one with the floral print, but the pattern keeps swimming in front of my eyes as I look down.

'You two are funny,' she says, a lopsided smile making her look even more of a naughty pixie than usual. 'You are closer than anyone I know, yet you pretend to just be friends.'

'We *are* just friends,' I argue, remembering as I say it just how badly I left things with him last night. Now that I know the truth about Nancy, everything else seems insignificant by comparison. I've been friends with Tom for so many years, and this is the first time he's ever done something to hurt my feelings. If I can't forgive him for liking my sister, then what kind of friend am I?

'You are lucky,' Claudette says then. 'I don't have many male friends that I haven't . . . You know?'

'Slept with?' I guess, and she nods.

'It makes me feel better about myself, to have male attention,' she confesses, sounding pragmatic. 'When I was younger, I used men to feel good – and I suppose I still do.'

'But you're stunning,' I tell her honestly. 'And so confident.'

'Pah!' she waves a vague hand in the air. 'All for show.'

'But I thought . . .' I begin, then have to stop because my ears have started ringing. There's a throbbing sensation behind my eyes and goosebumps all over my arms.

'Nancy, she is the same as me,' Claudette is saying now. 'Diego, Tom, Ignacio – she likes the way they make her feel.'

I need to sit down, I think, but I must have said it out loud, because Claudette has grabbed my elbow and is leading me around the corner to the steps leading up to the viewing platform.

'Here,' she instructs. 'Sit here while I go and fetch you some sweet tea.'

Black spots are popping up like spores in front of my eyes and I put down a hand to steady myself.

What is happening? I'm so tired, but I can't fall asleep. We have work to do, and Nancy needs me. I have to call my dad. Where's Tom?

Everything feels hazy and I'm suddenly shivering despite the heat. I try to stand up and move into the shade, but my legs don't seem able to support my weight, and I fold back over again, my face connecting with stone just as a pair of strong arms wrap around me. I'm aware of a strong scent of limes and of a Spanish voice shouting, and then there is just blackness.

38

I wake up without opening my eyes and lie still for a few minutes, waiting while my senses tune in to my surroundings. I know I'm not in the apartment, because the cushions below me feel squashy and unfamiliar, and I can just about make out the sound of a Spanish man shouting. I shift my head a fraction and sense rather than hear someone approach me and bend over. Lifting a tentative hand, the tips of my fingers encounter the firm thigh of someone solid, warm and unmistakably male.

'Hannah?'

I freeze, taking back my hand as the person standing over me crouches down.

'Are you awake?'

I open my eyes to find Tom's face a few inches away from my own, his kind eyes regarding me with concern.

'You fainted,' he says. 'Are you okay?'

I open my mouth to reply, but all that comes out is a croaking sound.

'I'll take that as a yes,' he retorts, and I detect a smile in his voice.

'Where am I?' I manage, glancing around. I can see that I'm in a small, rectangular room. There's a desk with a computer on it in the far corner, and two beaten-up old filing cabinets are hugging the wall next to a door.

'The ice-cream parlour in the square,' Tom says. 'Well, the office behind it, to be exact.'

I hear the crash of a milk jug against the chrome body of a coffee machine, and in a flood, it all comes back to me: the conversation with Claudette, sitting down on the steps, someone catching me as I fell.

'Who caught . . . ?' I begin, but stop as Tom stands up again, his knees creaking in protest.

'Theo, of course,' he mutters. 'Like the big hero that he is.'

'He's not a hero,' I say immediately, and again I see Tom smile.

'He carried you in here,' he admits, albeit begrudgingly. 'You were mumbling all sorts of weird stuff the whole time, and then you just fell into a deep sleep. That was about an hour ago, and once we knew that you were okay, none of us had the heart to wake you.'

'What stuff?' I ask, shuffling myself up on my elbows so that Tom can sit down beside me. Someone had the foresight to cover me in a blanket, and I pull it up around my shoulders now, scowling at the air conditioning unit as I do so.

'There was a lot of "I love you"s going on,' Tom says slowly. 'But you loving Theo is hardly news to anyone – including him.'

'I don't love him,' I argue, my voice small. 'I thought I did, but I honestly don't.'

There's a silence as Tom takes this in, his hand resting on my leg. It feels warm and pleasantly heavy, and I lean against him sideways with a sigh.

'I'm sorry,' he says then, turning his head so he can look at me. 'I hate that we argued.'

'I hate it too,' I agree, letting the blanket slip down a bit.

'Is Nancy okay?' is his next question, and I automatically shrink away from him.

'She will be,' I say, reassuring myself as much as him. 'We've sorted everything out, you'll be pleased to hear.'

'That's great,' he agrees, moving his hand off my leg and resting it in his lap.

'I'm glad that you and Nancy didn't . . . you know,' I say then, and Tom takes a breath.

'Oh?'

I nod my head up and down against the sofa cushion. 'Nancy is still in love with her ex-boyfriend,' I explain, telling him a half-truth. 'She's been trying to get over him by hooking up with other people, but it hasn't worked.'

'I see,' Tom is nodding. 'That makes sense.'

'She didn't mean to mess you around,' I hurry on, keen to gauge his response. Rather than look forlorn, as I suspected he would, Tom seems lost in thought, and I pick up one of his big hands.

'Are you upset?' I ask. 'About Nancy, I mean?'

He laces his fingers through mine, his thumb massaging the part of my wrist where my Indalo Man tattoo sits. 'I know you think I'm crazy about your sister, but mostly I was just worried about her,' he says. 'I could tell something was going on with her that wasn't quite right.'

'I was jealous of the two of you,' I whisper, making myself look at him.

He smiles. 'I know, but you had no need to be.'

'Am I that obvious?' I murmur, staring at the smooth

outline of his lips. I know his face so well, yet I haven't studied it like I am now for years.

'No,' Tom says, not letting go of my hand. 'But I know you, Hannah.'

He does, it's true.

'And?'

'And what?'

'Tom, I . . .' There are so many ways I could end that sentence, but I never get the chance, because he chooses that moment to slide his arm around my shoulders and pull me to him, hugging me tightly to his chest. I think about the night by the apartment steps, when I was on the verge of tears over Nancy going missing and Tom had held me as he is now, with such tenderness. Then I recall just how bad I felt when I discovered that he and Nancy had kissed. At the time, I thought it was because she was stealing away my best friend, but perhaps I was jealous for a different reason entirely.

'Claudette thinks we should get together,' I blurt, watching his eyes for a reaction.

Tom screws up his face in amusement. 'Really?'

'Yep. Apparently the two of us are in love, but in denial about the fact.'

'She said that?'

I nod. 'Just before I fainted.'

'Wow.' He braves a nervous laugh. 'So the idea was so horrible that it made you pass out. Well, there's a compliment if I ever heard one.'

'Oi!' I poke him. 'I don't think she was joking.'

'Claudette never jokes,' he agrees, but his eyes are more serious again now. He feels so solid and safe next to me, so familiar and comforting – and so unlike Theo, who it was impossible to properly connect with even for a second. When I'm around Tom, I feel connected to him all the time. It's as if the two of us have our own secret language that only we understand, and I realise now that I've missed it. I've missed him.

'I've missed you,' I admit, giving in to my thoughts, and he squeezes my hand.

'I've missed you too.'

Leaning in, he kisses the top of my head, my cheek, and the tip of my nose.

'I do love you,' I say, for the first time since I've known him, even though I've loved him for years. It should be the easiest thing in the world to admit, but even now my limbs are burning red-hot with mortification.

Tom pulls back to study my face.

'I love you, too, silly mare,' he says with a chuckle, meeting my gaze.

Instead of replying, I just stare at his lips, willing them to do what I suddenly want them to do so badly that it's making all the hairs stand up along my arms. Tom knows what I'm thinking, I can tell from the look on his face, but instead of desire I can only sense confusion.

Taking a breath, I shift around on the old leather sofa until I'm facing him.

'Do you want me to fetch you a drink?' he asks, his eyes straying to the closed door.

Back in Magaluf all those years ago, during that single week where I let myself believe that Tom and I could become boyfriend and girlfriend, I'd experienced lots of moments like this; moments where I imagined the very air between the two of us was bubbling with chemistry. I pictured myself kissing Tom, and him gathering me into his arms, so grateful that one of us had finally made a move. Back then I was too scared of being rejected and of ruining our friendship, and then the feelings I'd had that were so acute seemed to vanish overnight, so I put the whole thing down to a momentary lapse in brain function. Now, however, those thoughts are suddenly back, and this time I'm not scared of acting on them.

'Are you okay?' Tom asks now, his brow knotting as he looks at me. 'You've gone very pink.'

'Don't you think it makes sense, you and me?' I say, ignoring his comment about the colour of my face.

He looks at me like I've escaped from an asylum, but I blunder on.

'Don't you ever think about it?' I whisper, and he nods slowly.

'I suppose so – but you're my best friend, Hannah.'

I don't want to be like Theo, I realise. I don't want to mistake true love for friendship and end up losing the most important person in my life. Tom has gone a strange colour now, too, but it's more of a grey than a pink. He's never going to kiss me, I know that, but that doesn't mean I can't kiss him. Taking a quick, deep breath, I lunge myself forwards and close my eyes just as my lips connect with his. At first his mouth is hard and unyielding, but then he relents and his tongue collides with mine, our kissing hard and urgent and . . .

Oh. Dear. God.

'What's the matter?'

I've pulled away and am staring at him in horror.

'That was . . . We are . . .'

Tom pulls a face. 'Terrible?'

I flop backwards until I'm sitting down again, the abandoned blanket crumpled on the sofa between us.

'That was so wrong!'

There's a small beat of silence, and then the two of us are laughing, him with definite relief and me with a high sort of hysteria. What the hell was I thinking? Of course Tom and I aren't a thing. We're friends – we always have been.

'You really know how to flatter a guy,' he jokes then, and I laugh even harder.

'You must have thought I'd lost the plot!' I cry, and he smiles.

'You lost the plot years ago.'

'Oi!' I give him a light-hearted slap. 'At least pretend to be a gentleman.'

'Difficult when you're throwing yourself at me,' he quips, pulling a stupid face.

'Oi!' I scold again. 'You were the one kissing my nose and cuddling me.'

'I was just being affectionate!' he argues. 'God, can't a man enjoy a hug with his best friend without being made to commit a sexual act?'

'Hardly a sexual act,' I scoff, and he laughs.

'Oh, Tom,' I groan, headbutting him lightly on the arm. 'What are we like?'

'Fools,' he states, and we exchange a look that speaks volumes.

'We would have been great together, though,' I say sadly.

'We would,' he agrees. 'You're beautiful, Hannah, you should know that. And sometimes I wish I did fancy you as much as I love you. I've lost count of the amount of times I've looked at you and imagined what it could be like.'

'You want to try kissing again?' I ask dubiously, but he holds up a hand and laughs.

'No, thanks – I think I'm done.'

'You're an idiot,' I grin, and he winks at me.

'Takes one to know one.'

'We're going to be okay, though, aren't we?' I ask, all of a sudden overcome with worry. Losing Tom is not something I'm prepared to do – not now, and not ever.

'Of course we will,' he says, pulling me back across the sofa for a proper Tom hug. 'Now that you've finally stopped obsessing over Theo, you can go out and find yourself a proper boyfriend.'

I can't imagine anything more unlikely at this moment, but I let him think that his words have comforted me.

'And you?' I say, snuggling up against the reassuring bulk of him.

'Oh, you know,' he replies, digging me in the ribs with a finger. 'There's bound to be a woman somewhere in the world who enjoys bad dancing and even worse kissing. I just have to find her.'

'Good luck with that.'

'You'll laugh at this,' he adds. 'But I read this article the other day about soulmates.'

'Ha ha!' I joke immediately, but he cuts across me.

'It basically said that your soulmate could be anyone. It doesn't necessarily have to be someone that you are romantically involved with, just someone that you have a connection to which feels unbreakable and unique.'

'That's nice,' I agree.

'Like a best friend,' he adds, and I turn to face him.

'Like me?'

'Yes, Hannah,' he kisses the tip of my nose again. 'Exactly like you.'

39

Four months later . . .

'Hannah, did you forget the Manchego?'

'Shit! I mean yes – sorry!'

Theo narrows his eyes at me good-naturedly. 'Lucky for you that you're an excellent researcher.'

'Your best researcher,' I correct wryly.

'Yes, my best researcher.' He smiles easily and reaches past me to pick up the salted almonds off the counter. There's barely any room in the tiny office kitchen, and once upon a time this level of proximity would have had me licking the walls with lust. Now, however, I just lean politely to one side and try not to breathe in that delicious lime-scented aftershave of his. I might not fancy Theo any more, but my nose is still my nose.

'I can pop back out to the deli?' I offer, but he shakes his head.

'Don't worry – I think we have too much food as it is.'

He's not wrong. The worktop in here and the table in the screening room are filled with small plates of tapas-style food, and there are bowls of crisps and nuts, four huge jugs of sangria and some rather dubious-looking guacamole that Claudette brought in from home. I'm pretty sure guacamole isn't supposed to be brown and contain raw carrot, but there's no arguing with her. I'm almost jealous of Nancy, because at least she can use her pregnancy as an excuse for not eating it. The rest of us are going to have to hold our noses and swallow, or face the Claudette wrath, and the former is far less painful.

It was Theo's idea to host a mini-party to celebrate our little film being aired on TV, but it was Claudette's suggestion to invite Nancy and my parents. I still can't quite believe that my mum and dad are here in my place of work, and that the two of them seem genuinely happy to see each other. Perhaps it's the fact that my dad is becoming a grandparent first that's made my mum mellow a bit towards him. I'm not sure, but it is nice to have them all here for such an important moment.

I'm just tearing open yet another bag of cheesy puffs when my dad himself appears in the kitchen doorway.

'Do you need a hand, Muffin?'

I wish he wouldn't call me that. I'm very sophisticated and important these days, as I'm sure he's well aware. We've been spending a bit more time together over the past few months, and it feels good to have him here. It feels right.

'You can cut up some crudités, if you like,' I say, motioning to the packets of celery and sticks of cucumber on the side.

He steps forward and selects a knife from the drawer, then takes the celery over to the sink to wash it. He's tall, my dad, just like me, and has kept himself fit over the years. Aside from his thinning hair and the small beginnings of a paunch, he's actually in pretty good shape. My mum looks better, though, and she's glammed herself up specially this evening, although I think that has more to do with Theo being here than her ex-husband. It's my own fault, I suppose, for going on about how amazing he was for years. In fact, I suspect my mum is a little bit disappointed that things between Theo and me weren't destined to last – especially now she's met the man in question and been predictably charmed by him.

'In case I forget to say it later, I'm very proud of you,' my dad says then, taking me by surprise.

'Thanks, Dad.'

'No, I really mean it,' he says, frowning at my amused expression. 'And I don't just mean this documentary – which I'm sure is going to be amazing – I mean because of the woman you've become. You make me very proud to be your father.'

'Oh, come on, Dad,' I begin, but he silences me with a look.

'The way you stepped up and looked after Nancy,' he says. 'Well, it was just fantastic. I know things between the two of you have never been the best, but you were there for her when it really counted, and I know how much it meant to her. It meant the world to me, too, and to Susie.'

'It's no big deal,' I shrug, although we both know that it was at the time. When Nancy and I arrived back in the UK, our dad had been there at the airport, waiting for us. I knew that Nancy was afraid of telling him about the baby, but I also knew that the sooner we got it all out in the open, the better, so I called him before we left Mojácar and told him that he had to come, and that we had something we needed to tell him. Of course, the news had come as a huge shock to both him and Susie, but they were never anything less than supportive. Even before we left Spain, Nancy had decided that she wanted to keep her baby whatever happened, and from that moment onwards the only real emotion that all of us around her felt was pure excitement. It was a bit more complicated for poor Nancy herself, of course, because she still had the small matter of an errant ex-boyfriend to deal with. James had eventually agreed to talk, and Nancy had begged me to go along with her to act as mediator. That was a strange day, to say the least.

'Do you think they'll make it, her and James?' I ask my dad now, and he pauses with the knife in mid-air.

'Honestly, I don't know,' he says, a sigh escaping his lips. 'They seem okay at the moment, but a baby is a big game changer. It's impossible to know at this stage what will happen.'

'Is that what happened with you and Mum?' I ask quietly, finally asking the question that's been bursting to come out since that call I made to my mum months ago. 'Did I come along and ruin everything?'

There's a clatter as the knife drops on to the chopping board and my dad gathers me into his arms.

'Oh no. Hannah, you mustn't think that. It had nothing to do with you at all.'

'But you just said . . .' I argue, angry with myself now for turning the mood so sour.

I feel him take a deep breath.

'The truth is,' he says, letting me go so that I can look him in the eye. 'I kept making your mum unhappy, and I had no idea why.'

'But you fell in love with someone else,' I point out.

'Yes, but not for a long time after things had started to go wrong,' he replies. 'I know you hate me for what I did, but I don't want to stand here and lie to you.'

'I don't hate you, Dad,' I mumble. 'I never have – I just hate what you did.'

He nods then, a stricken look on his face as he recalls the hurt that his past actions must have caused.

'I've made a lot of mistakes in my life, Muffin, but choosing to leave your mum isn't one of them. What we had wasn't right, even if she thinks that it was. I desperately wanted to feel what I should have been feeling, but I didn't. It wasn't fair to either of us, or to you, that I stay – we would all have been unhappy.'

I'm not sure I believe this, and my face must have communicated the fact, because my dad looks suddenly as if he might cry.

'Don't get upset,' I say quickly, patting him awkwardly on the arm. 'It was all such a long time ago. I'm sorry – I should never have brought it up.'

'No, you have nothing to be sorry about,' he says. 'Just because I'm your dad, it doesn't mean that I'm perfect. I'm a human being, Hannah, just like you, and I stumble and I've hurt people and each time I hope that I've learned something new.'

'Do you think you're still learning?' I ask, and he nods again.

'Of course I am. And that's the thing about growing up, you see, it never really stops. There is always more to learn about yourself, but you can't put your blinkers on and ignore what's happening. You have to be honest with yourself and give yourself a break when things don't go as perfectly as you would have liked. And, most of all, you have to be brave. Nancy is going to have to be very brave from now on, too.'

'She already is far braver than me,' I tell him, thinking just how proud I am of my strong and beautiful half-sister, who still looks better than most people even now that she's eight months pregnant.

'I think you're braver than you realise,' my dad assures me, going back to his chopping. 'And you've discovered what it is that you're good at — it can take some people a lifetime to work that out.'

'I think they will make it,' I say then, answering my earlier question. 'James is on the phone every five minutes lately, checking Nancy hasn't gone into labour a month early. You can tell that he loves her.'

Dad chuckles at this, his eyes narrowing in the same way as my own do when I'm amused by something.

'Love isn't always enough,' he says.

I glance at him with disapproval. 'It's a pretty good starting point.'

'Yes,' he smiles, looking at me with pride. 'A very good starting point.'

By the time we've arranged the crudités, peeled the plastic off the top of the supermarket-bought dips and carried everything through into the screening room, there's only a few minutes left before the film starts. Rachel and Paul smile at me as I top up their glasses, and I thank them yet again for coming. What Rachel said to me during that awful phone call back in June, about Paul being intimidated by me, really struck home, and after I apologised to her, I asked to speak to him so I could make amends. He had joked that all the Spanish sun must have melted my brain – but if anything, I think it's been sharpened.

Nancy has commandeered the two-seater leather sofa in the corner, her legs stretched out so she can rest her swollen ankles and a bowl of olives balanced on her bump. The baby is fond of a kicking session, and my dad tells every single person they meet that his grandson-or-daughter-to-be is going to be a professional footballer when they grow up. I prefer to think of him or her as a martial arts expert, complete with tiny ninja costume, but that mental image understandably didn't go down too well with either expectant parent. Honestly, nobody seems to have a sense of humour when it comes to babies.

Theo is sitting in his big office chair, which he's wheeled through specially and positioned not far from the large pull-down screen. Unlike the rest of us in this room, he's already seen the finished film, but that hasn't seemed to dim his interest in the slightest. If anything, he's the most excited person here, and I feel a tingle of warmth as I take in the expression of happy contemplation on his face. He was a closed book to me for so long, this man, and now I feel like I can call him a real friend. Of course, the first few weeks back after the shoot were slightly awkward, but I didn't want to let what happened in Spain come between us or affect my ability to do my job, and so I just stopped thinking about it. That turned out to be a lot easier than I expected, and I think Theo is very grateful to me for being so professional about it all. Well, I know he is – he told me so himself the same day that he offered me a promotion. According to Theo, I am wasted being stuck in front of a computer all day, and he now wants me there on every shoot, doing interviews and giving Vivid Productions a more human face. I couldn't have designed my own dream role better, and in just a few weeks I'll be heading off to Thailand with him on a brand-new project.

I used to think that nothing meant more to me than Theo, but it turns out that he was actually way down the list, and the biggest surprise I think I've had since Mojácar is realising that little old me is actually fairly high up in the rankings after all.

Claudette has taken off her shoes and is sitting cross-legged on a stool, a straw connecting her mouth to one of the jugs of sangria which she's pinched off the table. In typical Claudette style, she's in the way of at least three other members of staff and is barking at people to pass her morsels of food so that she doesn't have to move. I notice that Sergio in accounts is watching her with a look of fascinated horror on his face, and I very nearly spit out my mouthful of crisps with laughter.

'Hannah, your phone's flashing at me.'

I hop down off my own stool and hurry across to where my mum is sitting in another of the office chairs, resplendent in a satin blouse decorated with strawberries which she's tucked into a dark red pencil skirt. Those zoga sessions are clearly paying off – she's looks bloody amazing.

'Thanks, Mum! Oh, it's Tom. It's Tom, everyone!'

There's a flurry of cheers as I press the button to answer and I can hear Tom's lovely booming laughter coming through the handset as there are cries of 'we miss you' and 'hurry home'. I glance at Theo.

'Five minutes,' he says, tapping his watch, and I slip quickly out of the room into the quiet corridor.

'How's it going?' I ask, beaming with pleasure at the sound of his voice. I've really missed the big scarecrow over the past month, even though I'd never tell him that.

'It's hot!' he declares, and I scoff at him.

'Well, durr – it's Sri Lanka.'

'I know,' he grumbles. 'But nobody told me how hot it was going to be. I mean, it's so humid over here that I feel like I live in the shower.'

'I've been spending lots of time in your shower,' I inform him. 'It's so much better than that dripping mould cave I had in Acton.'

'I hope you've been looking after the place,' he says sternly. 'If I come back in five months to find you haven't cleaned it, there will be big trouble.'

He's joking, of course, but I hope he knows just how grateful I am to him for letting me stay in his flat while he's away fulfilling his dream of travelling the world. It may be tiny and smell of chicken, but it's so nice to have a bit of independence at last, and London is finally beginning to feel like a home.

'Is it tonight?' Tom asks now.

I glance up at the clock on the wall.

'It's actually in about three minutes. I can't believe you're not here.'

'Me too,' he says, but he doesn't exactly sound devastated to be missing it.

'What's going on over there?' I ask. 'Is there's something you're not telling me?'

'No!'

'Out with it.'

'No!'

'Yes!'

Tom laughs. 'How do you do that?'

'Do what?' I say sweetly, examining my nails. I really should paint them more often.

'Do that thing where you read my mind.'

'Oh, *that*,' I reply breezily. 'You know, years of practice.'

'If you must know,' he says, his voice dropping an octave. 'I've met someone.'

'A *someone*, someone?' I exclaim and I hear his smile.

'Well, a someone who wasn't disgusted by my kissing technique, so that's a good start,' he says.

'You're never going to let me forget that, are you?'

'Nope.'

Tom starts talking to someone in the background, and I look again at the clock. Less than two minutes to go.

'Sorry.' He's back again. 'That was Sophie. We're just about to go to this bar with the rest of the crew.'

'You're up very late,' I remark. Sri Lanka is five hours ahead of the UK, which never fails to turn my brain into wire wool.

'Well, we took a nap earlier after—'

'I don't need the details!' I interrupt loudly, and he starts laughing.

'I was going to say, after we got back from the tea factory. Honestly!'

'Of course you were,' I say, but I'm smiling. 'Listen, Tom, the film's about to start. Will you call me tomorrow and let me know how your date went?'

'I told you, it's the whole crew – it's not a date.'

I blow a long raspberry into the handset and hang up – like I said, incredibly sophisticated and grown up – then allow myself a few seconds before I go back into the room with the others, my hand going automatically to the necklace I always wear, the one that Tom went back and bought me from the stall in Mojácar. Perhaps it's greedy to have an Indalo Man on my wrist and one around my neck, but as Claudette is always reminding me, a girl can never have too many good men in her life. And I'm happy that Tom has met someone – it is about time, after all. I was worried that the business with Nancy would set him back, but in true Tom style he has been nothing other than sweet to her since we got back from Mojácar. I don't even have to worry about whether this Sophie girl deserves him. If Tom likes her, then I already know she must be wonderful.

What I didn't tell Tom was that I have a date myself in a few days' time. I can't wait to hear what he says when I tell him it's with a friend of Paul's. He will probably rib me about it every day for the rest of my life – especially after some of the stuff I've said about Rachel's fiancé in the past. But I'm trying with Paul, I really am, and who knows – by the time he and Rachel get married next year, I may even have enough kind things to say about him to be allowed on the top table. As long as I'm not relegated to the bloody singles' table, I don't care.

'Hannah – hurry up!' yells Claudette, so loudly that it can't have been the first time, and I make it back to my stool just in time to hear everyone gasp as an image of Mojácar comes shimmering into view, and Claudette's sultry French accent fills the room.

'On the south-east coast of Spain, in the foothills of

Sierra Cabrera, there is a place both hidden and proud. A village that seems to shimmer as you look upon it, the cluster of white buildings a honeycomb shot through with moonbeams of colour . . .'

Even though I've heard these words before, they still cause every single hair to stand up on my arms, and from the looks on all the faces in the room, I'm not the only one who feels moved by the combination of Theo's script and Tom's stunning camerawork.

The food sits untouched on the plates and bowls as we all gaze at the screen, utterly enraptured by the story Claudette is telling. As the camera traces its way up and down those labyrinthine cobbled streets, I feel as if I can smell the bougainvillea and the jacaranda trees. There's laughter as Claudette recounts some of the more bizarre local legends, and tears when Elaine reveals her tragic story. In the end, it was she who contacted me to say was happy to appear undisguised, and I feel a new swell of unbridled pride at just how incredibly brave and honest she has been. Theo was right about her story bringing something special to the film, and he's edited it expertly so that her haunting words stay with you long after the scene has moved on.

The hour feels as if it's flown by, and when the credits eventually start to roll and I see my own name appear in the list, I'm happy to let the tears fall brazenly down my cheeks. There are a few hushed moments of humble silence, as everyone lets the enormity of what they've just seen settle into them, and then I'm almost deafened by a chorus of cheering roars.

My mum has wept all her mascara across her face and

Theo is busy wiping it off with the fancy hanky from his jacket pocket, his smile of pride so big that I can't help but match it with one of my own. Claudette has finished her entire jug of sangria and is crying noisily into the shoulder of Sergio in accounts, who is in turn grinning like a ventriloquist dummy that's swallowed a handful of Viagra. I look over at Nancy to find she is smiling at me, and when our eyes meet she winks and gives me a thumbs up. I know she loves Mojácar now just as much as I do, so the fact that she approves of the film makes me feel even happier than I already did. Rachel and Paul give me a high-five each, and my dad comes over for a hug, telling me over and over again how astounded he is at what we've all created, and joking that he finally forgives me for getting 'that bloody tattoo'. He's served me well over the years, my little emblem, but in the end, it wasn't me who needed protecting – it was my job to protect. For a minute, I'm simply content to sit and be with the people I care most about in the world, and my heart aches for Tom, who by rights really should be here, but is instead using part of his round-the-world sabbatical and all his own funds to help make a film for a charity in Sri Lanka. That's Tom, though, and I wouldn't want him any other way.

Theo puts down my mum long enough to fetch some champagne from the fridge, and before long the lot of us are dancing to Paul's rather eclectic iPod playlist, in between stuffing handfuls of leftover food into our gobs. There's a tense moment when my dad picks up Claudette's bowl of home-made guacamole and asks me loudly where I bought the dog vomit, but aside from that the mood is one of frivolity and relieved joy. We've all worked so hard to create something meaningful in record time, and it's more than paid off. Twitter is going berserk as viewers begin to declare the documentary everything from 'awe-inspiring' to 'magical' to 'spellbinding', and one especially impressed user makes Theo's night by tweeting, 'Give this film a BAFTA!' Even though I fear an accolade of that stature would send his already very large Greek ego soaring into a solar system in a galaxy far, far away, I can't help but cross my fingers and make a little wish that it comes true.

By the time I've kissed goodbye to Nancy and my dad, waved off Rachel and a very drunk Paul and put my rather unsteady and overexcited mum into a taxi, it's almost ten o'clock, but instead of heading back to the party room to join the others, I go over to my desk for a time-out. I've been so caught up with the preparations for this evening's screening that I've barely sat down since lunchtime, and my afternoon post is sitting in a small pile next to my keyboard. Ignoring all the boring envelopes, I select the stiff cardboard tube from the top of the heap and ease off the plastic lid.

There's a painting inside, and as soon as I start to unroll it I let out a yelp of joyful recognition. Elaine has captured me and Nancy perfectly, a faraway but contented expression on our faces. We even look like sisters, as Elaine's expert eye has noticed traits that I had never been aware of before – the tilt of our heads and the neat curve of our jawlines. My tan, which has been long since lost to the mediocre British summer, warms my slender limbs in the painting, while Nancy's dark, shiny hair seems to gleam with vitality on the paper. I'm just laying it out flat for a better look when the phone on my desk starts to ring.

'Vivid Productions,' I say, habit driving my hand towards the receiver before my brain has time to remind it of the late hour.

'Hello, is that the right place for the film about Mojácar?'

'The one that was just shown on BBC Two?' I enquire politely.

'Yes.' The caller sounds relieved. 'I was wondering if I could speak to whoever did the interviews.'

'That's me,' I tell her, opening a drawer and pulling out a stapler and a hole punch to anchor the painting and stop it from curling up at the edges.

'Hello?' I say, when the caller doesn't immediately reply. All I can detect is a strange sort of snuffling noise.

'Is everything okay?' I ask again, pulling Tom's chair across so I can sit down.

'Yes, sorry, it's just that . . .' She stops again, and I look up just in time to see Claudette emerge with her phone clamped to her ear. It will be Carlos on the other end – he calls her every night and she pretends not to care, but she's fooling nobody.

La Fuente looks so beautiful in the painting, and I find I can almost hear the water running as I gaze down at it. I've already booked to go back to Mojácar over Easter next year, but right now that feels so far away. The woman on the other end of the line has fallen silent again, and I force myself to give her my full attention.

'My name is Hannah,' I say gently, putting my spare hand over my ear so I can hear her better. 'I'm one of the team who went out to Mojácar to make the film you've just seen, so I'd be happy to help with any questions that you might have.'

There's another pause.

'Was there a particular reason why you called?' I try again, waiting while I hear her take a deep breath.

'The woman, in the film.'

'You mean Elaine?' I guess, my pulse starting to quicken.

'Yes, Elaine. This is going to sound crazy,' she says, a nervous tremble breaking through her voice. 'But I think she might be my mother.'

There are rainbows in the painting, hundreds of them, faint but unmistakable in the air around myself and Nancy. And high above the fountain, splitting the fresh blue of the Andalusian sky in half, there are two more. A double reminder of hope and of enduring love.

'Are you still there?' the woman asks.

'Yes, I'm still here,' I say quickly, watching my fingers shake as I pick up a pen and pull my notebook towards me.

'I've been looking for my mum for over twenty years,' she says now, her voice cracking. 'It felt like magic when her name popped on my TV screen tonight and I saw her sitting there, like a dream coming true right in front of my eyes – does that sound crazy?'

'Not at all,' I say, looking again at the rainbows that Elaine painted and giving in to a smile so big that it lifts my heart. 'That sounds just about right to me.'

Acknowledgements

Here it is, my third novel. THIRD! Can somebody pinch me, please? Right, my first thanks must go to you, dearest reader. Thank you for choosing this book and for allowing me the chance to whisk you away on an adventure. I really hope you enjoy it, and please do come and natter to me about it on Twitter@Isabelle_Broom – I would love to hear from you.

To my wonderful agent Hannah Ferguson, thank you for everything you do and for teaching me that no dream is too big. Thanks also to the amazing team at Hardman & Swainson and The Marsh Agency, all of whom are in fact superheroes masquerading as everyday folk – you heard it here first.

To my editor, Kimberley Atkins, you moved all the way to the other side of the world and STILL found time for me and for this book. There are very few people that I hold in higher regard than you, and I'm so proud of you for setting off on an amazing adventure of your own. This novel gained so much depth and integrity from you – not to mention a much-needed cull of adverbs! – and the two of us thank you dearly from the bottom of our booky boots. To the Penguin massive – AKA Maxine Hitchcock, Claire Bush, Sarah Harwood, Eve Hall, Sarah Bance, Emma Brown and Jess Hart – and to everyone else who helped get this book out into the world, you are all incredible. Thank you so much.

There are many great things about being an author, but one of the very best for me has been all the inspiring, supportive, kind, caring, funny and utterly brilliant friends that I've made along the way. There are far too many of you to list here, but I would like to send special thanks to Katie Marsh, Vicky Zimmerman, Rosie Walsh, Tasmina Perry, Giovanna Fletcher, Carrie Hope Fletcher, Fanny Blake, Kirsty Greenwood, Cesca Major, Hannah Beckerman, Kate Eberlen, Milly Johnson, Jane Fallon, Nina Pottell, Sara-Jade Virtue, Amy Rowland, Elizabeth Masters, Fran Gough, Francesca Pearce, Sophie Ransom, Anne Cater, Annette Hannah, Zarina de Ruiter and Linda Hill, not to mention all the bloggers and reviewing community who make time to read my books and spread the word. There will never be enough thank yous in the world for you all.

To my best friend Sadie, thank you for being the only person I can communicate with using weird grunting sounds alone. Let's promise to never stop being total weirdos. Same goes for you, Ian Lawton. I feel so lucky to have found you and to have you, Sarah and little Ethan in my life. I hope you know how much I love you all. To my uni crew, Ranjit, Sarah, Tamsin, Gemma, Carrie, Chad, Colette, Hack, Sue and Joe McStravick – you are all legends. To Dom and Tom, Corrie and Jamie, Alex H and Big Nurse G, Tammo, Linds and Rich, plus the beautiful Miss Molly Haynes and Charlotte McKeggie – who was the first to take me to magical Mojácar all those years ago – you are all glorious and I love you.

This book is all about what it means to be a sister, something I would have no idea about if it wasn't for my own dearest idiot sisters, Coralie, Heloise, Felicity and Bryony, who are all so brilliantly unique, funny and wonderful. To the rest of my family, both old and new, thank you for all the amazing love and support. And Mum, what else can I say except that I love you so very much indeed – then, now, and always.

He just wanted a decent book to read ...

Not too much to ask, is it? It was in 1935 when Allen Lane, Managing Director of Bodley Head Publishers, stood on a platform at Exeter railway station looking for something good to read on his journey back to London. His choice was limited to popular magazines and poor-quality paperbacks – the same choice faced every day by the vast majority of readers, few of whom could afford hardbacks. Lane's disappointment and subsequent anger at the range of books generally available led him to found a company – and change the world.

'We believed in the existence in this country of a vast reading public for intelligent books at a low price, and staked everything on it'
Sir Allen Lane, 1902–1970, founder of Penguin Books

The quality paperback had arrived – and not just in bookshops. Lane was adamant that his Penguins should appear in chain stores and tobacconists, and should cost no more than a packet of cigarettes.

Reading habits (and cigarette prices) have changed since 1935, but Penguin still believes in publishing the best books for everybody to enjoy. We still believe that good design costs no more than bad design, and we still believe that quality books published passionately and responsibly make the world a better place.

So wherever you see the little bird – whether it's on a piece of prize-winning literary fiction or a celebrity autobiography, political tour de force or historical masterpiece, a serial-killer thriller, reference book, world classic or a piece of pure escapism – you can bet that it represents the very best that the genre has to offer.

Whatever you like to read – trust Penguin.

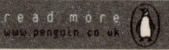

read more
www.penguin.co.uk